Hidden Secrets

Books by Jannine Gallant

The Siren Cove Series

Buried Truth

Lost Innocence

Hidden Secrets

The Born to Be Wilde Series

Wilde One

Wilde Side

Wilde Thing

Wilde Horses

The Who's Watching Now Series

Every Move She Makes

Every Step She Takes

Every Vow She Breaks

Hidden Secrets

Jannine Gallant

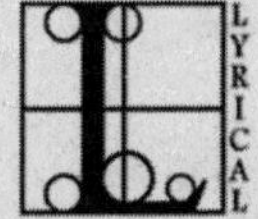

LYRICAL PRESS
Kensington Publishing Corp.
www.kensingtonbooks.com

LYRICAL PRESS BOOKS are published by

Kensington Publishing Corp.
119 West 40th Street
New York, NY 10018

First Printing: December 2018
ISBN-13: 978-1-5161-0378-2
ISBN-10: 1-5161-0378-5

eISBN-13: 978-1-5161-0379-9
eISBN-10: 1-5161-0379-3

10 9 8 7 6 5 4 3 2 1

Printed in the United States of America

To Pat. Your love and support mean everything.
I couldn't do this without you!

Prologue

He stabbed the shovel into the soft earth as the merciless summer sun beat down from a clear blue sky. Pausing to wipe his sweating face on the sleeve of his T-shirt, he glanced over at the body wrapped in an old sheet lying near the half-dug hole. A little of their normal coastal fog would have been welcome. Too bad nothing was going his way.

If luck were in his corner, he wouldn't be in the woods right now, far from the scene of the crime, slapping mosquitoes and burying a girl he'd always thought was pretty damn special. Not that he had much choice in the matter. Her death had been a horrible mistake. But if anyone discovered what had happened, the consequences would be even worse.

He flung another shovelful of earth and fought back the urge to let the tears burning at the back of his eyes fall. He'd do what needed to be done. Bury the result of an angry outburst where no one would ever find her. He dug furiously as the sweat ran down his back. Clods of dirt and stones flew, only to hit the ground with a solid thud.

God damn it! Why did this have to happen?

He stopped and lifted his face as a slight breeze rustled through the trees. Below him, the creek rushed over rocks, drowning the sound of his harsh breathing. Surely, he'd done enough. All he could possibly do. The hole stretched before him, five feet long and four feet deep. Her legs were bent a little, in the same position they'd been when she'd landed on the ground, her hands outstretched to ward off another blow.

Dropping the shovel, he knelt beside the girl and touched the sheet where it had come loose. Slowly pulling back the corner, he stared at her pale face and empty eyes. The bright sparkle that had been so much a part of Lucy's personality was gone forever. With a shaking hand, he brushed long, dark hair, matted with blood, off her face, and a glint of silver shone in the sunlight.

A silver chain with a heart-shaped pendant slid out from beneath the V-neck of her stained shirt. Lifting the silver heart, he turned it over. The initials L-E-G were engraved on its surface. After a moment, he let the pendant drop back against her chest and covered her face with the sheet before heaving her body into his arms. Staggering beneath the awkward load, he lowered her into the hole.

With each shovel of dirt he heaped on top, he buried the evidence of a singular loss of temper. An accident. But his stomach churned just thinking about the hint of excitement he'd sensed after it was over.

"No!" He shouted the word as he pounded down the soil covering her body. *It won't happen again.* His actions would remain a secret, hidden forever in the forest. Life would go on for everyone.

Except for Lucy.

Chapter One

Surrounded by barren fields, the dilapidated barn resembled something out of a low budget horror flick. Except the man approaching Paige looked more like a scarecrow than a serial killer. A red, plaid flannel shirt was cinched around his scrawny waist with a piece of rope, above high-water dungarees and cracked leather boots. A Trail Blazers cap shadowed his weathered face, which split into a smile as the old-timer held out his hand.

"You must be Paige Shephard from the antique store in town."

She grasped his calloused palm. "I am, and you must be Mr. Stillwater. Thanks for agreeing to see me."

"Call me Zeb. I appreciate you coming all the way out here. It's a bit of a drive from Siren Cove."

Paige stuck her hands in her jacket pockets as a cold breeze with a hint of rain rattled the dead cornstalks in the field behind the barn. "I travel all over the state looking for inventory to stock Old Things. A forty-minute trip is nothing. You mentioned wanting to sell part of your collection when we talked on the phone."

"I like to think I've been preserving the past for future generations, but my family says I'm just a packrat. Since I'm pretty certain they'll haul all my treasures to the trash dump the second they shovel me under, I'd rather sell now. None of my boys give a hoot about history."

Paige patted his flannel-clad arm. "I'll definitely see that anything I purchase goes to a good home."

His pale blue eyes twinkled. "I could tell we were two peas in a pod when we talked on the phone." He nodded toward the barn. "Let's get to it."

When he wheeled back the giant sliding door, her jaw sagged. The interior of the cavernous space belonged on an episode of *American Pickers* . . . or worse, *Hoarders*.

"As I mentioned, I've been collecting for a while now." Zeb's gravelly voice echoed with pride.

"I'll say."

The place was packed to the rafters with an assortment of ancient farm equipment, mining gear, the rusted remains of decades-old cars, household implements, and furniture. And that was just what she could see in the front of the building. God only knew what was hidden farther back.

"Wow."

"I know where everything is, so just tell me what you're most interested in acquiring."

"Nothing automotive or so big it won't fit in my shop." She took a few steps forward and pointed. "While that old plow is very cool, it would be too hard to display in my store. I'm more interested in smaller objects and furniture, but I have an eclectic selection of merchandise, so nothing is off the table, from butter churns to branding irons."

"I have several of both." He rubbed his hands together. "Follow me."

Two hours later, exhaustion weighed on her as Paige haggled over the price of a set of brass fireplace andirons topped by stag head finials with pointed antlers. "I'll tell you what. If you throw in the poker and shovel, I'll pay one hundred and fifty for the whole set."

Zeb removed his ball cap and scratched his bald head. "I suppose that's fair." Replacing the hat, he held out his hand. "Deal."

She shook it then gave him a fist bump. With the farmer's help, she hauled her purchase through rows of discarded furniture to the front of the barn. Glancing down at the pile of goods, satisfaction filled her to bursting. While Zeb was no slouch when it came to haggling, she'd make a good profit off this lot.

"It's past noon, and I'm hungrier than a bear fresh out of hibernation. Want to take a break and eat lunch? I have homemade chicken soup simmering in the Crock-pot."

"That's awfully nice of you, but I don't want to impose."

"No imposition. Heck, I'd enjoy the company." His expression was sober and expectant as he waited for her response.

"In that case, I'd love to try your soup."

This was far from the first time she'd stayed to eat a meal with an elderly client with too much time on his hands. Paige didn't mind in the least. She enjoyed listening to tales of life lived decades ago.

A misty rain fell as they headed toward the rambling farmhouse. While Zeb's home appeared to be in better shape than the barn, the place could have benefited from a fresh coat of paint. Her lips tightened. Maybe the family he'd mentioned wasn't any more interested in helping with home repairs than they were in his collection of antiques.

They'd just reached the front porch when a battered pickup turned off the access road and rattled down the rutted driveway to pull up next to her van. When the driver's side door opened and a tall man clad in grease-stained, gray coveralls emerged, Zeb's face brightened.

"Justin, I wasn't expecting you," he called out. "What a terrific surprise."

The man, probably in his early forties, would have been handsome if not for the hard look in eyes the same light shade of blue as Zeb's. A frown creased his brow as he approached, and he pushed a strand of brown hair that had escaped his ponytail behind one ear.

"I told you I'd be out to see you soon, Grandpa."

"Yes, but . . . it doesn't matter. You can have lunch with me and Paige. Do you know Miss Shephard? She owns the antique store in town. Paige, this is my grandson, Justin Stillwater."

"We haven't met, but I remember changing the oil in that van a few weeks ago."

"Nice to meet you." When Paige held out her hand, he shook it briefly. She turned to face his grandfather. "I won't stay since you have company. I'll write you a check and load up my van while you entertain your guest."

"But we've barely made a dent yet. I figured we'd dig farther back into the barn after lunch."

"What's going on, Grandpa? Are you selling your crap to this woman?"

"Not the crap. Just the good stuff. You and your brother don't want any part of it, and your dad can't be bothered to leave that hellhole in L.A. to visit us, so I'm clearing out what I can now."

Paige paused on the top step. "I can return another day, Zeb. I have an appointment later this afternoon, anyway."

"I suppose that'll be okay. I don't have much to occupy me on the farm now that winter's set in."

"Great. I'll print up a record of the sale for you while you and your grandson eat that soup." She gave him an encouraging smile. "I'm sure you two have plenty to talk about."

"You could join—"

"Don't press the poor woman, Grandpa. Besides, I'm sort of in a hurry."

A resigned expression filtered through the older man's eyes. "Fine. Come on inside once you have your van loaded and the receipt ready for me."

"I will." Paige flipped up the hood on her jacket and ran down the steps, happy to escape the awkward encounter. Zeb was a total sweetheart, but his grandson seemed like a jerk. She was halfway back to the barn when her cell rang. Fishing it out of her pocket, she checked the display and smiled. Quentin. About damn time he called her back.

"I was wondering if you'd fallen off the face of the planet."

"Sorry, I've been busy."

A hint of excitement in her best friend's voice made her pause, despite the rain coming down in a steady drizzle. "Did you get it?"

"We closed escrow this morning. The Poseidon Grill is officially the newest restaurant in my chain."

Paige let out a shout. "That's terrific! Why didn't you tell me they accepted your offer?"

"I didn't want to disappoint you if the deal fell through, and for a while there, I was afraid it might."

Happiness surged as she hurried toward the barn. "Are you moving back to Siren Cove?"

"For the foreseeable future. The restaurant needs some renovations before I can open for business. Plus, I have to hire a complete staff. I may crash with you for a few days while I look for a place to live, if that's okay?"

With a grunt, she slid aside the huge door. "You're welcome to stay with me as long as you need to, but I may know of the ideal place for you to rent. I'll check it out."

"You're the best. Thanks, Paige." He broke off for a moment as someone spoke in the background. "Damn. I have to go, but I'll be in touch."

"Okay. I'll talk to you soon." When the connection went dead, she returned her phone to her pocket.

Quentin Radcliff, her best friend since their pre-school days, was coming home. With a skip and a hop of sheer joy, she approached the towering stack of antiques she'd talked Zeb into selling. After pulling her laptop and portable printer out of the bag she'd left on the dusty floor, she sat on a hay bale and worked up a list of goods from the notes she'd taken earlier. Once she had a total, she wrote a check and folded both into an envelope.

Rising to her feet, she listened to the rain pelting against the metal roof. No way in hell was she hauling inventory through the current downpour. Instead, she pulled her keys from her pocket and ran toward the van. Once inside the dry interior, she started the engine and backed slowly across the yard to the open barn door, her attention glued to the rearview mirror.

When someone knocked sharply on her side window, she nearly jumped out of her skin. The van stalled. Pressing a hand to her chest, she glared at Zeb's grandson before opening the door and sliding to the ground. "Scare me to death, why don't you?"

"I told Grandpa I'd check on you." Justin paused just

inside the doorway and brushed water droplets off his hair as he stared past her at the stack of goods piled in the corner. "I hope you paid him a fair price for that stuff."

Paige bristled. "I assure you I don't cheat anyone. You can look at the receipt if you'd like." When he held out his hand, she maintained her temper with an effort and hurried over to the hay bale to scoop up the envelope. "Here."

Following her, he took it and studied the list while she carried a pair of silver candlesticks and an antique mirror to the van. "I don't understand half of this."

"I used a few abbreviations." She returned for a butter churn. "Do you want me to spell out each item?"

"I suppose not. I'll take grandpa the check."

"You don't have to bother. I need to speak to Zeb about a second appointment."

"Whatever." Justin shoved the paper into the envelope and dropped it on the hay bale. "I need to get back to work, anyway." With a brief nod, he stalked toward the door.

"Ass," Paige muttered beneath her breath. She finished loading her purchases into the rear of the van and shut the door. Flipping up her hood, she grabbed the paperwork, then ran across the yard to the house.

Zeb opened the front door just as she reached the porch. "All finished?"

"I am." She held out the envelope. "Here's your check. If you're interested in meeting again, I'm happy to come back whenever it's convenient."

He folded it into the pocket of his dungarees without looking at the total. "How about next week? I'll give you a call, and we can set up a time."

"Sounds good." Paige smiled. "I enjoyed meeting you, Zeb. I hope you had a nice lunch with your grandson."

"Justin couldn't stay to eat since he had to go back to work. He just wanted—" His voice took on a gruff edge. "It doesn't matter. Haggling with you was a real treat, young lady. I'll look forward to next time."

"I will, too. Bye, Zeb." Paige hurried back to her van, thankful the rain was easing up again. A glance over her shoulder revealed the elderly farmer hadn't gone inside, but leaned on the railing, his wrinkled face creased in . . . worry? She had a feeling his anxiety had nothing to do with her and everything to do with his grandson.

Once she reached her vehicle and started it up, she waved to Zeb before driving slowly down the rutted driveway. She couldn't adopt all her antique sources as honorary grandparents, but she could maintain a friendship with those who seemed most in need of a willing ear. Paige had a feeling Zeb fell into that category. She'd bet money the only reason his grandson had come out to see him was to hit him up for cash.

Turning up the radio, she sang along with a current chart-topper as she left the barren farm fields behind and turned onto the coast road leading to Siren Cove. Whitecaps topped a stormy sea that pounded the Oregon coastline, but the gray sky couldn't dampen her excellent mood. Having Quentin around fulltime instead of for an occasional visit would be terrific. While she adored Nina and Leah, both women were occupied with new husbands and didn't have a lot of time to just hang out anymore.

Despite her growling stomach, she made a left-hand turn into Nina's neighborhood once she reached town. She had a couple of hours before her next appointment, plenty of time to feel out her friend on the subject of renting her house. Pulling into the driveway of the old Victorian home, she parked next to Nina's Mini Cooper. Hopefully she wouldn't mind an interruption if she was busy painting.

Dashing through the rain from the van to the front porch, Paige gave a perfunctory knock on the door before pushing it open to step inside. "Nina, are you home?"

"In the kitchen."

"Good, you're not working." After pulling off her wet boots, she crossed the newly refinished hardwood floor to the arched doorway and paused. "Wow, it smells great in here."

Nina glanced up as she dropped a spoonful of dough onto a cookie sheet. "Chocolate chip. Keely will be home from school soon. Want one?"

"I should probably eat some lunch first." Wandering closer, she leaned against the island. "How's life?"

Her friend's green eyes sparkled. "Really great. Eloping was the right call. Teague and I are married without all the fuss, and after the nightmare his daughter and I went through last summer, she now has the stability she needs."

"That's terrific."

Nina slid the cookie sheet into the oven and set the timer. "Definitely. I'm happier than I've ever been. What's going on with you? You look like you're about to burst with news."

"Quentin closed escrow on the Poseidon Grill. He's moving back to Siren Cove."

"Oh, yeah? That's awesome." Crossing her arms over her chest, Nina grinned. "Having him around will be a boost to all of our social lives. The man certainly knows how to have a good time."

"True."

"What about the redhead he brought to Leah and Ryan's

wedding, the one with the funny name? Weren't they pretty serious?"

"Blaze? I think it's a nickname, and knowing her, probably one she gave herself. He broke up with her not too long ago. Then he dated a foreign model on the rebound, but that didn't even last a week. Last I heard he's between girlfriends."

"Interesting. Are you still seeing Ryan's rock climbing buddy, Tom?"

"No." A dart of pain slid through Paige's chest. "He was tired of the long-distance thing. Ryan mentioned he's dating someone else now."

"Why didn't I hear about this?"

Running a finger along the grain through the granite countertop, she shrugged. "You were on a tropical island saying 'I do' when we split up. I guess I forgot to mention it after you got back."

"So, both you and Quentin are currently single?"

"It looks that way."

"And will be living in the same town?"

"Yep." Paige glanced up. "Where are you going with this?"

"You two have been closer than most married couples since you were in diapers. It just seems like—"

"You're kidding, right? Why the heck would we want to ruin a perfect friendship by trying to make it something more?" She gripped the edge of the counter. "Do I look stupid?"

"Not in the least. Forget I opened my mouth."

"I will if you rent him your house."

The timer on the stove buzzed. Nina used a hot pad to pull the tray of cookies from the oven. "What are you talking about?"

Paige waved in the direction of the smaller home on

the opposite side of the cul-de-sac. "A couple of weeks ago, you mentioned you weren't sure what to do with your house now that you've moved in with Teague and Keely."

"True, but I still use my art studio over there."

"You have space here to set one up in a spare room. My guess is you haven't yet only because you can't be bothered."

Nina grinned. "You know me so well. Anyway, I'm not sure I want to rent that house. I kind of like not having neighbors in our little corner of the hood."

"Quentin needs a place to live while he's getting the restaurant up and running. Maybe he'll stay longer since he likes this area, but it won't be indefinitely. Also, we'll be invited to any parties he might have, so you won't be able to complain about the noise. Seems ideal since you know he'll pay his rent on time and not trash the place."

"You make a good point. Actually, several. I wouldn't mind the extra income. We could start a college fund for Keely, and you never know when—"

Paige's eyes widened. "Oh, my God. Are you pregnant?"

"Not yet, but we're trying. Both Teague and I want a baby before Keely's too many years older."

Rounding the island, Paige hugged her friend. "That's great. I'm so excited for you."

"Well, it hasn't happened yet. But to get back to your question, I'd be down with renting to Quentin. Next time he's in town, we can discuss it."

"Cool. I'll let him know." She glanced at the digital clock on the stove. "Damn, I need to get moving. I have to unload this morning's purchases, eat something, and then get to my next appointment. Busy day picking antiques."

Nina held out a cookie. "You should slow down and

smell the flowers. Or in this case, the sweet scent of chocolate chips."

With a laugh, Paige took the still-warm treat. "Thanks. Maybe one of these days, I will. Stranger things have happened, but I wouldn't count on it."

Chapter Two

Quentin Radcliff cruised down the coast road, singing at the top of his lungs to a U2 classic. As he shifted down on the approach to a tight corner, the engine of his Jaguar growled, but the tires held with only a slight squeal on the rain-slick highway. Maybe he was driving too fast for the shitty conditions, but where was the fun in life if you didn't push the envelope?

He hadn't planned to make the long trek from Seattle to Siren Cove when he'd rolled out of bed at the crack of nine after a late night, but that's exactly what he found himself doing. The challenge of opening a new restaurant awaited. The fact that the Poseidon Grill was in his old hometown only added to his enthusiasm. Even though his family had moved away twenty years before, this spot on the Oregon coast was the one place that felt most like home.

Maybe because Paige was there. The only person in the world he could tell all his troubles to. The friend who never judged. The woman he counted on to always have his back. Knowing his best bud would be within shouting distance was possibly the most satisfying part of this whole deal.

True, the new proximity would change the dynamics of their friendship. Hopefully for the better. She hadn't opened up a whole lot about her most recent breakup, and he couldn't help wondering why. With both Leah and Nina getting married in the past year, he'd sensed a tension in Paige. Possibly she needed a sympathetic ear right now nearly as much as he did.

When a small red fox darted across the road, he braked hard and skidded. Correcting with the skill born of long practice, Quentin slowed down a fraction. He might be fond of living life on the edge, but he wasn't a complete idiot. When his cell rang, he turned down the radio, put the call on speaker, and answered.

"What's up?"

"How would you like to move into Nina's place?"

Quentin couldn't repress a grin. "The woman is extremely hot, but her husband is a bad-ass firefighter and might not appreciate me poaching his wife."

He could almost see Paige's eye-roll.

"Hilarious. Her old house. She said she'd consider renting it to you."

"Oh, yeah? That'd be great. Much better than getting a generic apartment."

"You can talk to her about it when you get to town. Any idea when that might be?"

He glanced at the dashboard clock. "A couple more hours, give or take. I cut over to the coast. It takes longer, but the drive is more scenic."

"What! You're on your way here?"

"I'm anxious to get started on the restaurant renovations. It was a spur of the moment decision."

"No kidding. If I'm not back to my shop by the time

you arrive, just go on upstairs. Mindy's holding down the store while I'm out antique hunting and will give you my spare key."

"Thanks for being flexible about this. If you have plans tonight—"

"No, just a seller with a lot of potential. I'll be home in time for dinner."

"Maybe I'll swing by the grocery store first and cook tonight. Nothing fancy, but it seems like a fair trade for a place to sleep."

Her laughter made him smile.

"A Quentin Radcliff specialty—simple or not—sure beats the takeout I'd planned to grab on my way home. I'll see you in a few hours."

"Bye, Paige."

He disconnected and turned up the radio. When his phone rang again, he didn't even look at it before answering. "What did you forget?"

There was a moment of silence before a high-pitched voice whined in his ear. "Me? I didn't forget anything, but you sure as hell did. I had to find out from your manager down at The Zephyr that you left town *for good* without even calling to say good-bye."

Quentin released a long breath and prayed for patience. "Don't be so dramatic, Blaze. I'm hardly gone from Seattle for good. I'll be back in a few months, once I get my new restaurant up and running." His tone grew sharp. "Anyway, we're not together anymore, so I don't have to check in with you before I make a decision."

"You needed a break when things between us got serious. I understood, even though it didn't make me happy. But after your little fling with Inga, we talked about getting back together."

He ignored her tearful pleading, despite the sudden

ache in his gut. "You talked. I listened politely and said no. We're finished, Blaze."

"But—"

"Look, I'm driving. I have to get off the phone."

"Then I'll call you when you get to Siren Cove. We obviously need to have a serious conversation since you're being so unreasonable."

He gripped the steering wheel harder. "Calling me this evening is pointless since I'll be busy."

"You can't possibly be planning to work tonight."

"I'm making Paige dinner."

"Of course you are. I should have known you'd go running to *her*. She hated me from the start. If you hadn't let her opinion influence you—"

"I'm not having this conversation. You need to move on with your life. I am."

"I can't."

"Yes, you can. I have to go. Bye, Blaze."

Throwing the phone on the passenger seat, Quentin rubbed a hand across the back of his neck. "Damn. Damn. Damn." He felt like dog shit. Hurting a woman he'd once thought he loved was the last thing he wanted, but Blaze refused to accept the fact that their relationship was over.

Paige had tried to warn him months ago, but he hadn't listened. *Moron.* By the time he realized Blaze's need to constantly please him was brought on by a deep-seated dependency, bordering on psychosis, the damage was already done. Short of marrying the woman, there seemed to be no solution other than a quick, painful break.

Except Blaze wouldn't let go.

Just one more reason why getting the hell out of Seattle was a great idea. Maybe putting physical distance between them would help her find closure. He sure hoped so.

And the next time Paige gave him advice, he'd damn well take it.

Paige pulled up behind the moving van in front of Lola Copeland's home and parked. The Craftsman style house had a spectacular ocean view, which was probably the reason it had sold a few months after going on the market, despite the outrageous price tag. If Paige had an extra million lying around, she would have put in an offer on the place. Unfortunately, that kind of cash was far beyond her means.

After getting out, she slammed the door and headed up the walkway, passing two men straining under the weight of a floral-patterned couch. The older one nodded at her. The younger gave her an appraising look. Completely unwarranted, in her opinion. She wore jeans with a pair of tall, heeled boots and a cowl neck sweater. With strands of blond hair escaping her braided updo, she had a feeling she looked more messy than sexy.

Reaching the open front door, Paige gave a sharp knock and called out, "Miss Lola, may I come in?"

"Heavens, yes. How are you Paige?" No taller than Paige's diminutive five-foot two, the older woman was easily twice as wide. She hurried down the stairs, hands fluttering, her face creased in lines of worry. "This move will be the death of me. My daughter tells me I don't have room for half my furniture in the new place, so I need to downsize to get rid of a few things fast."

"I'll be happy to take a look at what you're selling."

"Good. Good." She reached the entry and kept moving. "Right this way. Most of what I plan to part with is in the dining room."

Paige followed her through the echoing house to a room crammed with furniture. "*Wow.*" She mouthed the word behind Lola's back.

"I had the movers put everything that's on the chopping block in here so they can load the van without making mistakes. I hope you can squeeze between the pieces."

"I can fit." She edged sideways around a massive grandfather clock. "Not all the furniture in here is old enough to interest me, though."

"I figured as much, so I taped prices on the pieces I thought you'd want. Much easier than haggling like a couple of Wall Street traders."

Paige eyed the sticky tag on an old treadle sewing machine and raised a brow. "That's retail, Miss Lola. I have to make a profit."

The woman's lips trembled. "You know I made some bad investments, right? This house was mortgaged to the hilt. I'm being forced to leave my home, the place where I raised my children and buried my husbands . . . all three of them."

Paige hoped she didn't mean the last part literally but refrained from asking. "I'm truly sorry for your misfortune, but I still can't pay you retail."

A sly grin curved Lola's lips. "It was worth a shot. You're a smart cookie, Paige. How about if I knock twenty-five percent off the total."

"I have overhead. Make it thirty-five, and we have a deal. That's a bargain, and you know it."

"Fine," she readily agreed. "You have me over a barrel since I'm in a rush to sell."

Paige winced. *I should have asked for forty.*

"Do you want the sewing machine? I remember my grandma using it to make doll clothes back when I was just a little bitty thing. I still have the doll. Frances was her name. She has a real china head. I put her in that armoire towards the back of the room."

"I'm interested in both."

"Of course, Frances won't come cheap since she has sentimental value."

"Why am I not surprised?"

Lola let out a loud, honking belly laugh. "Because you're sharp, like I said."

Three hours later, the movers had carried all her smaller purchases to her van, and Paige promised to return in the morning with a trailer for the armoire and sleigh bed. After typing up a list of goods and printing it out, she handed the proof of sale to Lola along with a check. "I wish you luck with your move. Nina mentioned you'll be living closer to your daughter now."

"I will, and I'm surely looking forward to spending more time with my granddaughter."

"I noticed you aren't selling any of Nina's paintings."

"Are you kidding? My hope is they'll be worth a whole lot more than I paid for them within a few years. Nina's making a real name for herself in the art world."

"She really is. I have a few pictures she gave me as birthday gifts, but I'd never part with them."

"You'd be surprised what you can do when push comes to shove."

"I suppose so." Paige paused in the yard beside a pile of trash bags and cardboard boxes filled with what looked like miscellaneous crap.

"My son promised to squeeze me into his busy schedule later and take a load to the dump." Her voice dripped sarcasm.

Paige bent to sort through one of the boxes and came up with a footed china cup with a spray of roses on the side. "If you don't want this teacup, I'll take it. I see that it's cracked, but it's a popular pattern."

"How much will you give me?"

The container also held a few other pieces of mismatched china, an old tennis trophy, a cookie jar in the shape of a beehive, and a pair of Egyptian themed brass bookends.

"Twenty bucks for the lot."

"Sold."

Paige pulled her wallet out of her purse, extracted a twenty, and handed it over. "A pleasure doing business with you Miss Lola."

"You bet. Have a nice evening, Paige."

Hoisting the cardboard box, she headed toward her van. "I intend to."

After dropping her final purchase on the passenger seat, she started the engine. Surely, Quentin would be in Siren Cove by now. When she reached Old Things, she turned down the narrow alley beside her shop and pulled to a stop near the back door. The rays of the setting sun reflected off the windshield of Quentin's black Jaguar parked in the small lot. Giving two toots on the horn, she turned off the engine, then slid from the seat to the ground. By the time she rounded the van to the rear doors, her old friend emerged from the store and scooped her up in a bear hug to spin her in a circle.

"Wow, it's good to see you. It's been too long."

She hugged him back then planted a quick kiss on his scratchy cheek. He smelled good and tasted like salt air. Maybe he'd been down to the beach for a stroll earlier.

"A couple of months, at least."

"I should have come for Thanksgiving, but I let Blaze talk me into going to her parents' place instead. Big mistake."

"Oh?" When he released her, Paige backed up a step and studied him.

His dark blond hair was cut shorter on the sides than when she'd last seen him. Trendy but neat. Kind of like the man himself. He wore jeans and an aqua-blue, button-down shirt, the same color as his eyes. While Quentin wasn't movie star handsome in the traditional sense, he oozed charisma. When he smiled, Paige was pretty certain every woman in the vicinity experienced heart palpitations.

Best friend or not, she was no exception.

But today, his eyes were shadowed, and fine lines radiated from the corners. Had he held her a little longer than normal? In general, Quentin liked his personal space.

"What's wrong?"

"Nothing I can't handle. I just have a lot on my plate with this new restaurant. Then there's Blaze . . ."

"I thought you broke up with her."

"I did the second we returned from our trip, but try telling her that. I hope hanging out here for a while will reinforce the message that we're through." He held up his hand. "And before you say it, yeah, you told me so."

She patted his arm. "I don't want to be right about these things, but sometimes I think I know what you need better than you do."

"Next time I'll ask your permission before dating anyone." Fisting his hands on his hips, he peered into the van. "Wow, that's quite a haul."

"I was on a roll today. Want to help me carry it inside?"

"Sure. I knew you'd find a way for me to earn my keep."

"Manual labor and cooking should do it. Take the other end of this cedar chest. The damn thing weighs a ton."

"Don't hurt yourself."

"Hey, I've been working out." She hefted her end as he maneuvered it through the door.

By the time they finished moving everything into the shop, exhaustion wore on her.

"Looks like that's it." Quentin slammed the rear doors. "I'd better hustle upstairs to finish our dinner."

"The smell has been taunting me." She hit the remote to lock her van and followed him inside. "What's cooking?"

"Roasted red pepper and tomato bisque. I'll throw together some grilled mozzarella and prosciutto sandwiches to go with it."

Paige groaned. "Your gourmet twist on tomato soup with grilled cheese. Have I ever told you I love you?"

"You're very free with your affection when I feed you." He slid an arm around her waist as they maneuvered through the storage room behind the shop toward the stairs. "The rest of the time, you give me grief."

"I only hassle the people I care about, so you can consider yourself lucky." She smiled. "Seriously, though, thanks for helping me unload. I'm beat. Did Mindy lock up?"

"She closed the shop a few minutes before you arrived. You bought a lot of inventory today."

"That load was only half of it. I had an appointment earlier today, too." She entered her apartment and dropped her computer bag and purse on the entry floor. "Not to mention, I have a third meeting with a potential source scheduled for tomorrow. That's it for this month, thank heavens. I'm not usually so busy, but I'm stocking up for Christmas sales. I put a good-sized dent in my inventory over Thanksgiving weekend."

Quentin headed into the kitchen to stir the fragrant

soup simmering on the stove. "Will having me crash here be an inconvenience?"

"Not in the least." She slid onto one of the bar stools at the counter and planted her elbows on the tile surface. "Do you want me to do anything?"

"Just keep me company while I cook. I bought wine. Do you want a glass?"

"God, yes. Haggling with Miss Lola is exhausting. Even after we agreed on a price, she kept badgering me for a better deal."

He smiled as he pulled a loaf of Italian bread and a bottle of merlot out of the pantry. "I hope this morning's client wasn't such a hard ass."

"No, he was a sweetie. Very reasonable, but his grandson was a jerk, insinuating I wasn't fair to the old guy. I don't take advantage of elderly clients. Or any client, for that matter. My reputation for square dealing matters to me."

After deftly removing the cork from the bottle, he poured a glass and handed it to her. "Everyone in Siren Cove knows you're honest. I trust you implicitly."

While he poured his own wine, she held up her glass. "To friends you can count on."

He grimaced. "It sure beats the hell out of love."

She took a gulp of her merlot, then ran her finger around the crystal rim. "Neither one of us has had much luck in that department."

"The single men around here must be idiots. You're smart and beautiful. I can't believe no one's snapped you up yet."

"True." She eyed him steadily. "Maybe one day they'll wise up."

Chapter Three

Quentin stood in the middle of the main dining room of the Poseidon Grill and surveyed his new kingdom. The place had spectacular ocean views, but the bar seating needed to be expanded. "If we take out that far wall into the room at the back, we'll have more usable space, and we can still use the upstairs area for private parties."

Jerry Favor, the local contractor, made a note. "Anything else in this section?"

"With the wall gone, I'd like to extend the bar to circle around." Picking up the pad of paper he'd laid on the shiny teak surface, he sketched rapidly. "Something like this is what I have in mind."

"That's doable." The heavyset man took the sheet from him and tucked it into a folder. "What changes need to be made in the kitchen?"

Quentin headed toward the opposite side of the dining area. "I'd like the wall separating the server station from our guests at full height. We aren't running a diner, for

Christ's sake." He kept walking past the line grill and the prep area to the storage room in the very back. "I want shelving added to the south wall. Also, the entire kitchen floor needs to be replaced since this linoleum is a hell of a lot older than I am. I want something seamless and durable."

Jerry scratched more notes. "Got it."

"I also want the carpeting removed from the stairs. We'll clad those in wood." Leaving the kitchen, Quentin returned to the dining room. "The whole interior has to be repainted, but there really isn't as much structural work as I expected. The place is solid. Oh, I'm going to need new fixtures in the public restrooms. I want granite countertops and above counter brass sinks to class up the place."

The contractor nodded. "I'll take some measurements before I leave. Bids on painting and new pavement in the parking lot shouldn't take long to get. I'll have an estimate ready for you in about three days."

"Sounds good." He shook the man's hand. "Take your time with those measurements. I have a few calls to make before I need to lock up."

"It won't take long."

After checking in with the managers at his other restaurants and settling a few minor problems, Quentin called Paige and smiled when she picked up on the first ring. "It's a little early, but do you want to go get some lunch?"

"Can't. I'm on my way back to the shop now with a couple of big pieces of furniture I picked up this morning, then I'm heading south to meet a client."

"Do you need help moving the furniture?"

"I borrowed Nina's open trailer along with her husband and a couple of his buddies from the fire station to do the heavy lifting."

"Oh." Quentin wasn't sure why he felt so put out that she hadn't asked him.

"Unless you're bored and want to drive down the coast with me. My appointment is about fifty miles from here."

"I'm never bored, but that sounds like fun. We can stop for sandwiches on the way."

"If you're still at the restaurant, I'll swing by to pick you up in about twenty minutes. Okay?"

"I'll be waiting." He disconnected and stuck his phone in his pocket. He had plenty of chores he could be doing, but hanging out with Paige would be a hell of a lot more fun than ordering dishes and linens for the restaurant. He did need to get an ad into the local paper for staff right away, but work on a website for the Poseidon Grill could wait one more day.

He'd made the call to the paper, let the contractor out, and locked the place up when Paige's van pulled into the parking lot. After opening the passenger door, he set his laptop case behind the seat and climbed in.

"At least the rain stopped. Cloudy beats a downpour."

"No kidding." Paige bumped through the potholes in the pavement and turned out onto the main road. "Yesterday morning was miserable."

He studied her profile as she leaned back in the seat and drove with confidence, the way Paige did everything. Despite her petite size—which he knew annoyed the hell out of her since people tended to associate little, cute, and blond with brainless—she was an intimidating force. When Paige wanted something, she didn't back down. Ever. As she smiled, intelligence shone in her eyes beneath upswept hair a few shades lighter than his own. She'd fastened her curls in some kind of fancy knot at the top of her head.

"Did you get the rest of your furniture moved into the shop?"

"You bet. While he was helping me, Teague mentioned something I hadn't heard about yet. They're having a bachelor auction at the Winter Ball in a couple of weeks."

Quentin grinned. "Is Teague wishing he hadn't jumped the gun and eloped with Nina?"

"Not in this lifetime. No, he was teasing his buddy, Mateo. Leah is on the organizing committee for the ball, and she badgered him into agreeing to be auctioned off. My guess is she'll be after you next."

"What?" He sat up straighter in his seat. "I don't want to be auctioned like a damn piece of meat. I did that once in Seattle, and this blue-haired old lady bought me. I spent our evening together fending off her advances."

Paige burst out laughing. "That's hilarious. I could actually see Leah's grandma getting a little frisky with a hot young guy."

"Evie? That woman is irrepressible."

"Lucky for you she has a live-in gentleman friend now, so you're probably safe."

He pointed out to sea where a whale breeched the surface. "Did you see that? God, I miss this area." Turning back to Paige, he shook his head. "I'll be plenty safe since I don't intend to let myself be coerced into volunteering."

"It's for charity. They're raising money for the local shelter to help battered women and children get back on their feet. How can you turn down such a worthy cause? I bet the ladies would pay top dollar for a date with a famous chef and restaurant mogul."

"Funny. I'm hardly in the same category as Gordon Ramsay or Bobby Flay."

"No, you're younger and better looking."

"True." Quentin couldn't hold back a grin. "Fine, I'll think about it."

"Great. I'll let Leah take it from here now that I've laid the groundwork."

"Tag team coercion?"

Paige took her attention off the road long enough to give him a contemplative look. "Whatever works. It's not like Siren Cove is overflowing with handsome, single men. If that were the case, I would have done my best to take one of them off the market by now."

"Instead, you've had to search further afield. Are you going to tell me what happened between you and Ryan's rock climbing friend?"

"Long distance dating wasn't working." Her tone was abrupt.

For some reason, Quentin felt like he was getting the air-brushed version of the truth. Still, it was clear he shouldn't push. "I'm sorry."

"Yeah, so am I. Tom is a good guy."

"Should I go beat him up for you?"

Her lips relaxed into a smile. "You sound like you're ten. Anyway, he scales cliffs for fun. That takes some serious upper body strength. I wouldn't want you to get hurt."

He snorted. "I'm a master at taekwondo. I expect I could hold my own."

"Okay, then. No, I don't need you to beat up anyone. I can take care of myself."

"Good to know."

After a moment of silence, she asked, "So, you ditched the model, huh? Any reason in particular? I saw a few photos of her. The woman is stunning."

"We had nothing in common outside of . . . never mind.

I wasn't comfortable talking to her the way I am with you. If I have to work at having a conversation, something is seriously wrong."

"I'd have to agree. But then, I'm pretty sure stellar conversationalist isn't your primary requirement for dating. You still think with . . . well, *never mind*."

He winced. "You make me sound like a complete douchebag."

"You'll be thirty-two in a couple of months. Professionally, you're extremely successful. Have you thought about settling down, getting married, having kids?"

"On occasion, but I'm in no rush. I enjoy my freedom."

"So, not a douchebag. Just a guy who doesn't want to grow up. As long as the women you date know that."

"I've always been pretty clear about my intentions . . . or lack thereof. Is it my fault if an occasional lady refuses to believe me?"

"Blaze?" she asked.

"Yeah. I thought we were on the same page, and I really liked hanging out with her. Then she started to get demanding and clingy and . . . well . . ."

"You called it quits rather than relinquish your hard-fought freedom." Paige's voice was flat.

"I certainly didn't want to hurt her." He slumped further down in the seat. "Blaze phoned again this morning, but I let the call go to voice mail. I don't know how I can be much clearer."

"Sometimes women *and* men are slow to accept what they don't want to hear. Maybe she just needs more time."

"I hope so. Meanwhile, let's talk about something else. The subject of my love life is fairly depressing at the moment."

"You mentioned getting lunch when you called me."

"Food." He straightened. "Now that's a topic close to my heart. Do we have time to stop before your appointment?"

"If we get takeout. There's a little hole-in-the-wall place a couple of miles from here that has excellent fish and chips."

"Sounds good. I need to fortify myself to watch you haggle over old, scarred furniture."

"You could probably learn a thing or two from me when it comes to the art of negotiation. Maybe take a few notes."

"This is why I love you, Paige. You don't get bent out of shape when I give you crap. You just fling it right back."

"Like a monkey in a zoo. Charming image."

"You'd make an adorable monkey." Narrowing his eyes, he pointed. "Hey, there's the fish joint. I'll admit I'm suspicious of a place with a flashing neon sign that says *eats*."

"I promise it's excellent. You'll thank me for this."

He smiled as she flipped on her blinker and turned off the highway. "I always do."

Thirty minutes later, Quentin was finishing up the last of the chips when they pulled up in front of an older house on a tree-lined street. Bicycles and red wagons cluttered driveways in neighboring homes, and yards were well maintained. The house in front of them seemed to be the exception, with shuttered windows, half-dead shrubs, and a dumpster squatting at the edge of the street. Other than a new SUV with dealer plates in the driveway, the place showed no signs of life.

Energized by the outstanding meal, he climbed out and

joined Paige at the front of the van. "If it wasn't for the car in the driveway, I'd think the place was vacant."

"The owner recently moved to an assisted living facility. I'm meeting her daughter and son-in-law. They want to clear out the house and sell it."

"From the looks of the neighborhood, it seems like a popular area with young families."

"One of the old sawmills outside of town reopened, which brought in a lot of new jobs." She opened the screen and knocked sharply.

A bolt slid back, and the door squeaked open. A middle-aged woman with faded brown hair gave them a hesitant smile. "Are you the owner of the antique store?"

Paige held out her hand. "Paige Shephard, and this is my friend, Quentin Radcliff. I figured we might need some muscle to move any heavy furniture."

She shook Paige's hand and then the one Quentin extended. "I'm Didi Goodman. My husband is here, too, so I'm sure we'll be able to manage without throwing out our backs."

"A big plus. Thanks for contacting me. I'm always happy to acquire new inventory for my store, though I'm sorry your mother has to leave her home."

"She's having memory issues. Early onset dementia." Didi let out a sigh. "Disposing of years of accumulation is a big job, and I just want to get it done. This way to the living room. We can start there."

Quentin stayed out of the way as the two women went straight to a wall of shelves filled with bowls and vases. When footsteps sounded behind him, he turned to glance over his shoulder.

A tall, thin man with a high forehead and horn-rimmed

glasses hurried down the hallway from the rear of the house. He held out his hand. "I'm Lucas Goodman."

"Quentin Radcliff." He shook the offered hand. "I'm just along for the ride and to help move furniture."

Lucas nodded toward the women. "They don't seem to need any assistance at the moment. I was out back, cleaning miscellaneous crap out of the shed."

"I'm happy to lend a hand since I don't have anything else to occupy my time."

"Sounds good." He raised his voice. "Honey, Quentin and I will be in the backyard clearing out your dad's junk if you want us."

Didi pulled a green dish down from one of the higher shelves and nodded. "That's fine, dear."

Paige met Quentin's gaze, but he just shrugged in response. He didn't mind getting dirty, and spiders didn't faze him . . . unless they were giant and furry. He'd take his chances in the shed rather than die of boredom listening to Paige and her client toss words like Spode, Waterford, and Depression glass back and forth.

The lawn behind the house was patchy and full of clover and dandelions. Lucas led the way past a picnic table to a shed built against a high board fence.

"The place has gone to hell in the last couple of years. We live over in Bend, and unfortunately don't get to the coast as often as we'd like." He pushed open the shed door. "Since Didi's brother spends most of his time in Salem, even when the government is in recess, we don't have a lot of help."

"I imagine dealing with aging parents can be a challenge." Quentin paused to look around for spiders before stepping inside. "Your brother-in-law is in politics?"

"State Senator."

"From this district? Mason LaPine?"

"That's right." Lucas picked a coffee can full of nails up off a workbench and dropped it in a partially filled wheelbarrow.

"I own a restaurant in Portland and met him at a fundraiser one time. He seemed ultra-confident."

"Mason is full of himself. He wants to run for governor." Lucas chucked wood scraps and a box of wire in after the nails. "There are a few decent tools I suppose we can sell. I'd keep them, but I'm not handy that way."

Quentin appreciated a man who wasn't afraid to admit his shortcomings. "I'm a hell of a lot better in the kitchen than a workshop, although I have a few skills. Just tell me what I can do to help."

Lucas glanced around. "If you really don't mind, all those gardening tools hanging on the wall need to go out to the SUV. I can use them at home since I'm thinking about putting in a small vegetable plot in the spring."

"I'm on it."

An hour later, they'd made serious progress, and Quentin was enjoying Lucas's dry humor. When he discovered an old wetsuit, a bamboo fishing rod, and a Hawaiian sling behind a tall red toolbox, he hauled them out. "What do you want to do with these? It looks like mice have been chewing on the wetsuit."

"The suit can definitely go in the dumpster." The older man frowned. "I don't remember Henry using that particular rod, and he sure as hell never went spear fishing. My father-in-law in a wetsuit would have been mistaken for a seal. The man was rather portly."

Quentin choked on a laugh. "The rod and spear look old enough to be interesting. If you want to part with them, I'll hang these on a wall at the Poseidon Grill."

"I heard that restaurant had sold after the last owner went to jail. You bought it?"

He nodded. "I'm looking forward to bringing the place back to life. The Poseidon Grill has been a mainstay for Siren Cove's tourism forever, and it's a favorite with the locals, too."

"Then I'd like to donate the rod and spear to the cause. I took Didi there for dinner the night we got engaged. I have fond memories of the place."

"Are you sure?"

Lucas waved a hand. "Absolutely. They can't be worth much, anyway. They're all yours."

"Thank you. The pair will get a place of honor on one of the walls. Maybe I'll put Paige to work looking for more vintage fishing gear to make a whole display."

"I like that idea."

Tucking the Hawaiian sling and the fishing rod beneath one arm, Quentin threw the wetsuit onto the pile in the wheelbarrow before maneuvering it out through the doorway. Once he'd stowed the spear and pole in the back of the van, he emptied the refuse into the dumpster.

"Want to take a break from hauling trash and help move some furniture instead?"

Quentin stepped toward the front stoop where Paige leaned against the doorframe. "Sure. Shall I call Lucas to come lend a hand?"

"I think we can manage between the two of us. I bought an old trunk, which isn't heavy, but I packed a bunch of breakables into it. Then there's a standing mirror and a corner cabinet. The rest I can carry on my own."

Leaving the wheelbarrow, he joined her. "Did you get some good stuff?"

"A few unbelievable pieces of china and glassware.

They cost me a bundle but are worth every penny. I'll have collectors fighting over them."

He slid an arm around her waist and squeezed. "So, the trip was worth it?"

"You bet. Let's load up and head home. We have an exciting evening of unpacking ahead of us."

Quentin rolled his eyes. "Oh boy. I can't wait."

Chapter Four

He couldn't freaking believe what had happened, although maybe he should have anticipated the possibility. Selling everything was inevitable, but he'd expected to have a little more advance warning. Obviously, he'd been an idiot to leave evidence behind. *The murder weapon*—his brain shied away from the term—had been well hidden all these years where no one would ever think to look for it.

He wanted nothing more than to forget that awful night, and the damn thing had seemed perfectly safe where he'd stashed it.

Better than trying to chuck it in the trash or a culvert when the cops were still sniffing around, looking for any connection to the crime.

He'd tried to wipe off all the blood and fingerprints, but with the DNA tests available now . . .

Damn. Damn. Damn.

He didn't know what exactly to expect. Hopefully he'd find the . . . *thing* where he'd left it. His skin crawled even thinking about touching the smooth surface. It couldn't be worth much, and surely the woman from the antique store had found better merchandise to buy. He'd take the last piece of incriminating evidence to the landfill and be done with it.

It was infuriating, knowing he had to deal with this crap now, when he had a shit-ton of work to do. But he didn't have any choice. He'd take care of unfinished business then move on with his life. Free and clear. At least for now.

Paige poured two glasses of chardonnay, stuck the cork back in the bottle, then returned it to the refrigerator. Carrying the stemware, she rounded the bar counter and headed into the living room. After handing one glass to Quentin, she settled beside him on the couch. "Did you choose a movie?"

"There's not much new available in romantic comedies." He sipped his wine and gave her a sideways glance before setting down the glass. "You're sure you don't want action adventure?"

"We watched car chases and gun fights last night. I'm in the mood for sweet and sentimental." Pulling her legs up beneath her, she curled into the cushions.

"Has anyone ever told you that you sit like a cat?"

She hid a smile. "No, but one guy I dated mentioned I growl like one when—"

"Oh, my God. Stop!" He clamped a hand over her mouth. "Way too much information. I don't want to imagine you and some dude getting it on. Save that kind of confession for Nina or Leah."

Paige pushed away his hand. "You're the one with the dirty mind. I was going to say when I try to program the TV. There are all those extra channels I don't want, and I can't get rid of them."

He held her gaze for a long moment. "Sure, you were." Finally, he looked away. "If it has to be a rom-com, how about an older one. Have you seen *He's Just Not That Into You*?"

"I'm a woman. Of course I've seen it. Not exactly sentimental, but I'd watch it again."

Picking up the remote, he clicked through the on-screen menu.

Curling tighter, she took a swig of wine. "The title might as well be my theme song."

When the opening music blasted through the speakers, he turned down the volume. "What was that?"

"Nothing. Get comfy and drink your wine. It's excellent, by the way."

"One of my favorites. It should go well with the cheesy premise to the plot."

"With jokes like that, it's no wonder you're still single. Now shut up and watch the movie."

He grinned back at her before stretching out with his feet up on the coffee table. "What's your excuse for not being hitched?"

"I don't need one. Men are idiots. Or at least the vast majority of them are. My BFFs seem to have found a couple of keepers."

"I thought I was your BFF."

She eyed him steadily. "You're in a class all by yourself."

"You make me feel so special."

They sat in comfortable silence as the movie progressed. Paige sipped her wine slowly and stared at the TV screen. *Guys who don't return calls. Boyfriends who're content with the status quo. Women who fool themselves into believing all is good when it isn't.* She could relate to each scenario.

Turning her head against the couch cushion, she narrowed her eyes at Quentin, who seemed more interested in playing on his phone than in the movie.

With his lifestyle, he could have starred in the film.

After a moment, he glanced up. "What?"

"Nothing."

"Doesn't seem like nothing when you're looking at me like I served up roadkill for dinner."

"Sorry. I was just thinking, you're a lot like most of the guys in this movie."

"I'll admit I haven't been paying much attention. Is that an insult?"

"Yes, but maybe I'm simply projecting."

He put down his phone, took her empty wineglass and set it on the table, then turned down the TV volume. Scooting closer, he pulled her against his shoulder. "Did that guy, Tom, hurt you? Is that what this is about?"

"A few things he said bothered me." She was quiet for a long moment. "Distance wasn't our only problem. He told me he couldn't compete with an ideal, and there wasn't much point in even trying."

Quentin tightened his arm around her. "What the hell does that mean?"

"That I know exactly what I want, and no mere mortal can live up to my expectations."

"Is it true?"

"I don't know." She rubbed her thumb back and forth over a spot on the knee of her pants. "Maybe. Probably. If he's correct, I'm doomed to living life alone. Forever."

He burst out laughing.

"Ass!" She shoved him away.

"Sorry! But you sounded so dramatic. Christ, Paige. You're beautiful and smart, entertaining and hot. I can't see you winding up as an old maid."

"So, I should give up on finding Mr. Right and just settle?"

"Or we can be each other's backup plan."

"I'm thirty-one. How long do you expect me to wait?"

"Good question. Forty seems like a reasonable number. I might be ready to settle down by the time I hit the big four-oh."

She threw a decorative pillow at him. "You're an idiot. My eggs would be petrified by then. What if I want kids?"

"Do you?"

"Yes, but maybe I should get a puppy instead. You used to say you wanted them—kids, not dogs. Has that changed?"

"I still do. Eventually." He poked her with his sock-clad foot. "What kind of puppy?"

Grabbing the remote, she turned off the TV as the credits rolled. "I'm going to bed."

"Hey, don't be mad. I'm just kidding." He lunged forward and grabbed her hand.

Off balance, she toppled onto him. When he wrapped his arms around her, she smashed her nose against his chin. "Ouch."

"Sorry." Bracing his foot against the coffee table to keep them from rolling to the floor, he regarded her with amusement. "Shall I kiss it and make it better?"

Before she could answer—or struggle upright—he pressed a kiss to the tip of her nose. Slowly his eyes darkened, and he adjusted his position to kiss her surprised lips that parted on contact. Whisper soft and tentative at first, he deepened the contact. Tongues touched, and Paige couldn't suppress a little moan.

His cell rang, and she jerked backward and fell over onto the floor when he released her.

His cheeks flushed as he snatched up the phone and slid his thumb across the surface without looking at it. "What?"

A high voice penetrated the silence, talking on and on as Paige scrambled to her feet. She rubbed her sore hip while her pounding heart slowed. With an effort, she wrenched her gaze away from Quentin's stunned expression. Since she didn't know what to say, escape to her bedroom seemed like the best solution. Turning, she fled.

Why the hell did he kiss me?

After quietly closing the door behind her, she leaned against it and simply breathed. The kiss was no big deal. A spur of the moment impulse. It wasn't like a single random kiss—*even if it involved tongue*—was going to ruin their friendship and make things awkward between them.

Was it?

She stripped off her clothes and dropped them into the hamper, then put on a pair of soft cotton shorts and a tank top, along with her fleece robe. She'd scurried into the bathroom and was scrubbing the enamel off her teeth when a knock sounded on the door.

"What?" she yelled through a mouthful of toothpaste.

"Are you okay?"

She spat in the sink. "Of course."

"Can I come in?"

She thought about it for a moment. "Sure. Join the party."

He pushed open the door and gave her a cautious smile. "You left abruptly."

"You were on the phone." Maybe if she didn't mention the kiss that had rocked her world, he wouldn't either.

"It was Blaze. That woman doesn't give up. She wants to come down here."

"And?" Paige rinsed out her mouth.

"What do you mean, *and*? I told her no way. I tried to be nice . . ."

"Maybe that's the problem. Nice is overrated."

"So, I shouldn't be nice and apologize for losing my mind and kissing you?"

There it is. He just couldn't leave well enough alone.

She decided to go for the direct approach. "Why did you?"

"You literally fell in my lap. Gut reflex when confronted with soft lips and even softer curves. I'm only human, and you were sitting on my—"

"Stop!" She held up a hand. "I'm taking my soft everything and going to bed. Feel free to shower. Cold is to the right."

He laid a hand on her arm as she brushed past. "It was an excellent kiss."

"I do most things well. Good night, Quentin."

"Night, Paige."

Minutes later, she lay in bed, not even close to sleep, while the water ran in the bathroom. Maybe he was taking a cold shower. Maybe the kiss had been all about hormones and the fact that Quentin currently wasn't getting any.

They'd been friends their entire lives. Best friends. She didn't want to screw that up with sex. Knowing Quentin's track record in excruciating detail, a romantic relationship between them wouldn't last since he obviously didn't want anything long term. She wouldn't let herself even think about the possibility. Instead, they would go back to what they'd always cherished. Friendship, pure and simple.

And maybe a little lonely.

* * *

Quentin stepped out of the shower, his skin covered in goosebumps, and grabbed a towel off the rack. After five minutes standing beneath the cold spray, he certainly wasn't tempted to do anything stupid with Paige. Rubbing vigorously to get the blood flowing again, he winced. In his current state, enticing *any* woman into his bed would be a challenge.

Wrapping the towel around his waist, he left the bathroom and headed to the second bedroom, which Paige used as an office and guest room. The futon was still folded out from the previous night, the covers in a rumpled mess. Clothes littered the floor. He wasn't exactly the neatest houseguest. Dropping the towel, he pulled on a pair of clean boxers, flipped the blankets into place, and climbed into bed. After a minute, he got up to lower the shade on the window to cut the moonlight streaming through. His hand stilled on the blind. With the moon shedding a silvery glow over the waves lapping the shore, the night was made for romance.

Which was the last damned thing he needed. He let the shade hit the sill with a thump and returned to his lumpy bed. Staring at the wall separating him from Paige and wondering what she slept in was just plain stupid. He wasn't going to start something with the one woman he'd loved forever. He knew she loved him back, but not in *that* way. Trying to change their friendship into something more would only end in both of them getting hurt since a whole lot of women had told him he sucked at relationships. Paige deserved better than his best effort.

Since he was lonely and horny, the solution to his problem seemed obvious. First, he needed to put some distance between the two of them, which meant calling Nina about renting her house. Second, he needed to find a willing woman who knew the score and didn't want anything serious, only a little extracurricular fun. With another female to distract him, he wouldn't let wine, the stupid rom-com, and the sweet vanilla scent Paige wore tempt him into making a move on his best friend.

With that settled in his mind, he closed his eyes, but it was a long time before he finally fell asleep.

After a restless night, he rose hours before his normal time as the scent of coffee teased him out of bed. Pulling on a pair of jeans and an old sweatshirt, he left his temporary quarters and headed into the compact kitchen. Paige stood at the sink wearing her fuzzy purple robe, drinking coffee, and staring out the window at an angry sea.

"Are you waiting for me to make breakfast?"

With a cry, she spun around and sloshed coffee. "Son of a bitch!" Setting down the mug, she shook her hand.

"Did you burn yourself?" Turning on the water, he took a gentle hold on her fingers and held them under the flow. "I thought you heard me coming."

"In bare feet? You didn't make a sound." She flipped off the faucet. "My hand's okay. Mostly, I was just startled."

"Sorry." When she turned away from the sink and brushed up against him, he stepped back. "I wasn't using my head. Will breakfast make up for my stupidity?"

That elicited a small smile.

"Depends on what you're making."

"Cinnamon apple crepes and scrambled eggs with gruyere and chives?"

"And you wonder why Blaze won't leave you alone. If you served oatmeal instead of ambrosia, you wouldn't have half the problems you do."

He reached for a mug off the rack beside the coffee pot. "Have you had my oatmeal? Talk about a secret weapon . . ."

"Just make the crepes. I'm going to go take a quick shower." Paige paused in the doorway. "Oh, I talked to Nina a little while ago and told her you're in town. She said to call her if you're still interested in renting her house."

Apparently Paige is also in a rush to get rid of me.

He poured his coffee then took a sip, eyeing her over the rim of his cup. "I'll do that."

"Great. I'll be back by the time those crepes are ready."

She disappeared before he had a chance to respond. The woman was definitely skittish this morning. Completely his fault, and past time to do something about it.

He chose three apples from the bowl of fruit on the counter, then dug through the utensil drawer for a peeler. He'd call Nina while he cooked, if he could find his cell. He snapped his fingers and strolled into the living room to scoop it up off the coffee table. Shocker, there was already a missed call from Blaze. Ignoring it, he scrolled through his contacts on the way back to the kitchen, put the phone on speaker, and dialed Nina.

She answered immediately without benefit of a greeting. "Paige said you'd be calling. Congrats on scooping up the Poseidon Grill."

"Thanks. I'm excited about it."

"Is this your fifth restaurant?"

"Sixth, but who's counting." He made short work of peeling the first apple. "Paige mentioned you might be willing to rent me your house for a couple of months."

"I could be persuaded."

He sliced the apple into a bowl and picked up a second. "Do I have to bribe you with food the way I do Paige every time I make a lame-ass move? Right now, I'm cooking her breakfast."

Her chuckle rolled across his senses. "I thought you were Mr. Smooth, Quentin. How'd you irritate Paige this quickly?"

He paused with the peeler hovering over the apple. "If she didn't tell you, maybe I—"

"Tell me what?"

He debated shooting his mouth off to Paige's friend, then shrugged. Maybe Nina would let him move in today if . . . "We were watching a chick flick—her choice, not mine—and drinking wine. I sort of forgot myself in the moment and, well, let's just say she'd probably prefer a little distance until the awkwardness wears off."

"Did you *sleep* with her?" Nina's shout practically deafened him.

"Of course not. I'm not a complete asshole. Give me some credit."

"Then, what—"

"It was a single kiss. Not a big deal." *At least it shouldn't have been a big deal.* "We just need a little space so we can return to normal."

"Is that what Paige wants?"

"Of course. The whole stupid situation was my fault. How much for rent?"

"Huh? Oh, uh, since I like you, two grand a month, furnished."

"That seems more than reasonable. When can I move in?"

"Today, I guess. I still have some art supplies and paintings stored in the second bedroom, but they won't take long to move. I'm working on setting up my studio here."

He finished slicing the apples, then added cinnamon,

sugar, and a little vanilla to the bowl. "Congratulations on your marriage, by the way. Teague's a lucky man."

"We're both lucky. You should try settling down with one woman instead of playing the field. You might actually like it."

"You could be right."

Chapter Five

Paige carefully unwrapped a Waterford crystal vase, set it on the shelf, then reached into the trunk for the next piece. Displaying the entire inventory she'd picked up recently would take time, but at least most of the smaller items from Margaret LaPine's home were clean. Unlike the collection from Zeb's barn. Removing years' worth of dirt and grime would take some effort.

Today, she was up for the challenge. Maybe scrubbing and polishing would work off most of her annoyance. She set a bone china cup and saucer next to the vase and wondered who she was more irritated with, Quentin or herself. He'd packed up his stuff and bolted after breakfast, but not before stripping his sheets off his bed and throwing them in the wash. A sure sign guilt was eating at him. Paige didn't want him to feel guilty. She wasn't certain what, exactly, she did want him to feel, but it wasn't guilt.

When the bell over the shop door jingled, she wiped her hands on the seat of her jeans and tucked a stray lock of hair back into the loose curls secured in a twist atop her head before heading up front to greet her customer. A man she didn't recognize stood with fists planted on his hips, surveying the store. If the scowl darkening his hazel eyes was any indication, he wasn't thrilled to be there.

Paige smiled anyway. "Welcome to Old Things. May I help you?"

"I hope so. A couple days ago, my mother sold a few pieces of furniture to you, along with a host of smaller items. I have reason to believe some of my personal possessions might have been included in what you bought."

"And you would be?"

"Baird Copeland. I had baseball cards and old comic books that are probably worth a fortune stashed in my childhood bedroom. I'd forgotten they were there until Mother dragged me over to haul her crap to the dump."

"Miss Lola mentioned you were helping her dispose of the trash. I can assure you I didn't buy any sports memorabilia or comic books."

"I know you didn't *intentionally* purchase them." He spoke slowly, the way he probably did when confronting a not too bright child. "But they might have been in a piece of furniture you bought. I can't remember exactly where I put them. It's been years."

Paige's hackles rose. "I'm currently preparing the new inventory for display. I don't expect to find your property, Mr. Copeland, but I'll certainly notify you if I do. If you'll leave a business card, I'll contact you."

"Maybe I could simply look through the pieces now."

"Everything I bought recently is in the storage room, and your mother's furniture is packed in with purchases from two other locations. Most of it isn't even accessible, and I have no intention of moving a lot of furniture when"—she broke off as the door opened with a jingle of bells and met Nina's questioning gaze—"when I have other customers."

"I guess I'll have to return later, once you've sorted out your storage problem." Pulling his wallet from the pocket of his slacks, he removed a business card and thrust it in her direction.

Paige took it. When he turned and brushed past Nina, Paige flipped him the bird. The door slammed shut with a clash of bells.

"Uh, bad timing on my part?" Her friend's eyes sparkled with amusement. "That guy looked familiar."

"Actually, perfect timing. He's Lola Copeland's son. The man practically accused me of stealing his old baseball cards, which he apparently stashed in a dresser at his mom's house."

"That's right, Baird. I met him once when I was delivering a painting to his mom. I'm going to miss her. She was a terrific customer."

Paige dropped the business card on the counter. "By the way, you're Miss Lola's financial backup plan. She's hoping to make a fortune selling your pictures in the not too distant future."

"Wouldn't that be wonderful?" Nina grinned. "Unlikely, but wonderful."

Paige's temper eased. "I may have been a little harsher than necessary with her son, but his attitude irritated me. And I wasn't in the best mood to begin with."

"About that . . ." Nina propped an elbow on the counter. "Quentin is officially moved into my old house. Should I have short-sheeted his bed before giving him the key?"

"What are you talking—oh." Paige's chin jerked up. "He told you about the kiss?"

"I think he was trying to spur me into moving my art

supplies out of the house so he could take possession immediately."

"Anything rather than face me tonight." Her cheeks heated. "Maybe Quentin was afraid I wouldn't be able to keep my hands off him."

"Paige, the man-eater on the prowl?"

She sputtered in laughter. "Okay, I'm being ridiculous. I can't help it. Who would have thought a simple kiss could be so awkward?"

Nina stared at her. "Was it?"

"Awkward? Not the actual kiss, but afterward . . ."

"Simple. Seems like with all the years of friendship between you two, neither of you would let a simple kiss bother you. He must have kissed you before?"

"On the top of my head, my cheek, the lips once when he was drunk after a rough breakup. He didn't remember doing it the next day. This was different."

"You two are so tight. You're not going to let—"

"Of course not." Paige rubbed her finger over a water spot on the mahogany surface of the counter. "Everything will be fine in a couple of days. We were both feeling a little vulnerable, that's all."

"If you say so." Nina straightened and took a step back. "I wanted to check on you, but I have a few errands to run."

"Go. I'm completely fine, and I have a ton of work to do. I need to organize my new inventory before I can decorate the shop for Christmas."

"Parks and recreation employees were out hanging wreaths and holiday lights up and down the street. The town is beginning to look very festive."

"Good. Tourists will be here in droves for the Winter Ball. Or at least I hope they will. And on that note, I'd better get busy."

"I'll see you later then. Bye, Paige."

"Bye, Nina."

Twenty minutes later, Paige was scrubbing tarnish off a pair of silver candlesticks from Zeb's barn when the bells jingled again. Swearing softly, she pulled off her gloves.

"It's just me," a voice called out.

"Oh, thank goodness."

A short time later, Mindy appeared in the doorway. "I finished quicker than I expected at the dentist. How's it going back here?"

"Slow. I have a lot of polishing to do, but the shop hasn't been busy this morning." Paige snapped her gloves back on and glanced up at her clerk.

In her sixties, Mindy had found retirement after a career in nursing tremendously boring. Active and friendly, the woman knew everyone in town and quite a bit about old furniture. Working part-time in the antique store had given her something constructive to do, and Paige some much-needed assistance.

"Thanks for hurrying back. You can help customers. That way I don't have to worry about getting filthy."

Mindy's light laughter bubbled up like champagne. "Since I didn't need Novocain, I won't even drool on the paperwork."

"Good to know. If you feel like taking a rag to the trunk I just emptied, the leather exterior needs to be wiped down with oil and the inside dusted."

"The steamer trunk near the front counter?" Her frosted hair fluttered as she waved a hand. "It's a beauty. I'll get right on it."

"Thanks, Mindy."

After her clerk disappeared, Paige went back to scrubbing. She'd just finished removing the last of the tarnish from the silver candlestick holders when the bells jingled again. Moments later, a male voice spoke rapidly in response to Mindy's greeting, too low for Paige to make out the words. Taking out a clean cloth, she wiped traces of cleaner from the pair of candlesticks. Pleased with the results, she removed her gloves.

"Sir, you can't go back there. I'll see if Miss Shephard has time to speak to you." Annoyance colored her employee's voice. She appeared in the doorway, brown eyes flashing.

"There's a Mr. Stillwater out front. He says you ripped off his grandpa, and he wants the inventory you purchased back."

"What the hell?" Paige pushed the stool away from the work bench and hopped to the floor. "I told that jerk I paid Zeb a fair price. I can't believe—" She stopped speaking as Mindy stepped out of the way to let her by.

No coveralls this time. Justin wore a suit and tie in addition to a pissed off expression.

"You cut your hair."

"What?" The frown deepened. "Lady, are out of your mind?" Before she could respond, his eyes cleared. "Oh, you met Justin. My brother and I are nothing alike. How you could mistake me for him is—"

"Did you come here for a reason, Mr. Stillwater?"

"I certainly did. That collection in Grandpa's barn is my inheritance. I won't have you robbing an old man blind. I took a look at the invoice you gave him, and you didn't pay him near what that crap is worth."

Paige held onto her temper. "I assure you I paid your grandfather a fair price. He was very happy with the deal we made."

"He's practically senile. You took advantage—"

"Do you have power of attorney for Mr. Stillwater?" Paige spoke loudly to cut him off.

"What? No. He's not—"

"Then I suggest you take your accusations and leave."

His eyes narrowed. "First, I'll retrieve my grandfather's possessions. I'll give you what you paid for them."

"No, you'll pay my asking price, after I clean up the pieces and display them for sale."

"Now you're just screwing with me."

"I'm in business to make money. Since you have no legal say in what your grandfather does, I'll thank you to leave now."

He clenched his hands at his sides. "I thought we could be civil about this. I'll make certain my grandfather doesn't sell any more of his antiques to you in the future."

"That's your prerogative, of course, but I didn't cheat Zeb. If you check around, you'll find other dealers wouldn't have paid more than I did."

Without another word, he turned and left. The door shut with a clash of bells.

"Wow, two for two this morning. I'm on a roll."

Mindy stared at her with wide eyes. "What are you talking about?"

"Baird Copeland showed up earlier, ranting about how his valuable baseball cards were stashed in a piece of furniture I bought from his mother. I looked through the armoire and dresser after he left and didn't find anything. My guess is they wound up at the landfill. After that encounter, I figured I'd dealt with my quota of idiots for the day."

"Jerk number two looked familiar when he walked in, but I couldn't place him at first. That was Jonas Stillwater. His twin brother, Justin, works down at Hank's garage."

When Paige headed toward the back of the shop, Mindy followed.

"I met Justin out at his grandpa's farm."

"I believe Jonas owns a small financial planning company up the coast somewhere. I haven't seen him in years."

"Zeb is a sweet old guy. It's too bad his grandsons are money-hungry assholes."

When the bells jingled again, Mindy lowered her voice. "Let's hope this isn't strike number three walking through the door."

Paige shook her head. "I couldn't be that unlucky."

The day passed quickly without any additional irate confrontations. By the time Paige was ready to lock up for the evening, she'd made substantial progress prepping the new inventory. A day spent with cleaning solvents was messy work, and she had quite a few more pieces that still required work. She'd left the ones with the worst rust in a container filled with white vinegar to soak overnight.

Mindy had gone, and Paige was flipping the sign in the window to 'closed' when Quentin parked his Jaguar in front of the shop. He stepped out onto the sidewalk, his blond hair gleaming beneath the streetlight as he hurried toward her.

She held open the door. "Did Nina kick you out of her house already?"

He grinned in response. "Not yet. I ran into Ryan and Leah earlier and made plans to meet them for happy hour at Castaways. Want to go with me? They have half-priced drinks."

She glanced down at her dirt-streaked jeans. "I need to clean up first."

"No problem. You know Leah will be late getting there."

"True. Come on inside. I'll lock up, and we can go out the back way."

Quentin followed her up the stairs then flopped down on the couch while Paige headed into her bedroom to strip off her filthy clothes.

"How was your day?" Quentin yelled from the other room.

"Not bad. With any luck, I'll have everything I just purchased ready for display in a couple of days."

"That's good. Are you almost ready?"

"Getting there." She obviously didn't have time for a shower. After dressing in a pair of black pants and a pink angora sweater, she headed into the bathroom to touch up her makeup and fix her hair, which was straggling around her face. With ease of practice, she secured it in a quick twist and snapped off the light.

Quentin glanced up from his phone when she entered the room. "That was quick."

"I'm nothing if not efficient." Pausing beside the coat closet, she bent to retrieve a pair of black heeled ankle boots. After tugging them on, she turned with a smile. "All set."

"You look hot."

"Hey, it's cold outside." She pulled her leather jacket out of the closet.

"I meant . . . never mind. Let me help you with that." He held the jacket for her to slide her arms through the sleeves.

Turning, she gave him a wicked grin. "You look pretty hot, too."

What an understatement. Wearing a button-down shirt a shade darker than his aqua eyes and a pair of dark jeans that hugged a superior ass, Quentin cleaned up nicely. But then, he always did.

Before she could open the door, he touched the back of her hand, his fingers warm against her skin. "Are we cool? I don't want any awkwardness between us."

"Of course." Standing on her toes, she pressed a kiss to his cheek. "Our friendship is bulletproof."

A weight she'd been carrying around all day lifted as she realized it was true. She and Quentin would always be just fine. "Let's go get that drink. Then we can talk dinner."

"For someone who can't weigh much more than a hundred pounds, you sure do think about food a lot."

"It's a curse being this small because I do like to eat. Especially when you're cooking." Taking the stairs at a quick pace, she avoided obstacles in the storage area to reach the rear door. "How're plans for the Poseidon Grill coming along?"

"Not bad." He stood close behind her while she locked up and then took her arm. "I offered the manager position to one of my people in Seattle. Braden's young and eager with a wife and new baby. He was thrilled with the opportunity and the promotion. Siren Cove is a great place to raise a family."

Paige turned her face up to sniff the salt-scented breeze blowing off the ocean as they walked the short distance to Castaways. "How about the rest of the staff?"

"I'll probably promote from within for the executive chef position, but we'll hire everyone else locally. My hope is a lot of the old crew from back when the restaurant was being run properly will return."

"I know a few former employees who are still looking for work. My guess is you won't have a hard time finding people."

"I hope not." He opened the bar door to a blast of

warmth. When Leah waved from a table near the windows, he guided Paige over with a hand on her back.

Leah rose and hugged Quinten first and then Paige. A quick glance toward Quentin followed by a questioning look spoke more clearly than words. Apparently Nina had mentioned the now infamous kiss to their mutual friend. Paige gave her a subtle thumbs-up. Relief eased across Leah's features.

When Quentin broke off a brief conversation with Ryan, Paige reached in for a hug. "I haven't seen you in a while."

"I spent some time in Portland last week on business. As soon as school lets out for the holiday break, Leah and I are heading over to my house in Sisters so I can do a little rock climbing."

Paige glanced from Ryan to Leah. "You'll be here for Christmas, won't you?"

"Sure. We'll return before the Winter Ball since I'm on the planning committee this year." Leah sipped her wine as the cocktail waitress approached. "What are you two drinking?"

Paige smiled at the older woman who stopped beside their table. "Hi, Janice. I'll have the house Chardonnay."

"A draft ale, please," Quentin added.

"Coming right up." With a quick nod, she hurried away.

"Speaking of the Winter Ball . . ." Leah pinned Quentin to his chair with a determined look. "We need bachelors to auction off for our fundraiser. I'm sure you'd love to participate."

"Can I just write a check instead?"

"That's not how it works. If we don't have enough men donating their *time*, the event will fall flat. It's one evening out of your life for the date. Who knows, you might even have fun."

"You're kidding, right? I'd rather pick up trash along the highway."

"I can arrange that, too, if you'd like." Leah's tone was completely serious.

Ryan took a swig of his beer. "You may as well cave in now. You know my wife won't back down until you do."

"Fine," Quentin said. "Sign me up. I'll probably survive."

"Way to be a good sport. I may even bid on you. The least I can do is run up your price since I have a feeling the winning bid will be more than I can afford."

"Gee, you're all heart, Paige." He smiled at the waitress when she returned with their drinks. "Thanks, Janice."

"You're welcome. Another round for you and Leah, Ryan?"

"We're good." Leah spoke before he could answer. "My mission here is accomplished, so we'll be leaving soon. I have English essays to grade."

"And here I thought you initiated a night out because you missed me," Quentin said as Janice departed.

Leah laughed. "That, too, but my duty on the committee is to round up victims . . . uh, I mean volunteers. You're a big score."

"I'll figure out a way to get even—I mean thank you—later."

Paige drank her wine while the others discussed a controversial film they'd seen recently, but her mind wasn't on the conversation. She loved hanging out with her friends, but it would be nice to have a man look at her the way Ryan watched Leah. Every time he glanced her way, his eyes softened, and a small smile curved his lips. Paige was pretty sure no guy had ever looked at her with such love and devotion. Which was probably why she was still single.

"You're awfully quiet." Quentin closed a hand over hers. "Usually you have an opinion on hot topics."

"Huh? Oh, I didn't see the movie. I didn't feel like watching it alone." She winced. "Wow, I sound pathetic. Maybe I really should buy myself a date at the Winter Ball."

Leah pushed her chair back. "Or quit being so damn picky. Men ask you out all the time. You should stop saying no."

"Maybe I will. Are you leaving?"

"Yep." She rose to her feet and waited for Ryan to help her with her jacket. "I have a bunch of essays to read tonight, along with a math lesson to plan."

"I'd rather scrub rust off a pair of andirons."

"To each her own." Leah dropped a kiss on Quentin's cheek. "Have a nice evening, and thanks for being a good sport about the bachelor auction."

"I don't mind doing my part for the good of the community."

Ryan pulled a twenty from his wallet and tucked it under his beer bottle. "Give that to Janice. Since Leah lured you here with an ulterior motive, seems like paying for drinks is the least I can do."

"True," Quentin said. "Go grade papers or whatever."

Ryan glanced over his shoulder as he left the table behind his wife. "I'm hoping for whatever."

Paige choked on her wine then sputtered and coughed. After a moment, Quentin pounded her on the back.

"Are you okay?'

"Yes," she croaked. After clearing her throat, she added, "I was thinking earlier that Ryan looks at Leah like the honeymoon isn't over yet. I bet he gets his 'whatever.'"

"Lucky guy."

"Lucky Leah." Paige polished off her wine. "Finish your drink, and then I'll let you buy me a burger."

"How about if I make dinner, instead? I went shopping earlier and bought prawns."

"My favorite. You didn't have to bribe me to get back on my good side."

"I just want to treat you the way you deserve."

Warmth filled her at the genuine concern in his eyes. "Maybe I'm the lucky one, after all."

Chapter Six

"Did you see that?"

Quentin pulled his keys from his pocket and glanced over at Paige. "See what?"

"I swear a light flashed inside my shop."

Turning to face Old Things, he frowned. "Are you sure? It looks dark in there to me."

"It was just for a second. There!"

A dim glow from somewhere near the rear of the shop appeared for a moment before it went out.

"Maybe a streetlight is reflecting off a mirror or something?"

"Then it would be steady since a mirror doesn't move around the shop on its own." Paige rounded his Jag and headed straight to the front door to rattle the knob. "The door is definitely still locked."

When a light flashed again, this time in a zigzag pattern, Quentin swore. "Damn it! Whoever's in there must have heard you. Stay here." He sprinted down the side alley and took the corner at full speed. In the dark, he cracked his knee on the trash bin. "Ouch! Mother fu—"

A door creaked open, and footsteps slapped the pavement. A darker shadow fled toward the rear of the parking lot. By the time Quentin hobbled to the low fence marking the cliff's edge, the intruder was halfway down the stairs leading to the beach.

"Son of a bitch!" Reaching into his pocket, he pulled out his phone.

"I already called nine-one-one." Paige stopped beside him and gripped his arm. "I guess he got away."

Quentin gritted his teeth. "Only because I slammed into the dumpster. My knee hurts like a mother."

When the roar of an engine sounded, they both turned to face the street. Moments later, a patrol car drove down the alley and stopped.

"That was quick."

"Not quick enough." Quentin limped toward the officer who exited the car. When a blinding light shone in his eyes, he raised a hand to shield them.

"Paige? What's going on?" The light lowered as the cop approached.

"Hey, Chris," Paige greeted the officer, a man they'd known since childhood. "I'd say it's good to see you, but it isn't. I had a break-in. The guy got away."

"You saw him?"

"It was too dark to make out any details," Quentin answered. "He ran down the stairs to the beach."

When Paige headed toward the shop, the officer laid a hand on her shoulder. "I want you both to stay back while I check it out. Someone else could still be inside."

She wrapped her arms across her chest and shivered. "I didn't think of that. Please be careful."

He spoke quietly into the radio at his shoulder as he approached the building.

"Are you okay?" Quentin slid an arm around her waist and held her close to his side.

"Sure. At least I think so." She let out a long breath and leaned against him. "I wonder what that creep stole. God, this sucks. I have a feeling I'm not going to get those prawns anytime soon."

"Really? Dinner is your main concern?"

"No, but if I think about the damage he could have done to some extremely valuable pieces while fumbling around in the dark, I might lose it completely."

"If anything's broken, you have insurance, but maybe he was a careful thief. I didn't hear any crashes before he bolted out the back door. How much cash do you keep in your register?"

"None. I always lock it in my safe when I close up at night." When the lights flashed on inside the store, Paige reached for his hand and held it. "Here comes Chris. Keep your fingers crossed the news isn't too bad."

The officer waved them over. "All clear inside. I checked upstairs, too, and your apartment door was still locked and hadn't been tampered with. I called this in. One of my colleagues will head down to the beach to look for the perp, but he's probably long gone by now." Chris Long met Quentin's gaze. "You said 'he.' The intruder was a male?"

"Definitely. He moved like a guy. The dude was probably my height but a little heavier."

He pulled out his notebook. "You're what, around six foot, a hundred and sixty-five pounds?"

"Close enough. The man I chased ran pretty fast, but it was only a short distance to the beach stairs. He could have been a teenager or an in-shape fifty-year-old."

"Anything else you can tell me about him?"

"I think he had on jeans and athletic shoes with fluorescent colors. I could see the blur of his feet when he ran. Some sort of dark jacket. I couldn't make out any other details."

"Great. Thanks." Chris turned toward Paige. "Did you see him?"

She shook her head. "I called nine-one-one while Quentin ran through the alley to the back of the building. He was gone by the time I followed." Impatience gave her tone an edge. "Can I go check out my shop now?"

"Sure. You'll need to make a complete list of anything missing. There's no point in dusting the whole store for prints since the merchandise has to be covered in them. But if you spot anything out of place, we can check for a match to known criminals." The officer held the door open. "Unfortunately, most experienced thieves are smart enough to wear gloves."

"Let's hope this one is an amateur or stupid."

Chris pointed. "Is this how you left the storage area?"

"It's more crowded than usual back here because I've been processing new inventory." Paige walked slowly around an armoire with one door ajar. "I thought both doors were closed, but I could be wrong since the latch is stiff. There's nothing inside the chest to take." She stopped beside a work counter covered in miscellaneous objects from china bowls to a branding iron. "I'd swear a few of these things have been moved, but I'm not sure which ones. I don't think anything's missing, but I can't be positive without pulling up my inventory."

"Don't touch anything." The cop laid a hand on her arm when she reached toward a cookie jar. "We'll do a walk-through of the main room before you check your computer records."

She headed toward the front of the shop. Her lips were pressed in a tight line, and the hands she clenched at her sides quivered. Quentin took one and squeezed it and gave her an encouraging smile.

"So far so good, right?"

Her responding smile seemed forced before she quickly looked away.

To his uneducated eye, the shop looked much the way he'd last seen it. Cluttered but not messy, the store reminded him of his grandma's attic. He was pretty sure a feeling of potential discovery was the ambiance Paige cultivated. When she tugged against his grip, he released her and waited while she roamed between pieces of furniture to study shelves filled with an assortment of smaller items.

Fifteen minutes later, she returned to his side. "Maybe I should go buy a lottery ticket, because boy do I feel lucky. I could swear nothing's missing, and he obviously didn't break anything in his search . . . if that's what the break-in was about."

"You think the perp was looking for something specific?" Chris broke off a brief conversation over his radio. "Any idea what, exactly?"

"I don't have a clue." She pointed to a small porcelain statuette of a woman in a bonnet resting on a nearby shelf. "That Hummel alone is worth a couple grand. How easy would it have been to slip into his pocket?"

Quentin stared. "Two thousand dollars, for that? I swear my grandmother has dozens just like it. Who knew?"

"Anyone who collects them. And potential thieves, you would think."

The officer cleared his throat. "Well, then, since I'm sure a thorough search of your records will take some time, do you want to give me a call tomorrow once you've finished?"

"Of course."

When Paige followed the cop toward the storage room, Quentin hurried to catch up. "How did the guy break into the building?"

Chris stopped at the open back door. Taking out his flashlight, he aimed the beam at the knob. "See those scratches. It looks like he picked the lock. You could use better security, Paige. A simple lock isn't much of a deterrent."

"Since I live upstairs, I figured that would make any potential thief think twice. Obviously, I was mistaken."

He gave her an up and down look. "No offense, but you aren't very threatening. Maybe if you had a guard dog for a pet, or a decent alarm system."

"I used to have one, but I deactivated it. I kept setting the damn thing off by accident. If I didn't live in the building, I'd reconsider." She leaned against the doorframe, and her shoulders drooped. "Hopefully we scared the potential burglar off before he took anything, and he won't risk coming back."

"Let's hope not. The department will notify other store owners in town to be extra cautious. We always have an increase in robberies during the holidays."

"Isn't that special? All in the spirit of giving, I'm sure. Thanks for your prompt response, Chris."

"You bet. I'll be in touch."

After the patrol car cruised out of the back lot, Quentin guided Paige inside with a hand at her elbow and shut the door. "Now what?"

"Let's see, I could spend the evening going through my inventory, or I could go eat prawns."

He grinned. "Let me guess . . . I should start cooking?"

"As soon as I do something about this door." Hands on her hips, she stared around the room. "Let's go with an old-fashioned fix." She took an ornate, straight-backed chair that was missing its seat out of the corner and dragged it to the door. "We can prop this under the knob."

"Good idea." Quentin locked the door then shoved the chair into place. "That ought to hold, though I doubt he'd have the balls to come back again tonight."

"I'm not taking any chances. The lock on the front door is much better and has a deadbolt. We can go out that way."

Before she could move, he wrapped an arm around her and hugged. "You need to take a deep breath and relax. I'm not sure if you're going to break or explode."

"Right now, I'd say it's a toss-up." She let out a long, slow breath. "Okay, I'll try not to fall apart on you. Let's get out of here. You can ply me with shrimp and wine, a perfect de-stressing combination."

"You've got it." Releasing her, he followed her to the door then waited on the sidewalk while she locked up. "Ready?"

"I should drive myself. Otherwise—"

"No, you shouldn't. You're still a little shaky. I'll bring you home."

"I'm not going to argue."

Minutes later, they cruised through town. When Paige maintained a tight-lipped silence, sympathy for her filled him. The whole break-in had taken a lot out of her, and he wished there was something he could do to ease her mind. He smiled when an idea formed.

"Turn." Paige pointed as she spoke.

"Huh? Oh, sorry." The tires screeched as he took the corner into his new neighborhood. "I wasn't paying attention."

"What's on your mind?"

He slowed to turn onto his street. "A surprise for you."

"Really? Seems like I've had enough suspense this evening."

"Too bad because I'm keeping this a secret until it's a done deal. You'll just have to put a lid on your curiosity."

"I'm too mentally exhausted to even wonder what the heck you're talking about."

He parked in the driveway of Nina's old home. Across the street, lights blazed in the Victorian house Teague had bought when he and his daughter moved to Siren Cove.

"Just give me that glass of wine you promised and let me chill in peace."

"I can do that." He opened the car door and stepped out.

Paige did the same. "You're the best. You know that, right?"

"I have my moments." He walked beside her up the brick path, unlocked the door, and punched in the code to turn off the alarm. "Nina has excellent security."

"Only because she thought she had a pervert stalking her last summer. The truth was even worse, but she didn't let it break her."

"You're easily as tough as Nina, so dealing with a wimpy burglar should be a piece of cake."

Paige flexed her arm. "Good point. I'll make that creep wish he'd never been born if he comes back."

"That's the right attitude. Come keep me company while I cook, and I'll pour you that glass of wine."

It didn't take him long to start some rice pilaf to go with the prawns and clean an assortment of veggies for a stir-fry. Paige was halfway through her Pinot Grigio and seemed to have shed her tension when a sharp rap sounded at the door.

He turned away from the prawns simmering in garlic

wine sauce and frowned. "That's strange. I'm not expecting anyone."

"Maybe it's Nina. Could be she forgot something in her rush to clear out her art studio today." Paige hopped down from the bar stool. "I'll go see."

A few moments later the door opened, and a female voice said something he couldn't quite make out. It wasn't Nina's voice, but it was extremely familiar. He closed his eyes and swore.

"Look who's here." Paige swept into the kitchen, followed by a tall redhead wearing a determined expression.

"Surprise!" Blaze hurried to his side and planted a kiss on his lips before he could fend her off.

"What are you doing here?" He scowled. "How did you even find me?"

Her trilling laughter filled the room. "Some clever detective work on my part. I could have called, but I wanted to see the amazement on your face when you opened the door. Of course I wasn't expecting Paige to answer my knock. It kind of ruined the drama of the moment."

"Oh, believe me, there'll be plenty of drama."

She ignored the irony in his tone and gave him a sexy look from beneath her long lashes. "I sure hope so."

A month earlier, everything south of the border would have leaped to attention at the promise in her deep chocolate-brown eyes. Thankfully, now he didn't experience so much as a twinge.

"I can see I wasn't meant to have prawns tonight." Paige turned her back and headed toward the door. "Blaze can eat my share."

"Hey, where do you think you're going?"

"Home."

"I drove you here," he protested.

Paige glanced over her shoulder. "I'll get a ride from

Nina. I can always count on her." Her tone dripped sarcasm as she continued, "Enjoy your *surprise*."

"You don't need to leave. This won't take long."

Her gaze dropped to his waist. "I'm not sure you want to advertise that fact. Nevertheless, I'm out of here."

"Very funny. Paige—"

The door slammed behind her.

"Your little friend didn't seem very happy to see me." Smug satisfaction glimmered in Blaze's eyes.

He didn't answer as he took a moment to cool off. Finally, he pointed at the stool Paige had vacated. "Sit. We need to clear up a few things, once and for all."

He sat on a rock and stared at the waves rolling onto the beach. Out of habit, he reached toward his shirt pocket before remembering he'd stopped smoking one hundred and sixty-eight days before. Not the first time he'd quit, but certainly the longest. The current situation was testing his resolve.

Instead, he pulled out a piece of gum, unwrapped it, and shoved it in his mouth. The burst of spearmint flavor did little to calm his jittery nerves. Hours before, he'd stood hidden in the darkness below the cliff face while a couple of cops walked the beach in search of the intruder who'd broken into the antique store. The official police presence was long gone now, but he was in no hurry to go anywhere. Instead, he contemplated his next move.

He'd pushed his luck, staying in the store as long as he had. To no avail. He'd searched through the whole damn shop then started on the back room, thinking maybe the little blonde hadn't displayed her new purchases yet. A work bench had been covered with various pieces that needed cleaning, but not what he was after. It got him to thinking, however. If luck was with him, the shop owner would clean all the fingerprints off the surface and any traces of blood still in existence from the crevices. Still, he'd rather be one hundred percent certain, and recovering the evidence was his primary goal.

Except the miserable thing was nowhere to be found. Maybe Paige had taken it up to her apartment. Which could either mean she intended to keep it for herself—though he couldn't imagine why—or she'd noticed bloodstains.

A chill slid through him. He wouldn't risk going back tonight, but he had to return soon. Before she realized what she had, or worse, turned it over to the police. He preferred to go when the woman wasn't home, but he'd do whatever it took to retrieve the last piece of evidence tying him to the night his life had changed forever.

Once he destroyed every trace of the crime, he could rest easy. At least for now. Until he saw the bloodlust burning in his eyes and knew he couldn't stop it. All he could hope to do was contain the damage afterward. As he had so many times before.

Chapter Seven

"Quentin is an idiot."

Paige smiled. "Not that I disagree with you, but why, exactly, does he get your idiot vote?"

Illuminated only by the dim glow of streetlights as they cruised into town, Nina's husband's good looks were plainly evident. With chiseled features and silvery eyes that saw far more than he let on, her friend had hit the jackpot when Teague moved to town. Besides being hot, the man was also nice. It was too bad he didn't have a twin brother.

"Quentin has the perfect woman for him directly under his nose, and he's too stupid to realize it. Not very astute, in my opinion."

"Blaze? That's right, you met her at Leah and Ryan's wedding. I don't know if I'd call her perfect. She's certainly beautiful, but she's a little too clingy for Quentin. He needs someone who can match his independence, a partner, not a doormat."

"I'm not talking about Blaze." Teague pulled up to the curb in front of Old Things and turned off the engine.

"I'm talking about you. From the minute I met the two of you, I thought you were a couple. It seemed so obvious."

Paige frowned. "Did Nina say something to you? Because—"

"No, she told me you're best friends, always have been. Nothing wrong with that . . . except it's a total lie."

"Just because I'm annoyed with him doesn't mean our friendship will be affected. I wouldn't let Blaze come between us, even if I do think Quentin's a fool not to make his feelings for her clear."

Teague leaned an elbow on the steering wheel and faced her. "Why don't you spell out your own feelings, then?"

"I have. I told Quentin that Blaze won't make him happy. He knows it, but—"

"Why haven't you confessed you're in love with him?"

Words died in Paige's throat as she stared back at him. "I'm not."

"Somehow you've persuaded my wife and Leah that's true. Hell, maybe you've convinced yourself." He shrugged. "I obviously don't know you as well as they do, being relatively new to the group, but I've seen how you act when Quentin's around. There's a lightness of spirit, I guess you'd call it, that I don't notice any other time. I suppose I could be wrong, but you glow like a woman in love. While you seemed to have a good time with Tom while you two were dating, he never made your eyes shine the way Quentin does."

"I do love him. I have as long as I can remember. But I'm not in love with him."

"Why not?"

"Because I don't want to be. Quentin sucks at cultivating lasting relationships, and most of the women he dates wind up getting hurt." She tapped her chest. "I'm too smart to do that to myself."

"You can't always pick who you fall for."

"True."

"Maybe he's only bad at commitment because those other women haven't been you."

Her smile was edged with irony. "I think you're giving him way too much credit."

He grinned in response. "You could be right. I like the guy. He's entertaining and sharp. Plus, he makes Keely laugh."

"Yes, he's amusing and good with kids, and I love him dearly. But in the interest of my mental health, I'll keep looking for a nice guy who has great abs and is almost as smart as me. Preferably one who likes romantic comedies, or at least pretends to."

"Paige?"

"What?"

"Good luck with that. You have high expectations." When he opened his door, the interior light flashed on. "I'll walk you up to your apartment to make sure all is clear."

"No need. If my burglar had returned, we would have seen some sign of movement inside by now. Anyway, I have to lock up."

"Then I'll wait here until your light comes on upstairs."

"That, you can do. Thanks for the ride home. I appreciate it."

"You're welcome. Nina is far better than I am at helping Keely with her costume for the Christmas play. Honestly, I was happy to escape."

"Your daughter will make an adorable tiger in *Christmas at the Zoo*." After opening the door, Paige slid to the sidewalk and gave him a final wave. Minutes later, she locked the front door behind her and made her way upstairs in the dark, familiar with each inch of her store. After entering her apartment, she flipped on a light and went to the front window to wave. With a tap of the horn, Teague drove away.

Strolling into the kitchen, she dropped her purse on the counter, opened the refrigerator, and stared at the contents. After a minute, she shut it. She wasn't hungry. She just felt numb. The life she'd built for herself had been invaded, and even though she'd been in no physical danger, the knowledge that she could have been shook her. Not to mention her parents would freak out when she told them about the intruder. Since they were currently on the other side of the country visiting her brother in Boston, she decided she could safely leave that phone conversation until morning without risk of them hearing about it through the local gossip grapevine.

After choosing an apple from the fruit bowl to serve as her dinner, she headed into the office-cum-spare bedroom Quentin had so recently occupied and sat down at her desk. After turning on the computer, she pulled up her inventory files and printed them out. The task of checking for missing items would be tedious. As a dozen pages landed in the tray, she took a bite of her apple and chewed furiously.

No time like the present. It wasn't as if she had anything better to do tonight. Nina was home with Teague and Keely, involved with family stuff, and Leah and Ryan were probably cuddling on the couch. God only knew what Quentin and Blaze were up to. Shouting wasn't his style. Maybe if he yelled at her, she'd actually believe he meant what he said about their breakup. On the other hand, if they had a civilized discussion over a glass of wine, and he was feeling lonely . . .

She shut down that train of thought as she snatched up the stack of papers and headed toward the door. She hadn't lied to Teague, not exactly. She didn't want to screw up her friendship with Quentin *or* get her heart ripped out of her chest. But knowing he was involved with another woman was always easier when he was over three hundred miles away in Seattle, and she was also dating someone. The current situation was just . . . awkward. Weird. Thinking about him and Blaze together stole the last of her appetite. She tossed the apple core in the trash on her way downstairs.

Since she wasn't a masochist, she simply wouldn't think about it. Because as much as she wasn't in love with Quentin, the idea of him being in love with someone else hurt. Even though it shouldn't.

She'd made serious progress and was on the fifth page of the inventory with nothing missing when a sharp knock interrupted her concentration. The paper she was holding slipped from her hand, and she was thankful it hadn't been the Fabergé egg she'd just checked off the list.

"What the heck?" She cautiously approached the front door and frowned.

Quentin stood outside with his face practically pressed against the window. Relief filled his eyes as she approached. He stepped back while she unlocked the door and opened it.

"What are you doing here? Did you bring me those prawns?"

"Why the hell didn't you answer your phone? You scared the crap out of me."

"You called?"

"About ten times, but you didn't answer." He brushed past her as he entered the shop. "I was worried the guy who broke in earlier came back."

Her heart melted a little at the hint of fear that made his voice gruffer than usual. "I guess I left it upstairs. I've been checking my inventory."

"Jesus, Paige, I probably have a few gray hairs now from picturing you chopped up in little pieces and tossed in the damn dumpster that maimed me earlier."

"Do you always suspect murder and mayhem when someone doesn't answer their phone?" She turned to head back the way she'd come and bent to pick up the paper she'd dropped.

He followed her, stopping to lean against a roll-top desk. "No, but it's been a shitty day. I'm glad you're in one piece. I guess I'll go home now."

"Where's Blaze?"

"I don't know. I assume she's at the Oceanside Inn. After we had a long discussion, I told her that was the best place to stay."

Paige turned to study him. "Are you okay?"

"Yeah. Not one minute of that conversation was pleasant, but I think I finally made my position clear. We aren't getting back together."

"And she accepted that?"

"Not at first, but I told her I was involved with someone else. For unknown reasons, Blaze can accept being dumped for another woman more easily than hearing our personalities don't mesh well, and we want different things out of a relationship."

"If that's the case, she needs to see a therapist."

"She wasn't buying it until I kind of hinted our friendship had turned into something more. Apparently, she had no problem believing that. She told me I was a bastard because I'd always loved you and not her, and then she left."

"Interesting."

"More like ugly. I didn't want to involve you, but I couldn't think of anything else to say. Then I called to apologize to you for the whole dinner fiasco, and you didn't answer."

"I'm sorry to have added to your angst. Maybe you should go home to bed. Tomorrow has to be an improvement over today."

"God, I hope so. It's late. You should get some rest, too."

"I will after I finish a couple more pages. I was on a roll before you showed up."

"Can I help?"

She stood on her toes to kiss his cheek. "Thanks for offering, but since you wouldn't know Chippendale from Hepplewhite, you wouldn't be much use. Go. Maybe I'll see you tomorrow."

He nodded. "Whatever. Good night, Paige. Make sure you lock up after me."

"I will. Good night, Quentin."

After the bells clanged, she strolled toward the front of the shop to lock the door. She probably shouldn't care so much that Quentin wasn't getting back together with his ex-girlfriend. When the perfect woman for him came along, she'd show him nothing but support. But she couldn't help hoping the right one would take her sweet time showing up.

Returning to her task, Paige picked up a statuette of an Egyptian Goddess and checked it off her list. Preferably, Quentin would discover true love *after* she finally found a man who could fill the emptiness in her heart. Because if the only man who could do that was Quentin, she was in serious trouble.

Quentin walked slowly down the row of cages, looking at one hopeful dog after the next. He suspected they all knew the drill and were putting their best paw forward in hopes of being chosen. He was tempted to take them all home.

Hardening his heart against excited barks and pleading eyes, he focused on his mission. Protection for Paige. He couldn't save every stray in the Siren Cove shelter. And the basset hound puppy Paige would find adorable wasn't going to bite a thief, although it might lick him to death. Neither would the lab with the goofy, doggy smile.

His steps slowed as he approached the cage at the end of the row. No furry face pressed against the bars. Instead, something that resembled a giant black mop lay on the cement slab near the back wall. When the beast shook its head, brown eyes that looked like they'd experienced a world of hurt gazed steadily at him from between straggling dreadlocks.

Quentin lifted the info card tied to the cage bars and scanned the contents. *Mixed breed Puli and Giant Schnauzer. Male, approximately three years old. Intelligent, loyal, can be aggressive. Minimal shedding. Leo is wary of men but friendly around women. He requires a fair amount of exercise.* His incarceration date was the previous August. After four months living in a cage, no wonder the poor guy looked like he'd lost all hope.

"Are you interested in Leo?" The shelter worker, who'd stopped to answer the phone after letting Quentin into the back area where the dogs were kept, hurried toward him.

The other occupants all barked a greeting. "He's not great with men, I'm afraid. I have a feeling he was abused by one before he came to us."

Quentin studied the big black dog as he rose to his feet and shook. Dreadlocks swung around his head and shoulders, but his back end had shorter, curly fur. His odd appearance might have something to do with why no one had wanted him.

"Actually, I'm looking for a pet for a woman friend. She owns a store in town and recently had a break-in. I want to get her a dog that won't be afraid to growl and bark if confronted by an intruder but isn't going to scare away her customers. Unfortunately, she doesn't have a huge apartment, and that guy is pretty big."

"Leo's just over a hundred pounds. He's been hard to place since he isn't overly friendly. But he's pretty well-behaved. If you're looking for a loyal dog that will protect your friend, this one would be ideal. As long as she takes him for regular walks, the space issue shouldn't be a problem."

The man reminded Quentin of a used car salesman trying to unload a lemon. But something about the giant mop appealed to him. "I assume he's housebroken?"

"Definitely. He also obeys basic commands and walks well on a leash without pulling, at least not too hard."

The dog had to weigh as much as Paige. Quentin wasn't sure who would be walking whom. He took a moment to wonder if she'd kill him for foisting this giant fleabag on her. He'd go with his gut, and his gut was telling him Leo and Paige were meant to be.

"I'll take him."

"You will?" The man's brows shot up in surprise. "That's great. This big guy deserves a good home. Let's go deal with the paperwork before we bring him out."

An hour later, Quentin drove through Siren Cove with Leo sitting on the front passenger seat of his Jag. The window was partway down, and his dreadlocks flapped in the chilly breeze. Better than putting up with the smell. Paige's new dog needed a bath. Quentin had stopped at the pet store to buy a giant bag of dog food, a couple of bowls, a collar and leash, and dog shampoo. He figured if he showed up with the required supplies, Paige was less likely to send him and Leo packing.

Taking the corner into his neighborhood, he eyed the dog, who eyed him back with supreme skepticism. His odds of getting bitten while bathing the fur ball were probably better than even, but a clean mutt would make a better first impression than a dirty, stinky one. And if he did get chewed on, at least Leo was current on his shots. Quentin had the bill to prove it.

He parked in his driveway and got out. Across the street, Keely turned cartwheels on the lawn in front of her house. Coco, her white and tan Papillion, frisked around the girl, emitting shrill yaps. Quentin could only hope Leo wasn't hungry because the miniature dog looked like a snack. After grabbing the bottle of shampoo, he slammed the door and walked around the front to let the big guy out. Holding tight to the leash, he headed toward the side of the house where a hose was curled near some shrubs.

"You got a dog!" Keely practically flew across the street with Coco in hot pursuit. "Can I pet her, Quentin? What's her name?"

"His name. Leo's a boy." He drew in a breath as the huge dog sniffed Keely's small one. Thankfully, there was no growling by either party. Apparently Leo got on well with other dogs. "You can pet him, but let him smell your hand first."

Keely did as instructed, her silvery-gray eyes sparkling with excitement. "He's kind of funny looking, like a lion, and he smells bad."

The dreadlocks did resemble a mane. "I'm going to hose him down before I take him to Paige. Leo will be her dog."

"I bet she'll love him." Keely danced in a circle, her long blond ponytail swishing. "Can I help you wash him? I'm good at giving dogs baths."

"Sure, but I'm not too certain how he'll like getting wet. Stay back until we see."

The dog behaved amazingly well throughout the ordeal. He didn't look thrilled, but he didn't try to bite anyone. It took three towels to get him semi-dry, but in the end, Leo smelled much better. Quentin and Keely, however, were both soaked.

"Tell your dad and Nina I'm sorry you got so wet."

"Daddy's at work, and Nina is painting. Me and Coco will go dry off."

"Thanks for your help."

"You're welcome. Bye, Quentin." After hugging Leo, she ran across the street and disappeared inside.

Feeling like he was leading a small pony, Quentin tugged Leo toward the door. Once inside the house, he left the dog to his own devices and ran upstairs to change. Ten minutes later, they were back in the car on the way to Paige's store. He parked on the street and unloaded the food and other paraphernalia before letting the dog out.

"Cross your toes this goes well, bud, or it's back to the shelter for you." The dog let out a low woof Quentin hoped indicated cooperation. After heaving the bag of food over his shoulder, he gathered up the rest of the crap and gave the leash a tug. "Let's do this."

The bells jingled over the door as they entered the

store. Behind the counter, Mindy's eyes widened as Leo dropped onto his butt to scratch.

"What an . . . unusual looking dog. Did you bring him down from Seattle, Quentin?"

"Nope. He's a Siren Cove specialty. Is Paige around?"

"She's in the storage room. Uh, you and your pal can go on back, I guess."

After setting down the food bag, Quentin gave the leash a tug, and the dog followed him through the rows of antiques. He smiled at two older women browsing near a shelf filled with china. The customers gave Leo a wary look as he passed but didn't run screaming from the shop. Considering that a good sign, Quentin paused in the doorway to the back room. Paige glanced up from sorting through a bin beneath her work bench, and the smile on her face morphed into a round *oh* of amazement.

"Who's your friend?"

"Leo. He's going to keep you company and scare away bad guys. I don't like the idea of you here alone without protection."

She rose slowly to her feet, never taking her eyes off the dog. "You're kidding, right?"

"Not in the least. I picked him out at the animal shelter an hour ago. Leo is all yours."

"He's as big as a moose. He'll destroy more merchandise than a dozen 'bad guys.' I like dogs, but I don't have time for one."

"You mentioned getting a puppy. The advantage to Leo is he's already house trained. No poop piles on your carpet."

She turned her narrowed gaze on him. "Take him back."

Leo let out a low moan and dropped to the floor.

"You hurt his feelings. The poor guy has been at the

shelter since August in a cold cell with no one to love him. You couldn't be so cruel."

"Damn it, Quentin!"

"Look at those sad eyes. How can you resist that face?"

"I can't even see his eyes through the fur. What the heck is he?"

"A Puli and Giant Schnauzer mix. He has character, and he loves women. Men, not so much. So far, he's tolerated me. Your customers weren't afraid of him since he doesn't look threatening like a Doberman or Pitbull, but the guy at the shelter said he'll be very protective."

She let out a long sigh as she came forward to rub Leo's ears. In response, he leaned against her leg. She staggered beneath his weight.

"See, he already loves you."

"Jerk."

"Hey, what did he do?"

"Not the dog. You. You know perfectly well I won't return him to the shelter, not after the sob story you gave me."

A relieved smile formed as Quentin reached across the dog to give her a quick hug. "I was counting on that. You two will get along great, and I'll sleep better at night knowing you have backup with sharp teeth."

"Let's hope he doesn't bite my customers by mistake."

"I'm pretty sure he's smarter than that. I'll go get his stuff, then take him upstairs. Do you have a few minutes to spare?"

"Let me finish what I was doing, and I'll come on up."

With a nod, Quentin prodded Leo to his feet. "Let's go, boy."

The dog followed him after a couple of tugs, and they climbed the stairs to Paige's apartment. Leaving him to sniff the room, Quentin ran back down and collected the food and other supplies. By the time he'd put the kibble in the pantry, Paige entered the apartment. She went straight to the big brute and scratched his ears. Leo moaned in response.

"He's not the best-looking dog on the planet, but he seems sweet. You should have asked before you committed me to a decade plus of dog ownership. How old is Leo, anyway?"

"Three." Quentin shut the pantry door. "Maybe, but I was afraid you'd say no, and I want you to be safe. Did that asshole steal anything really valuable?"

"I finished the inventory a little while ago. What's strange is he didn't take anything. I called Chris, and he said maybe we interrupted the thief before he had time to find whatever he was after. His theory is there's a specific item he saw and wanted. I have some pretty valuable pieces scattered in among the fifty-dollar vases."

"Then I guess you got lucky."

"Definitely. I just hope he doesn't return."

"If he does, you can sic Leo on him. So, you're doing okay?"

"Yeah, I'm fine." When her phone dinged, she pulled it from her pocket and frowned. "Mindy's texting me. Difficult client. I'll see you later, okay?"

"Sure. I'll give Leo some food and water and then take off."

She reached the door and looked over her shoulder. "We'll talk more about sharing dog duties. Bye, Quentin."

His smile dissolved. Apparently he and Leo would be seeing a lot more of each other. With a shrug, he filled the dog's bowls, patted his big head, and left the apartment. Nearing the bottom of the stairs, a loud male voice drowned out Paige's quieter tones. Several customers browsed between clusters of furniture, but the man near the storage room door talking to Paige looked familiar.

"You're welcome to look around on your own, Senator LaPine, but you can't go in the employee only areas." She pointed to the sign posted beside the door. "I'm also happy to help you locate something specific."

"My sister said you have a good selection of girly crap women like to put on shelves. I'm looking for something expensive for my wife."

"A Christmas gift?"

"More like a peace offering."

"Your mother had a lot of nice glassware and crystal. I'm surprised you didn't pick out a few items of hers for your wife."

His mouth twisted. "Believe me, Virginia would prefer to have something that wasn't my mother's. The two have never gotten along well, but they both love antiques."

"If you'll come this way, I'll show you a few things your wife might like." As she passed Quentin, Paige gave him a pained look.

He repressed a smile as he headed toward the door. With a wave to Mindy, who was manning the front counter, he left the shop. He wondered what their State Senator had done to piss off his wife. Based on a few comments made by his brother-in-law while they were cleaning out the shed, the man was something of an egomaniac.

And that reminded him he needed to take the fishing pole and spear out of Paige's van and put them up on the restaurant wall. At least he hoped they were still in her van. As he climbed into his car, which still smelled faintly of wet dog, he decided the chore could wait. He'd make her the dinner he still owed her after the previous night's fiasco, work out a custody arrangement for Leo, and ask her about the fishing gear tonight. Humming beneath his breath, he started the engine and pulled out onto the street. The day promised to be a good one.

Chapter Eight

Wearing heavy-duty rubber gloves, Paige pulled the branding iron out of the cleaning solution and swore. The top curve of the *S* had deteriorated past the point of repair. She'd been afraid that might happen, but leaving rust clinging to the surface hadn't been an option.

Good thing I didn't pay Zeb much for that piece. She dropped it into the barrel she used for trash. Metal clanged against metal.

From the old blanket she'd placed beneath her work bench, Leo raised his head and let out a low woof.

"Sorry. Did that clamor disturb you, boy? Better get used to lots of noise around here."

After rinsing the solution from a fireplace poker and shovel, she removed her gloves and carried the set of tools out to the show room. Rounding a tall grandfather clock, she smacked into a sturdy shoulder and wobbled precariously.

"Careful of the suit." Mason LaPine grabbed her arm to steady her. He eyed the poker. "I don't need any holes in my pants."

"Sorry, Senator. I didn't realize you were still here."

"I had to leave earlier to take a phone call, but I came back after a quick lunch. I've decided to buy that Fabergé egg for my wife."

"Excellent choice." Inside, she did a happy dance, but outwardly she maintained a serene expression. "The ornament is up front near the counter, not back here."

"I was just looking around . . ." His voice trailed off, and he pointed to a white marble cat. "Wasn't that statue my mother's?"

"Yes, it's a beautiful piece."

"I remember getting yelled at for touching it." He turned his back on the shelf. "I'll take that egg, now."

"Certainly." She hung the shovel and poker on a rack next to a butter churn—minus its plunger. The glue she'd used to repair the base of the cracked dasher should be dried by now.

LaPine cleared his throat. "I'm in a bit of a hurry."

Paige resisted the urge to roll her eyes as she led the way toward the front of the store. *Now he's in a rush?* Carefully, she lifted the ornate Fabergé egg from its stand and carried it to the counter. "Please wrap this for Senator LaPine and ring up the purchase, Mindy."

"Of course. What a beautiful piece. Your wife will love it, Senator."

"Let's hope," he grunted.

With a final smile, Paige returned to her work room and bent to scratch Leo's ears. "Score! That sale will keep you in dog food for a while."

After putting on her gloves, she pulled the andirons out of the solution in the soaking tub and studied them. The rust was gone, and the finials had cleaned up beautifully. She'd double her money on the pair.

When the landline extension rang on the wall next to

her, she tugged off one glove and answered it. "Old Things. This is Paige."

"Miss Shephard, Zeb Stillwater here. I know we talked about setting up a time for you to come out to the farm again, but . . ." Irritation laced the congenial man's tone as his voice trailed off.

"Is there a problem, Zeb?"

"You could say that. My grandsons don't believe I know the value of my own collection, which apparently means you're trying to cheat them out of their inheritance." His voice grew even gruffer. "Since those two are all I have in the way of family to keep me company in my old age, I'm going to pass on selling anything more. Let them deal with the lot when I'm gone."

Her heart ached a little for him. "I certainly don't want to come between you and your family, Zeb."

"I appreciate your understanding. You're a lovely young woman."

"And you're a real gentleman. Thanks for calling."

"You bet. Have a nice day."

When he hung up, she returned the receiver to the cradle. "Well, that sucks."

"What sucks?"

Paige glanced over when Mindy paused in the doorway. "A terrific source just dried up."

"That's too bad. What's with Senator LaPine? The man was acting kind of strange."

"My guess is a guilty conscience. He must have done something pretty awful if he needed to sooth his wife's ruffled feathers with a Fabergé egg."

"No kidding. Oops, the door bells are chiming. I'll talk to you later."

Paige cleaned the andirons and took them out to the shop, where she posted price tags on all her new acquisitions before returning to the storage room. Pausing in front of an armoire she'd acquired from Lola Copeland, she fisted her hands on her hips. The solid oak cabinet weighed a ton. Maybe if she took out the shelves and drawers, she and Mindy would be able to move it with a little help from Quentin the next time he stopped by. The shelves were easy to remove, but when she pulled out the bottom drawer, something rattled.

"That's weird." The drawer was empty, but the interior space wasn't as deep as she'd expected. "I wonder . . ." Paige felt along the edge until her fingers encountered a groove. Giving it a tug, she pulled out a false bottom. "Well, what do you know? The man wasn't lying."

A packet of baseball cards and a dozen comic books rested in the shallow space. In addition, several polished stones, a few Playboy magazines, and a silver letter opener were hidden in the drawer. The handle of the opener was fashioned in the shape of a naked mermaid. Apparently Baird Copeland had a healthy appetite for nude women when he was a teenager.

Leo stretched out on the blanket and rested his nose on his paws to stare at her, and Paige's heart melted a little as she met his wary gaze. "I guess I should tell Baird I found his baseball cards. Eat crow, so to speak. Every now and then, I do make a mistake."

Like believing she wanted a cute little puppy instead of an older dog. After a couple of hours spent with Leo, she wouldn't trade him for anything. The big, silly-looking brute needed her, and right now, being needed felt pretty damn good. Not that she intended to express that particular sentiment to Quentin. She'd rather apologize to Baird Copeland, and that was saying a lot.

After searching through a pile of business cards on the

work counter, she pulled out the one belonging to the lawyer and picked up the phone to dial his number. When his office assistant put her on hold, she gritted her teeth. Maybe she'd actually growled beneath her breath because Leo stood up and leaned against her leg. Burying her fingers in his dreadlocks, she wondered why no one had ever told her that petting a dog could ease away tension.

"What can I do for you, Ms. Shephard?" Baird's forceful tone replaced the easy listening music playing in her ear. "I don't suppose you found my property, which you claimed not to have."

"Actually, I did. You can hardly blame me for not knowing those cards were concealed in the false bottom of a drawer."

"I thought I checked . . . never mind." His voice grew less aggressive. "Was anything else in there?"

"The comic books you mentioned, a letter opener, some rocks, and several Playboy magazines."

"I'd appreciate it if you didn't share that piece of information."

Somehow, Paige doubted the existence of a nudie magazine would harm his reputation in legal circles. "I don't gossip about my clients, Mr. Copeland."

"Good to know. My schedule is packed right now, but I'll be by to pick up my stuff within the next few days."

"I'll keep everything safe for you until then. Have a nice day."

He hung up without responding.

She furrowed her fingers deeper into Leo's fur. "Some people are born jerks. I bet he doesn't pull any punches in the courtroom, either."

Paige went back to work. It was nearing closing time,

and Mindy had already left, when her cell rang. A quick look at the display made her smile before she answered. "Hey, Quentin."

"I owe you dinner. Are you and Leo busy tonight?"

Her smile broadened. "I did promise him a walk. The only one he's had so far today was around the parking lot to do his thing."

"We could go for a hike in the woods before dinner and eat a little later. I've been at the restaurant all day, so I'm not planning a fancy meal. Ribs and coleslaw."

Paige's stomach growled just thinking about it. "We'll be over shortly."

"I'll find a couple of flashlights. See you soon."

She set down her cell and glanced over at the dog. "Did you hear that? We have a date to eat ribs. I wonder if I can give you a bone."

Leo thumped his tail on the wood floor.

"Let's wrap this up and get out of here." She carried the last of her recent purchases out to the main room to display, including a few china cups with cracks she'd repaired and the freshly glued wooden plunger from the butter churn. Once she'd arranged everything, she locked the doors and took the bank deposit upstairs with her, only to realize her new dog hadn't followed. Turning, she shouted, "Leo, come here, boy."

After a few moments, he plodded up the steps. Giving him a pat on the head, she opened the door and ushered him inside.

"I'm going to take a quick shower, and then we'll hit the road."

The dog walked over to his bowl and flopped down.

"Uh, as soon as I feed you."

It was pushing seven before she'd made her deposit at the bank and turned into Quentin's driveway. Even the trip there had taken longer than she expected with the dense fog that had suddenly settled in. After letting Leo out of the van, she strolled up the path to the front door, gave a perfunctory knock, and walked inside. The sweet, spicy scent of barbecue sauce greeted her. “Honey, we’re home,” she called out in a high falsetto.

Quentin ran down the stairs wearing jeans and a heavy sweatshirt. He handed her one of the flashlights he carried and smiled. “Let’s go walk the dog.”

“The fog is pretty thick tonight.” She flipped up the hood on her fleece jacket. “I hope we don’t get lost, floundering in the woods.”

“We have our trusty canine to sniff out the trail home.” He rubbed Leo’s ears. “Ready to go?”

“Sure.”

Quentin led the way up the trail at the end of the cul-de-sac, flashing his light into the trees every now and then. “The fog is literally hanging in the branches. It looks a little creepy.”

Paige shivered. “Don’t say stuff like that. Now I’m expecting a werewolf to leap out onto the path, or maybe an escaped lunatic from an asylum.”

“Have you given up watching rom-coms for horror flicks?”

“Are you kidding? I’d never sleep again, but I have an excellent imagination. Apparently my dog does, too. Look at him. I’m not sure who would be protecting whom if we were confronted by a bear . . . or a serial killer.”

Leo pressed close to her side and whined every now and then. When the bushes at the side of the path rustled, he growled low in his throat.

Quentin turned. “See, he’s all business when it comes to threats. Even if the culprit is a squirrel.”

“Let’s hope it was only a squirrel.”

"Not enough noise to be a mountain lion," he teased. "You're a little jumpy this evening."

"I guess my nerves are still on edge from the break-in. Thankfully, today was relatively uneventful. Oh, I do need your help to move an armoire, if you don't mind stopping by Old Things in the morning."

"Not at all. Which reminds me—the Hawaiian sling and fishing pole Lucas Goodman gave me are still in your van. I forgot to take them out when we unloaded the other day. I'm planning a fishing theme for one wall when we decorate the restaurant."

"In that case, I'll be sure to snatch up any old poles or reels I come across when I'm buying for the shop."

"I'd appreciate that." Quentin stopped abruptly, and Paige slammed into his back. Turning, he slid an arm around her to steady her. "Sorry, I didn't realize you were following so closely."

"Between the dark and the fog, it's pretty creepy out here tonight."

He pulled her in closer to his side. "Isn't this the area where that psycho woman buried her little girl alive?"

"Are you trying to freak me out?" Paige's voice rose. "God, I don't want to even think about the nightmare Keely and Nina went through. Let's go back. Leo went to the bathroom in the bushes while we were discussing fishing gear."

Quentin tipped her chin up and frowned down at her in the glow from the flashlight. "You really are a nervous wreck. No more ghoulish topics. I promise."

"Thank you."

He left his arm around her once she'd prodded Leo to get him moving. "So, how do you like your new pet?"

She let out a sigh. "I'm a total sucker. You know I love him already."

"Does that mean the shared custody arrangement is off?"

"Nice try, but I can use help with walking him, especially during the next couple of weeks before Christmas, when the shop is busier than usual. Oh, and you may have to live here forever since shirking dog duties by going back to Seattle won't be an option."

His quiet laughter was muffled by the fog. "I hadn't thought about that angle. You're stuck with me for at least another month or two. After that, we'll talk."

She didn't really want to think about Quentin leaving, not when she was just getting used to having him around. With her mind occupied, she tripped on a root. Though Quentin grabbed for her, she went down hard.

"Son of a bitch!" Her right ankle throbbed as she sat up in the dirt and straightened her legs in front of her.

"Are you okay?"

When he bent over her, Leo growled.

"Easy, boy. I'm not going to hurt her."

"I twisted my ankle." Holding onto his arm, Paige pushed to her feet. "Damn it. That's what I get for not paying attention." She took a step and winced.

"I've got you." He swung her up into his arms and glanced over at the still growling dog. "Dude, if you bite me, I'm taking you back to the shelter."

"I'm okay, Leo." When the dog quieted, she hooked an arm around Quentin's neck. "You don't have to carry me, but I may need to lean on you."

"You don't weigh much. Just shine the light on the path so I can see where I'm going."

"If you say so. Damn. I hope my ankle isn't sprained." She clung to him as he maneuvered down the path behind the dog, the warmth emanating from him taking the edge off the damp, chilly air.

"We'll check it out once we get home. Ice it and wrap it."

Paige nodded and bumped her nose against his chin. He smelled . . . edible. A hint of spice clung to him that made her think of roasting nuts and pumpkin pie. She wondered if he tasted as good as he smelled. She was willing to bet he did, and the urge to find out—

"Earth to Paige. I asked if your ankle feels like it's swelling."

Her face heated in the dark. "My shoe feels tight. Ugh, I don't have time to be injured. Mindy has tomorrow off, and I was going to decorate the shop for the holidays."

"I'll come in and help you, but let's hope any injury is minor."

She rested her head against his shoulder and held the light steady as he left the woods and crossed the yard to his house.

"Can you get the door?"

She reached down to open it and laughed softly.

Quentin looked over at her as he followed the dog inside. "What?"

"I never expected you to be the one to carry me over the threshold."

"At least I don't have to fight through a big, fluffy dress to get to your ankle."

"If you were fighting through a big, fluffy dress, my ankle wouldn't be what you were after."

"You're right about that, but for the time being, let's concentrate on simply getting your shoe off." He set her down on the end of the couch and knelt beside her. "Yep, your ankle is a little swollen."

Paige winced as he untied her tennis shoe and carefully eased it off her foot. "I can't believe I was such an idiot."

"Give yourself a break. Well, not literally." He felt her ankle. "How much does it hurt?"

"About a four on a scale of one to ten. At least I didn't break it."

"It would probably be more like a seven if you'd sprained it. I think it's just twisted. A little rest and ice should fix you right up."

"Thank you, Dr. McDreamy."

He swatted her knee as he rose to his feet. "Didn't they kill him off? I'll go get you some ice and check on dinner."

Paige propped her sock-clad foot and fat ankle on the coffee table and waited for Quentin to return. *Since I can't do a whole hell of a lot else.* Frustration simmered. When Leo strolled over and plopped down on the floor beside her, she smiled. His unconditional love was growing on her by leaps and bounds.

"Here you go." Quentin draped a bag of ice wrapped in a dish towel across her ankle. "The ribs are done to perfection with the meat falling off the bones. I'll fix us a couple of plates, and we can eat in here."

"As long as we don't spill on Nina's couch, we're good."

"Yeah, I don't want to piss off my landlady and get the boot."

He returned a few minutes later with two plates heaped with ribs and coleslaw. Paige forgot about her ankle as her mouth watered in anticipation.

She took one of the plates from him. "If those ribs taste half as good as they smell, you'd better put them on the menu."

"They taste better." He set his plate on the coffee table. "Guard my ribs while I get you some ibuprofen and a glass of wine. Leo is literally drooling."

"I don't blame him. So am I." She patted the dog's head as Quentin left the room. "Don't worry, baby. I'll save you one."

The dog moaned and slobbered on her foot.

Quentin walked back in carrying two wine goblets he set on the table before handing her a couple of pills. "Maybe you shouldn't be drinking and popping pain meds."

"I doubt the combination of ibuprofen and a single glass of wine will kill me." Leaning forward, she picked up her glass and swallowed the pills with a gulp of excellent zinfandel. "Yum. Fruity."

He sat beside her. "You can always stay over if the combo makes you sleepy. I probably have a spare toothbrush."

"Since I wrenched my right ankle, I'm not sure driving home is even an option." She took a bite from one of the ribs and moaned. "These are so good they're practically orgasmic."

"Should I put that endorsement on the menu?"

She grinned. "Maybe not."

They ate in silence for several minutes before Quentin asked, "How does it feel?"

"Like I've died and gone to heaven."

"Your ankle, not your stomach."

"A little numb from the ice, but it doesn't hurt as much as it did." She licked sauce off her finger before holding out the bone. "Here, Leo." Surprisingly, he didn't try to bite her hand in his eagerness to grab the treat. "Good boy."

"The two of you have definitely bonded."

Paige pushed away the dreadlocks hanging in the dog's eyes as he chewed with enthusiasm. "We *get* each other, kind of like the relationship you and I have always shared." She regarded Quentin steadily. "His arrival has taught me an interesting lesson."

"I'm almost afraid to ask."

"Apparently, you can be replaced . . . by a dog. Who knew?"

Chapter Nine

Quentin slid his arm around Paige as she hobbled from the bathroom into the bedroom. His whole body heated as her breast pressed against his side. Minus the bra. Apparently, she'd taken it off, along with the sweater and pants she'd been wearing, after she brushed her teeth. Her current outfit consisted of one of his old college rowing club T-shirts and a pair of underwear. At least he assumed she was wearing underwear . . .

His grip on her tightened.

"I'm not going to fall on my face. Actually, my ankle doesn't feel half-bad. I could have gone home."

"And climbed all those stairs to your apartment? I don't think so." He released her as they reached his bed, which he hadn't bothered to make that morning. "Since you've taken it easy tonight, I bet your ankle will be nearly back to normal by tomorrow. No reason to push it."

"I guess not." She stretched out her uninjured leg to rub Leo on his belly with her bare toes. After Quentin made it clear Leo wouldn't be sleeping in his bed, the dog had taken possession of the bedside rug, as close to her as he could get. "I could still crash on the couch."

"I don't mind giving up my bed, even though I'm *re-placeable*."

She grinned broadly. With all traces of makeup washed away, she looked about twelve. At least from the neck up. For once, her hair was down, hanging past her shoulders in a pale cloud that brushed against her breasts clad only in his T-shirt, which was thin from years of washing. There was nothing the least bit childlike about her figure.

He tore his gaze away. "Do you need anything before I turn in?"

"No." Reaching out, she grabbed his hand and squeezed. "Sorry about the snarky comment earlier. Leo doesn't cook me awesome meals, so maybe I'll keep you around. Thanks for helping me out tonight."

"I'll always be available when you need me. You know that."

"Yeah, I guess I do. Right back at you, by the way."

Seeing the vulnerability in her eyes, he took a step forward and sat down beside her. "Is something wrong?"

"Not wrong, just . . . I don't know. Ever since you kissed me, I've been wondering . . ." A long breath slipped out in the silence. "Forget it. I'm being ridiculous."

He slid closer until their thighs touched. "No, you're not, because I've been wondering the same thing. Maybe it's time to resolve this."

Taking her chin in his hand, he kissed her. Slowly. Thoroughly. Pushing any concern about what he might be doing to their relationship to the back of his mind, he simply enjoyed the moment.

Until she let out a little moan that made him forget he was kissing Paige, his best friend. Instead, he was kissing

Paige, a woman who stirred his senses and made him crazy from wanting her. Deepening the kiss, he pushed her onto the bed and threaded his fingers into her hair. His whole body heated as her breasts pressed against him.

The low growl didn't penetrate his haze of desire until Paige wrenched her mouth away.

"Easy, Leo. I'm okay. Lie down."

The dog flopped onto the rug with a thump. When he shook his head, suspicious eyes narrowed on Quentin.

"Don't even think about it." Turning his back on the dog, Quentin tried to still his pounding heart with a few even breaths. "What are we doing?"

"Maybe something we should have done years ago. Instead of worrying about what could go wrong, we should have focused on what might go right."

"Your idea has a lot of merit." He kissed her again, taking his time, enjoying the taste of her and the little noises she made in the back of her throat. Finally, he raised his head. "You trust me, and I didn't want to risk hurting you. That's why I never made a move on you in the past. Not because I didn't think you're beautiful and smart and a hell of a lot of fun."

"Do you intend to hurt me now?"

"Of course not, but I can't seem to stop screwing up relationships. You know that."

"Yeah, I do, which is why I've been content to be best friends and nothing more. Most of the time."

"What does that mean?"

"I'm not going to lie to you. Watching you date other women hasn't always been easy."

"You dated other men."

"Sure, I did. Some of them were pretty great, but . . ." She slid her hands beneath his shirt, pressing warm palms against his bare skin. "Maybe we'll discover we click as a couple. Or maybe we'll realize we never should have left the friend-zone. But if we do this now, at least I won't keep wondering what could have been, and pushing other guys away because of it."

"And I won't compare every woman I date to you." He rubbed his thumb across her lips as he stared into determined eyes that held a hint of fear. "I do that, too, you know. After the novelty wears off, I start thinking you're funnier, or would understand what I mean without me having to explain, or that hanging out with you is infinitely more comfortable."

"If we don't survive as a couple, we'll go back to being best buds. Promise?"

He nodded, pretty certain neither of them believed their current friendship would survive a romance gone wrong. But they'd come too far and said too much to turn back now. They had to try. He wanted nothing more than to take his relationship with Paige to the next level. To wake up beside her in the morning. To hold the woman he'd loved for as long as he could remember close to his heart instead of at arm's length.

All I have to do is not wreck this.

He pushed away his concerns along with the T-shirt she wore, inching it across her smooth thighs and above the scrap of pink lace underwear. His breath came in ragged gulps as he drew the soft cotton over her belly until it caught on the fullness of her breasts.

"You are so incredibly pretty." He closed his palms over her then pressed his face against the softness of her breasts. "How did I resist doing this for all these years?" After pulling the shirt over her head, he paused to enjoy the view. "Sometimes, my lack of intelligence amazes even me."

"You've been too busy ogling gorgeous models to even notice."

Rising to his feet, he stripped off his own shirt and tossed it to the floor. "Don't knock yourself, Paige. I noticed and have been dreading the day some other guy became the most important man in your life. You're sweet and beautiful, inside and out."

"I've been worried about the same thing."

He unzipped his jeans and kicked them off his feet.

"That some woman would finally capture your undivided attention. Not that I didn't want you to be happy."

He let his boxers fall near Leo's tail before crawling back into bed and pulling her into his arms. "Maybe that's the most important thing we have going for us, knowing we each care enough to put the other's needs first."

"That's what loving someone is all about, isn't it?" Paige stretched against him and wrapped her arms around his neck.

"Yeah, it is." He couldn't talk anymore, could only give in to the need to be connected to Paige in the most intimate way possible.

When she reached one hand down between them, grazing tender flesh, he let out a yelp, but her objective was apparently the lace panties. After a brief struggle, there was nothing left between them.

For the moment, just holding Paige was enough. Until her lips found his, and the joy of kissing this woman filled his soul. Cupping her face in his hands, he tasted every crevice of her mouth as she wrapped her legs around him. When he pressed against her dampness, a modicum of sense stopped him.

"Protection." His voice came out in a husky whisper. Reaching out, he fumbled for the bedside drawer and pulled it open. While he grabbed a condom and ripped open the packet, she strung kisses along the side of his neck. Goose bumps broke out across his body, and he swore softly when the damn rubber slipped out of his fingers.

"I would have thought you'd be better at the technicalities." Her voice was tinged with a hint of humor.

"You're killing me here." With a herculean effort, he covered himself. "Finally."

"We've waited this long. A few more minutes isn't a deal breaker."

"Maybe not, but right now, I want you more than I've ever wanted anyone or anything. Ever." He kissed her again before pressing her into the mattress. "Ready?"

"Completely." The breath left her as he pushed inside. "Oh, God."

He paused to capture the moment in his mind, then closed his eyes and moved with Paige, building the feeling between them until he couldn't take any more. When she cried out softly, he stopped trying to hold back and shook with the intensity of his release. Sprawled next to her a few moments later, a feeling of peace settled over him.

She laid her palm over his heart. "Quentin?"

"Hmm."

"That was pretty darn special."

He tightened his arm around her. "Yes, it was."

Paige looped the strand of icicle lights over the hooks above the front door of her shop. When she moved the ladder to reach the next section, her ankle twinged a little.

"Should you be climbing that thing in heels?"

She glanced down at Nina, who was turning one of her big front windows into a winter wonderland filled with swirling snowflakes, frosted evergreens, and woodland creatures. "Most of the pain is gone, and the swelling was way down this morning, or I wouldn't have been able to wear these boots. Anyway, two inches is hardly a heel."

"If you say so." Nina went back to painting. "I'm glad you didn't hurt yourself any worse than you did."

"Me, too." Paige moved the ladder a few yards to drape lights above the finished second window depicting Santa's sleigh, complete with reindeer, flying across a full moon.

"Are you going to tell me why you haven't stopped smiling all morning? Not the reaction I would expect after injuring yourself." Nina held her paintbrush poised above a rabbit. "Quentin looked awfully happy, too, before he hustled off to meet with his contractor. If I didn't know better . . ."

Paige pulled her attention away and secured the end of the icicle strand at the edge of the building.

"Oh, my God, you did!"

She was saved from replying when a young woman clasping the hand of a toddler approached.

"Hi, welcome to Old Things. I hope you'll excuse the mess."

"No problem at all. The window scenes are absolutely gorgeous!"

Nina pulled a business card out of her back pocket and handed it to the woman. "If you're in the market for original art, give me a call."

"I'll do that, but today I'm Christmas shopping for my mother-in-law. She loves antique teacups, and I heard you had a nice selection."

Paige climbed down from the ladder. "I have some real beauties. Come on inside."

By the time she'd helped her customer and wrapped

her purchase in festive paper, Nina had finished the window. Paige was still debating what she intended to tell her. Thinking of Quentin in terms of more than friendship was still so new, she was almost afraid to talk about it.

When Nina entered the store, her eyes bright with curiosity, Paige brushed past her. "I need to bring in the ladder. I don't want any bad luck if someone walks beneath it."

"You're so not escaping this conversation."

"I didn't figure I would, but I'll bring in the ladder first. I need it to hang garlands from the top shelves to dress the place up in here."

"Don't forget the mistletoe. Although, maybe you won't need any."

"Funny." Paige stepped out onto the sidewalk and took a moment to admire Nina's finished artwork before folding the ladder. After carrying it inside, she leaned it against the counter. "You did a spectacular job. I have the best-looking windows on the block."

"You'll hand out my business cards to everyone who admires them." Nina's dark brows drew together over concerned eyes. "If you don't want to talk about . . . whatever . . . you don't have to."

Paige stuffed her hands in her pockets. "Quentin and I decided to give more-than-friends a try. We figured we owe it to ourselves to see if we can make it work."

"Well, it's about damn time. I wondered when you'd finally cave in and go for it."

"Give me some credit. You've seen the way he discards women. This could end in complete disaster."

"Or be the best thing that ever happened to you." Stepping closer, Nina slipped an arm around her and squeezed. "You've loved each other forever. Now you just have to figure out how to be *in* love."

"Honestly, I don't think it'll be much of a stretch."

Paige couldn't hold back a smile. "We certainly seem to have the chemistry part down pat."

"Always a plus, but there's a lot more to a relationship than great sex."

"Commitment is the hard part, at least for Quentin. The good news is I think he's had about enough of being single." She turned when thumps sounded on the stairs. "Did you meet Leo yet?"

Nina studied the approaching dog. "Keely hasn't stopped talking about how she got to help give him a bath. He's interesting looking."

"Leo is a sweetie." Paige scratched his ears when he came to lean against her leg. "I love him to death." After a moment, he left her side to go stand at the door. "Do me a favor and take him out to pee before you leave."

"I'll walk him down on the beach. I could use some exercise, too. I'm parked in back, so I'll let him in the rear door afterward."

"Thanks." Paige reached behind the counter for the leash and held it out. "And thanks for the artwork."

"My pleasure." Nina hooked the leash to Leo's collar. "I'll bring him back in a while."

The bells jangled as she left the shop. Paige hauled the ladder and a roll of ivy garland over to the front display shelves. A movement outside the window caught her eye, but she couldn't see the person clearly through the painted scene on the glass. Probably just someone admiring Nina's work. She went back to her decorating and was making good progress tacking the trailing vines in place with a stapler when a soft thump sounded from the storage room.

She paused with the stapler poised over her head. "Nina?" When no one responded and Leo didn't appear, she frowned. *Maybe I'm hearing things.* She went back to stapling, rather enjoying the satisfying thwack as she leaned precariously to tack down the end of the strand. Climbing off the ladder, she dragged it to the next section of shelves.

When she stopped at the end of the row, a faint scraping sound—a drawer opening or a box sliding across the floor—caught her ear. "Nina?" she called out.

Complete silence followed.

"What the hell?" Releasing the ladder, she ran through the shop. She paused in the doorway to the storage area before stepping fully into the room. The door to the parking lot was slightly ajar.

The hair on the back of her neck stood up. Before she could spin around, a large cloth dropped over her head, and hands shoved her to the floor. Fighting the sheet tangled around her, she rose to her knees to pull it off. The rear door was fully open, and footsteps pounded the pavement outside. By the time she scrambled to her feet and reached the parking lot, the area was deserted except for her van and Nina's Mini Cooper.

"Damn it!" Paige sprinted toward the stairs leading down to the beach. No one was in sight except Nina and Leo, far down the stretch of sand. Turning, she ran through the alley out to the main street and looked both ways. Other than a couple of teenage boys on skateboards, a middle-aged woman exiting the dress shop a block away, and a man in a black leather jacket talking on his cell beside a motorcycle parked behind a big pickup, the street was empty. The guy on his phone didn't even glance her way. After waiting a minute to see if anyone was lurking in a doorway, she gave up and entered her store by the front door.

A man stood at the counter. When the bells jangled, he turned to face her and scowled. "Do you always leave your shop unattended?"

Paige pressed one hand to her chest and gripped the doorframe with the other. "God, you scared me."

Baird Copeland tapped his fingers on the counter in an irritating rhythm. "I came by to pick up my possessions. What's your problem?"

"Were you just in my storage room?"

His hazel eyes narrowed. "No, of course not. I parked on the street, so why would I come in through the back?"

Paige let out a breath and realized her hands were shaking. Adrenaline had kept her going through the last few minutes, but now she felt like she needed to sit down. Or collapse. With an effort, she pulled herself together. "Someone was poking around back there. I chased him outside but didn't get a good look at him."

"Then how do you know it was a he?"

"I just assumed—"

"Look, I'm in a bit of a hurry. Can I get my baseball cards and the other stuff you found in that drawer?"

"Of course. Everything is in the back room." Paige led the way through the shop. When she reached the storage area, she frowned. "I left that crate under the workbench. If the creep sneaking around back here took anything—"

"I'm sorry for your troubles. If you'll give me my property, I'll get out of your way."

Baird didn't sound sorry. He sounded annoyed.

She held her tongue, stepped around the armoire standing in the middle of the room, then swore. "Damn it."

Several large containers had been opened and the lids left on the floor. The contents of the boxes were in disarray. She'd have to check her inventory to know if anything was missing.

Baird stepped up behind her. "My baseball cards."

"Oh, for God's sake." Standing on her toes, she lifted down a cardboard box. "Here you go."

Taking the box from her, he set it on a broken, slat back chair and sorted through the old Playboys before dropping them on the floor.

"Those were stacked neatly. The intruder must have looked through your box."

"If he took . . ." His voice trailed off on a grunt. "I guess not. The baseball cards are here." He flipped through the stack of cards before glancing her way. "I don't think any are missing."

"That's a relief. What about the comic books?"

He lifted them from the bottom of the box and counted. "Twelve. That seems about right. I bought them so long ago, it's hard to remember." His chin jerked up. "Didn't you mention a letter opener?"

"Isn't it in there?"

"Just a few loose rocks."

"That's weird." Paige peeked inside. "It was metal and not very old or valuable, so I can't imagine a thief would take it. Maybe he dropped it in one of the other boxes during his search. We can look for it, but it may take a while."

"I don't have time right now. If it turns up, you can let me know. But as you said, it wasn't valuable." He placed the magazines back in the box. "Thanks for contacting me."

"I'm happy to return your property." *And just as happy to see you leave.*

She followed him through the store and let out a sigh of relief when the door slammed shut behind him with a clash of bells. Simultaneously, the rear door opened, and feet thudded across the wood floor.

Not feet. Paws.

As she spun around, Leo loped in her direction. Paige bent to wrap her arms around her dog's shaggy neck and tried not to cry. "Where were you when I needed you, huh?" After a moment, she straightened. "Let's go see what that asshole took. My guess is whatever he was after was worth a whole lot more than a damn letter opener."

The tide had finally turned in his favor—or so he'd thought.

Seeing Paige's artist friend leave the shop with the dog in tow had seemed like a stroke of luck too good to pass up. Since he hadn't found the damn weapon in the rows of crap in the main room the last time he'd looked through the store, he'd wanted one more go at searching the storage area before he gave up his quest for good. But that big mutt the shopkeeper had acquired made timing a break-in tricky.

Bending, he picked up a shell and lobbed it out into the waves. His search had proved fruitless, and he'd damn near got caught in the process. Still, the risk had been worth it. He hadn't found what he was after, but his worry lessened with each passing day. Maybe Paige had discarded it as useless, and the object of his nightmares was currently resting in a refuse pile out at the dump. Even if he'd somehow missed seeing it during his search, surely she would have cleaned away any traces of blood by now. If she'd noticed anything suspicious, she would have contacted the cops. And he was damn certain news of that would have spread all over town.

He hadn't heard a single peep, which was excellent since he could tell the darkness was building again. He'd do everything he could to stop what was coming, or at least minimize the damage afterward, but sometimes he was powerless. Fear he'd pay the price for his failure ate at him. Not that worrying did a damn bit of good. It would happen again at some point, despite his best efforts. All he could really do was put off the inevitable.

Chapter Ten

An empty patrol vehicle was parked at the curb in front of Old Things. Uneasiness crept down Quentin's spine as he pulled in behind the cop car and turned off his engine. He had a feeling the officer who'd been driving it hadn't stopped by Paige's store to purchase antiques. Heart pounding, he slammed the car door and hurried up the sidewalk. The bells jangled when he entered, grating on his nerves. No one was behind the front counter.

"Paige?" he shouted.

Upstairs, muffled barking broke out. Footsteps sounded from the rear of the shop, the tap of the heeled boots Paige had been wearing that morning. When she appeared around a tall rack holding china plates, he let out a breath.

"Come on back. Chris Long is here."

Quentin rested a hand at her waist. "What happened now?"

"Someone was snooping around in my storage room earlier, while I was out front. I assume the same person who broke in before."

"Did he steal anything this time?"

Her brows drew together. "I don't think so. I was checking inventory while Chris took my statement. Whoever it was shifted things around, probably because he was looking for something specific and was in a hurry, but I've found just about everything on my list."

"Why the hell does he keep returning if it isn't to rob you?" When they reached the back room, Quentin nodded at the cop. "Hey, Chris."

The officer responded with a quick smile. "Good to see you, Quentin. I've noticed a lot of activity down at the Poseidon Grill. How're the renovations going?"

"Surprisingly, we're on schedule. I hope to open toward the end of January." Quentin tightened his hold on Paige. "What's going on around here?"

"My take . . . Paige must have something someone wants pretty badly." Chris returned his notebook to his pocket. "I'm glad you adopted the dog. Keep him close by when you're here alone."

Quentin glanced toward the ceiling as Leo let out a few more woofs. "Where was he when this creep showed up?"

"Nina took him down to the beach for a walk after she finished painting my front windows. I was putting up decorations in the shop and making quite a bit of noise, so I'm not sure how long the intruder was back here. When I finally heard something and ran to see what was going on, the guy tossed an old sheet I keep handy for refinishing projects over my head and pushed me down. At least I assume it was a man. He was certainly a lot bigger and stronger than me. Unfortunately, he was gone before I got untangled."

Anger burned through Quentin as he touched her cheek. "Were you hurt?"

"No, just pissed off. After I dealt with a pushy customer who came in while I was chasing after the jerk, I called nine-one-one to report the break-in or whatever you want to call it. The door wasn't locked when he entered."

"Keep the rear of the shop locked, even during business hours." Chris paused on his way toward the front of the store. "I'll let you know if anything turns up, and don't hesitate to call me directly if you get any strangers in the store who make you feel uneasy. If this was the same person Quentin caught a glimpse of the last time, he may try the direct approach next."

"I hope there *isn't* a next time. This sucks. I don't like feeling afraid."

"And I don't like that we don't know what the hell he's after. Maybe you have his granny's diamond ring hidden in a vase, or his grandpa's journal with a murder confession." Quentin followed Chris through the shop to the door. "You sure you don't have any leads?"

"I'm afraid not." He looked over at Paige. "Just take precautions to minimize your risk, and we'll keep a close eye on the shop for any suspicious activity."

She gripped the edge of the counter. "I'll stay alert. Thanks for coming so quickly today."

"You bet."

After Chris left the store, Quentin pulled her into his arms. "Are you okay?"

She leaned against his chest. "Yes, just angry and frustrated and a little scared. Next time I won't be so quick to send Leo off with someone else."

"Why'd you put him upstairs after Nina returned him?"

"He was growling at Chris. He obviously sensed I was upset and frightened, and he didn't want to let the man get near me."

"Good for Leo. I knew he'd be an excellent protector." Quentin stepped away from her as two women entered the store. "I'll bring him back down before I leave. I need to get some work done this afternoon, but I can bring my laptop here to plan menus."

"I don't need a babysitter, for heaven's sake."

"You said Mindy isn't coming in today, and I don't want you left alone. I'll be back shortly."

"Okay."

After Paige went to help her customers, Quentin ran up the stairs and entered her apartment. Leo shook the dreadlocks out of his eyes and gave him a cool look, but at least he came when Quentin called him. The dog followed him downstairs and into the back room. He even lay down on his blanket when Quentin pointed at it.

"Good boy."

"Oh, my God, he's so cute."

Quentin spun around. The younger of the two women who'd entered the shop stood behind him. She was in her twenties, pretty, with waist-length dark-brown hair. She blinked long lashes at him and smiled.

"Cute isn't exactly the word I'd use."

She gave Quentin a lingering glance. "He's adorable. I'm Clea, by the way. You look familiar."

Quentin shook the hand she held out. When she didn't release him right away, he gave a gentle tug. "Quentin Radcliff. I don't remember seeing you around town, but I only recently moved back to Siren Cove to open the Poseidon Grill."

"My aunt said the restaurant had a new owner. We didn't meet here. I was eating out with friends in Seattle, at The Zephyr, I think. You stopped by our table to ask how everything was. I remember thinking your eyes were a really unusual shade of blue. Striking."

He forced a smile, feeling a little uncomfortable as she took a step closer. A subtle scent of something flowery perfumed the air. “The Zephyr is another of my restaurants. I hope you enjoyed your meal.”

“Oh, I did, but then I always have a good time everywhere I go. I’m in the area through the holidays, staying with my aunt and uncle before I head to Europe in January. Maybe we could get together.”

“I’m sure you’d be a lot of fun to hang out with, Clea, but I’m dating someone.”

She gave him a half-smile. “Oh, well. Your loss.” When a woman’s voice called her name, she touched his arm. “Nice running into you again. Maybe our paths will cross in the future.”

“You never know.”

As the woman strolled away, he had a feeling she knew just how terrific she looked in the tight jeans that made the most of her assets. He let out a breath and decided it was a good thing he’d committed to a relationship with Paige since he was pretty certain Clea would be more than he could handle.

The bells over the door jangled as the customers left, and a few seconds later Paige appeared around the end of the aisle.

She pressed a hand to her chest. “Oh, my goodness, you surprised me. I thought you left a while ago.”

“I brought Leo down then talked to one of those women for a few minutes.”

“Ruth Merrick’s niece. Ruth is a regular customer. She just bought a gorgeous mirror for her entry and asked about antique ornaments.” Paige squeezed past him and bent to stroke Leo’s head. “I need to pick up a small tree for the shop before this weekend, so I can display my Christmas decorations. With the influx of tourists for the Winter Ball, ornaments will be hot sellers.”

"Maybe we can get a permit and go cut down a tree tomorrow, or do you have to work in the shop all day?"

"Mindy will be here, so I can take a few hours off." Her smile brightened her eyes. "That sounds like fun. An old-fashioned tree-hunting mission."

Reaching out, he pulled her against his chest and dropped a kiss on her upturned lips. "Then, it's a date."

"That looks like a good one." Quentin leaned his head back to eye the eight-foot-tall Sitka spruce squeezed between a couple of giants.

Paige turned to stare at him. "What part of small don't you understand? I want something about three feet high to put on a table in my shop."

"I meant for your apartment." He strolled around the tree, avoiding Leo, who was sniffing a nearby manzanita bush. "This baby is a beauty. Maybe it isn't perfectly symmetrical, but it has character. I don't like cookie-cutter trees."

As a cold wind whistled through the forest, she stuck her hands in the pockets of her jacket and shivered. "I don't usually bother to put up a tree in my apartment since I'm too busy during the holidays to enjoy it. Anyway, my parents are arriving home from their trip back East in a couple of days. I'll spend Christmas with them."

"Oh."

She joined him on the far side of the tree, where they stood knee-deep in ferns. "When I talked to my mom last, which was before we, uh . . ."

He turned to face her and grinned. "Did the deed?"

"Not exactly the way I would have phrased it, but yes. Anyway, I told her you'd probably be joining us for dinner. I hope that's okay?"

He slid his arm around her waist. "Of course. I don't want to go back to Seattle for the holidays. I'd rather spend them with you."

Warmth filled her, taking away the chill. She leaned her head on his shoulder. "Usually Leah and Nina and I spend Christmas Eve together. Now that they're both married, I imagine they'll want to do their own thing."

"I don't see why old and new traditions can't be combined. We'll cut down this baby, put it up in my house, and invite the group over for a low-key party. What do you think?"

"Sounds like an awesome plan." She tilted her head to stare up at the tree. "Will that thing even fit in your living room?"

"Sure. The ceilings are ten feet high. It's lucky we borrowed Teague's truck, though, since it would never have fit into your van."

Quentin picked up the saw he'd laid on the ground and went to work cutting down the spruce. Minutes later, the tree toppled over with a soft swoosh.

"Sweet. I'll take the top, and you can carry the trunk." Paige reached between the branches to get a good grip. She'd probably be covered in pitch, but she didn't care. Having a real tree for a change filled her with the spirit of the season. "I'm ready when you are."

Together, they carried the spruce back through the woods, following the dog who set a leisurely pace. Her sore ankle was starting to ache a little before they finally reached the dirt road where they'd parked. Bracing her legs and straining to hold up her end, Paige helped load it into the bed of the pickup.

Quentin wiped his hands down the legs of his jeans. "Good work. Now we need to find one for your shop."

"The Doug firs are thick down near the creek. I bet we

can find a small one if we beat our way through the bushes. This area is pretty open and picked over already."

He glanced at her across the tree in the back of the truck. "How's your ankle feeling?"

"It still twinges now and then, but I'm fine."

"Are you sure? I can—"

"I don't want to miss out on the fun. Anyway—" She paused. "Did you hear that? Sounded like a car engine."

"Someone else must be up here tree hunting."

A minute later an old pickup that looked vaguely familiar rounded the bend in the road and stopped behind them. When the engine cut off and doors opened, Leo growled low in his throat.

Paige laid a calming hand on his head and smiled when Zeb Stillwater climbed out of the passenger side. His grandson slammed the other door. The sharp click echoed through the forest.

"Well, hello there, Miss Paige. Fancy meeting you up here in the boonies."

"It's good to see you again, Zeb." She tightened her grip on Leo's collar. "Hush, baby. You don't need to growl at them."

"What a handsome boy." The older man approached and held out a hand. Leo sniffed it and stopped growling.

Paige touched Quentin's arm when he walked around the truck to her side. "Zeb, meet my friend, Quentin Radcliff. He just bought the Poseidon Grill and is in the middle of renovations. Quentin, this is Zeb Stillwater and his grandson, Justin."

Quentin shook hands with Zeb. "I've seen you around town a time or two."

Justin's blue eyes narrowed, and he pushed a strand of long brown hair that had escaped its leather tie off his face with an irritated gesture. "Probably."

When he didn't say anything further, Zeb rushed to fill the silence. "I see you already found yourselves a tree. We're hunting for a big one for the farmhouse, the same as we do every year."

"What a nice tradition." Paige smiled at him. "We still need to look for a small tree for my shop."

Justin lifted a hatchet out of the bed of his pickup and rested it on his shoulder. "We won't keep you, then. Come on, Grandpa. Let's go do this. I've got plans for this evening."

Zeb nodded. "Nice running into you, Paige. You have yourself a merry Christmas."

"Merry Christmas to you, too, Zeb."

After the two walked away, Quentin put a hand at her back and headed in the direction of the creek. "He seems like a nice old guy."

"Zeb is a sweetheart. I bought quite a few antiques from him not long ago. Actually, the day you arrived in Siren Cove. But his grandsons complained that I ripped him off, which I didn't." She scowled. "At any rate, he's not selling anything else. At least not to me."

"That's too bad. The man with him didn't have a whole lot to say."

"Justin's the sullen type. His brother, Jonas, is an even bigger jerk. From what I could tell, the only thing the two have in common is attitude."

"Unfortunate for Zeb." Quentin lifted a tree branch out of the way and ducked under it as they headed in the direction of the creek. "This area is pretty dense. What's Leo doing?"

The dog stood beside a manzanita bush and barked, tail wagging.

"I think a squirrel just ran in front of him. Hey, look at

that little fir over there." She pointed past the dog's up-ended rump. "It's the perfect size."

"I don't know. Looks kind of scraggly."

"There'll be plenty of room to hang all my ornaments. Once I get the tree decorated, it'll look great."

"I'm sure it will." He edged around the dog. "Move it Leo. That squirrel is long gone."

It only took a minute to cut down the small fir. Paige pushed her way through the dense underbrush to follow the dog down to the creek. She stopped on the bank to enjoy the sound of water rushing through the rocks below, while Leo stood belly deep in the current to get a drink.

"Pretty spot."

She smiled at Quentin when he reached her side. "Yeah, it is. Do you remember picnicking with our families in the woods when we were kids?"

"Fun times. I recall a water snake that swam over your foot while we were wading in the creek. You screamed bloody murder."

Paige shuddered. "I still hate snakes."

"Maybe we could make a day of it when I'm in town next summer." He gave her a nudge with his elbow. "We could find a private spot and go skinny-dipping."

The stark reality that he wouldn't be living in Siren Cove for more than a couple more months hit hard. Heaviness weighed on her chest. Of course she'd known his move here was temporary, and at least he intended to visit her, but still—

"There's some sort of chain caught on that branch." Quentin pointed toward a moss-covered log half submerged in the water beyond the dog.

Paige squinted as rays of sunlight broke through the

cloud cover to gleam off dull metal. “Maybe a bracelet or necklace someone lost?”

“Hold this, and I’ll go see.”

She took the handle of the saw he held out and waited while he picked his way down the bank. When he bent over the log, Leo strolled over to investigate. It seemed the dog was getting over his initial wariness of Quentin.

“It’s a necklace with a heart.” He waved the chain over his head. “I’m coming back up.”

Leo scrambled behind him and shook when he reached the top of the bank. Droplets of water flew everywhere.

“Ugh. Just what I needed, a shower.” She held out her hand. “Let’s see what you found.”

Quentin laid the necklace in her palm. A blackened silver chain curled around a flat heart-shaped pendant.

Paige flipped it over. “There are initials etched on the back, but it’s hard to tell what they are. They should be clearer once I clean off the tarnish.”

“The necklace looks old. Maybe you can sell it in your shop if it’s valuable.”

“No, this is a modern piece. It only looks like an antique because it’s so dirty. It’s probably sterling silver, and the pendant has some weight to it, so the necklace wasn’t cheap. Once I figure out the initials, maybe we can find the rightful owner. My guess is it belonged to someone who lives—or at least used to live—in town.”

Quentin glanced skyward as the shadows streaking the ground completely disappeared. “Those look like rainclouds to me. Let’s grab your tree and head back.”

“I’m ready to go.” She slid the chain into her jacket pocket and tucked her hand through his arm. “This was fun.”

He smiled down at her before bending to press a kiss

to her lips. "Yes, it was. But, then, we always have a terrific time together."

"Yes, we do." She didn't say anything else until they reached the tree Quentin had cut for her shop. "Do you need some help?"

"No, I've got this." He swung it up and balanced the fir over his shoulder. "Lead the way."

She followed Leo back toward the dirt track, thinking the dog had more sense than Quentin. What she really wanted to do was point out the obvious. If they enjoyed each other so much, why was he hell bent on leaving once the Poseidon Grill was up and running? Instead, she bit back the words. She wouldn't cling or push. Needy women irritated her, and she was determined not to be one.

If Quentin couldn't figure out what was in his own best interest, she wasn't going to be the one to tell him.

Chapter Eleven

Paige looked up from her work bench when the bells jingled in the front of the shop.

"Hi, Leah. I haven't seen you around lately." Mindy's greeting rang with enthusiasm.

"Ryan and I have been out of town," her friend answered. "Is Paige here?"

"She's working in the back, but I'm sure she'd love to see you. Go on through."

Paige pulled off her gloves and rose from her stool. Beside her, Leo stood up and shook. She laid a hand on his head. "Sorry, boy, but it isn't our walk time yet."

"Oh, my God. You got a dog!"

Paige gave Leah a hug when she entered the storage room. "I told you about the creep who broke into my store. Quentin was worried about my safety, so he adopted Leo for me."

"Hey, there, Leo." Leah scratched his ears. "He's sweet. By the way, I ran into Nina at the grocery store earlier. Seems the dog isn't your only big news."

"I take it she mentioned Quentin and I are sort of a thing now."

Leah frowned. "A thing? You've finally gotten together with the one man you've loved forever, and you're calling it a *thing*?"

"We agreed to give a real relationship a try." Paige's stomach knotted. "I hope we can work out the kinks. He still plans to move back to Seattle after he gets the Poseidon Grill up and running. Not to mention his track record with women sucks."

"But this is you, not some random woman. Give him credit for caring a whole lot more about you than a one-night-stand he met in a bar. Your friendship with Quentin has been going strong for the last thirty plus years, despite living in different states, so I feel pretty optimistic about this."

"I'm trying to keep a positive attitude and not overload him with expectations. How was your trip to Sisters?" she asked, abruptly changing the subject.

"Terrific. Ryan got his rock climbing fix, which made him happy, and I always enjoy spending time at his cabin away from the fog. By the way, *we* made having homes in two different locations work for us."

"That's because Ryan is flat-out awesome."

"True." Leah stepped closer to the work bench. "What have you got there?"

"Quentin and I found a necklace caught on a log in Stoney Creek when we were out cutting a Christmas tree yesterday. I'd just finished cleaning the tarnish off when you strolled in."

Leah picked up the heart and turned it over. "It's pretty. Are those initials?"

"Yeah. I couldn't read them before, but now that I've

cleaned the silver, they're more distinct. I was going to call you. Aren't L-E-G your initials?"

"That's right. My middle name is Evangeline after my grandma."

"I don't suppose you lost this up in the woods sometime during the last couple of decades."

"No, the necklace isn't mine." Leah frowned as she rubbed her thumb across the letters. "What's really weird is I remember a local news story about a girl who had my initials, back when we were kids. Her name was Lucinda Elizabeth something or other that started with a G. I commented on her initials to my mom, and she hugged me really hard and said she felt sorry for the mother of the other L-E-G. Mom looked so sad and held me so tight that the memory stuck with me."

Paige stared at the necklace as a chill slid through her. "What happened to Lucinda Elizabeth?"

"I'm not sure exactly, but I think she was a missing person."

"If this necklace belonged to that poor girl, she could have lost it years before she disappeared. Maybe they found her, and you simply didn't hear about it."

"That's entirely possible." Leah laid the heart back on the workbench, then bent to pet Leo again when the dog stood up and shook. "What are you going to do with it?"

"I guess I'll take it down to the police station. If the necklace is connected to a missing person case, they should be notified."

"Probably a good idea." Leah flipped a strand of her long hair over her shoulder. "Are you excited about the Winter Ball this weekend?"

"Sure. It's always fun to get dressed up for a change. Although, as things stand, I'm not so thrilled women will be bidding on Quentin. I'll have to bring my checkbook."

"You're going to bid on him?"

"Sure, but I'm not too certain I'll be able to afford him. Who else did you coerce into participating in the bachelor auction?"

"We have quite a lineup. Teague asked a couple of his buddies at the fire station to volunteer."

"Who doesn't like a hot fireman?" Paige smirked. "Just ask Nina."

"I know, right? Then there's Chris Long, everyone's favorite cop. Clayton Smith the business consultant Nina dated a time or two before she met Teague agreed to participate, and that new surgeon who moved here recently said yes."

"I haven't met him yet."

"Brandon Tate. He's very handsome and seems nice. Oh, and Jonas Stillwater. He doesn't live in Siren Cove anymore, but his brother still does. Jonas is a financial planner."

"I know who he is." Paige scowled. "He and Justin hassled me about buying their grandfather's antiques."

"Well, we weren't going to turn down any interested party. With Quentin, that's seven men. Hopefully we'll make lots of money for the women's shelter."

"I'm sure you will. Hey, do you and Ryan have plans for Christmas Eve? Quentin and I cut down a monster tree for his house and thought we'd have you guys, along with Nina, Teague, and Keely, over for a low-key holiday celebration. Quentin's cooking."

"Oh, wow, we'd love to. We're spending Christmas Day with Ryan's mom, my grandma, and her boyfriend, but that group is going caroling with some of their friends on Christmas Eve."

"Great. Let's plan on it, then."

"Ryan will be thrilled to know he has a good excuse to

skip caroling with the geriatric crowd," Leah said. "I should go. After spending time in Sisters, I have some catching up to do with the Winter Ball committee."

"If I don't see you before Saturday night, we'll hang out together at the party."

"You bet." With a wave, Leah headed back through the shop.

After her friend left, Paige pulled out her collection of antique ornaments and carried the box up to the front window where Quentin had anchored her tree in a stand and filled the container with water. With Mindy's help, she hung the ornaments, then stepped back to admire the results. "Very pretty."

"All you need are candles instead of electric lights to give the tree a truly authentic ambiance."

"And burn down the entire store in the process? I can live without that sort of dangerous charm." Paige smiled at a middle-aged couple who entered the store before turning back to Mindy. "I need to run an errand, if you don't mind."

"Of course not. I'll take care of everything while you're gone."

"Thanks. Leo's due for a trip outside, so I'll take him with me."

"Sounds like a plan. Have fun."

Paige returned the ornament box to her work room, pulled on her short wool coat, slid the silver heart necklace into the pocket, then hooked the leash to Leo's collar. "*Now* we'll go for that walk."

With the dog leading the way, she left the shop and headed down the sidewalk toward the end of the block. After crossing the street, she and Leo hiked up the slight incline leading to the police station and government buildings. The wind off the ocean blew in gusts, and she shivered as the dog stopped to lift his leg over a clump of weeds. When he paused to sniff a few times, she tugged him toward the long white building housing Siren Cove's city offices.

"I'd better tie you up out here." She looped Leo's leash around the empty bike rack a short distance from the front door. When he let out a gusty sigh and flopped to the ground, she patted his head. "You'll survive."

Inside the police station, the young woman behind the front counter slid back the glass partition and smiled at her. "Good morning. How may I help you?"

"I found a necklace that may belong to a missing person from around twenty years ago. I thought I should turn it in."

Dark brows shot up over surprised brown eyes. "That's interesting. I'll see if someone's available to talk to you."

"Thank you."

When she shut the partition window, Paige took a seat on one of the chairs in the waiting area. She'd just picked up a battered magazine when the door into the squad room opened.

Chris Long waved her over. "I didn't expect to see you here, Paige. I thought there was a conspiracy theory nut waiting to talk to me."

She dropped the magazine and stood. "How do you know I'm not?"

"Now that you mention it . . ."

"Hey, Leah's the one who put the idea into my head. I'm just passing along the necklace I found and her story." Paige followed him back to his desk and took the chair he indicated.

"Okay, let's hear it."

She reached into her pocket to pull out the chain and laid the silver heart on his blotter. "Quentin and I found this snagged on a log in Stoney Creek when we were cutting a Christmas tree yesterday."

Chris picked it up and turned it over. "There are initials."

"Yes, L-E-G. The piece was so tarnished I couldn't read the engraving until I cleaned it. I showed it to Leah because those are her initials, but she said the necklace isn't hers. This is where the story gets a little creepy. Leah remembered seeing a news clip about a girl who disappeared back when we were kids. Lucinda Elizabeth something."

"I don't recall a case like that, but it happened well before I became a cop. I can certainly look into it, but it would be a whole lot quicker if we had a last name."

An older officer who walked with a slight limp stopped beside Chris's desk. "I can offer a few insights." He held out his hand to Paige. "I'm Officer Cantrell. I've seen you around town for quite a few years now, young lady. My wife bought a lamp in your store that she just loves."

Paige shook his outstretched palm. "Nice to officially meet you. I've seen you around town, too."

Chris leaned back in his chair. "What do you know about the necklace, Art?"

"Nothing. It was the name that caught my attention. Lucinda Elizabeth Gordon. She'd just graduated from high school when she disappeared."

"A local girl?" Chris asked sharply.

The other cop shook his head. "No, she was from Portland, visiting her grandparents over the summer. Officially, she was listed as a runaway since there was no sign of foul play. But to my knowledge, the girl was never found."

Paige glanced between the two men. "The name Gordon

doesn't sound familiar. Do her grandparents still live in the area?"

"Her grandmother died a few years ago. I think Rupert Gordon moved to the senior apartments after his wife passed," Officer Cantrell said.

"Maybe I'll take this heart over there to see if he recognizes it." Chris looked across his desk at Paige. "If you don't mind leaving it with me."

"No, of course not." She rose from her chair. "My dog is tied up outside, so unless you need anything else . . .

"I'll write you a receipt for the necklace." Chris pulled a voucher book from his desk drawer and filled out a slip. "If you'll sign here."

Paige bent to scribble her name where he indicated. "If the necklace does belong to Lucinda Elizabeth, I hope you discover she was eventually found safe and sound."

"So, do I. Art will walk you out since he's already on his feet."

"I will indeed. Right this way, young lady."

Paige left the building a few minutes later and untied Leo. The dog shook the dreadlocks out of his eyes and gave her a look that made it clear he'd been left far too long.

"Sorry, boy. I tried to hurry." She urged him toward the road. "Maybe we should go say hello to Quentin down at the restaurant and see how the remodel is going. Mindy can handle the shop alone for a while longer."

Since the dog didn't argue, she turned south when they reached the main road through town and arrived at the Poseidon Grill a few minutes later. In addition to Quentin's Jaguar, a couple of work trucks were parked in the newly paved lot. The drone of a compressor and *whack, whack, whack* of a nail gun greeted her as she and Leo entered the restaurant. The wall behind the bar had been opened up into the back room, and a man with a tool belt slung low on his hips stretched to nail up trim. When he turned, Paige's jaw sagged.

"Since when did you turn in your spatula for a hammer?" she shouted.

Quentin adjusted the ball cap on his head and grinned. "Jerry and his helper are tiling the kitchen floor, so I decided to keep the progress going out here," he yelled back before bending down to turn off the compressor. Silence followed.

Paige rested her palm on Leo's head when he leaned against her leg. "I didn't know you could do carpentry work."

"Hey, I'm good with my hands. It's a gift."

"I'll vouch for that."

His aqua eyes darkened. "Come over here and say that."

"Maybe I will." She strolled closer and let out a little breath when he slid an arm around her and kissed her slowly. "You smell like sawdust. Kind of sexy."

"I'll keep that in mind." He dropped another kiss on her lips before stepping back a few inches. "What are you up to? Not working today?"

"I had to stop by the police station, then I decided to play hooky for a while longer and see how your renovations were going."

His hold on her waist tightened. "The cops, again? Something else happened?"

"No, nothing. The necklace we found in the creek yesterday might have belonged to a girl who went missing back when we were kids." She shared a brief recap of her conversation with Leah. "I gave it to the police."

"Well, that's kind of unnerving."

"Yeah, it is." Paige turned to survey the restaurant. "The dining area looks great with new paint. I like the pale green color, and I see you hung the Hawaiian sling and fishing pole. Where the heck did you find that old diving mask?"

He led her through stacks of chairs to the wall adjacent to the bank of windows overlooking the beach below. "It's a reproduction I ordered online. Not the real deal, but it's pretty cool-looking."

She touched the polished copper mask perched on a pedestal. "I like the fishing net and those glass floats, too. The whole theme really came together."

"I got those off eBay. Yeah, I'm happy with how it looks. As long as that fishing spear doesn't fall off the wall and stab someone, we're good."

"How much longer before the bar area construction is finished?"

"Around New Years is the goal. My contractor is staying on schedule, which is impressive, but he and his crew are taking time off over Christmas. The good news is we haven't found too many surprises other than some plumbing issues."

"That's excellent." She was pleased the renovations were going smoothly for him, or at least that's what she kept telling herself. She refused to think about Quentin moving home to Seattle. "I guess I should let you get back to your nail gun and go relieve Mindy."

He nodded, but instead of leading the way toward the door, he pulled her against his chest. "Thanks for stopping by. A surprise visit from you is always welcome."

"I'm glad I could brighten your day." She cupped her hand around the back of his neck and slid her fingers into his hair. "Are we still decorating your tree tonight?"

He nodded before leaning in to kiss her. "Seems like a good excuse to lure you over."

"You don't need an excuse."

"Then, I'll see you tonight. And Leo, too, since you two seem to be joined at the hip."

She rubbed her dog's ears. "Isn't that the point of a guard dog?"

"Yep. I'm glad he's keeping you company. Paige?"

She paused on her way toward the door and turned. "Yes?"

"Let me know what the cops find out about that necklace."

A shiver slid through her as she wondered about the teenage girl who might once have worn the heart pendant. "If I don't hear from Chris Long in the next few days, I'll call him and ask. Having held that necklace in my hand, I feel invested in the fate of its owner. Whatever that might be."

Hours later, when her cell rang while Paige was locking up her store, she was still thinking about Lucinda Elizabeth. The number wasn't one she recognized.

"Hello." Her voice was hesitant.

"Paige, this is Chris Long. I hope I'm not disturbing you, but I was wondering if I could get a little more information about the necklace you dropped off today."

She stilled, with her hand on the doorknob before flipping the deadbolt. "Of course. I'm happy to answer your questions, but I think I told you everything I know."

"Actually, I need to get an exact location from you." His tone was sober. "According to Rupert Gordon, that heart pendant did belong to his granddaughter, and unfortunately she was never located after the missing person's case was filed. At the time, there were reports she was spotted in Portland, so the officers handled her disappearance as a runaway. When none of the sightings turned up a solid lead, foul play was considered. However, there were never any real suspects. With the necklace as new evidence, we'll be reopening the cold case."

Paige braced her hand against the doorframe and stared out into the thick fog that had rolled in at dusk. "That's horrible. Was Lucinda wearing the necklace when she disappeared?"

"Her grandfather said she was. He had a picture of her wearing it that was taken a few days before she went missing, and he said she rarely took it off. She got it from some guy she was dating that summer."

"Did the police question this boy?"

"Her grandparents didn't know who he was, and that was back before kids posted every move they made on social media," Chris answered. "Her grandfather thought he might have been older than her, but he wasn't certain. He and his wife weren't at all happy about her sneaking around. They originally thought Lucinda had gotten mad and taken off without telling them. They reported her as missing a few days later."

"How awful. Not knowing what happened to her must have been the absolute worst." Paige leaned her cheek against the cold glass panes inset into the door, feeling a little sick. "I hope she wasn't a victim of that horrible cult that got busted last year."

"No, most of those remains have been identified, at least the more recent ones have."

"That's good, at least." Paige let out a long breath. "Do you want me to drive up into the woods with you to show you where we found the necklace?"

"I'd be grateful if either you or Quentin could come with me tomorrow morning."

"I'll see him within the hour and ask what his schedule is like. One of us will definitely meet you."

"I'd appreciate that, and I'll be in touch. Thanks, Paige."

"Have a good evening, Chris." She disconnected and stuck her cell in her pocket with a shaking hand. She didn't want to think about the young woman who'd disappeared, possibly to meet a horrifying fate.

It might be too late to save Lucinda. But maybe uncovering hidden secrets could still bring the lost girl some long overdue justice.

Chapter Twelve

Quentin wasn't sure if the red stain on his fingers was from cranberry juice or blood. As he threaded the needle through the berries and stabbed himself for the second time, he swore a little louder than he had a few minutes before.

"You know, they sell pre-made decorations that look exactly like this in the discount bin at the variety store."

Paige turned on the stepladder where she was winding the strand she'd finished around the upper branches of the tree and gave him a pitying look. "Plastic crap. I don't do fake if I can help it. All the ornaments I brought over are handmade, most of them created by yours truly in my younger days."

Quentin had no problem at all with plastic crap, but he kept his mouth shut. Lines bracketed Paige's tight lips, and her bright blue eyes were dark with shadows. The story she'd told him about the disappearance of the girl who'd owned the necklace was obviously still bothering her. She'd only picked at the chicken pasta dish he'd made for dinner, and he knew it was one of her favorites.

Under the circumstances, he was willing to bloody his fingers to make her happy.

He finally emptied the bag of cranberries, tied the thread in a knot, and cut it. Rising to his feet, he stepped over the sleeping dog and handed her one end as she descended the ladder. "Want me to walk the strand around the tree?"

"That would be great." She laid a hand on his arm as he squeezed past her. "You're being a really good sport this evening. I get the feeling you'd rather be stretched out on the couch watching TV than stringing berries and hanging stained glass ornaments I made when I was in high school art class."

"Nope. There's nothing worth watching on tonight." He cupped her chin with the hand that wasn't stained red and bent to kiss her. "Anyway, this was my idea." He couldn't stop the teasing smile that stretched his lips. "I should have known you'd want to decorate like it's the turn of the century . . . and not this one."

She smiled back. "True. You really should have."

He kissed her one more time, happy to have lifted her mood, then wrapped the cranberry string around the tree. Once they'd finished, he moved the ladder out of the way while Paige plugged in the lights. For several long minutes, he stood beside her with his arm looped around her waist, simply enjoying the beauty they'd created and having Paige by his side.

"You're right. This is a lot better than store bought decorations. Our tree has character."

She nodded and leaned her head against his shoulder. "Thanks for convincing me to do this. I guess I've made excuses not to decorate my apartment the last few years, simply because it's not much fun being festive by yourself. I'm glad you're here, Quentin."

"Me, too." Turning her to face him, he unfastened the clip holding her hair up on top of her head. Silky waves slid down over her back, and he buried his fingers in the soft mass. "Are you going home tonight?"

"I could be persuaded to stay."

He pulled her tight against him. "Yeah? What do I have to do to convince you?"

"Just kiss me."

"With pleasure." Moving his hand to tilt her chin, he kissed her, tasting every corner of her mouth. When Leo rolled over and kicked out with his hind leg, catching him in the back of the knee, he staggered against her and broke contact. "Damn dog."

Paige laughed softly. "He was your idea."

"Not one of my brighter moments." Quentin rubbed the pad of his thumb across her cheek. "Wanna go to bed?"

"We need to put away the ladder. Also, the dinner dishes are still in the sink."

He kissed her again. "They aren't going anywhere."

"True."

Releasing her only long enough to unplug the Christmas tree lights, he backed her toward the stairs. After turning off the lamp near the couch, plunging the room into darkness, he felt for her hand. "Right now, the only thing that matters is you."

With Leo clumping up the stairs behind them, Quentin led the way to his bedroom and turned on the bedside lamp. The soft light cast shadows across her face as she twined her arms around his neck.

"You're using a sleeping bag for a comforter?"

"Hey, at least I bought sheets. Anyway, the bag is down-filled and plenty warm, and I don't want a bunch of stuff to deal with when I move out. Thank God Nina left me her pots and pans to use along with her furniture, so I have something to cook with."

Paige backed up a step. "You don't have any intention of putting down a few roots while you're here?"

"I never have in the past when I've opened a new restaurant. Living in Nina's house, I have all the comforts of home without any of the hassle."

"And you don't feel this time is any different?"

He frowned at the edge in her tone. "You knew I wasn't moving here permanently."

She stared straight into his eyes, searching for . . . something. The light in them dimmed a little. "You're right, I knew that."

He stroked the hair off her cheek. "I'll still spend plenty of time with you. I'm not planning to walk away after the restaurant opens." He didn't want to think about not seeing Paige on a daily basis. Right now, he just wanted to live in the moment. "We'll work it out."

"I guess we'll have to, one way or the other."

"So, are we okay, despite the sleeping bag?" he asked, hoping to inject a note of levity into a conversation that had somehow gotten far too serious.

She took another step back. "Sure. I need to go brush my teeth."

"Your spare toothbrush is still in the bathroom."

"Great." Turning, she strode away, her back stiff.

Quentin clenched his fists at his sides and stared down at the dog stretched out on the rug. He knew what Paige wanted him to say. But as much as he loved her—and he was under no illusions about how he felt—he wasn't ready to commit to a major upheaval in his life. He was pretty happy with the way things were right now.

So why did his chest ache? He pulled off his shirt and

tossed it on top of the dresser, then pressed a hand to the skin over his heart, wondering if he had what it took to make her happy. Fearing he didn't, that he'd disappoint her in the long run, only sharpened the pain.

When she returned from the bathroom, he forced his concerns into a corner of his mind, determined to enjoy every moment with Paige. With her hair down, she looked sweet and vulnerable. And incredibly sexy.

He gave her a quick smile. "I'll be right back."

With a nod, she dropped to the edge of the bed and pulled off one boot. Quentin hurried into the bathroom and brushed his teeth in record time. The confusion reflected in his eyes made him wince. Apparently having a cavalier attitude about the future wasn't working so well for him, after all. When he returned to the bedroom, Paige was under the spread-out sleeping bag with the nylon material drawn up to her chin.

He unzipped his jeans and dropped them to the floor. "Cold?"

"I'm feeling a little chilly."

He yanked off his boxers before lifting the cover to slide in beside her. Reaching over, he snapped off the light, then drew her against his chest to run his hands up and down her bare back. "I'll warm you up."

"I'm sure you will." She burrowed even closer. "Whatever happens, this is worth it."

The catch in her voice ate at him. "You know I love you, right?"

She splayed her fingers against his heated skin. "I know you love me, but I'm not sure if you're *in love* with me. I guess we'll find out together."

"I don't see the difference."

"Not a surprise." She kissed the side of his neck.

He felt the contact all the way to the tips of his toes. Focusing on what she'd said required effort as her breasts rubbed against his chest. "What does that mean?"

She pulled back a few inches. "Honestly, I'm not certain you've ever been in love. So, when and if you do fall, who's to say you'd even recognize the symptoms?"

"What are you talking about?" He lined up all the body parts that counted, then held perfectly still to enjoy the connection. His mind fogged. He'd been about to make a point. Something about love . . .

"Quentin, stop. We need protection."

That brought him back down to earth. While he fumbled in the nightstand drawer, his brain cleared. "I've been involved with . . . well, let's not get into numbers. I've loved women in the past. Maybe not the way I care about you, but—"

She pressed her finger to his lips. "I know that. I don't think we need to talk anymore right now."

"Oh, thank God." He fumbled between them to put on the condom, then just held her. In that moment, it was enough.

Paige slid her hand into his hair and kissed him. "Is something wrong?" Her voice was a whisper, caressing his cheek.

"No, everything is right. Being with you is what I want. Don't doubt that. Ever."

"I don't."

When she wiggled against him, he gave up the fight to hold still and pushed inside her. *Home.* The word echoed through his head as he loved her. Making love with Paige was like coming home, and maybe that was what he needed to tell her. Except forming words was beyond his ability as he slid against her, building the tempo while perspiration dampened their passion-slicked skin. He flung off the cover and clung to her as he stretched the moment to the breaking point.

When she cried out, Quentin let himself go, holding tight to Paige as they both gasped and shuddered. As the minutes ticked by, he lay sprawled across the bed with her leg draped across his thigh until his damp skin chilled. She finally reached for the sleeping bag to draw over them, and it was all he could do to clean up before collapsing back against the sheets.

Paige cuddled close. “Quentin?”

“Hmm . . .” His voice slurred with sleep.

“Never mind.”

Paige stepped out of the police cruiser onto the dirt road and shivered. Wind blew through the trees with a hint of rain as Leo landed on the ground beside her with a thump. She grimaced. “I have a feeling we’re going to get wet.”

“Sorry to drag you out here.” Chris held back a tree branch as she headed into the woods behind the dog. “I appreciate your help.”

“Not a problem.” She pushed through waist-high ferns. “Quentin planned to come, but he got a phone call this morning from one of his restaurant managers. Some issue with a distributor he needed to straighten out immediately.”

“Is the Poseidon Grill his second restaurant?”

“Actually, it’s number six, with all of them scattered across Oregon and Washington. The logistics can be a juggling act at times. If he hadn’t committed to the bachelor auction tomorrow night, he probably would have driven up to Portland to handle the problem in person instead of dealing with it over the phone.”

The heavy cloud cover mirrored her gloomy mood.

This morning's phone call had been, literally, a wakeup call. Quentin's time was in high demand, and he carried a heavy load of responsibility. As much as she wanted to think she was a top priority in his life, she had a sinking suspicion she was just one of the many balls he was keeping in the air. Maybe his commitment-phobia in the past was simply his way of balancing an overburdened schedule.

"The guy always seems so lighthearted."

"Huh?" She jerked her attention back to Chris.

"Quentin strikes me as not having a care in the world. I didn't know he was running a conglomerate. The man has skills."

Paige couldn't argue that inescapable fact. Her internal temperature warmed as she thought about the skills he'd used the previous night. She was determined to focus on what they had together—not what they didn't have. At least for now.

"I volunteered for the bachelor auction, too." Chris broke into her thoughts. "I just hope someone bids on me, or I'm going to feel like a total fool."

"Are you kidding?" She turned around and grinned at his sheepish expression. "You'll bring in a pile of cash for the charity."

"I'll settle for not embarrassing myself." He broke off when she reached the creek bank. "Is this where you found the necklace?"

"Yeah, hooked on the log down there that Leo's sniffing. I wasn't sure if I'd be able to find the exact spot since there isn't a trail, but I figured he would."

"Great. You can go sit in the car if you'd like. I'll walk you back and unlock it."

"I'm fine here. It isn't raining yet."

"I don't think it'll hold off much longer. I need to take a look around, but I'll try to make it quick."

Paige dropped onto a large stone as he skidded down the bank to the water. She didn't want to ask exactly what he was looking for. She was pretty sure the answer would freak her out and only add to her current depression. Not that she had any reason to be depressed. It was her own damn fault for expecting to immediately turn her friends-to-lovers' relationship with Quentin into something a whole lot more. But it wasn't like she and Quentin had to start at the beginning and build slowly, the way she did in most relationships. She knew him better than anyone on the planet. Which was why she had no excuse for believing this time would be any different for him.

Below her, Chris walked slowly up the creek, along the water's edge. Leo deserted the log he was pawing and followed him. When her cell rang, she pulled it from her pocket, glanced at the display, and smiled.

"Hi, Mom. Are you home?"

"We rolled in around midnight. Leaving our car at your aunt's house in Portland was a smart move since our plane was late."

"How was your trip?"

"We enjoyed every minute of it. Having a long visit with your brother and his family was wonderful, but it's good to be home."

"I bet. Will I see you at the Winter Ball tomorrow?"

"Your dad and I wouldn't miss it." She hesitated for a moment. "Are you going with Quentin?"

"Yeah, we've been hanging out together quite a bit since he started renovations on the Poseidon Grill."

"I figured as much."

Something in her mother's tone made Paige sit up a little straighter. "What? You've always loved Quentin. I told him he could join us for Christmas dinner."

Her mom let out a sigh. "Of course we love him, and he's always welcome in our home, but . . ."

"Spit it out, Mom."

"When he's around, you blow off other men who are interested in you. The Winter Ball is a great place to start a new romance."

Paige rolled her eyes. "A few weeks spent with my niece and nephew, and you're back on the marry-off-Paige train?"

"I just want you to find someone who makes you happy. You deserve that, and I honestly don't know what you're waiting for. You've dated some really terrific men, but you always found a reason why they weren't *the one*."

Because none of them were Quentin. Still, she had no intention of getting her mother's hopes up. Not yet.

"Maybe you could let me worry about my love life."

"Fine. I have plenty to keep me busy. A pile of laundry is waiting, and I have all the Christmas baking to do. Your dad is picking out a tree today. Boy, am I behind on holiday preparation."

Paige opened her mouth to mention she was currently out in the same area before deciding to keep quiet. She wasn't in the mood to explain about the necklace. "You work best under pressure. You'll get it all done."

"Not if I don't get started. I'll see you tomorrow, sweetie."

"Okay. Bye, Mom." She pushed her phone back into her pocket and rose to her feet when a voice shouted farther upstream.

"Dammit, Leo. Get away from there!"

Paige slid down the slope to the creek and scrambled

across the rocks toward Chris and her dog. "Leo, come here," she yelled.

"It's okay," Chris called. "He stopped."

"Stopped what?" Paige was breathless when she reached Leo and laid her hand on the dog's rough fur. He whined a little as he stared upstream.

Chris turned slowly, scanning the trees closing in on the creek bank as the sky started spitting rain. "Damaging a potential crime scene. Can you take your dog back to the car, please? I'll be with you shortly."

"Of course, but . . ." Her voice stalled in her throat as she noticed the rounded shape embedded in the side of the creek bank. Dirt streaked the whitish-gray surface. It looked like—

Chris reached out and grabbed her arm when she swayed. "Are you okay?"

She couldn't stop staring. "Is that a skull?"

"Yeah, I'm afraid it is."

Paige shuddered. "Do you think it's Lucinda Elizabeth?"

Gently, he took her by the shoulders and turned her away. His voice was grim when he answered. "I don't know, but we'll definitely find out."

They'd found her remains. The news was spreading through town like wildfire. He'd heard it from a friend, who'd heard it from another friend, who'd heard it from a cousin who worked on the force. Despite the convoluted chain of gossip, he had no doubt the information was accurate. At the time, burying the body quickly, far from the scene of the incident, had been paramount. Somewhere no one would find her. And the dirt near the creek had been soft, easy to dig. Apparently storms and rushing water had eroded the bank over time, exposing what was left of her.

Damn bad luck is what he called it.

The wind blew off the ocean, chilling him to the bone. He could only hope any physical evidence had long since been destroyed in the years since he'd buried her.

After that first time, he'd learned not to panic, to dispose of everything incriminating, including the body, far more carefully. He always hoped there wouldn't be a next time, that he'd get over the deadly urge, but so far that hadn't happened. The best he could do was prolong the inevitable as best he could and clean up the mess afterward.

Because he couldn't live with the only alternative.

The timing for the discovery of those old bones couldn't suck more. He had a bad feeling another episode was nearing. The authorities would be asking questions and hunting for answers, digging up the past. Keeping old secrets hidden wouldn't be easy, and covering up new ones, well, he didn't even want to think about that.

Turning his back to the rolling waves as evening fell, he stared up at the row of lighted shops and singled out the building that housed Old Things. Damn Paige Shephard for dragging everything out into the open! Now, rumor had it she was somehow involved in the discovery of the body. He clenched his fists at his sides. If anyone deserved to come to a bad end, it was that meddling bitch.

Taking a deep breath, he let it out slowly. Right now, he couldn't think about anything but damage control. Yanking his keys from his pocket, he gave them a toss as he headed up the path toward his vehicle. He had a long night ahead of him.

Chapter Thirteen

Quentin straightened his tie before trying the shop door. Locked. After everything that had happened recently, he was glad Paige hadn't left it open for him. Glancing up at the light shining from her front room window, he pulled out his cell and called her. She answered on the second ring.

"I'm downstairs."

"I'll be right there. Well, as soon as I feed Leo."

"No rush." He tucked his phone into the pocket of his smoke-gray suit jacket and turned to gaze down the street. All the storefronts were illuminated with Christmas lights similar to the ones reflecting off Paige's painted windows. At the end of each block, wires had been hung across the street with wreaths placed in the center, and the light posts were wrapped with gold and silver garlands. Siren Cove was definitely decked out for the holiday season.

Street traffic was heavy this Saturday night with the influx of tourists attending the Winter Ball. He appreciated the boost to the local economy, but he could do without the hoopla. Especially since he'd be front and center, strutting his stuff for the highest bidder.

When the door opened behind him, he turned and stared. Paige wore a form-fitting dress in bright red with a plunging neckline that more than hinted at the curves beneath. The hem stopped a few inches above her knee, displaying shapely legs. His gaze lowered to her high black heels, and he couldn't help wondering how the hell she could walk in those things. Instead of a coat, she had a black, fake-fur scarf draped over her shoulders. Her hair was piled on her head in a series of twists and curls that had probably taken her forever to achieve. Whatever effort she'd expended had been well worth her time.

"You look extremely hot." Sliding an arm around her waist, he bent to kiss her.

"So do you." She was breathless when he released her. "I hope I have enough cash in my account."

"What are you talking about?" After she locked up, he strolled to the passenger side of the Jag and opened the car door.

She slid onto the leather seat. "My guess is the winning bid for you will be extremely high. After tonight, I may not be able to afford to buy you a Christmas present."

He couldn't help grinning. "Hey, it's for a good cause, right?"

"Right."

He ran around the front of the car, climbed in, then started the engine and turned out onto the street. They headed through town toward the country club where the Winter Ball would be held. As he drove, he snuck glances at the spectacular neckline of her dress, which did nothing but make him want to turn around and go back to her place. Gripping the wheel, he searched for something to say that wouldn't make him hornier than he already was.

"Uh, is this the first time you've left Leo alone for any length of time?"

"Yep. He looked sad as I was leaving, but I trust he won't destroy the place while I'm gone. He's a good boy."

The subject of the dog exhausted, he gave up on the mundane and took one hand off the wheel to rest it on her thigh where the dress had slid up. "I can't believe how amazing you look. Was I blind all these years, or just stupid?"

"Do you really want me to answer that?" Her voice held a hint of humor.

"Probably not. Okay, we'll talk about something guaranteed to cool my libido. Have you heard whether they've identified those bones yet?"

She gathered the wrap closer around her and shivered, despite the heat blasting through the vents. "I think they're running DNA tests. Chris said he'd let me know what he could, but somehow, I don't think we'll be privy to all the details of the investigation. Honestly, I'm not sure I want to know."

"Okay, I'll shut up, then. There's no reason to think about anything depressing tonight. I just want us to have a good time. I'd also prefer not to look stupid while I'm being auctioned off like a side of beef. Those are my two main goals for the evening."

She turned to face him, and the dashboard light illuminated her smile. "You won't look stupid. But if you lose the jacket and tie, and undo a few buttons on your shirt, you'll probably fetch a heftier price."

"How about if I just do a striptease on the stage?" Sarcasm rang in his voice.

"Take a page from the *Magic Mike* playbook." Her soft laughter filled the warm interior. "Then I really wouldn't be able to afford you."

He pulled into the parking lot and turned off the engine. In the darkness, he ran his hand farther up her thigh. "I think I'll save any stripping strictly for you."

She unsnapped her seatbelt and leaned in for a kiss. "I like that idea."

He would have been happy to make out in the car for a whole lot longer, but she pulled back and reached for the door handle.

"We're already fashionably late, if the number of cars in the lot is any indication. We'd better go inside."

He reluctantly released her. "Sure. It should be a fun party."

After Quentin locked the Jag, he took her hand and ushered her toward the lighted building. Inside, music and the din of conversation echoed through the lobby decorated with a giant fir tree. They turned in their tickets at the door and greeted acquaintances as they made slow progress through the crowd. The dining room was set up with a buffet, and servers roamed among the attendees, offering appetizers. He snagged a shrimp wrapped in prosciutto and took a bite. "Not bad."

"Not bad? These things are awesome. I could eat a dozen." Paige wiped her fingers on a napkin after finishing her own shrimp. "Do you want to eat first or dance? Sounds like the band is in full swing in the other room."

"I could be persuaded to show you off on the dance floor."

"Sounds good, just as soon as I say hello to my parents." She pointed toward a large table in the center of the dining room. "They're over there with some of their friends."

"Sure. I haven't seen your mom and dad since Leah and Ryan's wedding last summer."

He followed Paige through the crowd and stopped behind her when she reached the table. Ava Shephard jumped up from her seat to hug her daughter. The woman was small and blond and spunky, like Paige. Quentin had spent as much time in Ava's kitchen as he had in his own during his early years before his family moved to Seattle. Paige's father was slower to rise to his feet, but his smile was warm and his grip firm as he shook Quentin's hand.

"How are you, Son? It's been a while."

"Too long. It's good to see you, Sheldon." He clapped him on the back before swooping in to hug Paige's mom. "I've missed you both."

"I was thrilled to hear you're opening up the Poseidon Grill again." Ava gave him a smacking kiss on the cheek before stepping back. "I guess you'll be in town more often now."

"I certainly plan to be."

Paige leaned against her dad after he gave her a quick hug. "It's like old times . . ." She met Quentin's eyes. "Sort of. Anyway, we just wanted to say hello. We'll let you get back to your meal."

"The dinner is excellent," Sheldon said. "Make sure you eat before they clear away the buffet."

Paige laughed as she took a couple steps backward. "Have you ever known me to turn down good food? We'll eat after we check in with a few people."

"Go. Have fun." Her mom waved them away. "I know you don't want to hang out with us old folks."

"You'll never be old, Ava." Quentin slipped his arm around Paige. "You're young at heart."

"You bet I am." Her mother's laughter followed them as he guided Paige away from the table.

"Way to score points with my mom. They both love you, even though she thinks you scare away men who might want to marry me and produce grandchildren."

He stopped in his tracks. "She said that?"

"Pretty much. I didn't tell her we're . . . uh . . . hooking up. I figured that information is on a need-to-know basis, and my parents don't need to know."

Quentin pulled her in closer as they edged around a group of new arrivals on the way to the ballroom. He wasn't sure how he felt about Paige keeping her parents in the dark regarding their dating status. Almost like she was ashamed of him. *Or maybe she simply doesn't trust what we have will last.* Completely his fault, if that was the case. He opened his mouth to say something—anything—reassuring, and struggled for the right words.

"Oops, excuse me." Paige paused, as the blond man she'd brushed up against turned. "Oh, hello, Baird. How's your mom settling into her new home?"

The man, probably in his mid-forties, wore an Italian suit that Quentin was pretty sure cost five times the price of his off-the-rack model. A tall woman with long, blond hair and a wary expression clung to his arm. He wasn't sure if she was the guy's wife, his date, or his daughter.

"She's happy living closer to my sister," he answered abruptly. "Enjoy your evening." Propelling the woman with a hand on her back, the two walked away.

"Who was that?" Quentin asked.

"Baird Copeland. I bought a bunch of furniture from his mother. He's a lawyer here in town, and he was irritated with me because he left some stuff in one of the drawers. Like that was my fault." Her voice held indignation.

"And the woman?"

Paige rolled her eyes. "Trophy wife. Hey, Ryan and Nina are over at the bar. Let's go hang out with them."

The moment to tell Paige how he felt was gone. Now obviously wasn't the right time to have a serious conversation. He wasn't sure if he was relieved or disappointed.

As they approached the bar, Leah set down her wineglass, slid off the stool, and gathered Paige in for a quick hug. "Oh, my God, you look gorgeous."

"So, do you. That emerald shade does amazing things for your coloring."

Leah did look beautiful, and it wasn't just the shimmering green dress that left her back bare. Her brown eyes glowed with happiness as she drew Ryan over next to her and tucked her hand through his arm. There was an air of confidence about her, the look of a woman who knew she was loved.

By contrast, a subtle tension filled Paige. She smiled and chatted happily with Leah while Quentin ordered drinks, but the sense of peace surrounding the other woman was missing as Paige fidgeted with the napkin the bartender laid in front of her.

Guilt ate at him.

"How're the renovations going?"

Quentin tore his attention away from Paige and glanced over at Ryan. "Better than I'd hoped. How was your trip to Sisters?"

Quentin paid for the drinks while Ryan made an amusing tale out of a climbing misadventure. "I was literally stuck between a rock and a hard place—for two hours. Luckily I didn't break something getting out."

"Was Leah freaking out?"

Ryan gave him a self-deprecating grin. "Thankfully,

she was Christmas shopping and didn't even realize I was late." He took a swallow of his beer. "Congrats. I hear you and Paige are, uh . . ."

"Yeah, we are."

"I guess Teague wins our bet. He swore you two would get together before the year ended. Nina and Leah and I told him if it hadn't happened by now . . ."

"Apparently, I'm a little slow." Quentin looked toward the entry. "Here come Teague and Nina now."

Paige broke off her conversation to turn around on the bar stool. "And I thought we looked amazing. Nina throws on a little black dress I swear she's had for the last ten years, slaps on some smoky eyeshadow, and puts supermodels to shame."

Leah laughed. "Completely unfair, I agree."

"We're finally here." Nina squeezed past Quentin and Ryan and plopped down on the empty barstool next to Paige. "Babysitter issues. Stella's out of town for the holidays, and the high school girl we hired to watch Keely was late." She smiled at the bartender when he gave her an enquiring look. "Just a sparkling water for me. I plan to be the designated driver tonight. Teague?"

He rested a hand on his wife's shoulder. "Any decent draft beer. Surprise me."

"You've got it." The man moved away to fill their order.

After a few minutes of casual talk, Quentin pressed a hand to Paige's back as the band struck up a slow Eric Clapton tune. "We were planning to dance. Shall we?"

She nodded. "I love this song."

Taking her hand, Quentin led her through the crowd. Once they reached the dance floor, he pulled her into his arms, determined to make her feel as special as she was.

"The song is appropriate because you're definitely beautiful tonight."

"Thank you." She leaned her head against his shoulder as they swayed to the slow music. "This is nice. Especially after the break-ins in my shop and finding those bones . . ." She shivered and tightened her grip on him. "It feels good to relax and enjoy myself."

"You always go full speed ahead." He rested his cheek on her hair and breathed in the light scent of honeysuckle. "Do you ever take a day off just to chill?"

"Not in recent memory." She pulled back a few inches from him. "Do you?"

"Not exactly. I guess neither of us is big on down time. My schedule used to piss off . . ." His voice trailed away as his gaze landed on a woman with her back to him on the other side of the room. Even in the duskiness created by colored strobe lights flashing across the vaulted ceiling, he was pretty sure he couldn't mistake that mane of red hair.

"Who?"

He looked down into Paige's inquiring eyes. When he glanced up again, the woman was gone. "Never mind. I think we both should take some time off to do something fun."

Surely that wasn't Blaze . . .

Paige's fingers teased the back of his neck as they danced. "After the holidays, maybe we could get out of town for a few days before the restaurant is ready to open."

"Somewhere tropical to escape from the January rain and gloom."

"God, that sounds wonderful."

"I'll look into it." He cupped the side of her face in his

palm and kissed her as the song ended. After a second kiss, he pulled back. "Since making out on the dance floor would probably be frowned upon, maybe we should go eat dinner before the auction starts."

"Fatten you up for the bidding war."

"I was thinking more along the lines of needing all the strength I can muster."

"There's nothing to worry about. I fully intend to win that date."

He slid his arm around her and guided her through the other couples. "Good, because I'm counting on it."

Paige stood in the crowd with Nina, Teague, and Ryan while the price on a date with the town's new surgeon rose. He was handsome in a boy-next-door sort of way that obviously appealed to the single women in the room. A month before, Paige probably would have bid on the man.

"Sold to the lady in the silver dress!" Their state senator, Mason LaPine, was acting as the MC for the auction, in addition to promoting his run for governor every chance he got. The man oozed charisma, and his voice rang out as his gavel hit the podium. "Leah Alexander will collect your winning bid at the table in the back. Let's have a big round of applause for Dr. Brandon Tate."

The lucky woman with the winning bid was a good friend of Paige's who owned the dress shop in town. The crowd clapped and cheered, along with a few catcalls, as the doctor took a bow and Regan headed toward the far end of the room to pay for her date.

"Yay, Regan! You go girl," she called out as her friend breezed past.

Regan flashed a broad smile. "It's not often Siren Cove has a new, eligible bachelor in town. Nina snapped up the last one before the rest of us got a chance."

"Isn't that the truth." Ryan slapped Teague on the shoulder. "Quentin and I don't count, since we're old faces making a comeback."

"I knew if I didn't act fast, someone else would make a move on my future husband." Nina touched Paige's arm. "Doctor Tate was bachelor number four. When does Quentin get auctioned off?"

"I think Jonas Stillwater is next. Then Quentin." Paige pointed toward the stage. "Yep, there's Jonas. The guy is good looking, but he was a total jerk about the antiques his grandpa sold me."

"His brother Justin is over at the bar. The guy worked on my car last month when I had problems with the transmission," Nina said. "He treated me like I wasn't quite bright just because I asked a few questions."

Teague slid his arm around her. "Let's face it, babe, when it comes to cars, you're—"

"Don't say it! Well, not unless you want to sleep on the couch."

"I'll shut up." He kissed his wife.

"Stillwater isn't getting as much interest as the surgeon." Ryan said. "I guess a date with a doctor is more exciting than one with an investment advisor. Who's the pretty brunette bidding on him?"

Paige turned to follow the direction of his eyes. "That's Clea Merrick. Her aunt is a good customer of mine. She bid on Chris Long, too, but his sister's old college roommate scooped him up."

"Well, it looks like Clea just dropped out of the bidding again," Nina said.

"Sold to the woman in blue!" The senator's gavel struck the podium. "Congratulations on your purchase, young lady."

"Young?" Teague snorted. "LaPine really is shopping for votes. That woman looks like she's in her sixties."

"Let's give Jonas a round of applause," the senator called.

Paige clapped as Jonas Stillwater left the stage. "He didn't look super thrilled."

"Karma's a bitch. That's what he gets for thinking you'd cheat his grandpa." Nina clutched Paige's arm a little tighter. "Here comes Quentin. Are you bidding on him?"

"Of course. Oh, damn."

"What's wrong?" Ryan asked.

"Does he have to smile and look so freaking hot?" She groaned. "This is going to cost me a fortune."

From the stage, Quentin searched the crowd until he saw her. He gave her a quick grin as LaPine went through his spiel.

"Opening bid starts at a hundred bucks. Okay, ladies, who wants a date with our executive chef and restaurateur?"

Paige held up her hand and waved. On the other side of the room, a voice called out, "Two hundred."

"That's what we like to see. Let's make some money for the local women's shelter!"

Paige gritted her teeth. "Three hundred."

"Four hundred," the same high voice shouted.

"It sucks being short." She poked Teague. "Can you see who's bidding against me?"

"She has long red hair. Hey, I think that's the woman Quentin brought to Leah and Ryan's wedding."

"Blaze? Are you kidding me?" Paige raised her hand. "Five hundred!" she yelled.

The crowd cheered.

"Do I hear six?" LaPine's smile broadened. "Apparently Quentin is a hot commodity, ladies. So far, our highest winning bid was five-fifty."

"Six hundred!"

"Geez, I guess Blaze doesn't mind spending a fortune to spend an evening with her ex." Nina gave Paige a sympathetic look. "You know you don't have to go broke winning him, right? It's just one date that won't mean anything."

"I know, but—"

"A thousand dollars."

The crowd went still before bursting into applause. On the stage, Quentin's eyes widened.

"Who was that?" Paige shouted to be heard over the commotion.

Ryan stretched to see. "The young brunette who bid on Stillwater earlier."

"Clea Merrick?" Paige's shoulders sagged. "I give up. She's a trust funder. I certainly can't afford to outbid her if she wants Quentin that bad."

"Does anyone want to top that generous bid?" When the senator looked her way, Paige shook her head. He turned toward where Blaze was standing and raised a brow. "No? Okay, sold to the beautiful lady in the gold dress. You've won yourself a date with Quentin Radcliff. How about a round of applause, folks?"

Everyone clapped and cheered as Quentin gave a thumbs-up and left the stage.

Nina nudged her arm. "It's not all bad. At least the women's shelter will benefit."

"In a big way." Paige shrugged. "Whatever. It's just a date, and I certainly trust Quentin, even if Clea is young and extremely hot."

Ryan patted her back. "So are you. Anyway, you're the one Quentin cares about."

"True." She forced a smile she wasn't feeling. "When it comes to the big picture, one date with that woman won't change anything. Nothing at all."

Chapter Fourteen

Quentin held his cell clamped to his ear with his shoulder while he buttoned his shirt. “I can come over after my date with Clea, if you want.”

Paige was quiet for a moment. “I’m actually pretty tired. The store was slammed today with last-minute shoppers looking for that perfect gift, so I’ll probably be asleep by then.”

He closed his eyes and let out a frustrated breath. “I wanted to wait until after Christmas for this date, but Clea insisted on going before. She suggested Christmas Eve, and I flat-out refused.”

“It’s not your fault I didn’t pony up the cash to win you. Have fun tonight, and I’ll see you tomorrow.”

“Okay. Hey, I love you.”

“I love you, too. Bye, Quentin.”

He dropped his phone on the bed and rubbed the back of his neck. Paige had been quiet the previous evening after they left the ball. He knew she didn’t blame him for the auction fiasco, despite winding up in a bidding war with his ex-girlfriend and Clea. But she certainly hadn’t been thrilled when the younger woman had run over to plant a kiss on his surprised lips before dragging him away to schedule their date. Even though Paige had asked him up to her apartment to spend the night after the ball, he'd gotten the feeling her heart wasn't really in it.

"Damn."

When the doorbell rang, he frowned. He was scheduled to pick up Clea in a half-hour, and he certainly wasn't expecting anyone. He left the bedroom and ran down the stairs to throw open the door. His eyes widened.

"Blaze, what are you doing here?"

She swept past him without waiting to be asked inside. Reluctantly, he shut the door behind her.

"I'd hoped we would have plenty of time to talk about our future on the date I planned to win." Her brows drew together. "Obviously I can't catch a break, so I decided to drop by instead."

"I have to leave in a few minutes, and I see no reason why we need to have a conversation since I'm pretty sure I made my feelings clear during the last one."

"Too bad because I do. Can we sit down?"

He let out a sigh. "Sure, but we'll have to make this quick. Clea is expecting me, and since she spent a thousand bucks on this date, I should probably be on time."

Blaze curled up on the couch. "You're going out with her so soon?"

"Her choice."

"I bet Paige isn't any happier about how the auction turned out than I am."

Quentin refrained from responding. "What did you come here to talk about?"

"When I heard you were in the bachelor auction, I figured it meant you were over Paige and had come to your senses. The woman is a yawn-fest."

"Look, if you're going to badmouth Paige—"

"God forbid. No, I'm here to tell you I finally get it. I watched you two together at the party last night. When you look at her, it's clear you honestly care how she feels."

"When we were together, I cared."

"Maybe, but it wasn't even close to the affection and concern you show Paige. So, while I had high hopes you'd realize you were totally missing out with me, this time I'm leaving under no illusions."

"You'll be a whole lot happier with someone else. Honestly."

"I'm sure you're right. You're a hell of a lot of fun, Quentin, and you were great in bed, but I want to be loved. So, I'm out of your life as of now." She rose to her feet.

He followed her to the door but refrained from touching her. "I hope you find a guy who will make you happy. You deserve it."

"Thanks. A word of warning . . . Don't do anything stupid with that rich girl. I recognize the type. She's used to getting what she wants, and I have a feeling that's you."

"I have no intention of screwing up my relationship with Paige."

Her eyes were sober but without a trace of tears. "Have a merry Christmas."

"You, too, Blaze. Take care."

He shut the door behind her and leaned against it, feeling like a chapter of his life was finally closed. He'd get through this date with Clea tonight and then focus on making things right with Paige. Blaze had made him feel like a jerk. Probably because he was one.

Squaring his shoulders, he pushed away from the door

and grabbed his leather jacket from the closet. After making sure he had his wallet and keys, he locked up the house and strolled out to his car. A chill in the air sent a shiver through him, but the sky was filled with stars without a hint of fog. Minutes later, he was cruising down the highway toward Clea's aunt and uncle's home. The house was fifteen miles north of town, set on a small rise with a huge expanse of lawn and a view of the ocean. He stopped at the end of the driveway in front of the wood and stone structure. Before he could turn off the engine, the front door opened and Clea emerged. Leaning over, he pushed the passenger door ajar as she reached it.

His date settled on the seat and gave him a thorough inspection in the illumination from the floodlights. "You look great. Worth every penny of the grand I spent."

"I'd tell you you're gorgeous, but that would be an understatement."

She wore a white dress that rode up her thighs as she leaned back in the seat, and she hadn't bothered to bring a coat, despite her bare arms and the cold temperature. Long, wavy brown hair slid over her shoulders, and her breasts pressed against the rounded neckline that revealed plenty of cleavage. It was clear she wasn't wearing a bra. Reaching over, he turned up the heat.

"I'm looking forward to this. Where are you taking me?"

"I thought we'd keep driving north and have dinner at a really spectacular restaurant on Yaquina Bay in Newport."

"One of yours?" Her voice held a sexy purr.

"No, but it's still good."

During the nearly hour-long drive, they talked about Clea's travels abroad. The woman was entertaining and funny. If he wasn't committed to Paige, he probably would have been interested in a whole lot more than one date. But while Clea was certainly beautiful and witty and extremely hot, his attraction to her was superficial. She didn't tug at his emotions the way Paige did.

"We're here. Finally. I'm looking forward to your hands being occupied with something other than driving."

When he met her gaze as he helped her out of the car in the restaurant's parking lot, her eyes held the promise of all sorts of fun, but none of the commitment and love Paige had to offer. He ignored her provocative comment.

Inside, the hostess seated them at a table with a view of the bay. Quentin ordered a bottle of chardonnay and wild salmon, while Clea chose fresh halibut. With the low lighting, soft music, and intimate banquet seating, the ambiance was made for romance. As they sipped the wine, they kept the conversation light, discussing their favorite movies.

"Rom-coms are my weakness. I love *When Harry Met Sally*. What about you?" She scooted closer to him on the bench seat until their legs touched, and gave him a lazy smile.

He wanted to inch away but was already pressed up against the wall. Her perfume teased his senses, something rich and exotic. "Uh, maybe you and Paige should hang out together. She likes chick flicks, too. Me, I like action movies. *Die Hard* springs to mind."

Her throaty laugh filled his ear as she laid a hand on his thigh. "I can think of all sorts of comments to make about that title, but I don't want to make you blush."

Words failed him, and he feared his neck was turning red. When the server approached with their food, he let out a relieved sigh. Thankfully, Clea moved over a few inches and finally gave him room to breathe.

The meal and the wine were both excellent. He stopped after two glasses, but Clea finished the bottle. Her eyes held a lazy softness that hinted at trouble.

"I saw a sign for live music at one of the bars we drove by. We could go hang out and listen to the band," he offered as he slipped a credit card into the folder the server left on the table. What he really wanted to do was take Clea home, but she'd paid a thousand dollars for this date. Ending it so soon seemed like bad form.

"I'd rather go straight back to your place, maybe have a drink and get comfortable."

She rubbed her palm up and down his thigh beneath the tablecloth. He clamped down hard on her fingers as they moved even higher.

"We aren't doing this, Clea."

"What? Just a little harmless flirting . . . for now."

He snatched up the bill folder when the server returned. After adding a tip and scribbling his signature, he handed it back to the man. "Thank you. The meal was delicious."

"I'll be sure to tell the chef. Enjoy the rest of your evening."

"Oh, I intend to," Clea chimed in.

Quentin didn't say another word until they'd left the restaurant. He opened the car door for her, shut it once she was settled, then ran around to his side and climbed in. Finally, he turned to face her. "It's not that you aren't extremely tempting, but our date isn't going to end with me taking you back to my place."

"It wouldn't be the first time I invited a man up to my room at my aunt and uncle's house. Not even the first time this trip. They go to bed early and don't ask questions."

"Not happening, Clea."

"God, I thought you'd be fun. Why do you have to be so uptight?"

"When we met at Old Things, I told you I was involved with someone. Paige and I are in a committed relationship."

Clea's eyes narrowed. "What she doesn't know won't hurt her, and I'm not going to kiss and tell."

"*I* would know, and I don't cheat."

"It's not cheating if you're just having a no-strings attached good time."

"I guess we see relationships differently." He started the car engine.

"Obviously, I misread you." After that, she was silent as he drove out of the lot to head back through town. When they reached the tavern where the live music placard was displayed, her head snapped around. "You can drop me off here."

"What?" He slowed to a stop when the light changed from yellow to red and turned to face her. "I'll park and walk in with you. We don't have to leave town right now if you want to hang out and listen to the band, maybe dance a little."

"No offense, Quentin, but I'm kind of over this date. I saw someone I know going into the bar, so you don't have to worry about how I'll get home."

When the light turned green, he made a U-turn and parked on the street. "I'm not going to ditch you in a strange town with no transportation because you thought you saw someone you know."

"You don't have a whole lot of choice since I insist." She patted his leg. "I plan to have fun tonight, with or without you. Don't sweat it."

Irritation fought with a sense of responsibility. Not that he could force her to return to Siren Cove with him, but still . . . "Humor me, okay. Go inside and see if this man will give you a ride home. If everything's cool, I'll take off."

"Fine." She opened the door, got out, and then bent down to look in at him. "We could have had quite a night. My guess is you'll regret your decision."

"I don't think so."

"Whatever. Bye, Quentin."

After Clea ran across the street, he drove around the block and parked in front of the tavern. A minute later, she came outside, and he lowered the passenger window. "Well?"

"The guy is stoked to see me, and he'll make sure I get home safely."

"All right." The thought of leaving any woman alone bothered him, but she disappeared inside the building before he could argue. After a moment, he closed the window and pulled out onto the street. "Shit." He reached the highway and had driven halfway across the Yaquina Bay Bridge before he decided he simply couldn't do it.

Damn, Clea and her stinking money! If she hadn't bid such a ridiculous amount on him, he would be hanging out with Paige right now instead of worrying about a woman with the morals of an alley cat. He pounded his fist on the steering wheel and winced. When he reached the end of the bridge, he turned around and headed back the way he's come.

It was going to be a long evening.

Blood soaked the sand and had spattered huge pieces of driftwood with spray. Cleaning up the mess wasn't going to be easy. He shivered in the early morning chill as he snapped off the flashlight after surveying the work ahead of him. At least the chances of anyone wandering down to this stretch of beach at such an ungodly hour were remote.

He'd known the episode was imminent. All the indications had been there, but he hadn't been able to stop the madness. Now, all he could do was damage control. At least this time he'd killed her outside instead of somewhere incriminating. Still, the risk of DNA evidence was always possible. Best to eliminate all traces of blood, along with the body, before someone opened a missing persons case. By the time he finished cleaning up, no one would ever suspect this place had been the scene of a crime.

Based on the wild partying the girl sprawled face down on the sand was known for, the police weren't likely to start searching for her the second her aunt and uncle reported she hadn't returned home. Hell, they might not even call the cops for several days.

Hunching his shoulders against the wind, he went to work, scrubbing down the driftwood and boulders at the base of the cliff with buckets of seawater and bleach. The sky was beginning to lighten by the time he finished. Hurrying now, he carried buckets of contaminated sand out into the surf. Waves smacked against his boots as he flung the contents into the water as the tide receded. Nothing left to do now but remove the body.

With the wind flapping the tarp, he spread the square of plastic out beside the dead woman and rolled her body into the center. Long, brown hair tangled across her face, which was as white as her dress had once been. Now, the clinging material was caked with damp sand and stained a dark red.

This time, he'd used a knife to slice across her throat. He wasn't particular about his weapons. Any sharp object that would get the job done, or a blunt one for that matter, was acceptable. Whatever was handy. The satisfaction came in watching the life force fade away, not in the method he used.

A psychiatrist would probably have a field day analyzing him.

He rolled up the bundle and secured it with a rope, then hauled away more of the sand that had been stained beneath her body. It was pushing seven before he finally finished. Gathering up the cleaning materials, shovel, and buckets, he shoved them in his pack with the flashlight and took a long look around. Nothing but pristine beach for as far as he could see. Except for the bulky package. After shrugging on the pack, he heaved the tarp-wrapped body over his shoulder and thanked God she was light. He'd ditch the last of the evidence somewhere a rushing creek wouldn't expose bare bones in the future. He was too smart to make the same mistake twice.

In an hour, the job would be finished . . . until the next time.

Chapter Fifteen

Wearing a bright red Christmas dress, Keely ran through the entry, chasing Leo, Barney, and Coco. Leo skidded on the hardwood floor as he took the corner into the kitchen with Leah's big mutt in hot pursuit. Not to be outdone by the larger dogs, the little Papillion barked like a lunatic.

"Keels, please!" Teague shouted over the commotion as he carried a stack of dirty plates from the dining room table to the kitchen sink. "Find something quieter to do."

The girl stopped beside Nina and scrunched up her nose. "No fair. You're all talking about boring, grown-up stuff, and I don't have anyone to play with."

"True." Paige scooped leftover scalloped potatoes into a container. "It really isn't fair. I don't mind the noise, and she's having fun with the dogs. Christmas should be about kids enjoying the excitement of the season."

"It's tough to contain all that anticipation." Leah took Keely's hand. "I'd much rather play Go Fish with you than clean the kitchen. I'm sure there's a deck of cards around here somewhere, and the dogs can take a breather."

Quentin paused from loading the dishwasher. “There’s a deck in the cabinet by the TV.” He smiled at Ryan, who was hovering near the refrigerator. “Why don’t you go play with them? This kitchen isn’t big enough for everyone to help out.”

“I scrubbed pans before we ate, so the dishes won’t take long.” Paige shooed Ryan toward the doorway. You, too, Teague. Go have fun with your daughter. It’s Christmas Eve.”

Keely released Leah’s hand and skipped across the floor, her shiny dress shoes clicking against the wood. “Once my baby sister comes, I won’t have to hang out with only grown-ups. Too bad she won’t get here for months and months.”

Everyone turned to stare at Nina and Teague as his daughter disappeared around the foot of the stairs into the living room.

Nina laid her palm across her stomach. “I guess the cat’s out of the bag. We were going to wait until after the holidays to tell you. I didn’t want tonight to be all about us.”

“You’re pregnant?” Paige practically shouted as she dropped the serving spoon and ran across the kitchen to hug her friend.

Leah wrapped her arms around both of them in a three-way hug. “I’m so happy for you. The baby’s a girl?”

“We have no idea. It’s way too early to tell.” Teague’s smile was so wide he looked like he might burst. “Keely’s just wishful thinking.”

Nina laughed. “She says boys are nasty, so if this is a baby brother, we’ll have our work cut out for us.”

“I thought we were going to play Go Fish,” Keely shouted from the other room. “I found the cards.”

Leah backed out of the embrace and wiped away a few tears. “Whatever this baby is, I’m thrilled for you.”

"So are we." Nina leaned against her husband as Paige released her. "But we don't want to make a huge deal about it in front of Keely, not yet, anyway. She isn't used to sharing the limelight, and I have a feeling there'll be a few challenges ahead."

"You'll meet them head-on like you do everything." Leah squeezed her arm. "I've seen plenty of kids at school go through the trauma of a new baby in the house, and they all survived the transition. Right now, I'm going to go play cards with the little princess."

"If you don't need me to help . . ." Nina glanced toward Quentin.

"Go, all of you. Paige and I'll finish the dishes. Put your feet up or whatever it is pregnant women do. Congrats, Teague."

"Thanks."

Ryan rested a hand on his friend's shoulder and spoke in a low voice as the two men headed into the living room.

"They'll be next." Paige snapped the lid on the potatoes and put the container in the refrigerator.

"Huh?" Quentin took the baking dish from her and set in in the sink.

"Leah and Ryan. I bet they'll be pregnant in no time."

"I guess that's one reason to get married. I enjoy kids. Someday, I'd even like to have a couple. Right now, I can't imagine fitting them into my schedule." He squirted soap into the dish and picked up the scrub pad to tackle the baked-on cheese. "Why are you looking at me like that?"

"Sometimes the crap you say amazes me. You don't squeeze children into your life like leftovers in a too-small bowl. You make them a priority."

"Which is why I'm not ready to have any."

"I guess not." She looked away. "I'll go wipe off the table while you wash that pan."

"Okay." He reached out and snagged her around the waist as she passed him, then kissed her thoroughly. "Thanks for helping me out. I know I can always count on you."

Her insides quivered as he released her. She wanted so badly to stay irritated with him, but he made it damn hard. Still, she couldn't simply ignore their different priorities.

Maybe for the next couple of days, I can.

They finished the cleanup with only minimal conversation. The silence was easy between them, and the rousing game of Go Fish in the other room provided plenty of background noise. After she'd dried the last pan, and he'd wiped down the stove, they joined their friends in front of the Christmas tree.

"Is it present time?" Keely asked, dancing around the room. The dogs scrambled up off the rug and joined her, barking in excitement.

Quentin winced. "Maybe we could put them outside."

"Good idea." Teague left the couch and herded the dogs toward the front door. "I don't know why we let them in to begin with. The rain stopped hours ago."

When he returned, he glanced toward the tree. "I see a couple of gifts under there with Keely's name on them." He smiled at Paige and Leah. "That was awfully nice of you."

"Are you kidding? Shopping for a little girl is a blast." Paige settled on the floor and let the periwinkle folds of her dress slide over her knees. "Nina and Leah and I have been exchanging gifts for as long as I can remember. We couldn't leave Keely out."

"I don't see anything with my name on it," Ryan jokingly complained.

Leah poked him. "Start your own gift exchange. Ours is girls only."

He pulled her in close and kissed the top of her head. "No worries. I'll get the only thing I want later tonight."

Her response was lost as Paige handed a gift to Keely. The girl squealed as she ripped it open. "You got me a crown? It's so pretty."

Paige smiled. "It's a tiara to go with your princess dresses. Every princess should have a special crown."

"You know her so well." Nina adjusted the tiara more securely on her stepdaughter's head. "What do you say?"

"Thank you." Keely scooted across the rug to hug Paige.

"You're welcome, sweetie." She handed over an oblong box wrapped in bright Santa paper. "What did Leah get you?"

"I'll find out!"

While Keely thanked Leah for the light-up wand and waved it over her head, the women opened their gifts from each other. Every now and then, Paige glanced at Quentin as the men discussed the football season. He seemed to be having a good time.

A few minutes after he rose to his feet and stepped over wrapping paper to head into the kitchen, she put aside the soft scarf and earrings she'd received to follow him. Pausing inside the doorway, she studied his expression before entering the room. "Is something wrong?"

Quentin sliced the chocolate cheesecake he'd baked earlier. "Of course not. I figured I'd serve dessert now since Teague and Nina will probably want to take off soon. Keely seems to be winding down."

She leaned against the counter. “If you were in Seattle for Christmas, what would you be doing?”

“Probably hanging out at my restaurant, maybe going to a club with friends afterward.”

“Not much like the family-friendly party we have here.”

He transferred the dessert plates to a tray. “Siren Cove isn’t exactly a hotbed for nightlife. Anyway, I’m having a good time. Ryan and Teague and I all have different interests, but we still click.” He nodded toward the coffee pot. “Do you want to grab some mugs? I made decaf, and we can doctor it with shots of Kahlua. Well, not for Nina, but the rest of us.”

Paige prepared a second tray with the coffee paraphernalia while he decorated the slices of cheesecake with raspberries. “Those look beautiful.”

“They’ll taste even better.”

“I get the feeling this is all pretty tame for you.”

He set down the bowl of berries and turned to face her. “Tame isn’t a bad thing.” He stepped closer and cupped her chin. “If I wanted wild, I could have had it last night. I didn’t. I’m enjoying this . . . and you. Honestly, hanging out with our friends for a quiet evening beats the hell out of partying in the city.” He bent to kiss her and smiled. “Maybe we’re all getting old.”

“Somehow, I don’t think you’re ready for a rocking chair on the front porch just yet.”

“No, and neither are you. Maybe you and I aren’t on the fast track toward diapers and formula like the others, but that doesn’t mean we can’t appreciate a night like this.” He stepped back. “Is the coffee tray ready?”

“Yeah, it is.” She followed him into the other room, thinking about what he’d said. Keely sat on the couch next to her dad with her head resting against his shoulder.

Paige's heart melted a little. She was pretty sure she was ready for what her best friends had. But Quentin obviously wasn't.

They ate the delicious cheesecake, drank their spiked coffee, and reminisced about past Christmases until Keely fell asleep. After exchanging hugs and handshakes all around, Teague carried his daughter home, with Nina by his side. Ryan and Leah left a few minutes later, and Quentin let Leo back inside. The dog shook his head and glared at him, then walked over to sit at Paige's feet.

"I don't think your buddy liked being left out in the cold."

"He's getting spoiled. He thinks he's a person."

"A dose of reality is good for everyone now and then."

She leaned back against the couch cushions. "I can't argue with that. Having unrealistic expectations isn't healthy."

He crossed the room, nudged Leo out of the way, and sat down beside her. "You've been acting a little strange all evening." He picked up her hand. "Not to the others, just me. Are you pissed about that whole stupid date I went on with Clea?"

"Of course not. I'm the one who asked you to volunteer for the bachelor auction in the first place. It's certainly not your fault Clea outbid me."

"Nothing happened between us. You know that, right?"

She twined her fingers through his and squeezed. "I trust you completely. Always have, always will."

"Then what—"

When the doorbell rang, Leo leaped to his feet and barked like a trained attack dog.

"Nina must have forgotten something." Paige reached out to lay a calming hand on her dog's head. "Quiet, boy."

Rising to his feet, Quentin headed to the entry. Paige

closed her eyes and contemplated her options. Starting a discussion—which was sure to lead to an argument—about their future on Christmas Eve didn't seem like a great choice. Better to wait, even if her insides were tied in knots . . .

The front door squeaked as Quentin opened it. "Hey, Chris, this is a surprise. What brings Siren Cove's finest out on Christmas Eve?"

"I was hoping for a few minutes of your time, if you don't mind answering some questions."

"Of course not. Come on in. Paige is here."

Paige sat up straighter and held onto Leo's collar as Chris Long entered the room behind Quentin. "Did you need to know something else about the necklace we found in the woods?"

"No, this doesn't have anything to do with that." He glanced at Quentin and shifted from one foot to the other. "Uh, can we speak privately?"

Quentin stopped beside Leo as the dog lay back down on the floor. "What's this about?"

"Clea Merrick."

"I don't mind talking in front of Paige. I took Clea out last night on the date she won at the Winter Ball. What the hell did she say that would involve the police?"

"Nothing, since she's gone missing."

Quentin's face lost some of its color, and he dropped down onto the couch beside Paige. "Shit."

"This isn't an official case yet since she hasn't been missing for forty-eight hours, but I told Ruth Merrick I'd see what I could find out. Apparently, this isn't the first time Clea has disappeared with a man for several days, but her aunt swears she wouldn't have blown off their Christmas Eve dinner without a word. She's understandably worried."

"Did she tell you I took Clea out last night?"

Chris nodded. "She also said her niece never came home afterward."

"Dammit! I didn't want to leave her at that bar, but she insisted. When I went back for her—"

Chris's eyes darkened, and he took a notebook and pen out of his jacket pocket. "Maybe you could start at the beginning of your date and fill in the details."

Quentin's hand shook when he ran his fingers through his hair and let out a harsh breath. Paige scooted a little closer and laid her palm on his thigh.

"I picked her up around seven, and we drove to Newport. We ate at a restaurant on Yaquina Bay."

"Which one?" Chris asked.

"The Bayview Inn." Quentin looked over at Paige. "To be honest, we argued. Let's just say we had different expectations for how the night would end, and Clea wasn't happy."

"You expected her to sleep with you." Chris's voice cooled.

"I'd rather not discuss it."

"Look, you volunteered to have this conversation. I'm happy to bring you down to the station if—"

"I don't want to disrespect any woman, but I'm not going to take the heat for Clea's questionable social habits, either. She wanted to hook up. I told her I was involved with Paige."

"Then what happened?"

Quentin told him about dropping Clea off at the bar.

"And that was the last time you saw her?" Glancing up, Chris kept the pen poised above his notebook.

"Yes, but I did return to the bar. I'd driven over the bridge when guilt got the better of me. I didn't like the idea of leaving a woman alone in a strange town that way, so I drove back. I'd probably been gone about twenty minutes, total."

"You didn't talk to Clea when you went back to the bar?"

"She wasn't there. I checked around inside and asked the bartender if he'd seen her. He hadn't but said he'd been busy. I asked a woman if she was in the ladies' room. She wasn't. At that point, I figured she'd simply taken off immediately with the man she said she knew, so I gave up and went home."

Chris stopped writing in his book. "Were you here when Quentin got back from his date, Paige?"

"No, I'd had a long day. I was at home asleep."

He eyed Quentin steadily. "What time did you leave the bar the second time?"

"Probably around ten thirty. I got home well before midnight."

"Clea didn't mention the man she saw by name?"

"No, she didn't. I shouldn't have left her there by herself."

"Clea is an adult and has a right to make her own decisions, no matter how stupid they might be." Paige shivered, despite the heat in the room. "You couldn't force her to go with you."

"I guess not."

Chris put the notebook back in his pocket. "Thanks for talking to me. I imagine she left the tavern of her own volition. The bartender would surely remember any kind of confrontation."

"She was definitely happy to see the guy she noticed."

"If she doesn't come home before the forty-eight hours are up, we'll officially open a missing persons investigation. Stick around town since I'll probably have more questions for you."

"I'm not going anywhere." He stood and followed the officer to the door.

Chris glanced back over his shoulder. "Have a merry Christmas, Paige."

"Thanks. You, too, Chris. I sure hope Clea shows up soon so her aunt and uncle can enjoy their holiday. Ruth is a nice woman, and Clea should know better than to worry them."

"I'm hoping for the best, too." He nodded at Quentin. "Sorry to burst in on your evening, but I appreciate your cooperation."

"No problem. Good night." He shut the door behind the other man, then stood for a moment with his head hanging.

Page joined him and wrapped her arms around him to lean her forehead against his back. "I know you're concerned, but don't be. Clea strikes me as the type of woman to think about her own pleasure first and not to give a crap if she worries the people who love her."

"An accurate assessment. Still, I had a bad feeling about leaving her at that bar."

"That's because you care about people. You have a conscience."

Quentin turned around and pulled her close against his chest. Warmth radiated from him as he rested his cheek on her hair and let out a sigh. "She told me I'd regret my decision not to bring her back here last night. Turns out, she was right."

Chapter Sixteen

"Dinner was excellent, Ava. Thank you both for including me." Quentin smiled at Paige's mom and dad sitting across the table from them, before reaching beneath the tablecloth to squeeze Paige's hand. "You make me feel very welcome, just like you did when I was a kid and both my parents were working long hours."

"That's because we still consider you part of the family." Sheldon rose to his feet and clapped him on the shoulder on his way around the table. "Don't get up. I'll bring in the pie."

Paige pressed her free hand to her stomach. "After all that turkey, I don't think I can eat dessert. I'm stuffed."

Her mother gave her a teasing smile. "It's blackberry, your favorite."

"In that case, maybe I can make a little room."

"I figured you could." Ava sipped her after dinner cream liqueur. "I didn't want to bring this up during our meal, but I heard some strange gossip at the Winter Ball. Rumor has it someone found a skull out in the woods. I don't suppose either of you knows what that's all about?"

Paige seemed to shrink against her seat. "Unfortunately, we do."

"It's true, then? My goodness, how awful."

"What's awful?" Sheldon returned with a beautiful, lattice-topped pie in one hand and a carton of ice cream in the other. "Did I miss something?"

"The rumor we heard at the party about the skeleton." Ava sliced into the pie he set down in front of her and lifted out a piece. She frowned as she eased the oozing berries and delicate crust onto a plate. "Is something wrong, Paige?"

"No, not really." Her grip on Quentin's hand tightened. "Actually, I'm the one who found the skull. Well, Leo uncovered it, but I was with him and Chris Long at the time."

Her dad held a scoop of ice cream poised over the slice of pie. "Are you okay, honey? Why didn't you tell us sooner?"

"It's not a big deal, but the whole situation freaked me out. After discovering the necklace and hearing the story about its owner, the sight of that curved piece of bone felt a bit personal."

Ava's eyes widened. "There's obviously more to the gossip than I imagined, but if you'd rather not talk about it . . ."

"I can see you're dying of curiosity. You tell them, Quentin. I'm going to eat my pie and have another liqueur."

"Are you sure?"

"Yep." Releasing his hand, she took the plate her mother passed across the table.

"All right." While he ate his dessert, he explained about finding the necklace with the L-E-G initials, turning it over to the police, and Paige's trip back to the creek with Chris Long.

"Wait a minute, the necklace you found near the skull

belonged to Lucy Gordon?" Ava dropped her fork, and it clattered against her plate. "That's horrible!"

Paige straightened in her chair. "Lucinda Elizabeth Gordon, but I don't think the authorities have confirmed the skull belonged to her yet. Why? Did you know her?"

"I worked on several charitable events with Lucy's grandmother. Poor Liz was devastated after her granddaughter disappeared. I can't even begin to imagine her pain." Ava's blue eyes darkened. "Actually, you two knew Lucy, as well."

Quentin frowned. "We did?"

"She babysat for you just a few days before she disappeared. Quentin, your mom was working day shifts at the hospital that week, and your dad was gone on an overseas trip. I had jury duty and needed someone to watch you both. Liz told me her granddaughter was in town for the summer and would be happy to make some extra money babysitting."

"Lucy?" His voice rose. "Lucy our babysitter was Lucinda Gordon?"

"I vaguely remember having a sitter one summer a couple of years before you moved to Seattle. She took us to the pool when I wouldn't stop begging."

"We were nine at the time, and she was practically an adult." Quentin's stomach knotted. "Lucy had long dark hair and a beautiful smile. The age difference didn't matter to me in the least. After the first day we spent with her, I was completely in love."

"I remember you kept doing stupid stuff to try to impress her." Paige set her glass down with a thump. "How come no one ever told me she disappeared?"

"We didn't tell either of you. You both liked her a lot and were disappointed when my jury duty ended. You would have been devastated if we'd mentioned her disappearance." Ava's brows pinched. "Although on the last day Lucy watched the two of you, something was bothering you, Quentin. You wouldn't come tell her good-bye before she left."

He could picture the scene clearly, despite the twenty plus years since that day. Lucy had hugged Paige then smiled her beautiful smile at him. He'd hung back and clenched his fists in his pockets, hurt and angry because she'd let a man kiss her.

"I was jealous. Lucy had a boyfriend, and my nine-year-old heart was broken."

Paige pushed away her half-empty dessert plate and turned to stare at him. "How did you know she was dating someone?"

"I saw him. Well, I saw his back. Lucy disappeared outside, so of course I followed her a few minutes later. She was under the big willow tree in the front yard with a man, and they seemed to be arguing. Then the guy grabbed her and kissed her. I was all ready to charge across the lawn to defend her honor when she wrapped her arms around his neck and kissed him back. After watching for a few minutes, I felt a little sick, so I went inside."

Paige touched his arm. "You should tell that story to the police. Chris said Lucinda's boyfriend was a suspect at the time, but no one knew who he was."

"I only saw the dude from behind. He had brown hair and was big. Then again, I was a kid, so my perception could have been all off. Every grown man seemed big to me."

"Paige is right," Sheldon said. "You should call the police. They may have suspects you don't know about, and even a little information might point toward one of them."

Quentin nodded. "I'll call Chris Long in the morning."

"Well, this was certainly a less than pleasant way to

end a lovely Christmas day." Ava pushed back her chair and stood up to collect the pie plates. "I'm sorry I asked about that rumor."

"I'm not, Mom." Paige rose to her feet, as well. Her hands shook a little as she rested them on her hips. "Maybe what Quentin saw that day will help solve an old case and bring justice for Lucy. Let's go finish the dishes, then Quentin and I need to take off. It's getting late."

"You don't have to—"

"Yes, I do have to help." She disappeared into the kitchen behind her mother.

Quentin stared at the wall and frowned as bits of the conversation his babysitter had had with her boyfriend echoed through his mind.

"I won't do it."

". . . no damned baby . . ."

"If you're serious about me . . ."

"What's bothering you, Son?"

He jerked his attention back to Paige's dad. "They were arguing about a baby. I didn't understand what it meant at the time, but in hindsight, maybe Lucy was pregnant, and the guy wanted her to get an abortion."

Sheldon was silent for a minute. "You think he might have killed her because she refused?"

"I don't know what to think. It was so long ago, and I could be misremembering. I never thought about Lucy again after that summer."

"Tell the police what you know. It's their job to sort out the facts and come to the truth."

Quentin did his best to shake off his sour mood and smiled. "I guess so."

"Not to change the subject, but I couldn't help noticing your friendship with Paige seems to have changed course.

I know my daughter is a grown woman who makes her own decisions, but a father can't help worrying." Sheldon turned his empty liqueur glass between his fingers. "You mentioned going back to Seattle after the Poseidon Grill has its grand opening."

"I always spend a lot of time traveling between my restaurants to keep them running smoothly." His defenses rose. "As much as I'd like to spend more time here, I can't change that."

"I understand your work is demanding." He met Quentin's gaze. "Does Paige realize you have other priorities?"

"She knows I can't shirk my responsibilities. Believe me, the last thing in the world I want is to hurt her."

"I don't doubt that for a minute since I know how much you've always loved my daughter. As long as you both have the same expectations and she's happy, I'm happy."

"That's my goal, to make Paige happy." When Sheldon rose to his feet, Quentin stood, too. "Traveling for work as much as he did, my dad was out of town more often than not while I was growing up. You always jumped in to help out when I needed a male role model and Dad wasn't available. If I've never told you before how grateful I was, I'd like to now. It meant a lot to have you come on my Boy Scout camp-out with me and help me with my pitching when I was playing baseball."

"I was glad to do it, and I knew you appreciated having me stand in now and then. Your father thanked me more than once. He regretted missing out on so many important moments in your life. That was the main reason your family moved, so he wouldn't have to travel as often for work."

"I was pretty angry when we left Siren Cove, but I ended up liking Seattle. Mostly, I missed Paige, but our friendship survived the separation."

"You two always had a special bond." Sheldon looked up when his wife and daughter returned, followed by Leo. "Are the dishes finished? I was just planning to come in and help."

"*Sure* you were, Dad." Paige reached up to kiss his cheek. "We forgive you this time."

"Are you taking off?"

"Yep. I have to work in the morning. I expect it'll be busy, and Mindy took a few days off to visit her family."

Quentin followed her to the entry, shook Sheldon's hand, and gave Ava a hug before thanking her again for the meal. Once Paige had told her parents good night, he carried the load of gifts they'd opened earlier in the afternoon out to his car. After Leo scrambled into the backseat and they were settled, he started the engine and pulled out onto the street.

"What a relaxing day, well, except for the discussion over dessert." Paige shifted to look over at him. "I hope you weren't too bored."

"I wasn't bored at all. Your parents are family to me."

"That's good to know, since my mom is wondering when we plan to have the wedding. She suggested Valentine's Day would be very romantic."

"What?" He braked hard at the stop sign and stared at her. "How did you answer that?"

"Relax. I told her it isn't happening."

"You did?" He couldn't help feeling a little put off by the finality in her tone. "Maybe not right now . . ."

"Because as much as I love you, I've come to the conclusion you aren't husband material. Today pretty much cemented that knowledge in my mind."

He opened his mouth, then shut it to put a little thought into what he was going to say. They were halfway back to her apartment before he spoke. "I'm not sure if I should be insulted or relieved you don't sound angry with me. I'm leaning toward the former. Can I ask what I did to make you think I'm such a jerk?"

"Not a jerk. You're just not ready to make a commitment. You gave me a plane ticket to Hawaii for Christmas."

"We talked about a tropical vacation later in the winter." He gripped the steering wheel a little harder. "I thought you liked my gift."

"I do like it. We'll have a great time."

"Why do I hear a *but* in your voice?"

"No *but*. We'll definitely have fun. We always have a blast together. I'm not sure if I'll still be sleeping with you in February, but that doesn't mean we can't take a friendly vacation."

He felt like his head might explode. He pulled into the alley next to her shop and parked in the lot behind it. Once he turned off the engine, he didn't make any move to get out of the car even though Leo hung his head between their seats and panted.

"Why wouldn't we be sleeping together? If there's one thing I do know—and I'm beginning to think there's one hell of a lot I don't—it's that we're perfect together in bed."

"Yeah, we are, which kind of sucks."

He pressed fingers to his temples. "You're going to have to explain that one."

"My expectations for the next guy might be a little unreasonable."

"The next guy . . ." His voice faltered.

"Yeah, the next guy." She reached over and laid her

hand on his thigh and patted it. "All these years I've been rejecting men because they weren't you. Now that I know without a doubt you and I have different goals, I think I'm finally ready to give someone else a chance. Taking our friendship to the next level was the smartest thing I ever did. It freed me from false expectations."

"So, you plan to date someone else?" Anger coursed through him just imagining Paige with some asshole. "Does this guy have a name?"

"Not yet. I intend to keep my options open."

When Leo gave a snuffling whine, Quentin felt like doing the same. "Why?"

"Because I *do* want to get married and have kids. I want what Leah and Nina have. You don't."

"Oh." All the built up, self-righteous indignation dissipated like fog in a stiff wind. Pain took its place to eat at him. "So, you're breaking up with me because I don't want to have kids anytime soon?"

"We're not breaking up. We'll always be friends. Nothing will change that. Ever. I'm not even opposed to continuing our physical relationship while you're still here in town. As you pointed out, the sex is great." She unfastened her seatbelt. "Are you coming inside or not?"

Catching his breath became an effort as he digested everything she'd said. "Uh, I guess so." Once he opened the car door and stepped out, Leo clambered across his seat to leap to the ground. The dog had probably scratched the leather, but at the moment, that didn't seem like his biggest concern.

He helped her carry in the armload of gifts from her parents, leaving the display board of vintage fishing lures she'd given him in the trunk. "Those lures will look terrific on the wall in my restaurant."

"I'm glad you like them." She juggled her load to unlock the back door.

After the dog pushed past him, Quentin locked up again and followed her up the stairs. "You know, you never explained why the plane ticket I gave you sealed my fate."

She glanced over her shoulder as she entered her apartment. "If you were committed to a future with me, that plane ticket would have been a ring."

He backed up a step, feeling like he'd been punched in the gut. "You expected a proposal?"

Her smile held a hint of regret. "No, Quentin, I honestly didn't. But I've been thinking long and hard about what I do want. I'm not upset with you. I'm irritated with myself."

He shut the door and leaned against it. "Why would you be angry with yourself? I don't want that. I'd rather you were pissed at me."

"I know you better than I know myself, so I was an idiot to have expectations that aren't even close to being in your wheelhouse."

He pushed away from the door to set down the soft wool blanket and boots he was carrying. "Drop that stuff and let's go talk."

"Okay." She piled books and a couple of sweaters onto the stack, then took his hand to walk into the living room. She curled up on the couch and eyed him steadily when he sat next to her and braced his elbows on his knees. "I had my say. Talk."

"If you want to get married, we'll get married."

"No, we won't." She held up her hand when he opened his mouth. "I know you love me and would do anything for me, but that isn't what I want. I don't want you to be guilted into doing something that isn't right for you.

Maybe in five or ten years you'll want to settle down and have a family. I don't want to wait that long."

"So, you're going to keep sleeping with me until you find a guy who *is* ready?"

She scowled. "If you say it in that tone, I sure as hell won't."

"Sorry, but I don't like the idea of you with someone else."

"And I'm not crazy about knowing you'll go back to your love 'em and leave 'em ways the second I cut you off. We'll both simply have to get over it." Her eyes filled with determination. "Maybe it won't be easy, but that's what's going to happen."

"Shit." He flopped back against the couch. "I was so damn happy with the way things were going."

"I know you were. I'm happy right now, too. There's no one I'd rather be with than you, and you know that. But I can't fool myself into believing a casual relationship where we see each other as much as possible, but our lives aren't connected on a daily basis, is going to be enough once you open the Poseidon Grill and return to Seattle."

"What if I make Siren Cove my home base instead of Seattle?"

"That would be huge for you, Quentin."

"I know, but your livelihood is here. Your family and best friends are here. I can't exactly ask you to pack up and move."

"I'd think about it under the right circumstances."

He studied her vulnerable face that reflected every emotion she was feeling. "I guess you would move for me, which makes me feel like a total douchebag."

She smiled. "Sometimes you really are."

"Gee, thanks." He was quiet for a moment as Leo rolled over and moaned in his sleep. "You're entitled to one hundred and fifty percent of my attention, and not a bit less. If I can't give that to you, I don't deserve you."

"Probably not."

"Do you want me to take off?"

She scooted toward him and threaded her fingers through his. "No, because for right now, you're still living here in Siren Cove, and I intend to simply enjoy having you around. It would be ridiculous to expect us to return to being just friends while we see each other on a daily basis. Neither of us would be able to pull that off."

He squeezed her hand a little harder. "I know I wouldn't."

"So, we won't even try. Once you leave town, we'll go back to the way things used to be between us. Maybe I'll meet a guy who's willing to give me one hundred and fifty percent, and you'll find another extremely sexy and slightly crazy woman to date. One day, I might even be willing to listen to your woman problems again and give you sane dating advice you probably won't take."

"If I was smart, I'd listen. If I was smart, I'd make a whole lot of changes."

Her eyes were shadowed with regret. "I don't want to change you. Then you wouldn't be the man I love."

He lowered his gaze to the floor. *Maybe not, but I'd probably be a hell of a lot happier in the long run.*

Chapter Seventeen

Dim light slanted through the blinds as Paige lay in bed with her head pillowed on Quentin's chest, wondering if she'd made a huge mistake. *Isn't something better than nothing? Will I ever love another man the way I love him?*

His warm palm rested on her back. As his breathing changed from sleep to wakefulness, he stroked a thumb up and down her spine. An ache settled low in her belly and spread. When he rolled her beneath him and kissed her, she wrapped her arms around his waist and held on tight.

Finally, he pulled back a few inches to smile down at her. "I can't imagine a better way to begin my morning."

"Me, either."

He nuzzled the side of her throat, then worked his way south to her breasts. As he took one tip into his mouth, she drew in a sharp breath and pressed her heels hard against the mattress.

"Not everyone is lucky enough to have this." He switched to her second breast.

"I know." She gritted her teeth and focused on not coming unwound. "But sex isn't everything."

He stopped what he was doing to glance up at her with a teasing smile. "Are you sure?"

"Maybe right this minute I'm not." When he pushed hard between her legs, she nearly melted. "But I will be once I get out of this bed."

Rocking slowly against her, he went in for another long, drugging kiss. "Maybe we should stay here all day then."

"Can't. I have work." Her voice came out in a harsh pant. "Are you trying to kill me?"

He reached for the nightstand drawer where he'd left a stash of condoms. "Only if dying of pleasure really can happen." After ripping open the packet and covering himself, he gathered her close. "It's certainly the way I'd like to go out."

He did have a point. "I'm willing to take the risk."

"Me, too."

When he buried himself deep inside her, all coherent thoughts fled. She focused on each fleeting moment, the feel of his hard chest pressed against her breasts, the scent of their lovemaking. As the tension inside her built, nothing else mattered.

She cried out and clung to him as her body shook. Moments later, he collapsed on top of her with an explosion of breath. After a minute, he rolled them both to their sides. Perspiration dampened their skin until they stuck together.

Paige didn't care in the least.

"You really want to give this up?" A long sigh stirred her hair.

"Not want. Need."

"I'm not going to push you to change your mind. Not

right now anyway." He tilted her chin to kiss her. "I should jump in the shower and then get going. I have a call scheduled with my manager at The Zephyr in an hour."

"And I need to open my store."

He tossed back the covers and slid to the edge of the bed. His feet came down beside Leo, who was snoozing on the rug below them.

"Remember, you need to go talk to the police about Lucy and her boyfriend."

Quentin's shoulders stiffened. "Damn. I'd forgotten about that." He glanced back at her and grimaced. "I'll make time."

"Okay." Her euphoria of a few moments before had faded, and each breath she took hurt her chest. *Or maybe my heart.* "I'll go make coffee."

With a nod, he crossed the room and disappeared into the bathroom. When the shower turned on, Paige flopped against the pillows and focused on not crying. After all, it had been her idea to keep sleeping together.

Putting off the inevitable, one night at a time.

After a couple minutes of self-pity, she forced herself out of bed and threw on a robe. By the time Quentin joined her in the kitchen, she'd fed the dog and made the coffee. When he reached across her for a mug, she breathed in his fresh scent. Somehow her floral shampoo didn't smell girly on him.

"Do you expect the shop to be busy today?"

She sipped her coffee. "Lots of people are off work all week, so there'll be good-sized crowds strolling through town, looking for something to do. Plus, I'll have a few returned gifts. The good news is most people wind up buying something even more expensive in exchange." She set down her mug. "I can make eggs if you want."

"Nope. All my notes for the call are at my place, so I'll

grab something to eat there. I have a personnel problem to iron out with my manager, and I'm trying to avoid taking a trip to Seattle."

"Oh. I guess I'll see you later then."

He took a few more swallows of coffee before putting his mug in the sink. On his way past, he wrapped an arm around her waist and kissed her. "I'll call you."

"Okay. Have a good day."

After the door shut behind him, Paige glanced down at Leo. "*Have a good day,*" she mimicked. "Who am I, June Cleaver? Ugh."

The dog stretched out across the floor with his nose on his paws. When she caught a glimpse of worried brown eyes through the dreadlocks, she smiled. "No reason to be alarmed. I won't send you packing along with Quentin. We're in this together."

Deciding she couldn't face the thought of food, Paige showered and dressed for work in a wool skirt, bright red sweater, and boots, then took Leo for a stroll around the parking lot. Shivering in the damp air, she hurried the dog inside and promised him a better walk later. She'd no more than plugged in the Christmas lights and turned around the open sign when her first customer walked in.

The morning was chaotic, and it was noon before the most recent batch of browsers departed. Feeling a little lightheaded and wondering why she'd been stupid enough to skip breakfast, she ran upstairs to grab a bagel and a bag of baby carrots. When the doorbells downstairs jangled, she swore beneath her breath as she sprinted back down with her snacks. Pasting on a smile, she searched for her customer. Rounding a tall armoire, she nearly ran into a well-dressed woman wearing a suit and heels. Not the usual attire for someone vacationing on the coast . . .

"Welcome to Old Things. May I help you find something?" Paige asked.

"You have a few interesting pieces here." The dark-haired woman glanced around. "Some total crap, too, but I wouldn't expect otherwise. My husband bought me a Fabergé egg. Since we're staying in town for a few more days, I thought I'd check out your store for myself."

Paige's smile remained in place, despite the crack about her merchandise. "You must be Mrs. LaPine. How do you like your egg?"

"It's stunning. I was wondering if you have any decent antique jewelry."

"I don't have anything really valuable since I don't carry that kind of insurance, but some of my collection is set with semiprecious stones." Paige showed her the display of necklaces and broaches near the front counter. While the woman picked through the jewelry, Paige surreptitiously munched carrots.

"I wasn't sure buying a vacation home in this area was the right choice. But Mason has always been fond of Siren Cove." She held a pair of garnet earrings up to the light. "These have potential."

"I didn't realize you and your husband had a residence here."

"We bought Lola Copeland's house. The place has beautiful views. We didn't budge on our offer, and she finally accepted it."

"I know Miss Lola. Actually, I acquired some of her furniture when she moved."

"Mason mentioned his sister sold some of his mother's glassware to you when they were cleaning out her house. I didn't care to take any of it. His mother and I don't exactly have the same style."

"We all have different tastes." When the senator's wife

approached and laid the earrings on the counter, Paige wrapped them in tissue. “These are beautiful.” She took the credit card Mrs. LaPine handed her and rang up the sale. “I’m Paige Shephard, by the way. Will you be in town for a while?”

“The State Senate is on winter break, so we’ll be here through the New Year. Of course, Mason still has some traveling to do, what with his run for governor on the horizon.” Her lips tightened. “I’m Virginia.” She held out her hand. “Nice to meet you.”

Paige shook her hand. “Likewise. I hope I’ll see you again soon.”

“I may be back, since there isn’t a whole lot to do in Siren Cove but shop.” She accepted her package. “Have a nice day.”

“You, too.” After the door closed behind her, Paige winced. Virginia LaPine was definitely on the abrasive side, which wasn’t ideal for the wife of a political figure. Still, who knew what the woman had to contend with.

Paige doubted anyone but her closest friends would be able to tell the weight of her recent decisions had crushed her spirit. Maybe not even them since she would make every effort to hide her pain. She knew what had to be done, but this time the right choice just might kill her.

Quentin slouched in an uncomfortable orange chair in the waiting room at the police station and stared out the window. His mind was on Paige’s decision to cut him loose instead of his upcoming conversation with the cop. Not surprising, since his thoughts had been on Paige all day. Surely there was something he could do to change her mind without wrecking her chance at happiness . . . and making his own life miserable.

Since no brilliant answers presented themselves, he surged to his feet when Chris Long appeared in the doorway.

Chris waved him over. “Hey, Quentin. Come on back. I hear you have information about the Lucinda Gordon case.”

“I’m not sure how helpful it’ll be to your investigation, but I figured I should share what I remember of Lucy.”

Chris’s brows rose. “Lucy? Wait. Hold that thought until we get to my computer.”

Quentin followed him into the squad room and dropped into the chair across the desk from him. A pile of neatly stacked folders rested on one edge, along with a coffee mug with brown stains on the sides.

Chris typed on his keyboard for a moment before glancing up to regard him steadily. “Let’s hear what you know about Lucinda. You couldn’t have been very old when she went missing.”

“I was nine.” Quentin related his memories of his babysitter and the meeting with her boyfriend beneath the willow tree.

“I’ve studied the old case files. Apparently, no one knew who Lucinda was dating that summer, or if they did, they weren’t talking. You’re saying you heard her arguing with a man about a baby, and you actually saw this guy?”

“Only from behind. I didn’t see his face.”

Chris’s blue eyes narrowed as he leaned back in his chair. “Did anyone else see him? Were any of the neighbors out in their yards?”

“I don’t remember anyone being around. It was midweek, and most of the people on our street worked. Old Mrs. Harris, who lived two houses down from the Shephards, might have looked out her window, but she must be dead by now. She seemed ancient back then.”

He jotted something on a notepad. "Paige didn't come outside with you?"

"No, she was watching cartoons. I left her in the living room to see where Lucy went."

"Why is that?" Chris asked.

"Lucy was a beautiful girl, and I had a huge crush on her." Quentin grimaced. "Seeing her kiss that guy destroyed those feelings. I remember being pissed off for the rest of the day."

The cop typed for another minute. "Let's work on a description of the man. How tall was he in relation to Lucinda? Was he skinny or heavy? What color was his hair, and what was he wearing?"

Quentin closed his eyes and tried to picture the scene. "Lucinda came up to the man's chin. She stood on her toes to kiss him. I don't remember him being skinny or fat, just average. I think his hair was brown. He had on a ball cap, but his hair came down over his neck. He was wearing jeans and a white T-shirt that had some sort of blue logo on the back. I don't remember what it was because I wasn't paying attention." He stopped speaking and opened his eyes.

"That's a pretty good description, considering you were nine years old when this happened."

"Lucy left an indelible impression on me. I bet you remember your first big crush."

"I might. All right, what about a vehicle? Was there a car parked on the street in front of the house?"

Quentin searched his memory. "Lucy's little blue car was parked nearby. I don't remember the make. There was a motorcycle behind it. Black, I think, but I couldn't see it very well from where I was hiding in the bushes."

"I'm impressed. Most adults who've witnessed something only a few hours before don't have that kind of recall. Anything else you want to tell me?"

"Not that I can think of." He paused for a moment. "Actually, yes. I was in the living room watching cartoons with Paige when I heard the motorcycle roar away. Lucy came inside a minute later. Her eyes looked kind of red, like she'd been crying. She didn't say anything, just went straight to the bathroom down the hall. When she came out, she'd fixed her makeup. I felt bad that she was upset, but I was still too angry about that kiss to forgive her."

"Did you see her again after she left the house that afternoon?"

"No. Ava Shephard mentioned this happened a few days before Lucy disappeared. She might be able to give you an exact date. I know it was in August."

"You've been very helpful. We'll follow up on this information to see if her grandfather can remember anyone Lucy associated with that summer who rode a motorcycle."

"I'm glad I came by." Quentin pushed back his chair and paused with his hands pressed against the chair arms. "Did Clea Merrick show up at her aunt and uncle's house?"

"No, and none of her friends or relatives have seen her." Chris's lips tightened. "We've officially opened a missing persons case. The tavern where you left her was closed yesterday for Christmas, but I'll head up to Newport in a couple of hours to question the employees and the evening crowd. Maybe someone will remember seeing her and the man she was with. If you're planning to leave town, I'd appreciate it if you'd check with me first. I expect I'll need to speak to you again once I get a statement from the bartender. I'll give you my cell number."

Quentin typed it into his phone. "I'll be around. If I do

have to go anywhere for business, I wouldn't be gone for more than a couple of days."

"Do you take these trips often?"

Something in his tone set Quentin's teeth on edge. "Not lately. My focus has been on getting the Poseidon Grill open."

"When will that be?"

"Hopefully during the second half of January. Once I have a firm date, I'll schedule a grand opening." He pushed to his feet. "If you don't have any further questions . . ."

"No, that'll be all. For now." Chris stood. "I'll walk you out."

Quentin left the police station a few minutes later and drove straight to Castaways. After hearing Clea was still missing, he needed a drink. He parked his Jag on the street and entered the bar, where clusters of patrons sat with glasses and bottles in front of them. Most were watching the college football game between two west coast teams blaring on the televisions spaced around the bar. He didn't see anyone he knew, and Paige wouldn't close her shop for another hour.

Resigned to drinking alone, he slid onto a bar stool beside a well-dressed woman sipping a martini while she tapped on her phone. On his other side, two guys who looked vaguely familiar were in a heated debate. Quentin ordered a draft from the bartender and glanced up at the game. As he sipped his beer and brooded, the conversation between the two men caught his attention.

"Christ, Jonas. You skipped out on Christmas dinner with Grandpa to go to the track. Real nice."

"I had a good tip. Too bad it didn't pan out."

"You're an idiot."

"Who are you to talk?"

The guy with the shorter hair had been in the bachelor auction. Quentin was almost positive his brother was a mechanic in town. While they were pulling cash from their wallets to pay their bill, his cell rang. After glancing at the display, he swore softly.

"What's up, Blaze? I thought you intended to move on with your life."

"God, you can be a jerk. Merry Christmas to you, too."

He let out a sigh. "I'm sorry. I'm having a shitty day, and seeing your name pop up on my phone was a surprise. What can I do for you?"

As the two men walked away, a middle-aged man with dark blond hair took one of the vacated stools. "Barkeep, can I get a shot and a beer over here?"

"I'll be right with you, Mr. Copeland."

Between the roar from the TV as one of the teams scored, and the exchange next to him, Quentin missed Blaze's response. "I couldn't hear you, Blaze. It's a little loud in here."

"I said I can't find one of my diamond studs. They were expensive, so I want it back. The last time I wore those earrings was on a date with you. I probably dropped it in your townhouse."

He rubbed the back of his neck while the guy on the stool to his left glanced his way. "I didn't find your earring."

"You didn't look for it, either. Can I get into your place? Is the spare key still under the flowerpot?"

He didn't really want her in his home, but he was even less enthused about debating the issue. "I moved the key before I left for Siren Cove. Now it's under that decorative rock by the clump of ferns to the right of the door.

When are you planning to go over to look for the earring?"

"Excuse me. I think I left . . . There they are." The clean-cut brother swooped down to grab a ring of keys from under the barstool beside Quentin.

His twin stood behind him, tapping his foot. "Can we take off now?"

"You've got somewhere better to be?"

Quentin returned his attention to Blaze. "Sorry, when did you say? Tomorrow evening? Sure, go look for it."

"Where are you that's so noisy?"

"Castaways. Make sure you lock up after you leave."

"Drowning your sorrows, Quentin? I'm not an idiot. Of course I'll lock up. Have a good evening."

She hung up before he could respond. He set his phone on the shiny surface of the bar and grimaced. Since he'd taken her name off his approved guest list, he'd have to call the manager so they'd let her into the complex.

"Woman problems?"

Quentin glanced at the man on the nearby stool as he downed the shot the bartender set in front of him. "Something like that."

"Don't feel alone. Most of us have women issues." Turning his shoulder, the guy picked up his beer and focused on the football game.

Truer words had never been spoken.

Chapter Eighteen

He needed a distraction. A fall guy. Anything to divert the cops from the truth. With two ongoing investigations, the police just might get lucky.

He stared straight ahead at the stretch of freeway, his teeth clenched as he fought off a headache. He was sick to death of damage control. According to word on the street, if it weren't for Paige Shephard and Quentin Radcliff and their damn Christmas tree hunt, Lucy's death would still be buried deep in some dusty file. Instead, Chris Long was sniffing around, questioning people she'd hung out with that summer.

His grip on the steering wheel tightened as he shot around a big rig. Then there was Clea. Lucky for him, Radcliff was bound to be the prime suspect in her disappearance, thanks to his date with her. All he needed to do was fan those flames.

The moron had practically handed him the perfect opportunity on a silver platter. Follow-through was the key now. Getting the address to the man's townhouse had taken very little effort. It was almost a crime how simple it was these days to track down personal information. Not that he was complaining. As long as Radcliff spent enough time alone to blow up any alibi, his plan was pretty much foolproof.

Leaning back in his seat, he tried to relax as he considered his next move. Another woman would disappear in the space of a week, and the cops would focus their attention on the only person with a connection to both. Chances were good, no new evidence would turn up in the investigation into Lucy's death. He couldn't be that unlucky after all these years. If all went well, the cops wouldn't look past the obvious. He'd be safe once again.

When the door to her shop opened, Paige paused with her red marking pen hovering over the after-Christmas sale sign she was creating. "Leah, it's good to see you."

Her friend flipped long, wind-blown hair over her shoulder as she approached. "I thought I'd stop by after fighting the crowds at the grocery store. Has your shop been busy?"

"Extremely. You caught me during a lull."

"Good. We can have a chat." She dropped her purse on the counter and leaned on her elbows. "Have you heard the latest gossip spreading through town? People are freaking out, and I don't blame them."

"About what?"

"Clea Merrick, the woman who bought a date with Quentin at the bachelor auction, has apparently gone missing. She disappeared four days ago and hasn't been heard from since."

Paige's shoulders slumped. "Chris Long stopped by after everyone left the party on Christmas Eve to talk to Quentin. Since they've officially opened an investigation, he told him he'd probably have more questions. Quentin is pretty upset because Clea disappeared the evening he took her out for their date."

A memory of the previous night flashed through Paige's mind. Quentin hadn't said much after showing up at her apartment, but his tension was palpable. They'd gone to bed early, and he'd simply held her through the dark hours. She was pretty sure he hadn't slept at all.

"I had no idea." Leah laid a hand on her arm. "I can imagine he's feeling sick about it."

"Clea was annoyed because Quentin wasn't interested in taking their date any further than dinner. She insisted he leave her up in Newport, and apparently that's when she disappeared. Quentin is blaming himself."

"How horrible." Leah's brown eyes were wide with shock. "Surely the cops don't believe—"

"God, I hope not. Quentin is cooperating fully with their investigation, of course."

"At least he has you in his corner. That's got to be a comfort to him right now."

Paige ran a finger along a scratch in the surface of the counter.

"What? You're behind Quentin one hundred percent, aren't you?" Leah asked sharply.

The ache in Paige's chest that never seemed far away intensified. "Of course I am."

"Why do I hear a *but* in your voice?"

"We aren't going to work out as a couple. I told him so on Christmas Day."

"Why not?" Leah's tone held frustration and a hint of anger. "What the heck did he do to you?"

"Nothing. This is my choice, not his."

"Then I don't get it."

When Leo strolled out of her storage room and walked

over to lean against her leg, Paige buried her fingers in his fur. "Leo knows I'm upset, but it isn't Quentin's fault. Ironically, I made my decision because of you and Nina."

Leah jerked back. "Me? What did I do?"

"You're so damn happy with Ryan, and Nina's pregnant." Paige's voice broke. "I want that kind of stability. I'm thirty-one years old, and I'm tired of feeling like I'm always looking for something that isn't there. Quentin loves me, but—"

"He doesn't want to get married and have kids?"

"Not right now. He casually threw out a *we'll get married if it'll make you happy* proposal, but it's not what he really wants. Maybe in five years—or ten—he'll be ready. By the time he gets his crap together, I'll be too old to have a baby."

"That sucks." Leah rounded the counter and hugged her.

"Yeah, it does, and I'm not stupid enough to set myself up for heartbreak down the road. I'd rather get it over with now."

"You'll still be friends with him, won't you?" She sounded like she wasn't too sure she believed it.

Paige stepped back. "Yeah, we will. I won't give up our friendship, but I'm going to find a guy who'll make me happy, even if it kills me."

"That's the spirit." Leah rolled her eyes. "You make it sound as enticing as eating liver."

"Said like a true vegetarian. Once Quentin opens the Poseidon Grill for business and heads back to Seattle, I'm going to make dating some serious contenders my number one priority."

"Good for you, but why wait? If the jerk doesn't know how badly he's blowing it with you, he doesn't deserve your consideration."

"We're kind of still sleeping together, so it might be a little awkward."

"Are you kidding me?" Leah's voice rose.

"Hey, I'm weaning myself off Quentin slowly. Going cold turkey would be . . ." Paige fluttered a hand. "I don't have that kind of strength. This is what I want."

Sympathy filled her friend's eyes. "If you say so, but don't miss out on an opportunity if it presents itself. You never know who might walk through that door."

Paige smiled. "Not a lot of hot guys in their thirties are antique buffs, but I'll keep your advice in mind."

"You do that." Leah pulled out her phone. "Damn, I'm running late. I told Gram I'd have lunch with her, and I have to go home to put away my groceries first. Are you going to be okay?"

"I always am. Tell Evie I said hello."

"Will do." She stepped around the dog on her way to the door. "I'll talk to you soon."

Paige nodded. Once the door shut behind her friend, she pressed her fingers to her eyes. She refused to cry and screw up her makeup. Again. When the bells jingled, she jerked her hands away from her face. The professional, welcoming smile faded as Chris Long entered her store.

His somber blue eyes met hers. "How are you, Paige?"

"Uh, fine. Why do I feel like you have bad news?"

"I guess I don't make much of an effort to hide my feelings around my friends. Unfortunately, this visit is work related." He turned to survey the shop. "If you have customers . . ."

"Not at the moment. Should I sit down?"

"You'll be fine standing since I'm sure you're expecting my news. The department put a rush on the DNA results for those bones we found in the woods. Confirmation came in this morning. They belonged to Lucinda Gordon. I wanted to tell you in person since you were key in the recovery of her remains."

Paige braced a hand on the counter. "I was afraid you had bad news about Clea Merrick."

His lips tightened. "We're still investigating her disappearance."

This time his expression gave nothing away. Paige swallowed. "What's going to happen now . . . about Lucy?"

"We've reopened her missing persons case as a homicide."

Any response stuck in her throat. The word homicide sounded so very ugly.

Apparently, Chris wasn't expecting a comment. "Based on a fracture to her skull, it's been determined she was killed by a blow to the head. I'd like to get a statement from you about the time she babysat you the summer she went missing."

Paige felt for the stool behind her and eased onto it. Her legs shook as she crossed her ankles. "I don't know what I can tell you that'll help. I didn't see her talking to her boyfriend that day."

"But you might have other relevant information. Did Lucinda have a cell phone? Not everyone was attached to a phone back then."

Searching her hazy memory, she came up with an image of Lucy lying on a towel on the concrete apron of the public pool, her cell clutched in her hand, while she and Quentin tried to dunk each other in the deep end. "Yeah, she did. I remember her using it while we were at the pool."

"Did she call anyone by name during that conversation?"

"I couldn't hear her. It was unusually hot, and there were a lot of kids at the pool that day, laughing and shouting."

"Did Lucy meet friends while you were there?"

Paige shook her head. "Not that I remember." She paused as a recollection formed. "We were getting ready to leave, and she told me and Quentin to go change into our clothes so we wouldn't get her car soaked from our wet bathing suits. I couldn't find my underwear, and I was embarrassed I might have dropped them by the pool. I left the changing room to go look for them, and Lucy was standing by the fence, talking to someone."

"A man?" Chris's voice was sharp.

"I think so. I couldn't see him even though Lucy's head came over the top of the fence, so he must have been sitting on something."

"Like a motorcycle?"

"That makes sense. Anyway, she said she took a test and it was positive. The male voice swore, words I'd never heard before. I stood there staring until Lucy turned around and noticed me. She looked mad. She asked me what I was doing." Paige let out a breath as the memory unraveled. "I saw my underwear under a lounge chair and scooped them up, then ran back to the changing room."

"Was she still talking to the man when you came back out?"

"I don't think so. I only remember the first conversation because later I asked Quentin if he knew what a—uh, excuse my language—a cocksucker was. His face got red, and he told me not to say that again."

"Do you remember Lucy talking to anyone else while she watched you? Maybe a girlfriend?"

"I honestly don't. The only time we left the house was to go to the pool, and that was because I begged so hard.

I think it was the second of the three days she sat for us. While we were hanging out at home, no one ever came over. Well, except for the man Quentin saw, but I didn't know about him at the time."

Chris stepped back from the counter. "Thanks, Paige. You've been very helpful. Your story corroborates what Quentin told me."

"You think the test she mentioned was a pregnancy test?" Her voice rang hollow in her ears. "That asshole killed her because she was pregnant."

"I probably shouldn't speculate, but it's beginning to look that way."

She rubbed her hands up and down her arms as a chill shook her. "That's just sick. Will you be able to find her boyfriend after all these years?"

"I damn well intend to try." He squeezed her shoulder as his eyes filled with compassion. "Are you okay? You look a little pale."

Everyone seemed to be asking her that question. First Leah, and now Chris. Maybe because she was anything but okay. Maybe because she was sad and discouraged.

"This year, the holidays have been anything but joyful, all things considered." She tried to smile as his eyes darkened. "But I'll be fine."

"I hope so. Feel free to call me anytime if you need to talk."

Before she could answer, the door opened. Quentin paused on the threshold.

"Am I interrupting something?"

Chris took his hand off her shoulder and backed away as Paige stepped down from the stool. "No, we were finished talking." He studied Quentin for a moment. "I had a conversation with the bartender last night. He remembers you, but not anyone resembling Clea Merrick."

Quentin entered the shop and let the door shut behind him. "I told you that."

"Strangely, no one at all remembers seeing her. Not the cocktail servers, any of the regular patrons I contacted, or the members of the band who were playing that night. It's almost like she wasn't there." Chris paused for a moment. "The waiter at the restaurant where you ate dinner does remember her. He said you two looked pretty cozy."

Quentin jammed his hands into his pockets. "Clea made a few advances. I told her it wasn't going to happen. I can't help what our situation looked like."

When the bells jingled again and an elderly couple entered, Quentin held the door wide before moving out of the way.

Paige forced a smile for her customers. "Welcome to Old Things. Please just ask if I can help you find something."

"Thank you." The diminutive woman studied the police officer as she leaned on her walker. "We're browsing today, but I'll let you know if I have any questions."

Chris cleared his throat. "I'll be in touch, Quentin. Expect a call from me in the next few days."

"I may need to leave town."

"Oh?" He paused with his hand on the doorknob. "Why's that?"

"Issues at my Seattle restaurant. I'm waiting for a call now, but chances are I'll need to head up there immediately."

"How long do you expect to be gone?"

Quentin stepped past him to stand beside Paige. Tension radiated from his stiff shoulders. "I'm not sure. Hopefully no more than a couple of days."

"I have your cell number. I'll contact you if need be." Chris smiled at Paige. "Thanks again for your help."

"I appreciate you keeping me in the loop. Bye, Chris."

"What loop is that?" Quentin asked as the door shut behind the officer.

"The DNA test came back." Paige stopped speaking as the door opened again and three women entered. "Hi, welcome to Old Things. Please let me know if I can be of assistance."

A tall blonde spoke up. "Actually, I'm looking for red Fiesta dinnerware. The pieces made back in the thirties, not the more recent stuff. Do you have anything?"

"I have a couple of bowls you might like." Paige gave Quentin an apologetic look before smiling at her customer. "I'll be with you in just a moment."

"You're busy. Come on, Leo. We'll wait in the storage room."

"Thanks." She squeezed past him and led the group of women to her dishware selection. By the time she'd rung up their sale, the older couple had chosen the white marble cat she'd bought from Margaret LaPine's daughter. "It's a beautiful piece. I hope you enjoy it."

"Oh, we will." The elderly woman beamed. "It looks just like our Fluffy who died nearly fifty years ago. I have a whole collection of cats."

Paige handed the reinforced bag over to her husband. "Be sure to come back the next time you're in town."

"You can count on it." The woman waved one arthritic hand. "This place is a treasure trove."

Once the customer had maneuvered her walker through the doorway, Paige headed toward the back of her store. Quentin sat on a stool at her workbench with his cell clamped to his ear. When she retreated a step, he waved her forward.

"I'll be there this evening, Val. Yeah, we'll get everything straightened out. This isn't your fault. I'll talk to you soon."

Paige leaned against the doorframe as he dropped his phone on the bench. "What's going on?"

"An employee is threatening a sexual harassment suit if we don't pay him off."

Her brows shot up. "Him?"

"Yeah, him. Val, my manager, has been trying to handle the complaint for several days now, but the situation has gone south. I need to personally step in."

"Was he harassed by another one of your employees?"

"I did some digging, and the guy is up to his eyeballs in debt. I think he's looking to make a quick buck." Quentin stood. "Still, I need to get to the bottom of the situation. If the man was sexually harassed, someone is going to get fired, and I'll report it to the cops. If he wasn't, the idiot is going to wish he hadn't taken me on. Either way, I'll deal with it."

"One more piece of bad news. This day just keeps getting better and better."

"You said something about DNA results."

"They identified the bones Leo found at the creek. Someone killed Lucy and buried her up in the woods."

"She was murdered?"

"According to Chris, someone hit her over the head and cracked her skull. They're still trying to identify her boyfriend. He questioned me about what I remembered from that summer. Unfortunately, it wasn't much."

"Is that what he was doing?"

She stuck out her foot to rub Leo's belly when the dog rolled over. "What do you mean?"

"Long was questioning you? When I showed up, it looked like he was asking you out."

“You mean like how the waiter said you and Clea looked ‘cozy’ together.”

“Hey, I told Clea to back off. If I hadn’t, she might not have gone missing.”

Turning away, Paige blinked back tears. “Whatever. I guess you’d better go home and pack if you’re leaving shortly.”

He stepped up behind her, hauled her back against his chest, and held on tight. His breath brushed her ear. “Sorry. I guess seeing you with another man, even if his intentions were innocent, made me a little jealous.”

“I’m not planning to date Chris, for heaven’s sake. He used to have a thing for Nina. Even if she didn’t reciprocate his feelings, it’d just be . . . weird.” She rested her cheek against his chest. “You should go.”

“I know.” Turning her fully in his arms, he tipped up her chin to kiss her. “I wish I didn’t have to leave right now. We need to talk.”

“Why? We’ve said everything that needs to be said. Several times.”

When the shop bells jangled again, he swore. “No, we haven’t.”

“I’ve got to go take care of my customer. You have to deal with your restaurant. Right now, that’s what’s important.”

He pressed another hard kiss to her lips. “No, Paige, not by a long shot.”

Chapter Nineteen

Quentin slowed his car to turn into the complex where his townhouse was located. As he approached the guardhouse, he frowned when no one stepped out to greet him. “What the hell?” He rolled down the window and craned his neck to see into the lighted booth. Definitely empty.

As he eased the Jag forward, a gangly figure wearing a navy uniform blazer loped across the lawn. Quentin braked to a stop. “Evening, Danny. I was wondering where you were.”

“Sorry, Mr. Radcliff. I think I ate a bad burrito. I’ve been running back and forth to the restroom all night.” A scruffy beard didn’t do much to cover a bad case of acne on his youthful face. “I wasn’t expecting you home tonight. How was your trip to Siren Cove?”

“Filled with ups and downs. Actually, I’m only back in Seattle for a day or two. Did you happen to see Blaze come through here earlier this evening?”

The kid nodded. “She showed up a couple of hours

ago. I hope it's all right that I let her in. She said you okayed it, and she was pretty insistent."

"I meant to call and put her on the list, but I got distracted and never followed through. Thanks for bending the rules." Quentin leaned his elbow on the open window. "If you don't feel better soon, call for a sub for the rest of your shift."

"I might have to do that. I'm sorry I wasn't here to greet you."

"No worries." He shifted into gear. "By the way, do you know when Blaze left?"

"Actually, I didn't see her come out. She might have passed through while I was using the can. I tell you, that burrito did a number on me." Danny's eyes widened. "In fact . . ." He took off, running toward the office where the nearest toilet was located.

Feeling sorry for the poor guy, Quentin hit the gas and cruised down the curving street toward his townhouse. A touch of the remote sent the garage door trundling upward, and he pulled his car inside the empty space. He hoped to hell Blaze wasn't still there. After the day he'd had, the last thing he wanted was another confrontation.

He stepped out onto the concrete floor, lifted his overnight bag from the backseat, and slammed the door. A moment later, he entered his home through the short hallway next to the laundry room and flipped on the kitchen light. "Blaze?"

His shout was met with silence.

"Thank God." He dropped his suitcase next to the island and opened the fridge. After surveying the skimpy contents, he pulled out one lone beer and popped the top. Taking a swallow, he headed into the living room where a single light had been left burning.

Throw pillows were in disarray on the couch, and the lamp on the end table was pushed clear to the edge. Dirt stained the rug below the dead poinsettia perched on the raised hearth. The plant had been a gift from one of his suppliers, and he'd forgotten all about the damn thing when he'd left town.

Apparently, Blaze had knocked it over while searching for her earring and hadn't bothered to clean up the mess.

"Whatever." He was too tired to care. Dropping onto the couch, he closed his eyes. His townhouse didn't feel like home. Maybe because Paige wasn't sitting beside him. He took another swig of his beer before pulling out his phone. After eleven. He wondered if she was already asleep. Just imagining her wearing a soft T-shirt that rode up over her panties as she curled beneath her quilt gave him a boner.

God, he missed her. He couldn't imagine how empty his life would be without Paige as an intrinsic part. Maybe marriage and kids hadn't been on his radar up to this point, but he might have to rethink his priorities. Paige seemed pretty damn certain about what she wanted . . . and it wasn't him.

He wanted to talk to her about all the thoughts swirling through his head, but not over the phone. He needed to look into her eyes and see her emotions reflected in their blue depths. But first, he had to figure out exactly what he was willing to sacrifice to make a future together happen.

"Asswipe," he muttered beneath his breath. If he was still thinking in terms of sacrifice, he had a long way to go. By the time he got to where he needed to be emotionally, Paige would be hitched to some other dude and have a baby or two.

His temples throbbed, and he rubbed them.

Just seeing Chris Long standing so close to her had lit his fuse. He couldn't imagine how he'd react to Paige in a wedding gown, walking down the damn aisle toward a man who'd spend the rest of his life making her happy. Not unless that man was him. He could almost picture himself in that scenario. Almost.

When the landline sitting on the end table beside him rang, he opened his eyes. No one called his landline. He'd meant to cancel service and hadn't gotten around to doing it yet. He glanced at the caller ID on the display. Not Paige. A number he didn't recognize. With a shrug, he picked up the receiver. Anything, even some idiot trying to convince him to upgrade his internet service, was a welcome distraction from his current, depressing thoughts.

"Hello."

"Is this Quentin?" a hesitant female voice asked.

"Yes. Who's this?"

"Blaze's friend, Jazmin. We met a couple of times while you two were still together. Is she there?"

"I'm afraid not."

"We had plans for tonight, but she said she had to stop by your townhouse first to look for something." Jazmin raised her voice as the background noise escalated. "Since she never showed up at the nightclub, I was worried."

"Did you call her cell?"

"Of course. I've been trying it for an hour, but she doesn't pick up. Once, when her battery was dead, she called me from your house phone, so I had the number. I'd hoped she was still there."

"The guy manning the gatehouse said she arrived over two hours ago, but she was gone before I got home. Sorry I can't be more help."

"I guess she changed her mind about clubbing this evening. Still, it isn't like Blaze to blow me off. Sorry to bother you."

"No bother. I'm sure Blaze simply forgot or double-booked with someone else. She did that a few times while we were dating."

"I hope that's what happened. Bye, Quentin."

"Bye, Jazmin." Quentin hung up the phone.

Slowly he rose to his feet. He wouldn't wake up Paige when she was sure to be sleeping, no matter how much he wanted to hear her voice. Instead, he'd go to bed and try to forget about how screwed up his life was right now. He had a meeting with the employee who was making allegations of harassment scheduled for the following morning. If all went well, he'd be able to head back to Siren Cove afterward. If it didn't . . . well, he'd face that problem when it happened. No point in anticipating trouble.

When his cell rang, Quentin answered it, despite the fact he was on the freeway, driving way faster than the speed limit. After two solid days of ugly conversations, all he wanted to do was go home to Paige.

"Quentin, this is Chris Long. Are you still in Seattle?" The voice on the other end of the line was curt.

Reducing his speed, he put the phone on speaker. A reflex action to obey the law when talking to a cop. His lips twisted in grim amusement. "Actually, I'm on my way back to Siren Cove. I should be there in a couple of hours."

"Do you mind coming in to speak with me when you get here?" His tone didn't make it sound like a request.

"Not at all, but it's Saturday. Don't you ever take a day off?"

"Now and then. I'll expect you later this afternoon."

Before Quentin could ask what he wanted to talk about, the line went dead. No doubt Chris had more questions regarding Clea. Not that there was any new information Quentin could contribute. With each passing day, his fear that something truly awful had happened to the woman increased. Sometimes the world just flat out sucked.

Leaving the phone on speaker, he called Paige.

"Hey. Are you on your way home?"

Just the sound of her voice softened his mood. "Yes, but your buddy Chris wants to have a chat when I get there. I'm not sure how long that'll take, but I'll stop by your shop when he's finished with me."

"Okay. Mindy's here, so I can take off a little early, maybe make you dinner for a change."

The tension flowed out of him. "That sounds great."

"How'd everything go at the restaurant?"

"It took a whole lot longer than I'd hoped to uncover the truth, but we finally got there. Basically, an employee was trying to shake me down for a cash settlement. After extensively questioning my staff, I came to the conclusion he was a lying sack of shit, and I told him he could file criminal charges and prove he'd been sexually harassed. At that point he backed off, and I fired him."

"Will he turn around and sue you for wrongful termination?"

"I'm not too worried about it. He's the type who looks for easy money, not a court battle. Anyway, I filed a report with the police to cover my ass. Waiting to get that handled was part of what took me so long."

"I'm glad you got to the bottom of it."

"I am, too. Problems like this are the downside of being a business owner."

"Makes me glad I only have Mindy on my payroll."

"Lucky you. Hey, I need to get gas at the next exit. I'll see you this evening, okay?"

"Okay. Bye, Quentin."

She hadn't told him she loved him. An oversight on her part, or was she already putting up walls? Then again, he hadn't expressed how he felt, either. Not in words, anyway.

Quentin brooded the rest of the way to Siren Cove as the sky above him darkened with clouds. He drove straight to the police station when he reached town and ran through the parking lot in the drizzling rain, happy to enter the warm interior of the building.

The young woman at the front counter opened the glass partition and smiled. "Officer Long is expecting you, Mr. Radcliff. I'll let him know you're here."

"Thank you." He dropped onto the same orange chair he'd occupied the last time he'd come by and waited for Chris to summon him. As the minutes ticked by, his impatience grew. Finally, the interior door opened, and Quentin rose to his feet.

Not Chris Long. Chief Stackhouse. The older man waved him forward. "Come on back, Quentin. We appreciate you stopping by."

"I'm happy to help in your investigation, but I'm not sure what more I can contribute. I've already told you everything I know about that evening."

"Which evening would that be?" The chief gestured for Quentin to precede him toward his office where Chris Long waited.

Quentin nodded at the man before taking the chair Stackhouse pointed to. "December twenty-third. The night Clea Merrick went missing. Isn't that why you wanted to talk to me?"

The chief sat heavily on his desk chair. His sharp gaze

never wavered from Quentin's face. "We may get around to Miss Merrick, but right now we'd like to know about the last time you saw your girlfriend, Blaze Campbell."

"Why? What happened to Blaze?"

"We're not too sure. It appears no one has seen her since she went to visit you at your townhouse in Seattle on Thursday night."

Quentin gaped at him. The chief's eyes were hard as stone. When he glanced over at Chris, the man's expression gave nothing away. Not a hint of sympathy showed in the tight line of his compressed lips.

"I didn't see her. Blaze called me about a missing earring before I even knew I was needed in Seattle. I told her she could look for it at my place, but she was already gone when I arrived."

"Is that right?" The chief sounded skeptical.

"Yes, that's right. I don't understand. If Blaze is missing, why didn't the police in Seattle question me about it? I was down at the precinct nearest my restaurant half the morning, filing a report on another matter?"

"Interesting. Apparently, you'd finished your business before this came to our attention. Officers went to your townhouse and found it empty. When they questioned your manager at The Zephyr, she said you'd left for Siren Cove. That's when they got in touch with me, and I asked Chris to call you."

Quentin's pulse throbbed at his temples. Taking a couple of calming breaths, he focused on bringing down his soaring blood pressure. "The cops in Seattle think I had something to do with Blaze disappearing?"

"You told her friend she was at your home on Thursday evening. The gate attendant confirmed it."

"Jazmin called me because Blaze didn't show up at the club that night. Maybe she simply had a date that stretched into the next day and forgot she was supposed to meet her friend."

"Certainly possible, but her boss confirmed she wasn't at work yesterday, and she didn't call in sick. He was concerned. Jazmin Washington reported Miss Campbell missing after stopping by her apartment this morning and finding no sign of her."

Quentin lifted both hands. "I don't know what to tell you. We broke up quite a while ago. Of course I'm concerned about her, but I don't know where she might be."

"Chris mentioned she was at the bachelor auction, bidding on you. Strange behavior for an ex-girlfriend, don't you think." The chief's gravely tone deepened. "Makes me think you two still had some sort of connection."

A sick feeling tightened Quentin's gut. "She stopped by my house the evening after the Winter Ball. She'd come to town, hoping to get back together. Based on what she saw at the party, she finally realized I was in love with Paige. She said she wouldn't bother me again, and that's the last time I saw her."

"Wasn't that the same night you took Clea Merrick out to dinner?" Each word out of Chris's mouth hit like a sharp blow. "Kind of a coincidence, don't you think, that you were the last person to be seen with Clea. Then days later, your ex-girlfriend shows up at your townhouse and hasn't been heard from since."

Quentin clenched his hands together on his lap as a chill shook him. "I had nothing to do with either of those women disappearing."

"So you keep saying, Son." The chief leaned back in his chair, and the leather creaked. "I want to believe you, but I'm not too certain I do."

"Am I under arrest?"

"No. Not yet, anyway."

Quentin surged to his feet. “Then I don’t intend to answer any more of your questions, at least not without a lawyer present. And in case you’re wondering, I plan to call one.”

“That’s your right, of course.” Stackhouse looked him straight in the eye. “But refusing to cooperate with the police only makes you look guilty.”

“I’ve cooperated, but I’m not going to let you find a way to twist my words into some sort of admission of guilt.” His voice escalated. “I haven’t done anything wrong.”

“If you have nothing further to contribute, I’ll walk you out.” Chris pushed away from the wall and touched his shoulder. “Let’s go.”

Quentin’s legs trembled as he crossed the parking lot to his car a couple minutes later. It took two tries to hit the right button on his remote to unlock the door. Tugging it open, he collapsed onto the driver’s seat. He couldn’t believe what was happening. Couldn’t comprehend that a woman he’d cared about might be in trouble. His stomach threatened to rebel, and he took short, fast breaths to stem the rising bile. Tears dampened his eyes, and the hand he used to brush them away shook.

Finally, he started the engine and turned toward the main drag. The open sign still hung in the window of Paige’s shop, but a light shone from her apartment above it. Hopefully, she was upstairs alone because indulging in meaningless chit-chat with Mindy was beyond him. He drove slowly down the alley and parked in the back lot. It took another minute to compose himself before he got out of his car and slammed the door. The back entrance was unlocked. He entered through the rear door, flipped the deadbolt, then headed up the stairs.

Damn careless on Paige’s part, since anyone could

have entered her building. When he reached the landing, Leo let loose a barrage of barks. At least the dog was paying attention to intruders. Quentin went inside without bothering to knock.

"Quiet, Leo." When the dog stopped barking, he rubbed his ears.

"Quentin?"

"Yeah." He followed her voice and his nose to the kitchen where Paige was stirring a pot of chili. "Smells great." He wasn't sure if he could force down food, but he'd try.

"Thanks." She turned with a smile that slowly faded and dropped the spoon on the counter. "What's wrong?"

"Blaze is missing. She stopped by my townhouse shortly before I got there to look for a lost earring, and no one has seen her since."

Paige pressed a hand to her mouth. "Surely Blaze just went off with a friend and didn't bother to tell anyone where she was going?"

"God, I hope so." He slumped against the counter. "The police have another theory."

"What's that?"

"They don't like the coincidence of Clea disappearing while on a date with me, and now Blaze turning up missing when she was last seen at my home."

"Oh, no." Paige backed up a step. "Chris can't think you . . ."

"Not just Chris. Chief Stackhouse was there to interview me, too, and they both looked pretty damn grim. Honestly, I don't blame them."

"But you would never hurt a woman!" Her voice was fierce as she practically spat the words.

"Thank you for that." Quentin took three steps forward and pulled her roughly against his chest. "Thanks for your unconditional trust."

"Did you expect anything less?"

"No. Even though I've done my best to break your heart, no."

"One has nothing to do with the other, but why don't you blame the cops?"

The fact that she hadn't denied he'd hurt her destroyed what little composure he was clinging to. "I feel responsible for leaving Clea alone that night, and I wouldn't be surprised . . ." He stopped speaking to swallow the hard knot of fear burning in his throat.

"What are you trying to say, Quentin?" Paige asked softly as her grip on him tightened.

"I'm afraid some sick freak wants me to look guilty and snatched Blaze to turn attention fully on me. I feel like I'm being used as a scapegoat."

Chapter Twenty

Paige scrubbed the crusted-on scrambled eggs with so much force she was probably taking some of the finish off the pan. Still, ruining a skillet was better than breaking her fist by punching a wall. Too bad she didn't feel any less frustrated. After rinsing the abused pan beneath the running water, she set it on the drainer and turned off the faucet.

Quentin rested his hands on her shoulders and kneaded the tight muscles. "Hey, being pissed off isn't going to help. You look like you're ready to explode."

"Probably because I am." She wiped down the counter and tossed the sponge into the sink. "I thought I'd wake up this morning, having conquered the desire to take a swing at someone—preferably our police chief. Wrong again. I'm still plenty mad."

He turned her around and smiled down at her. "We need to harness all that righteous indignation for good. You could help me clean the walk-in refrigerator down at the restaurant, or maybe scrape what looks like a year's worth of grime off the grill. My goal today is to get the kitchen appliances I didn't replace ready for use."

"How the hell can you act like everything is normal? I don't get it."

"Because if I let my anger take over, I'll lose my mind."

"We can't just sit back and wait for Chief Stackhouse to arrest you." Her voice rose. "We need to freaking do something."

"Like what? No one can prove I kidnapped either of those women—or worse—because I didn't."

"Well, someone sure as hell did. While I'd love to believe both Clea and Blaze simply took off of their own volition and will turn up again when they feel like it, that scenario doesn't seem very likely. If the cops are focused on you as a suspect, they probably aren't looking for the person who's actually responsible."

"We don't know that." Quentin hesitated for a moment. "At least I hope they're out following other leads."

Paige glanced at the digital clock on the stove. "I have an hour before I need to open my store. Let's figure this out."

Taking her arm, Quentin tugged her toward the living room, detoured around Leo stretched out on the floor, and pressed her down onto the couch. "What's on your mind?"

She hadn't slept at all, not with anger and fear for Quentin whirling through her brain like an approaching storm. Her eyes felt grainy from exhaustion, and she was pretty sure she looked like crap, but her thoughts were sharply focused on protecting the man she loved. At the moment, nothing else, including their relationship problems, mattered.

"If someone wanted you to look responsible for Blaze's

disappearance, they had to know you'd be in Seattle. Who did you tell about your plans?"

"You and Val. Oh, and Chris Long. I imagine Val mentioned it to most of the staff at The Zephyr."

"How could anyone in Seattle have had something to do with Clea walking into that bar in Newport to hook up with a man she said she knew?"

"I'm not sure, but Clea is acquainted with a lot of people. She travels extensively. The guy she saw could have been from anywhere." Quentin rested his elbows on his knees and frowned. "Maybe there isn't a connection between the two women. Maybe it's all just a great cosmic coincidence, and I'm caught in the middle."

Paige snorted. "I don't believe in coincidences. I think you were right with your first theory. Some asshole picked up Clea that night and . . . hurt her. When the police started asking questions, he looked for a stooge."

"Why would he choose me, unless Clea told him we'd been out together?"

"Half the town probably knows about your date. Hundreds of people attended the Winter Ball and saw her place the winning bid at the auction. When she didn't come home that night, her aunt and uncle undoubtedly spread the word you were with her when she disappeared. Gossip in this town has a life of its own."

"If you're right, that would mean the man she saw either lives in Siren Cove, or at the very least, is in town for the holidays. If he was looking for a way to focus attention on me, what better way than to make another woman I used to date turn up missing?"

"Blaze was last seen at your townhouse in Seattle. How in the world would anyone in Siren Cove know she'd be there?" Paige slammed her fist down on the couch cushion. "I don't get it."

"I do. Shit."

She turned to stare at him. "What do you mean?"

"I was at Castaways when Blaze called me. She wanted to look for a missing earring at my place. Son of a bitch!" Quentin surged to his feet. "I told her where the key was hidden. Anyone at the bar could have overheard me. A football game was blaring on the TV, and I had to practically shout."

"How would someone listening to your conversation know who you were talking to?"

"I'm pretty certain I used Blaze's name while I was on the phone. It's pretty distinctive. Also, she was here for the bachelor auction and bid on me. It wouldn't take a rocket scientist to figure out who she was and my connection to her."

"This is crazy." Tears threatened. Breaking down wouldn't help Quentin.

"Psychopaths generally are." He paced across the room and back. "If we're right, it's entirely my fault some bastard grabbed Blaze."

"We should tell the police. Maybe they can—"

"Find a new way to blame me? I'm not talking to anyone. Except a lawyer." When he kicked Leo's rawhide bone, the dog lifted his head and gave his dreadlocks a shake. "Do you know any good criminal defense attorneys? The ones I've worked with in the past are corporate, and I have a feeling I need a shark."

"Ryan has connections. Talk to him, but I think we can figure this out ourselves. Who was nearby while you were on the phone?"

"I don't know. The bartender was certainly close enough to hear me. There was a blond guy on the stool just down from me." Quentin stopped pacing and stared at the dog. "Two brothers were looking for keys one of them had dropped, and a woman wearing a suit was drinking a martini on the other side of me. It's possible someone else walked by and paused to listen. If so, I didn't notice them."

"Okay, let's start with the ones you do remember. Did you recognize any of those people?"

"The guy who dropped his keys was in the bachelor auction. I don't remember his name, but I think his brother is a mechanic here in town."

Paige sat up straighter. "The Stillwater brothers? Jonas was in the auction, and Justin has done maintenance on my van. I bought antiques from their grandpa a while back."

"Yep, that's right. The blond guy next to me looked familiar, too, but I can't place him. He's probably in his forties, maybe a little older than the two brothers. The bartender referred to him by name, but I was talking to Blaze and honestly don't remember what it was."

"Who was tending bar that evening?"

"Not the owner who's usually there. This was an older guy with a snake tattoo on one forearm."

"Sounds like Abe. Maybe I'll go ask him a few questions. He and my dad golf together once in a while, so I'm sure he wouldn't mind talking to me."

"I guess it can't hurt to fish for information, but don't you need to work today?"

"I'll head down to Castaways this afternoon since Abe usually works the early shift. Mindy is coming in around noon, and she can handle the store on her own."

"You actually think one of the men at Castaways was the person Clea saw that night?"

"I don't know." Something she couldn't quite grasp niggled at her brain. If she wasn't so damn tired . . . "Who was the woman?"

"Huh? Oh, the martini drinker? I don't have a clue.

She was middle-aged, and her suit looked expensive. Maybe the bartender would know."

"I'll definitely ask him."

"Why bother? Clea didn't chase after a woman that night."

Paige stood up and rounded the coffee table. "No, but the woman could have mentioned the conversation she overheard to someone. I want to cover as many bases as possible."

"I guess we have to start someplace. If you find a connection—"

"I'll tell Chris Long. He's not a bad guy, Quentin. He'll listen to a reasonable argument."

"If you say so. Uh, I think your hour is about up."

Paige stepped over Leo and checked the digital clock on the stove. "I need to open the store. Can you walk my baby for me?"

"Sure. Then I'll go scrape the damn grill. If Mindy is working with you today, maybe I'll take Leo to the restaurant for company. It's Sunday, so the construction crew won't be around."

"Thank you." Paige stood on her toes to kiss him. "We'll figure this out."

He wrapped his arms around her and turned the quick peck into something a whole lot more meaningful. Finally, he rested his forehead against hers. "I hope so. What I really want is for Blaze to show up, perfectly safe and embarrassed as hell for worrying everyone."

"Me, too. I don't want to think about the possibility of anything else, but my main concern is you."

"Thanks for having my back."

She came down off her toes and pressed her face to Quentin's neck where his pulse thrummed strongly beneath her cheek. "Always."

* * *

When Paige walked into Castaways, Abe smiled. He set down the glass he was drying and waved her over. "Isn't two o'clock a little early to be drinking?" His dark eyes sparkled with amusement. "Or is this just one of those days?"

"Both." She planted her elbows on the polished surface of the bar. "Actually, I came to ask you a couple of questions."

The only other occupant of the bar, an old-timer who had to be in his eighties, was working on a crossword puzzle a few stools down while he sipped what looked like scotch. He didn't even look up.

"Ask away. What did you want to know?"

"It's about last Wednesday afternoon." She lowered her voice. "My friend, Quentin was in here—"

"You don't have to whisper. Morris is half-deaf and never bothers to turn on his hearing aid."

"Okay." Paige gathered her thoughts. "My friend, Quentin, the guy who bought the Poseidon Grill—"

"I know who he is. I remember him coming in a few days ago. He looked none too happy, if I recall right."

"I expect he didn't. Anyway, a blond man sat down next to him. Quentin said you addressed him by name but couldn't remember what it was."

Abe's salt and pepper brows shot up. "Why do you want to know who was hanging out in the bar that day?"

"Quentin had a conversation on his cell, and he was wondering who might have overheard him. It's kind of a long story, but trust me, this is important."

"I've known your dad for years. Of course I trust his little girl." He picked up another glass and rubbed it with the cloth. "Let's see, I remember the Stillwater brothers were arguing about something. They left, and Baird Copeland sat down. He was shouting for service before I even had a chance to say hello."

"Baird was the blond guy Quentin remembers?"

"Must have been. I'm pretty sure your friend left not long after that."

Paige straightened. "Interesting. Okay, there was a woman wearing a suit on his other side. I don't suppose you know who she was?"

Abe grimaced. "I don't want to talk out of turn on that one."

"I don't intend to tell anyone but Quentin. Was she incognito or something?"

"No, nothing like that, but Senator LaPine probably wouldn't like gossip getting started about his wife's drinking habits. Since they've been vacationing in town, she's been something of a happy hour regular."

"Really, Virginia LaPine? She told me they bought Miss Lola's house. Was Baird there to see her?"

"They briefly acknowledged each other but didn't talk. Don't go thinking they're having some sort of affair. I didn't get that impression at all."

Paige raised both hands. "Hey, I don't spread tawdry gossip. Not my style." She hesitated for a moment. "Quentin's in a bind over that phone call. Knowing who else may have heard his conversation will help. At least I hope it will."

"I remember he was talking to someone named Blaze. The only reason I recall the name is because it's unusual. I was busy, so whatever else he might have said I didn't catch."

"Thanks for your help, Abe. This gives me a place to start."

"Next time you talk to your dad, tell him I want a rematch on the golf course."

"I'll do that."

She left the bar and paused out on the sidewalk, wondering what to do next. After morning showers, steam rose from the pavement as the sun broke through the clouds. The heels of her boots clicked against the concrete as she slowly headed back toward her shop. Her first instinct was to go straight to the police station to talk to Chris. But what exactly could she tell him other than that a few people may have overheard Quentin's phone call? Not exactly incriminating evidence.

When her cell rang, she pulled it out of her coat pocket and glanced at the display. Speak of the devil . . . She swiped to answer. "Hi, Chris, what can I do for you?"

"I was wondering if I could have a minute of your time."

She stared down at her feet. "I'm pretty pissed off at you right now. How you could believe Quentin—"

"This isn't about Quentin. It's regarding Lucinda Gordon."

"Oh." She let out a breath as some of her anger receded.

"Can I stop by your shop?"

"I guess so. I was running an errand, but I'll be back in a couple of minutes."

"Thanks. I'll see you shortly."

She wasn't sure if she should be curious or worried about Chris's visit. After entering the store to a clash of bells, she pulled off her wool coat and hung it on the tree near the door. Mindy hurried out from the rear of the store but slowed her pace as Paige turned around.

"Oh, just you." She lowered her voice. "I have a live one in the back, looking at that big armoire."

"Sweet. I'll leave you to close the sale. I have to run upstairs for a minute." Paige stepped out of the way as

Chris Long pushed open the door. She gave him a quick smile. "I need to follow up on something with Chris."

"No problem. Take your time." After giving a brief nod to the cop, Mindy headed back the way she'd come.

"Let's talk in my apartment. I don't want to scare away customers with a police presence, and I assume you want this to be a private conversation."

"Sure." He followed her up the stairs. "Sorry to disturb you at work."

She entered her apartment with the officer at her heels. "I've been disturbed since Quentin showed up here yesterday evening after being interrogated by you and Chief Stackhouse." She turned around to face him. "But, you said this isn't about Quentin."

Chris shut the door. "Look, we were doing our job, questioning a man we have to consider a suspect. The fact that I actually like Quentin has nothing to do with it."

"He would *never* hurt a woman. Never." She whirled around and came to a jerky stop in front of the coffee table. "Have a seat."

He took the only chair in the room after she dropped onto the couch. "I hope that's true. I don't want to see your life turned inside out, and I know it would be if he's guilty."

She worked to compose herself. "What did you want to ask me? You said it has to do with Lucy."

The sympathy in his eyes was replaced by speculation. "Something's been bothering me. Those break-ins you had—twice someone searched your shop before you found that necklace and turned it over to me. Since then, I assume you haven't had any more problems with intruders?"

"No." She frowned. "What does one have to do with the other?"

"I don't know. The timing just seems strange. I don't suppose you bought a bunch of old jewelry right before those break-ins. I can't help thinking someone was after a specific item. If the intruder thought you had Lucinda's necklace, he'd have no reason to look again once news broke that the police had it in their possession. Who knows how many people Lucinda's grandpa mentioned the necklace to."

"An interesting theory, except I didn't buy any jewelry. I did do quite a bit of picking shortly before the break-ins." Her eyes widened as the connection her brain had been looking for earlier clicked into place.

"What's on your mind, Paige?" His voice was sharp as he sat forward.

"Nothing. Uh . . . nothing. Do you have any potential suspects who might have been dating Lucy that summer?"

"How about if you tell me where you acquired inventory in the days before the first break-in."

Chris didn't seem inclined to share information. Why should she?

"I bought quite a selection of antiques from Zeb Stillwater, mostly household items. I also acquired furniture and a few odds and ends from Lola Copeland before she moved. Then I took a trip south to Margaret LaPine's home, where her daughter and son-in-law were preparing to put her house on the market."

"Is Margaret LaPine Senator LaPine's mother?"

Paige nodded. "He knew about the sale. His mother is in assisted living now."

"Any jewelry purchased from Mrs. LaPine?"

"A lot of dishware and knickknacks, along with a few small pieces of furniture. No jewelry."

"Thanks for the information. I appreciate it." Chris stood.

"Any red flags? Is one of my customers . . . or maybe a relative . . . on your radar?"

"You know I can't discuss an ongoing investigation."

"I figure you owe me."

"You're pushing the bounds of our friendship, Paige."

She followed him toward the door. "You did that first when you questioned Quentin like a common criminal."

"As I've already mentioned, the chief and I were just doing our jobs. If he's innocent, he has nothing to worry about."

"Unless someone is doing everything he can to make Quentin look guilty. While you're focused on him, the person responsible is out there somewhere." She shivered. "Possibly looking for another victim."

Chris paused with his hand on the doorknob. "Is that what you believe?"

"Damn right it is. I hope you'll at least think about the possibility."

"Despite your worst fears, cops aren't stupid." He glanced back over his shoulder as he walked out of the apartment. "We'll find the asshole responsible for making those women disappear. You can count on it."

Chapter Twenty-one

"Let me get this straight. Chris thinks you might have bought something shortly before the break-ins that someone wanted back."

Quentin crossed bare ankles on her coffee table and flipped Paige's purple robe over his thighs, feeling like an idiot. After spending the whole day scrubbing appliances, he'd gone straight to her apartment. A mistake, since she'd refused to let him sit on her furniture in his filthy, grease-stained clothes. While she tossed his shirt and jeans in the wash, he'd showered and put on the fuzzy robe, since nothing else she owned fit him.

"Chris wondered if I'd acquired any jewelry recently, which I hadn't. His mind was on Lucy's necklace." Paige eyed him from her corner of the couch. "The fact that I find you hot when you're wearing my robe must mean something, but I'm not sure I want to analyze exactly what."

He let the edge of the robe slip open a little farther. "Come over here and say that."

"Stop. I thought you wanted to hear about the investigation."

"I do. Go ahead. What else did Siren Cove's super cop have to say?"

"Sarcasm doesn't become you. Chris didn't *say* anything, but he perked up when I told him who I'd bought inventory from recently. For a police officer, the man doesn't have much of a poker face."

"So, there's a possibility you purchased something incriminating at one of those three picks, and someone connected to the seller is on Chris's radar?"

Her brow wrinkled, the way it did when she was thinking. Quentin had a hell of a lot of respect for Paige's powers of deduction, but his focus was on the curve of her breast beneath the clinging sweater she wore.

"Both Stillwater brothers were pissed their grandpa sold me pieces from his collection. Maybe price wasn't the real issue. Zeb could have parted with an object one of them wanted to stay buried in his barn. Then there's Baird Copeland, who made a huge fuss about getting back his baseball cards and comic books. Could be that's not all he was after."

"What about Mason LaPine?" Quentin dropped his feet to the floor and sat up straighter. "Did he have a beef with his sister for selling their mother's stuff?"

"He didn't act like it, but he hustled into the shop soon afterward and spent a long time looking around before he bought that Fabergé egg. If he didn't find what he was really after, he might have broken in later to look again."

"Any one of them could have been the intruder. I don't suppose you bought a knife, a wrench, a candlestick, or maybe a led pipe from one of them?"

"I think I did purchase a candlestick, Professor Plum." Her smile broadened. "Or should I call you Miss Scarlet?"

"Funny." The gravity of the situation sucked the

humor out of him. "Let's think about what we know. Three of those men most likely overheard my conversation with Blaze."

"Don't discount the senator. His wife could easily have mentioned it to him."

"Okay, for the sake of argument, let's say all four of them could have known where Blaze would be the night she went to my townhouse." He scowled down at the rug where Leo was stretched out with his nose on his paws. "If our previous logic follows, one of those men was trying to set me up because the cops were investigating Clea's disappearance."

"God, it's hard to believe an upstanding citizen might have . . ." Her voice cracked. "Okay, I'm just going to say it. One of them is either holding Clea hostage, or he murdered her. She might not have been the first."

In the silence that followed her statement, Leo rolled over and moaned.

"We know someone who lived in or around Siren Cove killed Lucy all those years ago. Look how long it took to find her body. Any number of victims could be buried in the woods."

"Right now, I think we need to focus on the present and who had opportunity since that's what impacts you."

"I suppose we can ask around to see if any of those men have an alibi for the night Clea disappeared or the evening Blaze was at my townhouse."

"Or I could report our suspicions to Chris. I kept my mouth shut earlier, but it wasn't easy."

Quentin pushed a hand through his hair as frustration simmered. "We have no proof of any wrongdoing, Paige, only suspicions."

"The cops may know things we don't, like who Lucy

hung out with that summer. If it was one of the men in question . . .”

“There’s no evidence one crime has anything to do with the other.” He stood up and held out a hand. “We can do a little digging, though.”

She clasped his palm and rose to her feet. “What do you have in mind?”

“We can search your shop for whatever the intruder might have been looking for.”

“If he didn’t find it, how likely is it we will?”

“I’m sure you have an inventory list for those last three picks. All we have to do is check off each item and pull out anything that looks like a possible murder weapon.” He slid an arm around her waist as he stepped around the dog. “I’m surprised Chris didn’t search your store while he was here.”

“I had customers at the time. Doesn’t mean he won’t come back. The problem is I clean everything I buy before displaying it. We’re not going to find blood traces on that candlestick I mentioned.”

“Don’t the cops have special UV lights or chemicals to detect blood?”

“They do on TV, but that’s the extent of my experience with crime scenes.”

He smiled down at her. She looked cute when she was irritated, but he didn’t figure he’d earn any points making that observation out loud. “Okay, I’ll concede we may not be able to do this on our own. If we find anything that looks promising, we’ll let your good buddy Chris check it out.”

“Now you’re being smart.” She pulled away from him and let her gaze roam over the loosely belted robe. “Are you going downstairs dressed like that?”

Quentin's gaze dropped. "I'd probably get arrested if anyone looked through the window. Do you think my clothes are ready yet?"

"Let's hope."

"If they're not, we can talk about our future, a subject you seem hell bent on avoiding."

She turned away from him. "I love you, Quentin, and I don't want you to get arrested, but I haven't changed my mind about—"

"Maybe I have."

"You're under a lot of stress. Your judgement is probably compromised as a result."

The woman was making him crazy. "We can still have a discussion—"

"The dryer shut off a little while ago. I'll go check on your clothes." She bolted from the room and returned a minute later with his jeans and shirt draped over her arm. Whatever she was feeling was masked by a defiant gleam in her clear blue eyes.

Reluctantly, he dropped the subject. For now.

"Thanks." Taking the clothes, he retreated to her bedroom to dress. By the time he finished, she was at her computer typing something. Pages spit out of the printer into the tray.

"I printed my recent purchases to make this search easier." She scanned the list. "Geez, a bunch of these things would work as a blunt object, but I'm pretty sure most of them were on display during the first break-in. A few, I was either cleaning or repairing, or maybe hadn't gotten around to putting out on the shelves. Seems more likely they would have escaped detection during the intruder's search." Her tone held a no-nonsense edge.

"That makes sense."

She followed him through the apartment to the door. "I

hope we're not wasting our time, but I'd love to give Chris a good reason to suspect someone other than you of committing crimes around here."

"No kidding." Quentin flipped on the light at the bottom of the stairs. "Okay, where do we start?"

"The stuff from Zeb's barn has the most potential. I bought a fireplace poker and shovel, either of which could definitely brain someone."

"Talk about a convenient weapon. I say we set them aside to test for traces of blood. Where are they?"

"In the northwest corner of the shop." Paige led the way. Reaching an area containing household items, she pointed to a pair of andirons with sharp finials next to the fireplace tools. "I got those from Zeb, too. And I'm pretty positive they were soaking in cleaning solution to get the rust off when the first break-in occurred."

"Well, hot damn. We have ourselves a contender. Was anything else in that solution?"

Paige scanned her inventory sheet. "Crap. There was a branding iron, but it wasn't salvageable so I tossed it. I wrote it off as a loss."

"I guess we'd better hope that wasn't what we're looking for. Anything else from the Stillwater place?"

"The silver candlesticks I mentioned, but I know they were on display. Nothing else strikes me as a potential blunt object."

"Let's be thorough and take the candlesticks with us. This place is like a rabbit warren. He could have missed seeing them."

"I guess so. They're up closer to the front of the store."

Quentin hefted the fireplace tools and andirons and carried them to her work room. By the time he dropped off his load, Paige had the candlesticks tucked under her arm.

"I bought mostly bigger pieces of furniture from Miss Lola. She did part with an antique doll after a lot of bargaining, but even with the china head, it doesn't have much potential as a weapon." She frowned at the list. "I paid her twenty bucks for a teacup and a pair of bookends in a box of miscellaneous crap. The bookends are heavy."

"Where are they?"

She searched the shelves and pointed. "Up there."

"Jesus, these could definitely kill someone. What else."

"There was more in that box, but . . ." She snapped her fingers. "A ceramic cookie jar. I think it's still in my workroom. There was also an old tennis trophy."

"Oh, yeah? Most trophies have sharp edges."

"I should have asked Baird if it was his when he came to get his baseball cards and comic books." Her eyes widened. "There was a letter opener in the false bottom of the drawer with those cards, but it disappeared. The damn thing must be somewhere, unless my thief stole it the second time he searched the place."

"Not a blunt object, but definitely a deadly weapon. We can search for it again."

"All right, let's move on to Margaret LaPine's property. Mostly I bought china and glassware from her daughter, all extremely fragile. Also some small furniture. Nothing that would . . . wait." Her finger hovered near the bottom of the list. "There was a white marble cat, plenty heavy enough to kill someone, but I sold it to an older couple just the other day. Damn."

"Like the branding iron, we'll have to hope it wasn't what we're looking for. Did you have it on display when the creep broke in here?"

"I'm pretty sure I did."

"Then, let's not worry about it. What else?"

"Nothing lethal. Maybe Mason LaPine is in the clear."

"God, I'm an idiot." Quentin smacked himself on the side of the head. "Truly too stupid to live. Remember the fishing pole and the Hawaiian sling I got from Lucas Goodman while we were cleaning out the shed? Talk about a deadly weapon."

"That spear certainly qualifies. Maybe our guy didn't kill poor Lucy with it, but that doesn't mean he didn't murder someone else and want it back."

"I'll take the spear down from the display wall in the morning. Are we finished here?"

"As soon as we look for the letter opener." When a thump sounded from the back of the shop, her words ended on a squeak.

"What the hell?" Quentin closed his fist around the pyramid bookend and pushed her behind him. Trying not to make a lot of noise, he hurried through the shop. He reached the foot of the stairs and let out a burst of laughter. "Leo is the guilty party. He bumped into your stool and knocked that empty box onto the floor." Reaching down, he rubbed the dog's ears.

"He was probably lonely upstairs." Paige's hand shook as she set the candlesticks next to the andirons on the bench. "I have a bad case of the jitters. This sucks."

When a knock sounded on the rear door, she let out a screech, and Leo leaped to his feet, barking like a lunatic.

"Quiet!" Quentin shouted. He pushed the dog away and unlocked the door.

"Should you open it?"

"Criminals don't usually knock." He swung the door wide.

Chris Long eyed the dog warily when he gave a few

more woofs. "I called your cell, Paige, but you didn't pick up. When I saw the light on down here I thought I'd check to see what was going on."

"I left my phone upstairs. We were . . ." She hesitated and glanced at Quentin.

"Go ahead and tell him our crazy theory. Why the hell not?" Gripping Leo's collar, he dragged the dog away. "I'll put the beast upstairs."

If the cop had come to arrest him, surely he wouldn't have given him an opportunity to escape. Tugging the uncooperative dog behind him, he entered Paige's apartment and shut the door. After giving Leo a treat, he drew in a few calming breaths as his anger simmered. Maybe the police had reason to suspect him of foul play or whatever the hell they wanted to call it, but he sure didn't have to like it. Plus, the fact that Paige seemed inclined to turn to Chris every time she had a problem was beyond irritating.

Or maybe I'm simply jealous.

Stupid, but he couldn't help it. Her plan to date other guys made his blood boil. After taking another minute to compose himself so he wouldn't say something guaranteed to get his ass thrown in jail, he headed downstairs.

When he entered the storage room, Chris gave him a cool look before returning his focus to Paige. "I'll take these items down to the station to spray with luminol. If there are any traces of blood present, we'll know."

"Thank you." When Quentin stepped up behind her, Paige relaxed against him. "Quentin can bring you the Hawaiian sling tomorrow. And the letter opener, if we're able to find it."

"I'm honestly not too concerned about either of those."

Quentin wrapped an arm around Paige's waist and eyed

the cop. "Why's that? They aren't blunt objects? Or you're giving Mason LaPine and Baird Copeland a pass?"

"Currently, they aren't relevant to our investigation."

Which didn't answer my question. Quentin decided not to push his luck. "Did Paige tell you all four men could have known Blaze was at my townhouse the other night?"

"She did. We'll look into it."

"I hope so. Since I know I didn't make those women disappear, someone else must have. I don't like thinking that the man responsible is out there, a danger to the public. Anyway, maybe there's still time . . ." He had to stop speaking to steady his voice. "They could be alive."

"The investigations into both women's disappearances is active and involves several law enforcement agencies in two states. We haven't given up hope of finding them alive, not by a long shot."

"It's good to know you aren't focused solely on Quentin."

"I know this isn't easy for either of you." When Chris turned to Quentin, any sign of sympathy faded. "However, we feel pretty confident we can close these cases soon."

"I sure hope so." Paige sounded drained.

Apparently, the man noticed her exhaustion. "I'll let you lock up and go to bed. Just give me a minute to bag these." He slipped each item into an evidence bag and gave Paige a receipt when he was finished. "You saved me quite a bit of work by taking the initiative with your search."

"It was Quentin's idea," she answered.

"So, I guess that means I either think like a cop . . . or maybe you have the mind of a criminal."

"Sometimes, that's how we have to think." Chris headed

toward the door and paused with his hand on the knob. "Have a good night. I'll be in touch."

"I bet you will," Quentin muttered beneath his breath. He only hoped it wouldn't be with an arrest warrant.

When he opened the door, muffled sobs came from the interior of the shed. Feeling his way in the pitch dark, he set down water bottles and a bag of food. The confined area stunk to high heaven. Apparently, the woman had relieved herself in the pail he'd left for that purpose. As soon as he untied her gag, she started jabbering.

"If you're going to kill me, just do it and get it over with. Why torture me like this?"

Her shrill cry grated on his nerves.

"Or let me go. Please, please let me go. This is *insane*. I don't know who you are or why you'd want to lock me up. *Please* let me go." She broke down in another crying jag.

He shut the door behind him, and lowered the wooden bolt into place, then kicked the side of the shed. The woman inside stopped her blubbering. Small relief. He had to make a decision soon about what the hell to do with her. He couldn't keep her locked up indefinitely.

Hopefully the cops would arrest Quentin before too much longer. He'd practically served the moron up on a silver platter. That would take some of the pressure off. He'd been extremely careful to keep his identity hidden from the woman, but releasing her didn't seem like a viable option. His mind shied away from the alternative.

He shivered against the cold wind as he waited for her to eat the food he'd left so he could replace the gag. For now, he'd simply do nothing. Time might not be on his side, but it was all he had.

Chapter Twenty-two

Monday morning brought howling offshore winds that chilled Paige to the bone as she planned her strategy. Chris had called earlier to say none of the objects she'd turned over to him showed any traces of blood. When she'd questioned him about what the police intended to do next, he'd hedged. Not a good sign.

A shiver slid through her as she hurried down the sidewalk toward Baird Copeland's law office. After Quentin left for a meeting with his contractor, she'd bolted out of the shop, intent on her own agenda. Too bad she hadn't taken the time to grab her warm coat. Her leather jacket might look great with jeans, but she was freezing her ass off.

Better than getting it chewed by Quentin. At the moment, he wasn't her biggest fan. He'd been pissed when she refused to have a serious talk about their future over breakfast. She'd scampered downstairs where Mindy and a few random customers acted as a buffer between her and certain heartbreak.

Paige took an extra-long stride to avoid stepping on a crack and hugged her arms tighter across her chest. She'd known exactly what he was going to say. And she wasn't at all certain she had the strength to resist him. Quentin intended to offer her everything she wanted, everything she needed. She could see the determination in his eyes, along with a hint of martyrdom. No way in hell was she going to rope him in against his will, even if he swore it was what he wanted. In the long run, they'd both be miserable.

Instead, she'd save him from himself. And possibly from the police, if she could pull this off. Arriving at her destination, she pushed open the door into blessed warmth. The young, dark-haired woman sitting at the front desk smiled at her as she shut the door against a rogue gust of wind.

"Wow, it's really howling out there. May I help you?" She clicked the mouse and frowned at the computer screen. "I don't believe Mr. Copeland has an appointment. There isn't anything on his schedule."

"That's because I don't have one." She crossed her fingers behind her back. "Is he available?"

"No, he took an early lunch today, and his afternoon schedule is full."

Paige nearly sighed in relief.

"Darn it. I just had a quick question for him." She prayed her acting skills were up to the task. "We had a late meeting last week after hours, and I think I might have left my wallet. I can't think of any other place I could have lost it."

The young woman's lips compressed, and she gave Paige a cool look. "Mr. Copeland didn't mention finding a wallet."

"Would you mind taking a look in his office? Maybe he put it in a drawer and forgot about it."

"I suppose so." She pushed back her chair and stood. "You can have a seat in the waiting area while I look."

"Thank you."

Paige waited until the receptionist disappeared down a hallway she assumed led to Baird's lair before racing around the desk. The attorney's schedule was still up on the computer screen. With a few clicks, she found the previous Thursday's entries and scanned through his day. He'd had a conference call scheduled at one o'clock, and then a four o'clock appointment with a Mrs. Jones. There was no way in hell the man could have driven to Seattle and beaten Quentin to his townhouse unless he'd cancelled his last client.

When the sharp rap of heels sounded on the wood floor, Paige clicked back to the current date, then hustled around the desk and stopped to study a seascape on the side wall. She smiled when the office assistant appeared. "Do you know if this is by a local artist?"

"I'm really not sure. I didn't find your wallet."

"No? I was positive . . ." Her forehead crinkled. "I wasn't carrying a purse that day. I'd shoved my wallet in my coat pocket. Out on the sidewalk, I bumped into a woman just leaving the office. Maybe my wallet fell out and she picked it up. Do you remember if Baird had a meeting late Thursday afternoon?"

"He did, but I'm certainly not allowed to give out private information about his clients. I'm sorry I can't be of more assistance."

"I already cancelled my credit cards, but I guess I'll have to go to the DMV to replace my driver's license. What a hassle." Paige gave the woman a bright smile. "Thanks for trying."

"I'll let Mr. Copeland know you stopped by Miss—"

"Oh, no need to concern him. Thanks again for your help." She bolted out the door as the wind practically wrenched it from her hand. She slammed it shut. "Well, that settles that. Mission accomplished."

She paused on the sidewalk as two older men approached. When the one wearing overalls glanced her way, she smiled. "How are you, Zeb?"

"Paige, it's good to see you. Actually, I intended to get in touch with you this week. I've decided I still want to sell a portion of my collection. Those grandsons of mine can kick up a fuss if they like, but I honestly don't see why they should care. Anyway, I could use a little spare cash right now."

"I'm definitely interested."

"Do you know my old friend, Morris? We go way back to our Korean War days in the same unit." Zeb raised his voice. "Morris, this young lady owns the antique store in town."

"How do you do?" The old-timer who'd been sitting at the bar when she questioned Abe stuck out his hand.

Paige shook it. "Nice to meet you, Morris. Thank you for your service. You, too, Zeb. Any idea when you'd like me to come out to the farm?"

"How about after New Year's? If you aren't busy on the second, I'm free."

"I can make that work. Maybe around two?"

"Good. Good. I'll see you then."

As the two men ambled away, she hurried down the street in the opposite direction. It was all she could do not to fist-pump the air. Zeb had given her a perfect opportunity to question him. Hopefully he'd know where Jonas and Justin were the night Blaze had gone missing. She'd already narrowed the field by one.

Minutes later, she entered the shop. The bells clanged as she pushed the door closed against the wind. "Those things are starting to annoy me."

Mindy looked up from the shelf she was dusting. "They're pretty loud, but isn't that the point?"

"I guess so." When the bells jangled again, she turned and smiled at Quentin. "How did your meeting go?"

He shut the door behind him. "Excellent. The final inspection is scheduled for next week. I should be able to plan the grand opening on Martin Luther King weekend."

"That's great. Will you have all your staff in place by then?"

"I will if I hustle." His brows rose as he studied her. "Did you go somewhere? You look a little windblown."

Paige stepped in front of the antique mirror hanging near the counter and let out a yelp. Hair straggled from what had once been a neat twist. "Crap. I'm going to run upstairs and fix this mess."

When she reached her apartment, she paused to pet Leo before heading into the bathroom. She'd taken down her hair and was brushing it out when Quentin stopped in the doorway behind her and met her gaze in the mirror.

"You can't avoid me, you know. I intend to have a serious conversation."

"I eliminated one of our suspects this morning."

He stiffened against the doorframe. "What the heck are you talking about?"

"Baird. I went down to his law office and did some fast talking. Who knew I have serious acting skills?" She fastened her hair in a topknot and stabbed a few pins into the slippery mass to hold it in place. "Anyway, I took a look at his calendar for last Thursday. He had a late appointment on his schedule, and I verified it with his receptionist. He couldn't have been at your apartment that evening."

"I can't believe an employee would discuss her boss's clients."

"She didn't. It took some creativity on my part to get that information. Oh, I also ran into Zeb Stillwater on my way back to the shop. He wants to sell more of his stuff. We're meeting the day after tomorrow, and I intend to find out where his grandsons were when Blaze and Clea disappeared."

"Good God, Paige. Why don't you take out an ad in the paper asking if any of these men is a murderer? You're about as subtle as a freaking wrecking ball."

"I didn't give Baird's receptionist my name. Even if he does figure out I stopped by his office, why would he care? The man isn't guilty of anything but being a jerk. As for the Stillwater brothers, I doubt Zeb will tell them about our appointment since they were so against him selling anything. He won't want to create a problem."

"A waste of time since I doubt their grandfather is privy to their schedules."

"If he doesn't know, no harm no foul. I'll find a different way to get the information."

"Obviously, you're on a mission." When she edged past him, Quentin slid an arm around her waist. "So am I. I've been doing a lot of thinking since Christmas."

She reached up and stroked his cheek with her fingertips. "I know you have. I also know you want to make me happy."

"Of course I do, but this isn't just about you. It's about me and what I want." He tipped her head back to look into her eyes. "I don't think I can live without you, Paige. Life would just flat out suck."

"You won't have to. I don't intend to give up our friendship."

"I want more than friendship. Since we—"

Her heart ached as his eyes clouded. "Started sleeping together?"

"I was going to say became a couple, but it's more than that. We're bonded in a way I've never experienced before. I don't want to give that up. Hanging out alone in Seattle, I realized there's nothing about my old life I'm not ready to change. It doesn't begin to compare to what I could have with you by my side."

"I feel the same way, but—" When her phone dinged, she let out a sigh and pulled it from the back pocket of her jeans. "Mindy needs my help downstairs."

"We'll go out tonight for New Year's Eve and talk. Or maybe I'll buy a bottle of champagne and cook. We can continue this discussion at my place."

She nodded and stood on her toes to kiss him. "I almost believe you mean what you say."

"That's because I've never been more serious about anything. Nothing has ever mattered this much to me."

"I love you, Quentin. We'll work this out. For now, though, can you . . ." She waved a hand toward the dog as she stepped back.

"Sure. I'll take him for a walk. Go help Mindy."

She practically ran down the stairs, her feet barely touching the treads. Maybe she'd been too quick to judge his state of mind. Maybe—

Rocking to a halt, she nearly ran into a woman standing at the end of a row of shelves. "Sorry, I should slow . . . Oh, hi, Mrs. LaPine. Can I help you find something?

"Actually, I just wanted to ask you a question. Mason and I are looking for a few pieces of original artwork for our place here. An acquaintance mentioned a local woman, a friend of yours, does some nice work. I was hoping to get her contact information."

"You must mean Nina Hutton. I have a few of her business cards up front. Her paintings are gorgeous. Actually, I have a couple of them in my apartment if you want to see an example of her work."

The woman's eyes brightened. "That's very accommodating of you."

"Not a problem. Right this way." Paige stopped at the base of the stairs as Quentin and Leo descended. "Mrs. LaPine, this is a friend of mine, Quentin Radcliff. He bought the Poseidon Grill and will be reopening it in a couple of weeks."

"Please call me Virginia. I'll look forward to checking out what you've done with the place the next time we're in town." She frowned. "You look familiar. Maybe we've met before?"

"It's a small town, so possibly we've crossed paths. Nice to meet you, Virginia. Come on, Leo."

He gave Paige an enquiring look on his way past. She shrugged in response. With any luck, she'd be able to pump the senator's wife for information on her husband's whereabouts. Fate seemed to be smiling on her today.

"Right this way." When Paige reached the top of the stairs, she led Mrs. LaPine into the living room and pointed to a painting of the three Sirens. Nina had painted the cove at sunset, and the combination of pinks and purples was spectacular. "What do you think?"

"It's beautiful. Your friend isn't afraid to use vibrant colors."

"No, Nina puts her personality into her work. You mentioned your next trip here. Are you and your husband leaving soon?"

"Yes, the state legislature will be back in session after New Year's. He's on a few important committees, and he's anxious to get back to work."

Paige injected a note of sympathy into her tone. "I imagine he's always busy. Has he had to travel much since you got here? That must not be easy for you."

"Just a one-day trip to Salem for a meeting the day after Christmas. This has actually been a pretty relaxing trip." She glanced over. "You said you have two paintings?"

"The other one is in my bedroom." Paige led the way. "The subject is a field of poppies Nina painted down on the California coast."

"I'm impressed. Your friend is very good."

"I'll get you her business card. I have some in my desk."

Paige led the woman back downstairs and then helped another customer while her mind clicked over the facts. If Virginia LaPine was telling the truth, her husband was in the clear. That left the two Stillwater brothers. Trying to imagine which one was capable of kidnapping two women and doing God knows what to them made her stomach ache. She needed to speak to Chris Long about what she'd learned.

During a lull in customers, she called his cell phone. When he didn't pick up, she waited for the beep. "Chris, this is Paige. I did a little investigating—" The door opened, admitting a trio of middle-aged women, chatting and laughing together. "Uh, could you stop by later. Thanks."

With a sigh, she stuffed her phone back into her pocket and went to help her customers. By the time she finally turned the closed sign around and urged Mindy to go enjoy her evening, she was mentally and physically exhausted. And she still hadn't heard back from Chris.

"Maybe the man actually took a day off," she muttered as she headed upstairs. "Or, he's just sick to death of hearing from me."

She dropped onto the couch, tipped her head back against the cushion, and closed her eyes. When her phone rang, she didn't bother looking at the display before answering. "Hello."

"Did you close up shop for the year?"

Just the sound of Quentin's voice improved her mood. "Yes, thank God. We're closed tomorrow for the holiday, and I'm ready to ring in the new year with you."

"Good, because dinner is cooking, and I'm about ready to pop the cork on a superb bottle of champagne. By the way, your dog is stretched out on the kitchen floor, trying to trip me. We took a long walk in the woods earlier."

"That sounds lovely. I wish I could have gone with you."

"It did help me solidify my thoughts. I know exactly what I want." His voice deepened. "When are you coming over?"

"As soon as I change my clothes. I hope casual is okay since I'm not up to looking fancy tonight."

His soft laugh sent a tingling warmth through her. "I'm pretty sure Leo won't mind if you don't dress up. As for me, I don't care if you dress at all."

She smiled and opened her eyes. "That could be awkward on the drive over if I get stopped. I'll see you in a few minutes."

After stripping off her jeans and tailored shirt, Paige pulled on yoga pants and a comfy sweatshirt. Then she exchanged her heeled boots for a pair of ballet slippers and literally let down her hair. With a huge sigh of relief, she grabbed her keys and purse and headed downstairs. On her way through the storage room, she paused beside the workbench were the inventory sheets she'd printed out the previous day were still spread across the surface. Snatching them up, she shoved the papers into her bag before locking the rear door and battling the wind on her way to her van. Minutes later, she turned into Quentin's neighborhood and navigated the streets to the dead-end cul-de-sac. The outdoor flood lights illuminated the walkway and cast shadows across the lawn. She slammed her car door and practically skipped up the path.

A delicious aroma greeted her as she entered the house. Leo's nails scraped against the tile as he raced out of the kitchen and stopped to lean against her leg.

Paige rubbed his big head. "Hi, baby. How was your day?"

"Not bad. How was yours?"

She glanced up and smiled at Quentin. "I was talking to the dog, but good to know. Mine was busy. Whatever you're cooking smells amazing."

"I roasted a chicken and stuffed it full of herbs. Come have a glass of champagne and tell me about your busy day." When she reached his side, he took her chin in his hand. Bending, he kissed her until she was breathless.

Paige wrapped her arms around his neck and kissed him back. "You taste good."

"Chocolate covered strawberries. I ate one."

"That sounds better than . . . well, maybe not sex, but most anything else."

He laughed and squeezed her waist. "You can have a few while I put the food on the table. Dinner's almost ready."

While they ate, she told him about her conversation

with Virginia LaPine. "That's two down and two to go. One of the Stillwaters must be guilty. I called Chris Long earlier, but he didn't get back to me."

"It's not like the boy scout to slack off when you send out a distress signal. Maybe he's out partying tonight."

She choked on a mouthful of green beans. "I can't picture Chris with a noise maker and party hat on New Year's Eve, but I guess it could happen. Cut the guy some slack. He hasn't arrested you."

"At least you didn't say yet."

"He's not stupid. Hopefully the police are following their own leads and narrowing in on the freak who kidnapped those women."

When the doorbell rang, Leo jumped up from beneath the table. The china rattled as he galloped to the door, barking.

"Who do you think that is?" Quentin pushed back his chair and followed the dog. "Maybe Nina and Teague decided to drop by to celebrate."

"I should have called them—Leah and Ryan, too—and invited them all over." Paige laid her napkin on the table as she rose to her feet. "This damn tension has been distracting me from the important things in life, like friends and family."

Quentin glanced over his shoulder. "My hope is we'll get back to normal soon." He pushed Leo out of the way and swung open the front door.

Chris Long and an older cop stood on the doorstep. Neither smiled.

"Happy New Year, officers. What can I do for you? If you're looking for Paige, she's inside."

"Actually, we're looking for you." Chris stepped across the threshold and gripped Quentin's arm. "Quentin Radcliff, you're under arrest for assault with intent to do bodily harm and the kidnapping of Blaze Campbell. You'll be coming with us."

Paige's chair crashed to the floor as she rounded the table. "Are you kidding me!"

When Leo bared his teeth and growled, the older officer spoke sharply. "Control your animal."

Lunging forward, she grabbed her dog's collar. "This is crazy!"

Before Chris could snap a pair of handcuffs around his wrists, Quentin touched her cheek. "Hey, everything will be okay. Not exactly how I'd planned to end the evening, but I'll be fine. I promise."

As the two cops led him away, Paige gripped the doorframe while tears ran down her cheeks. "I love you. We'll fix this."

"I love you, too."

Chapter Twenty-three

Quentin sat alone in a room with a table, three straight-backed chairs, and a single overhead light. Horizontal metal blinds covered the windows facing the hallway he'd passed through on the way from his holding cell. There wasn't a mirror on the wall, so he assumed no one was observing him. Apparently, Siren Cove wasn't as high-tech as the average police drama on TV.

He slid deeper into the chair. Maybe he should be more concerned than he actually was after being processed and stuck in a jail cell for the night, but at the moment, mostly he was simply pissed. When he'd asked Chris about getting out on bail, the man had rolled his eyes. Obviously the cops didn't cut you loose the minute someone showed up waving a checkbook the way they did on TV, either. He was beginning to think Hollywood should do their homework.

Or maybe no one had tried to bail him out.

When the door opened, two men entered the room and took seats across the table from him. Neither looked familiar, but based on the hard looks they gave him, he was pretty sure both were cops. When he'd contacted Ryan Alexander with his one phone call, his old friend had promised to use all his connections to round up a kick-ass defense team. He couldn't help wondering what the hell was taking him so long.

"I'm Detective Raleigh, and this is Detective Overton. We're here from Seattle to ask you a few questions."

Raleigh looked like a linebacker. The chair beneath him squeaked when he moved, and his nose had probably been rearranged on his face more than once. His partner was a good-looking black man wearing an expensive suit and an impassive expression.

"Shouldn't I have an attorney present before I answer any questions?"

Overton adjusted the cuff of his shirt. "That's your right, of course, but you told the arresting officers you had nothing to hide. The sooner you answer our questions, the faster we can clear this up."

Raleigh crossed muscled arms over his chest, straining his jacket seams, and tilted his chair back. "Since you say you're innocent, what do you have to lose?"

"I *am* innocent. Oh, what the hell, ask away."

"Good decision." Overton pulled a small recorder from his pocket and set it on the table, then stated the date, time, and occupants of the room before giving Quentin a long, measuring look. "What time did you arrive at your residence in Seattle on the night of December twenty-seventh?"

"It was probably around eleven. You can verify the exact time with Danny, the kid who was working the gate that night."

"So, you don't deny you were there." Raleigh's tone made it a statement, not a question.

"Why would I deny it? I already told Chief Stackhouse and Officer Long I was at my townhouse that evening.

Anyway, you could easily confirm my presence. I was in Seattle for a couple of days last week, dealing with an employee problem."

"You didn't go up there to see Ms. Campbell?" Overton didn't so much as blink.

"No, I didn't. Blaze had mentioned she intended to stop by my place to look for an earring she'd lost back when we were dating. I took the phone call from her when I was having a beer down at Castaways on Wednesday. I told her where I kept my spare key. You can verify the conversation with the bartender. He probably overheard me, along with a few other patrons who were nearby."

"So, it was purely a coincidence that you drove up to Seattle when you knew she'd be in your home?" Raleigh's tone was infused with disbelief as he leaned back, lifting the chair legs off the floor.

"Not a coincidence. My manager at The Zephyr called me about a situation she couldn't handle. An employee was claiming sexual harassment, so I drove up there to straighten out the problem. I filed a report with the police. You can check—"

"Was anyone with you on Thursday evening? Did you speak to anyone when you arrived?" Overton interrupted.

Quentin stared at the man for a moment before answering. "I was alone. The only person I spoke to, as I've told you, was Danny when I came through the gate. Oh, I also took a call from Blaze's friend, Jazmin Washington. Blaze was late meeting her at a club, and she wondered if she was still at my townhouse."

"Are you certain Ms. Campbell wasn't there when you arrived?" The chair creaked ominously as Raleigh dropped the legs to the floor with a thump. "Maybe you two argued? I understand she turned up in Siren Cove more than once after you left Seattle. Maybe you were sick of her bothering you? Could be she was causing conflict between you and your new girlfriend."

"That's an interesting theory. A complete load of crap, but interesting. Can I ask you something?"

"Go ahead."

Quentin turned to face the well-dressed member of the team. Instinct told him he was the more dangerous of the two. "Officer Long said I was charged with assault and kidnapping. Why would you believe I injured Blaze if you haven't found her yet?" Sweat dampened his palms as he held the man's gaze. "If you found her, she would have told you I had nothing to do with her disappearance. If she was—"

"Dead?" The detective's voice hardened. "If we found her lifeless body, why weren't you charged with murder? Is that your question?"

"Yes." He balled his hands at his sides. "Look, Blaze and I broke up after Thanksgiving, but I still care about what happens to her. Knowing she's missing, and that it's probably my fault—"

"Your fault?" Raleigh slammed his muscled forearms down on the table. "What the hell did you do to her?"

"I didn't do anything, but if the asshole who took Clea was trying to throw the cops off his track, he damn well succeeded. You people are wasting time talking to me when you should be looking for the person who's responsible."

"Let's talk about Clea Merrick," Overton said in a cool tone. "Seems like spending time with you isn't exactly healthy, Mr. Radcliff."

"I've told the local cops everything I know about that night. Repeating myself doesn't seem very productive."

Before Overton could respond, the door swung open,

and a man with salt and pepper hair cut short above narrowed gray eyes entered. He looked vaguely familiar. An image of this man standing on the steps of a court house, talking to the press about the high-profile case he'd just won, flashed through Quentin's brain. Ryan had come through for him, after all.

"My client won't be answering any further questions." The attorney pulled a business card from the pocket of his pale gray suit and dropped it on the table. "This interview is over."

Irritation flickered through Overton's eyes, along with resignation. "Your client agreed to speak to us."

"Without his attorney present? You should know better than that. I've spoken to a judge about a bail hearing, and even that was a challenge." His lips clamped tightly together. "Since today's a holiday, the earliest court date I could get was tomorrow. Sorry about that, Quentin. The timing for this arrest was poor. Probably intentional on the part of the police so they could keep you locked up an extra day."

Overton's brows drew together. "I resent the implication. We couldn't charge him until we got the DNA test results back."

"What DNA results?" Quentin asked. "Don't I have a right to know what's going on since I'm the one stuck in a jail cell?"

"Your attorney will be privy to all the evidence soon enough," Raleigh answered. "He's got a damn ringer on his team. Perfect."

Quentin glanced at the business card still lying on the table. Vincent Gatti. Hadn't this man defended some mob boss? Not that he intended to complain about the lawyer's morals if he got positive results.

"I've already taken a look at the so-called evidence.

They found blood at your townhouse, Mr. Radcliff. The search warrant was issued on pretty flimsy grounds, and I can probably get anything they found thrown out in court."

"Whose blood?" A hollow roar filled Quentin's head. "I didn't notice any blood when I was there."

"Blaze Campbell's blood. That was the DNA evidence they were waiting for," Gatti answered. "Dirt from a plant covered the stain. I might argue my client isn't stupid. If he'd intended to cover up evidence of a crime, he would have done a better job."

Quentin rose to his feet on shaky legs. "How much blood?"

As both cops stood, Raleigh let out a snort. "More than you get scraping your knee, that's for sure. There was blood, all right, and plenty of it."

Paige left the police station so angry she wanted to scream. Despite pleas and badgering on her part, no one would let her see Quentin. As the shadows on the sidewalk lengthened, she kicked a tuft of grass growing up through a crack. If Chris Long had shown his face while she was arguing with the woman behind the front counter, she probably would have slugged him.

"This bites!" Her words carried on the breeze. A pair of pre-teen boys strolling in the opposite direction elbowed each other and grinned. Maybe shouting out her frustration wasn't the best idea. Instead, she needed to do something proactive.

Something other than cry. Paige sniffed hard and dug in her purse for a tissue. Her fingers closed around folded papers. Jerking them out, she glanced down and stopped walking. The inventory sheets. If she could tie one of the Stillwater brothers to a crime, even if it was an old crime, maybe the cops would consider someone other than Quentin as a prime suspect in the current one.

Once a predator, always a predator, was the way she saw it. And if Chris pulled his head out of his ass long enough to take a good look, maybe he'd see it that way, too.

With determination in her stride, she hurried toward her shop. Thank God, she'd decided to close Old Things for the holiday. Putting on a cheerful face for customers would have been far beyond her acting ability.

When she reached the store, she unlocked the door and held it open as Leo came bounding outside. "Okay, we'll take a quick trip out back to go pee, but that's it for now."

While the dog sniffed the bushes near the stairs leading to the beach, Paige crossed her arms over her chest to ward off the cold and stared out across the water at the Sirens as the sun set into a bank of fog. Darkness shrouded the cove. She'd been looking forward to a day spent alone with Quentin and had hoped they could hash out some sort of compromise for their future. Instead, she'd been left with this God-awful fear and uncertainty. Sometimes life flat-out sucked.

"Come on, boy. Let's go inside." With the dog following behind her, she crossed the parking lot to the back door and unlocked it. Entering the store, she flipped on lights before removing the inventory sheets she'd returned to her purse. Flattening them on her work bench, she discarded all but the page with purchases she'd made at Zeb's farm and read through each listing. Nothing she hadn't already turned over to the cops looked promising as a weapon.

"Damn. What am I missing?"

Sleeping Beauty might have fallen victim to a spinning wheel, but since this wasn't a fairytale, Paige lined through that entry on her list. She also crossed off a set of needlepoint cushions. A three-legged stool could have potential as a blunt object if someone swung it by one leg. Taking the list with her, she headed into the shop to find the stool. When she reached the row of small household items, she let out a sigh. Short and squat, with a patchwork cushion to pad it, the footrest was far more likely to mess up someone's hair than kill them.

"There has to be something . . ." She checked off a decorator hatbox, then let her pen hover over the entry for a butter churn. Turning, she walked down the aisle and stopped in front of an oak churn banded in iron. "I'm a complete idiot."

Leo wandered over to lean against her leg as she removed the top and pulled out the dasher. Turning the long stick upright, she examined the round disk at the bottom. She'd glued the cracked edge back together, and the repair was nearly invisible.

Talking to Chris wasn't something she wanted to do, not after watching him escort Quentin into the back of his patrol car. But she might have to swallow her anger and ask him to test the dasher for traces of blood. Clenching her fist around the handle, she carried it through the shop to the storage room and pulled out her phone.

When the bells over the front door jingled, Leo growled. Damn it, she'd forgotten to re-lock the door when she'd let the dog out earlier. Apparently, someone didn't care that the sign in the window clearly stated her business was closed.

"I'm sorry but we're closed," she called out. When no one answered and the bells didn't ring again, she laid down the dasher, pushed her phone into her pocket, and headed into the shop. Her footsteps slowed. "Hello, is anyone here?"

An echoing silence rang in her ears before a quiet curse and the scrape of a shoe against wooden floorboards made her scalp prickle. Leo lunged forward as the lights went out, plunging the room into blackness. She let out a yelp and grabbed a handful of the dog's fur.

Leo pulled from her grip and shot away, his bark deep and furious. Disoriented in the dark, Paige held her hands out in front of her face and staggered toward the rear door, only to slam up against a solid body. She screamed and kept screaming until an arm clamped across her neck.

Leo leaped against her attacker, and they both went down hard.

"God dammed, mother fu—"

Leo let out a loud yelp as Paige scrambled to her feet and ran. Shoving open the back door, she raced across the parking lot to the beach stairs and hurried down them. Heart pounding, she gripped the railing in the dark. Footsteps slapped the pavement above her. She was halfway to the bottom when barking erupted, followed by a shout and a whimper.

Reaching the beach, Paige pulled out her phone and dialed nine-one-one while she ran. When the operator answered, she gasped out each word. "An intruder entered my store and attacked me."

"Ma'am, where are you. Is this person still a threat?"

"I ran down the stairs behind Old Things, and I'm on the beach now. My dog slowed him down." Sobs choked her. "That freak hurt my dog. I can't hear him anymore, but the waves are crashing pretty hard."

"I'm sending help now. Try to find somewhere safe to hide until the police get there, and stay quiet."

Paige ran harder, a stitch in her side making breathing difficult. When she reached an area with large boulders beneath the cliff, she struggled up through the softer sand and crawled behind one of them. In the direction of the stairs, a light flashed and bobbed.

A whimper slipped out as she clutched her cell.

"Ma'am, did you find someplace safe?"

"I'm hiding in the rocks by the cliff," she whispered. "He has a flashlight, and he's looking for me."

In the distance, a siren wailed. Moments later, headlights glowed through the fog. Doors slammed, and voices shouted. Twenty yards away near the water's edge, the flashlight snapped off. Feet pounded the sand up the beach. Paige waited until the sound faded before grabbing hold of a rock to pull herself upright on trembling legs.

"He ran off, and the police are here now."

"If you're certain you're safe, go identify yourself to the officers," the dispatcher said.

"Thank you for your help." She hung up and shoved her phone in her pocket, then hurried back down the beach as flashlights bobbed on the staircase. When a beam hit her in the eyes, she raised her hand to shield them. "I'm Paige Shephard. The intruder ran north up the beach."

"I'll stay with her," a familiar voice answered.

Two figures took off at a dead sprint, while a third stopped beside her and lowered the beam. "Are you okay, Paige?"

"Chris?"

"Yeah. I was off-duty and driving into town when I

heard the call on the scanner. I hauled ass over here. What happened?"

"Oh, God, I think he hurt my dog. I have to go check on him." She ran toward the stairs while Chris kept pace beside her.

"He was lying at the edge of the parking lot when we arrived. We nearly tripped over him, but he was definitely still conscious since he growled at us."

Paige let out a cry and panted up each step. She was gasping for breath by the time she reached the top and knelt beside Leo. "Are you hurt, baby?"

Chris shone his light on him when the dog whimpered. "It looks like his side is cut. There's blood on his fur."

"I've got to get him to the vet."

"The clinic will be closed at this hour, but the owner lives next door. We'll roust him out of his house to take care of your dog." Chris pushed her aside. "Let me load him into my car. I also need to check in with the other officers. They'll want an official statement from you."

Leo growled when the cop tried to lift him, and Paige couldn't hold back the tears running down her cheeks. "Easy, baby. He isn't going to hurt you . . . or me." Jogging ahead, she opened the rear door and climbed into the backseat. When Chris eased Leo in beside her, she held his head on her lap and stroked his ears.

Blood streaked the seat beneath the dog. Pulling off her jacket, she tried to wrap the heavy wool around him to stop the flow of blood as her tears came even faster.

"Don't fall apart, Paige. We'll get your dog fixed up. Can you tell me what happened?"

She met Chris's gaze in the rearview mirror. "He saved my life. I was in my shop, looking for something, when the bells over the front door jangled. My fault since I hadn't locked the damn thing. I called out, but no one answered.

When the lights went off, I freaked out and ran toward the back of the store. I smacked into someone, and he grabbed me with an arm around my neck. That's when Leo attacked him."

"You think the intruder in your shop wanted to kill you?"

"I'm pretty sure he's killed before." She let out a shuddering breath as Chris parked in front of the dark veterinarian clinic. "And now I think I can prove it."

Chapter Twenty-four

What had he been thinking! Finding the front door to Old Things unlocked had seemed like a gift. One last shot at locating the freaking churn dasher. In his haste, he'd forgotten all about the damn dog. Peeling off the gauze pad, he winced at the sight of ragged flesh. He hoped to hell the mongrel was current on his shots.

At least the cops had arrested Radcliff. Suspicion had been placed squarely where he wanted it. In this whole stinking nightmare, one thing, and only one, had gone the way he'd planned. His stomach roiled as he thought about the redhead. Granted, she was locked up tight, but he couldn't keep her there forever.

When the front door swung open without any warning, he spun around, his heart pounding. Not the cops coming to arrest him for breaking and entering. Just his brother.

"What happened to you? That looks nasty."

"I tangled with a dog. Have you ever heard of knocking? Jesus, you scared the hell out of me." He turned back to the first aid supplies on the table and the task at hand.

"If you don't want people to walk in, you shouldn't leave your door unlocked."

No shit. An unlocked door had caused his current problems. He daubed antiseptic ointment on his arm. "Help me with a new bandage. Using one hand is awkward."

"You should have that bite looked at. Whose dog took a piece out of you? If I were you, I'd sue the owner."

After his brother taped the pad in place, he rolled down his shirt sleeve and lied. "I think the mutt was a stray." *God knows I've had plenty of practice altering the truth over the years.*

"Even worse. What if it has rabies?"

"I'll take my chances. Did you drop by for a reason?"

He shrugged. "Your funeral. You're the one who'll be foaming at the mouth. Yeah, I'm here for a reason. I went over to Grandpa's first thing this morning to see if I could convince him to sign the power of attorney papers we talked about."

"Did he sign them?"

"No. He's a stubborn old fart. He says he isn't senile yet. I found him out in the barn, hauling a bunch of crap up closer to the main doors. He'll likely have a heart attack, lifting dead weight that way."

Dread tightened like steel bands across his chest. "Why was he doing that?"

"He plans to sell more of his antiques to that woman, Paige Shephard. He says he needs the cash and that she won't rip him off, so we don't need to worry." His brother leaned against the wall and regarded him steadily. "I guess as long as he isn't getting cheated, it's not a big deal."

Not since the damage is already done. Still, if the woman

went snooping around the farm while she was there . . . "When is Grandpa meeting her?"

"Later today. Hey, why don't you go talk to him about the power of attorney papers? He might listen to you since you've always been his favorite."

"I might do that."

"I need to head into work. If you start salivating, you'd better sign up for those shots."

"Funny. I'm not going to get rabies."

Paige Shephard seemed like the type to be a responsible dog owner. He was far more concerned about what she might find at the farm. He'd take a trip out there, just to make certain she didn't stick her nose in where it didn't belong. Again.

His brother stopped halfway across the room. "Don't you have to work today?"

"I'm taking some sick time. My arm doesn't feel so great."

"I'll catch you later, then." He left, slamming the door shut on his way out.

With his head throbbing to match his arm, he dropped onto the nearest chair and propped his good elbow on the table. He had some decisions to make. He needed to decide just how far he was willing to take the cover-up he'd orchestrated.

Not that he didn't already know the answer. His nerves were as raw as the damn dog bite just thinking about it. He'd take it as far as he had to. Anything less wasn't an option.

Quentin walked out of the police station, not exactly a free man, but close enough. His attorney had posted his bail. At the moment, breathing the damp, salt-scented air and listening to his shoes slap against the sidewalk as he headed toward the main drag and Paige's shop was all that mattered. He felt free.

Sure, he had to meet with Gatti in a few hours to discuss his defense, but he'd insisted on some time to himself first. Uneasiness tightened his gut as he picked up his pace. When he'd mentioned going to see Paige while Chris Long was processing his paperwork, the cop had gotten a strange look on his face and mumbled something about a butter churn. Quentin couldn't help wondering what the hell was up now, but he hadn't asked. All he wanted to do was hold Paige in his arms for an hour or two and block out the rest of the world, not look for new problems. A few minutes later, he opened the door of the antique store, his heart beating faster in anticipation.

Mindy turned in his direction and beamed. "Quentin, they released you! Paige has been worried sick."

"My lawyer arranged bail. Is she here?"

"She's in her apartment with Leo. Go on up and surprise her."

He nodded and wound his way through the aisles toward the stairs. When he reached the top, he gave a perfunctory knock and walked inside.

"Mindy?" Paige called out.

He turned into the living room. "Nope, just me."

She stared at him for a moment as tears filled her eyes. Setting her laptop on the coffee table, she leaped up from the couch and threw herself into his arms. "Why didn't you call me?"

"I wanted to see you here, where we could be alone, not down at the police station." Cupping her face in his hands, he kissed her. "God, I missed you."

"Was it horrible?" She stroked his cheek as her tears subsided.

"The food sucked." He smiled at her. "I offered to cook, but they wouldn't let me near the knives."

"How can you make jokes? I've been freaking out."

"Hey, I was locked up in a Siren Cove jail cell, not doing hard time at Pelican Bay. The mattress was lumpy, but I survived."

"Tell me what happened. Did they drop the charges?"

"Nope, I'm out on bail."

"I thought for sure if they found blood on that dasher . . ." Her voice trailed off when Leo moaned. Turning in his arms, she spoke to the dog. "Are you okay, baby?"

Quentin glanced over her shoulder, and his brows shot up. A bandage covered a shaved portion of Leo's side.

"What the hell happened to him?"

Paige slipped out of his arms and knelt beside Leo to stroke his dreadlocks. "He defended me last night and got a knife in the ribs for his effort. According to the vet, the tip glanced off a bone and didn't hit any organs. Leo was lucky. He's going to be sore and on painkillers for a while, but he'll be okay."

"Jesus." He studied her from head to toe. "Were you hurt?"

"No. The man entered my shop when I was downstairs trying to figure out what the heck he'd been looking for when he broke in last month. The freak flipped off the lights and grabbed me while I was trying to get away. That's when Leo sprang into action."

Quentin sat on the rug beside her, patted the dog, then slid an arm around her waist. Just thinking about what could have happened to her made his mouth dry. He tried to swallow. "Did you see him?"

"No, it was too dark. I ran down to the beach and called the cops. The asshole got away before they arrived."

Pulling her tight against his chest, he rested his cheek

on her hair. “This is so messed up. I should have been here.” When he slammed his fist against the floor, the dog whined. “Sorry, boy, but I want to punch something.”

“I know how you feel. I couldn’t stand the thought of you being in jail, which is why I was trying to do something, anything to help.” She ran a shaky hand through her hair. “When I found that dasher . . . I don’t know. Maybe I was wrong about everything since Chris hasn’t called.”

He clamped his teeth together to keep from speaking his mind as his temper soared. He couldn’t believe she’d called the jerk who’d arrested him. But picking a fight with Paige was the last thing he wanted.

“Are you taking the day off?”

“Sort of. I picked Leo up from the vet earlier and wanted to spend some time with him, so Mindy’s covering the shop. This afternoon, I have an appointment with Zeb Stillwater.”

He pulled back to look her in the eyes. “Absolutely not. If one of his grandsons—”

“They won’t be there, and I want to see if Zeb knows where Jonas and Justin were the nights Clea Merrick and Blaze went missing.” She jerked her gaze away from his. “The police certainly aren’t asking any questions since their focus is on convicting you.”

“You don’t know one of them won’t be there!” he practically shouted.

“I don’t care. I *hate* that the police suspect you. Maybe I can—”

“The risk isn’t worth it.”

“Then come with me.”

“I can’t. I have a meeting scheduled with my attorney.” Quentin ran a hand through his hair and blew out a frustrated breath as helplessness gripped him. “He wants to set up an immediate hearing date to get the charges against me thrown out based of the fact the police had no grounds for a warrant to search my townhouse."

"That sounds promising."

"Yeah, but we have to go over a few things first. I already put off the meeting to come see you. Gatti will go ballistic if I blow him off again."

"You should talk to him. The sooner the better."

"Then cancel your meeting with Stillwater."

Paige stroked Leo's ears while she appeared to give his suggestion some thought. "What if I take along a friend. Would that ease your mind?"

"Not much. I'd rather you didn't go."

"I appreciate that, but I'm not cancelling." Her tone rang with stubborn determination. "I'll call Nina to see if she can drive out to Zeb's farm with me."

Arguing seemed pointless. Finally, Quentin nodded. "When's the meeting with your attorney?"

"In a couple of hours. Right now, I want to finish the conversation we were having when the cops showed up at my door. One thing about being stuck in a jail cell, it gave me plenty of time to reflect on all the idiotic choices I've made in my life."

"I figured you'd want to . . ." She nodded toward the bedroom.

He couldn't hold back a smile. "Oh, I do. No reason we can't do both." Standing, he pulled her up off the floor.

"At the same time?"

"Why not. If I'm going to bare my soul, I might as well bare the rest of you while I'm doing it."

"I could get behind that. Or maybe in front of it."

Quentin held on tightly to her hand as he led her into the bedroom. Pausing beside the bed, he brought her hand to his lips and kissed it. “I need to shower first. I smell like that holding cell.”

“I’ll call Nina while you’re in the bathroom.”

Cupping her chin in his hand, he kissed her. “Bring Teague instead, if he isn’t working. Please.”

“Okay.”

Quentin took a quick shower to wash the scent of industrial cleansers, burned into his nostrils, out of his head. Paige’s floral shampoo did the trick, even if he did reek of honeysuckle when he finished. After shutting off the water, he gave his head a shake, sending water droplets flying. He stepped out of the shower, dried off, then wrapped the towel around his waist before leaving the steamy room.

The leggings and sweater Paige had been wearing were folded on the top of the dresser. In their place, her fuzzy purple robe was cinched around her waist. She had her back to him and her cell pressed to her ear.

“I’ll stop by to pick you up in a couple of hours, then. Thanks, Ryan, I appreciate it.”

When she set down her phone, Quentin dropped his hands onto her shoulders. “Ryan’s going with you?”

“Teague was at the fire station, and Nina has to pick Keely up from school. Leah is working, but Ryan was happy to take a break from his coding project to help me out.”

“Good.” He bent to kiss the back of her neck, then pulled the pins from her hair to release the soft mass. “I still don’t like the idea, but I feel better about you going out there now.”

“Me, too.” She turned in his arms and nuzzled her face against his bare chest. “You smell good.”

“I smell like a girl, but I honestly don’t care.” He pushed

her back onto the bed and dropped down beside her. "Did I mention I missed you?"

Her smile made his heart ache with love for this woman.

"I believe you did."

"I love you, Paige." He ran his finger across the swell of her breasts beneath the lapel of her robe. "I honestly can't live without you. I don't want anyone else. Only you."

"I feel the same way. I love you, too. I've always loved you, but—"

He lifted his finger from the tip of her breast to press it against her lips. "No buts. Maybe when I moved to Siren Cove a month ago, I wasn't ready to settle down and be a full-time adult. But things have changed since then."

"It's been less than a month." Her eyes held skepticism as she met his gaze head-on. "You might believe that now—"

"I don't *believe*. I *know*. I don't want another man to be the one who makes you happy while I go back to Seattle to act like an immature jerk who doesn't know what he needs. The only thing I wanted while I was sitting in that jail cell was to go home to you."

She stroked the side of his face. "You have six restaurants. You can't spend all your time here. You have a lot of staff whose livelihoods depend on you devoting your attention to your businesses. If you don't, they'll flounder."

"There's some truth to that, but Seattle doesn't have to be my home base. I'm also thinking about selling a couple of them so I'm not spread so thin. I can live in Siren Cove and travel when I need to. If I want this enough, I can make it work, and believe me, I want it."

"But you said—"

He closed his eyes. “I said a lot of stupid shit. I don’t need you to remind me.”

“This decision seems rushed.” Her forehead creased. “You’re responding viscerally to being arrested. Once the crisis is over, your perspective will be different.”

“Don’t use your psych degree on me. You may be smart, but you’re way off base with that analysis.”

“I am?”

He cupped her face in his hands and kissed her, taking his time. “Yes. This so-called crisis only made me take a hard look at what I already knew. You’re the most important person in my life. Always have been, and always will be. I’m not making any sacrifices. I’m simply trying to hold on to my only true shot at happiness. I’ll keep begging if you want.”

“I’ll pass. I don’t want to torture you unnecessarily.”

“Then say you believe me. Tell me I can stay right here where I belong.”

“That’s all I want, Quentin. As for the future, we can work out the details after this nightmare is over and your name is cleared. I still can’t believe the cops arrested you. How stupid are they, anyway?”

“Pretty clueless.” He nuzzled her neck, kissing his way down the length of it. “I can only assume the truth will come out. I just hope it’s sooner rather than later.”

She nodded and closed her eyes when he spread her robe open, baring her beautiful body. Paige was perfection. He wanted to kiss each curve, to love every inch of her. He imagined her stomach, round with a baby—his baby—and the idea didn’t terrify him. Not much anyway. Before he could tell her any of it, she tugged his towel loose and rolled over to lay on top of him. All coherent thought disappeared.

Their lovemaking felt almost reverent. He wrapped

her in his arms and took care to show her just how much she meant to him with every stroke of his hand along her body and kiss he pressed against her soft lips. He loved her slowly, with enough passion to make him crazy with need. He held on, waiting for her to reach completion, relishing in each cry wrenched from her throat before he let himself go. Lost in Paige.

For several minutes afterward, they lay melded together on the bed while their skin cooled and heartrates slowed. Cradling her close, he let out a sigh that stirred her hair.

She kissed his chest. "If I can have this—you—for the rest of my life, I'll never need anything else to be happy."

"We'll always have each other." He tightened his arms around her. "Nothing will ever come between us. I promise. Nothing."

Chapter Twenty-five

"It's okay, Ryan. Honestly." Paige propped her elbow on the steering wheel and stared out over the fog-shrouded cove.

"Mom swears she didn't hit her head hard when she fell, but—"

"Of course you should go check on her. Hopefully she's fine, but you should still check to make sure."

"I hate to bail on you." Ryan's voice held an edge of stress. "If Quentin is that worried about you going out to the Stillwater farm alone, maybe you should cancel your appointment."

"Quentin is being overprotective." Paige crossed her fingers as she lied to one of her oldest friends. "I'll call someone else to go with me if it'll ease your mind."

"It will. I'm really sorry about this."

"Don't be. Take care of your mom, and let me know how she's doing, okay."

"Sure. Talk to you later, Paige."

She hung up and stuck her phone into her pocket before starting the engine. She didn't have time to round up a babysitter for herself, especially when she didn't believe she was in any real danger. There was absolutely no reason for either of Zeb's grandsons to be at his farm in the middle of a work day.

Even if one of them shows up, he can't exactly murder me in front of his grandpa.

Not certain she believed her own argument, she released the emergency brake, drove through the alley beside her store, and turned out onto the street. Thankfully, Quentin had left for his meeting with his attorney before Ryan called her. She wasn't in the mood for an argument, and she damn well intended to question Zeb.

Her grip on the steering wheel tightened. Despite the poor visibility, she accelerated on the straight stretch of road leading out of town. Quentin still faced criminal charges, and two women were missing. If she was lucky, she'd dig up information that would spur the police into arresting the person who was really guilty. If she had to take a minor risk in the process, she didn't give a damn.

A frown pinched her brows. It was strange Chris still hadn't called. Maybe he was too busy arresting some other innocent person. Paige brooded the rest of the way to the rutted access road leading to the Stillwater farm. After bumping down the long drive, she parked in front of the barn and climbed out of her van.

The big red door slid open, and Zeb emerged. "Welcome. Welcome. Happy New Year, Miss Paige," he called out.

"You, too, Zeb." She tucked her hands into her pockets and shivered in the cool dampness as she approached. "The fog is thick today."

"Ain't that the truth. It's a little warmer in the barn. I've kept the door shut and the space heater on."

"I appreciate that, but this place is huge."

"Don't you worry. I brought quite a few good pieces I thought you might like up front. You can start there instead of fighting your way through my . . ." He paused, and his eyes sparkled. "Not junk. Let's call it less desirable merchandise."

She laughed and patted his arm as he shut the door behind them. "That was thoughtful of you, Zeb. Anyway, you know what they say about one man's junk being another man's treasure. In my eyes, your barn is filled with treasure."

"That's why I like you and was prepared to buck my grandsons over this." He led the way to a variety of items neatly lined up on the scarred wood floor. "That, and I could use a little extra income to help pay the bills."

He'd given her the perfect opening.

Paige picked up a metal weathervane fashioned in the shape of a galloping horse. "This is beautiful. I can easily sand off most of the rust. What do you think, twenty dollars?"

"I'd like to get thirty for it."

"Since I like you, too, Zeb, I'll give you the thirty."

He shook her outstretched hand. "Now that we have the ball rolling, how do you like that cast-iron boot scraper?"

"It has definite potential." She lifted the heavy object and studied the craftsmanship before giving him an innocent look. "Did you spend a lot of time with your grandsons over the holidays, or were they busy?"

"I saw them off and on. Justin had Christmas dinner with me, but I didn't see Jonas until a couple of days later. He spent the evening trying to convince me to sign power of attorney papers. Those boys think I'm senile, but I still have all my marbles."

"Was that Thursday night?"

"I think so, why?"

"No reason. How about fifteen for the boot scraper?"

Zeb removed the wool hat he was wearing and scratched the back of his neck. "That seems fair."

"Deal. Now, about those wind chimes . . ." Paige haggled for another hour, until Zeb seemed to be running out of steam. "Let's call it a day. After buying the pair of end tables and the curio cabinet, I won't have any room left in my van."

He leaned on the handle of the broom he'd used to clear away cobwebs on their foray in search of the cabinet. "I guess you can come back again another time."

"I'd be happy to." She eyed the glass fronted display cabinet before checking her watch. *Time to get moving since she had the information she was after.*

"I don't suppose you have a dolly handy. We're going to need one to move that thing."

"Actually, I believe I do. At least I used to have a hand truck. I think it's in one of the sheds out back of the barn, with a bunch of other equipment I don't use often. I haven't had an occasion to go out there in a while, not since we harvested the last of the hay. You'll see the sheds over near the fence line."

The man looked slightly unsteady on his feet, and the bright enthusiasm in his eyes had faded.

"Tell you what, Zeb. I'll pack the smaller items into my van and then walk back to the house with you to settle up. Afterward, I'll go search for the dolly. You look like you could use a break."

"I don't have the stamina I used to, that's for sure, but I'm not completely useless. Let's get your van loaded, young lady."

Twenty minutes later, they left the cold to go inside his house.

Paige printed out a receipt for the goods she'd purchased, wrote Zeb a check, and handed it over. "It's been a pleasure doing business with you, sir."

"I enjoyed your company." He sat in his recliner with his booted feet propped on the footrest and the remote resting on his lap. "If you can't find that hand cart, you just let me know. Once I've had a little breather, I should be able to help you carry the cabinet. It isn't that heavy."

"I'll do that. You take care, Zeb."

Paige left the house and hurried across the yard, pausing when the rumble of an engine caught her attention. The sound faded, and she wondered if she'd imaged it. She couldn't see more than a hundred yards in the heavy fog, but surely headlights would be visible if someone had turned down the access road to the farm. She reached her van and put her computer and printer on the front seat. The door creaked when she shut it.

There's nothing to freak out about, Paige. Quit imagining boogeymen where they don't exist.

It was the damn spooky atmosphere, with tendrils of fog swirling clear to the ground, that was making her jumpy. Zeb would have said something if he was expecting company.

When her cell rang, she pressed a hand to her chest and swore. On the second ring, she pulled it out of her pocket and glanced at the display. Chris Long. *About damn time.*

She swiped to connect. "Hello, Chris. I was wondering when you'd call."

"Sorry. It's been a hell of a day, first dealing with Quentin and his pushy lawyer this morning, then assisting at several accidents caused by the fog. I didn't have time to spray the churn dasher with luminol until a couple of hours ago."

"And?"

"I found faint traces of blood, but there isn't enough to run a DNA test."

"You aren't going to follow up on this?" Her voice rose along with her temper. "Are you kidding me?"

"I didn't say that. It actually adds a little more evidence to an ongoing investigation, but I can't discuss that with you. However, I did feel I owed you an answer regarding the dasher."

"You think? My dog got knifed in the ribs thanks to that damn thing." Her teeth chattered in the cold as she left the van. "I can tell you one thing. Jonas Stillwater has an alibi for the night Blaze disappeared. He was with his grandpa."

"God damn it, Paige. I heard through the grapevine you were asking questions down at Baird Copeland's law office."

"Yep, he's in the clear. So is Mason LaPine. That only leaves one suspect. Justin."

"When did you talk to Zeb Stillwater?" Chris's voice was abrupt.

"Not long ago. He sold me a few antiques."

"I want you to stay out of this and let the police do their job. You don't know what the hell you're getting into, and you could wind up like those other two women if you continue to push your luck."

Paige rounded the corner of the barn. "Does that mean you think Quentin is innocent?"

"Let's just say I have a few questions that haven't been answered."

"I guess I'll have to be satisfied with that. For now."

"Stay away from the Stillwaters. Do you hear me?"

"Loud and clear. Bye, Chris." She hung up before he could ask her where she was. She'd get the curio cabinet loaded into her van and take off.

Vague shapes appeared in front of her out of the fog. As she drew closer, a trio of sheds became visible. She headed toward the largest one and pulled open the door. Like the barn, the interior was packed full, but not with antiques. The shed held various pieces of equipment, car parts, and the promised dolly. She squeezed past an old bumper and two giant tractor tires and wheeled the hand cart toward the door. When the edge caught on a piece of rebar leaning in the corner, the whole stack went down with a crash.

"Jesus. The place is practically booby-trapped." After picking up the rebar, she maneuvered the dolly out the door and down the short ramp to the ground.

A muffled cry caught her attention, and she paused to glance around. Not the wind since the fog hung in a dense curtain, possibly even thicker than it had been earlier. Driving back to town would be a bitch.

The faint mewling came again. Maybe a cat trapped in one of the other outbuildings? As Paige turned toward the nearest shed, her phone rang. She pulled it from her pocket and smiled.

"Hey, Quentin. Is your meeting over? How'd it go?"

"Good. We just finished up. Gatti is one smart lawyer. Are you at home?"

"No, I'm still at the farm, but I'm leaving shortly. I wouldn't turn down help unloading my van, though. I acquired some good stuff. Anyway, I want to hear what your attorney had to say about your defense."

"When will you be back?"

"Probably in about an hour. I'll have to drive slow in this fog."

"Why don't you call me after you drop Ryan off, and I'll meet you at the store."

She hesitated a minute. "Sure. I'll do that." *I didn't lie to him, just omitted a few facts.* "I love you," she said softly.

"I love you, too. Drive carefully."

"I will. Bye." She stuck her phone in her pocket and glanced in the direction of the shed. Had that been another cry? She headed toward the small building. No way was she leaving a cat stuck out here, even if she was in a hurry to get back to town and see Quentin.

When she slid back the wooden bolt and pulled open the shed door, a stench smacked her in the face. Covering her nose, she retreated down the steps. Not a shed, an outhouse. The mewling sound grew louder as Paige stepped farther away from the odor. She had no intention of fishing in a pit toilet for a cat.

Muffled sobs sounded from the interior of the small space.

"Oh, my God." Dragging in a deep breath, Paige ran up the steps. In the dim light, a huddled figure in the corner was just visible. With a cry, she dropped to her knees beside the woman as she raised her head.

Paige brushed hair from her face and worked on the knot holding a gag in place. "Blaze?"

When she pulled the cloth loose, the woman's voice came out in a croak. "Get me out of here before he comes back."

"Are you tied?"

"My wrist is chained. The key is by the door."

Paige rose to her feet and turned to grab a metal ring hanging on a hook. "Got it."

Blaze held out her hand, and Paige fumbled to unlock the manacle around her wrist. "Did Justin Stillwater do this to you?"

"I don't know. I've never seen his face. He wears a ski mask when it isn't dark."

The lock clicked open, and the heavy chain dropped to the floor.

"Let me help you up." Paige put an arm around the other woman as she staggered to her feet. Holding her tight, she practically dragged her down the steps. "Can you walk?"

"I don't know. My legs are cramped from sitting still for so long. I could only move a few feet."

"We'll take it slow." Paige held Blaze upright as she stumbled along beside her. "There's dried blood in your hair and all over your shirt."

She coughed a couple of times. "I must have hit my head when he took me from Quentin's townhouse. The last thing I remember was looking for my earring before I woke up shackled in that hellhole."

They'd made it halfway back to the barn. Heart pounding, Paige tried to move a little faster as fear clawed at her. If Justin showed up . . .

"Did he feed you? It's been nearly a week."

"Yeah, he'd untie the gag to give me food and water. But he wouldn't let me out to go to the bathroom." Her voice broke, and she nearly fell as she tripped on a clump of dead grass. "That freak said he'd let me loose when it was safe, but I didn't believe him."

"You're safe now. That's all that matters We'll get away from here and then call the police."

"I'm so thankful you found me. I was losing my mind."

"I can't begin to imagine how terrified you were. Was anyone else ever in the shed with you?"

"No."

Paige couldn't think about what had happened to Clea. She needed to focus her attention on getting Blaze and herself safely away from the farm. "Almost there. Just a few more yards."

She reached the corner of the barn and stopped. A car was parked beside her van. Not the older truck Justin Stillwater had been driving the last time she'd been here. A blue Lexus. The car was empty, and no one was in sight.

"Shit." She spoke in a whisper. "I don't know who that is, but let's not risk it. We need to get the hell out of here."

Blaze ran beside her toward the van, crying softly. An engine rumbled from somewhere out of the thick fog. Paige jerked open the passenger side door and boosted the other woman onto the seat. As she ran around to the driver's side, a battered pickup drove into the barnyard and stopped just short of her rear bumper, blocking her in.

"No!" Paige turned and ran, sprinting toward the road.

Behind her, a car door slammed, and boots pounded the gravel driveway. She increased her speed, her breath coming in harsh gasps. She wasn't even halfway to the highway when he grabbed the back of her jacket. A seam ripped, but he didn't let go.

Paige slammed up against the man's chest as he gripped her around the waist with his other arm. Kicking his legs, she struggled to get loose.

"God damn it. Stop that." He gave her a hard slap to the side of her head.

Ears ringing, she continued to struggle until something cold touched her throat. The flat blade of a knife rested just below her chin. Her heart nearly burst as she quit struggling and held perfectly still.

"I don't want to hurt you, Paige. If you cooperate, maybe I won't have to."

"Like you didn't hurt Blaze? What about Clea? What did you do to her?" She walked steadily in front of him, despite her shaking legs, as he prodded her back toward the farm. She needed time. Enough time for Quentin to get worried and come looking for her, or for the police to arrive. *Please. Please. Please.*

"Blaze is fine. I never harmed Clea, or any woman, for that matter. I didn't ask for this to happen. Damn it to hell! I thought I could take care of the problem without anyone else having to die."

Justin's voice held a hint of panic, but the knife at her throat didn't waver. One slip, and she could bleed out. Paige kept walking, slowing her pace, praying Blaze hadn't been too weak to go for help. Surely whoever was inside with Zeb would call the police. She'd run in the opposite direction to give Blaze time to reach the house.

Her hope faltered as they neared the barn. Jonas stood beside the van, holding Blaze in a tight grip. The woman's eyes were wide with terror, and a piece of duct tape covered her mouth.

"Your brother is crazy," she shouted. "He kidnapped Blaze, and God only knows what happened to Clea Merrick. You have to help us, Jonas. The man is sick."

"Do you hear that, Justin? You're the sick one." Jonas grinned. "All this time, you've been telling me I'm the one who needs help."

"Where's Grandpa?" Justin's tone was tense.

"He's inside watching TV. I turned up the volume, so he probably didn't hear anything before I shut this one up. If I have to—"

"No! Let's get them out of here now. Then we'll decide what to do."

Jonas shrugged. "Suits me." He stared straight into Paige's eyes, his gaze cold and hard. "Keep your mouth shut, or he'll cut you. Got it?"

She nodded as the flat blade pressed against her throat.

Jonas glanced at his brother. “Load her into the back of the van and tie her up. We’ll take them someplace where they won’t be found.”

“I guess we don’t have a whole lot of choice. Move it Paige. Even if I wanted to, it’s far too late to turn back now.”

Chapter Twenty-six

Quentin hurried down the sidewalk after leaving his meeting with Gatti. He and his attorney had planned out a solid defense, but the man had assured him the chances of his case actually making it to court were slim. Things were looking brighter, both for getting the bogus charges against him dropped and for his relationship with Paige. Still, worry nagged at him as he headed toward her store. Something in her tone when they'd talked on the phone had made him think she wasn't exactly lying, but possibly evading the truth. He wondered what the hell she'd neglected to tell him.

A Jeep slowed beside him and pulled to the curb. Quentin met Ryan's gaze when he leaned over and rolled down the passenger side window.

His anxiety ramped up a notch. "You're supposed to be with Paige."

"My mom slipped on her front steps and banged her head earlier today. Paige told me she would ask someone else to go out to the Stillwater farm with her. Can you pass along the news that my mom is fine?"

"I'm pretty sure she didn't call anyone. I don't have my car. Can you—" Quentin held up his hand as he jerked his cell from his pocket and dialed. After several rings, Paige's recorded message clicked on, and he waited impatiently for the beep. "Paige, call me. Now, damn it. Pull over if you're driving in this fog."

"What's going on?"

"Hopefully nothing, but she lied about you being with her, and now she isn't answering her phone."

"Get in. We'll go find her. Better to be safe, right?"

With a nod, Quentin pulled open the door and slid onto the seat. "I'm sure she's fine, but I'd rather make sure."

"I get it. Believe me. The Stillwater farm is north of town, right?"

"Yes. I think it's about a forty-minute drive." He tried to calm his jumping nerves. "Thanks, I appreciate this. I also appreciate you jumping onboard to hire Gatti. The man knows his business."

"You'd do the same for me. I'm happy to help."

They drove in silence as Ryan navigated through the thick fog. Every now and then, they passed an oncoming vehicle, but none of them were Paige's van. As the minutes ticked by, the knots in Quentin's stomach tightened. He tried her phone again, but this time it went straight to voice mail. He left another message and hung up.

"We should have passed her by now based on when she said she'd be back at her shop."

Ryan glanced over at him before returning his attention to the short strip of pavement visible in the headlight beams. "Maybe she was delayed leaving the farm or is simply driving really slow. This fog is awful. I wouldn't expect her to answer her cell if she's on the road."

"I guess not."

Another five minutes passed. Quentin pressed his foot against the floorboard, trying to urge more speed out of the vehicle.

"Dude, I can't see shit. If I drive any faster, I'm afraid we'll wind up in a ditch."

"Sorry. It's just . . ." He broke off as headlight beams approached. As the car drew closer, the distinctive *L* emblem on the front of the blue luxury vehicle was just visible through the fog. Following close behind the Lexus was a van.

"There's Paige. Thank God. Can we—" Quentin leaned forward, practically pressing his nose against the windshield, and swore.

"Are you sure it was her van? I'm almost positive a man was driving, although I didn't get a good look at him."

"It was her van. Turn around, for God's sake."

"I will. Damn it!" Ryan slowed as a big rig rumbled by. "Hold on and pray no one is coming."

He made a U-turn, the Jeep's tires crunching on the gravel at the edge of the road.

"Shit. There's no way we can pass that truck, is there?" Quentin asked, as Ryan accelerated and fell in behind the semi.

"Not unless you have a death wish. I can't even see the road ahead, let alone oncoming cars. Killing ourselves isn't going to help Paige."

Quentin's hand shook as he reached for his phone and scrolled through his contacts.

"Are you calling nine-one-one?"

"It would take too long to explain, and they probably

wouldn't consider this an emergency. I'm calling Chris Long directly, if I can find the number . . . there it is." He tapped the number and put the call on speaker, hoping to hell the cop would answer his cell.

"Long here."

"It's Quentin Radcliff. Paige went out to the Stillwater farm earlier and—"

"I talked to her."

Quentin gripped the armrest. "When was that?"

"Probably an hour ago."

"Damn it! I'd hoped—"

"What's wrong?" The officer's tone was sharp.

"I just passed her van, headed back toward town, but she wasn't driving, and she isn't answering her cell. Paige thinks one of Zeb Stillwater's grandsons might have kidnapped Clea and Blaze. I have a feeling she's right."

"Where are you? Do you have her van in sight?"

"We're probably twenty minutes from town, but there's a semi between us and her van. It drove past before we could turn around, so the asshole driving her van could be pulling away from us. He was following a Lexus."

"A blue one?"

"Yes, why?"

"Jonas Stillwater owns a blue Lexus."

"Fuckin' A! God damn it!"

"I'll head out now and call for backup. I'll also see about getting a unit out to the farm to see what they find. Unless those boys turn off the highway, we should be able to pull them over before they get into town. Are you driving your Jag?"

"No, I'm with Ryan Alexander in his Jeep."

"If I don't see the van before I pass you—"

"Let's hope that doesn't happen."

"I'll be in touch."

When Chris disconnected, Quentin closed his eyes. "Justin must be driving the van if his brother is in the car."

"The police will stop them." Ryan spoke with quiet confidence. "There aren't a lot of places he could turn off the road between here and Siren Cove."

"God, I hope so."

Quentin's chest ached, and it was all he could do not to swear at the trucker in front of them when he downshifted with a muffled roar to take a corner at a crawl. A couple of cars passed heading north. Each time he gripped the armrest a little tighter. When red and blue lights flashed ahead through the fog, he let out a shaky breath.

Ryan took his foot off the gas. "Maybe the police stopped them."

Quentin didn't answer. Moments later, a patrol car pulled even with the Jeep. Chris Long leaned out the open window and gestured at them to turn around.

"Doesn't look like he spotted the van."

"I'm afraid not, but the good news is the fog seems to be lifting slightly." Ryan found a wide spot and made another U-turn, then stopped behind the cruiser parked on the side of the road.

A door slammed, gravel crunched, and Chris ducked to look in at them when Ryan rolled down his window. "I figured you were behind that truck. It was the first one I saw."

"No sign of the van ahead of it?" Quentin forced an even tone.

"I'm afraid not. They must have turned off somewhere along this stretch. Did you see headlights veer away from the road?"

Ryan shook his head. "No, but with the fog . . ."

"You can't see more than about twenty yards, if that, although it's not quite as thick as it was a few minutes ago." Chris backed up a step. "We'll check every possible side road for the last ten miles. Most of them lead to isolated homes or parking areas above the beach. I have an APB out on Paige's van, so highway patrol will spot them if they get back on the road."

"What about the backup you called for?" Quentin asked.

"Too damn many accidents. No one is available right now, and I didn't want to waste time."

"Finally, we agree on something." Quentin eyed the man steadily. "Splitting up seems smart. We can cover twice as much territory."

After a moment, Chris nodded. "Only on the condition you stay back and call me if you spot Paige's vehicle. Those two may be armed, and they're certainly dangerous. Do I have your word?"

"We don't want to jeopardize Paige's safety," Ryan answered. "We won't do anything stupid."

"Fine, I'll take the first road. You take the second, and so forth. Stay in contact."

As the cop walked away, Ryan reached over and gripped his shoulder. "We'll find her."

Words stuck in Quentin's throat, and he could only jerk his head in agreement. They'd find her, and when they did, he had no intention of keeping his distance. His only goal was to make sure the woman he loved was safe . . . and make the son-of-a-bitch who'd taken her pay.

Paige sat on the damp sand, her arms bound around a boulder at the base of the cliff. A short distance away, waves crashed against the beach. Blaze faced her, tied to a giant chunk of driftwood, her eyes wide with terror in her pale face. The tide was coming in.

"We're screwed. The police will find their bodies at some point, and as Paige pointed out, plenty of people knew she was out at the farm." Justin practically had to shout to be heard over the rush of water surging ever closer to the cliffs.

"No one will be able to prove she didn't leave the farm of her own free will. Radcliff is out on bail. Maybe the police are stupid enough to believe he dumped the women here. A love-triangle gone wrong." Jonas jerked on the ropes binding her wrists, checking to make sure they were tight around the rock.

The damp cordage dug into her skin, and Paige couldn't hold back a whimper. "You're hurting me."

"Not the way I'd like to."

His cool tone sent a shiver through her that had nothing to do with the biting wind that was finally blowing the fog inland.

"You won't get away with this. You'd be far better off letting us go."

"I think I'll take my chances. I'm amazingly adept at avoiding trouble." He stepped over her legs and paused beside his brother. "I'll go wipe down the van to get rid of any prints since you were stupid enough not to wear gloves. Keep an eye on them until the tide does its job, and then we can get the hell out of here."

"Sorry if I'm not as experienced as you are when it comes to . . ." His voice cracked as he shouted, "Fuck you, Jonas. I never wanted this to happen."

"You're the one who grabbed the redhead. How did you think that would turn out?" Before his brother could answer, Jonas headed up the steep path leading to the top of the cliff.

"You don't have to do this. You can untie us right now." Paige tugged at her ropes. They didn't budge.

"Family first. He's my twin."

"He's sick. He needs help. You haven't done anything wrong, but if you kill us, you'll spend your life in jail."

"Oh, I've done plenty I regret." Justin brushed wind-whipped hair that had pulled loose from his ponytail out of his eyes. "I've covered up my brother's crimes for years. I kept hoping he would—"

"That he'd stop? He won't." Paige met his gaze and held it, trying her best to appeal to some shred of decency in the man. "Not unless you take a stand."

"That one isn't as innocent as he pretends. He kidnapped me and locked me in the shed. I recognize his voice." Blaze kicked sand in his direction. "Asshole. This is all your fault."

"The cops were asking questions. I'll admit I panicked. I was trying to shift their attention, and it worked. They arrested Radcliff. I planned to let you loose just as soon as I found that churn dasher." He turned away from Blaze to face Paige as the words spilled out. "If you hadn't bought the damn thing from Grandpa and then found Lucy's skull, nothing from the past would have been dredged up. I was afraid the cops would question the wrong person and figure out Jonas dated her that summer."

"What the hell is he talking about?" Blaze shouted.

"Paige knows. Blame her if you want to throw stones."

"Was Lucy the first one?" The salt air stung her eyes. "Did Jonas kill Clea?"

"Yeah, Lucy was the first, and Clea was the last."

"She could be if you untie us, Justin. You're not a bad person. You're loyal to your brother. I get that."

"Even though he's a freak and a murderer!" Blaze let out a cry as a rogue wave soaked her legs.

"There were traces of blood on the dasher. I turned it over to the police, so it's only a matter of time before they test it for DNA. The butter churn was in your grandpa's barn. Jonas isn't going to be able to weasel his way out of this. Even if you let us die, he's going to prison. You both will. They'll be able to prove he killed Lucy and her baby."

"Baby? What baby?" Justin frowned, his brows drawing together over worried eyes. "There was no baby."

"Lucy was pregnant. Didn't you know? Your brother wanted her to have an abortion, and she wouldn't. That's why he killed her."

"He said it was an accident. He didn't mean to hurt her." Justin's face crumpled. "But I could see in his eyes that he liked it. He couldn't let go of the rush, so a few years later he did it again."

"And you helped him cover up his crime. You have to stop him, Justin," Paige pleaded. "Don't you see, this has to end."

"Damn, brother, have you been shooting off your mouth?" Jonas reached the bottom of the trail, a scowl flattening his lips.

Paige hadn't heard his approach. She'd been so focused on trying to change his brother's mind, she'd been oblivious to the real danger. When Jonas narrowed his blue eyes against the punishing wind, her skin crawled. This man had no compassion. He wouldn't hesitate to kill again.

Justin sidestepped the oncoming tide. "She says the police have evidence. Maybe we should—"

"Maybe you should stop listening to a lying bitch whose only goal is to work you."

"You don't believe her?"

"Hell, no." Jonas turned his attention toward the waves washing up on shore, the line of wet sand stretching closer with each surge. "It won't be long now. Fifteen minutes, tops."

Blaze let out a shriek as water drenched them both before sucking back out to sea.

"Are we just going to stand here and watch them drown? I don't think I have the stomach for it."

Jonas rolled his eyes. "I guess we can take off since your nagging is a complete downer. How we came out of the same womb, I'll never know."

"You can't leave us here!" Blaze shouted, her teeth chattering. "You can't."

"I'm not in the mood to listen to her whining, anyway. Let's go." Jonas turned and headed back up the trail.

"No! No!" Blaze screamed.

Paige wrenched against the rope holding her arms in place. If she could inch them upward even a little . . . The rope caught on a rough protrusion and refused to budge.

"I'm sorry. Honestly, I am. I'll insist he gets the help he needs. I'll—"

"Then save us, Justin. Do the right thing."

"I can't." The words seemed to be wrenched from deep within him before he turned away and hurried after his brother.

"Now what? Are we going to just sit here and drown without doing anything?" Blaze sobbed. "I've been trying to twist my hands loose, but the damn rope seems to get tighter the more I pull on it."

"Maybe I can cut myself loose." Paige sawed back and forth against the jutting edge of the rock holding the thick cord in place. "If I could see what I'm doing, it would help."

Blaze turned her face to wipe her tears on her shoulder. "It looks like the rope is fraying a little. Can you rub faster?"

"I can barely move my hands. They're going numb." Paige gritted her teeth as a wave submerged her waist-deep in water.

"Oh, my God, you have to try harder!" Blaze shouted.

Staring at the Sirens far out in the cove, Paige concentrated on keeping the rope in the exact same spot as she rubbed back and forth. The sharp rock gouged her wrist, and warm wetness streamed down her arm. She didn't stop. Wouldn't give up.

Quentin. She loved him so much.

"Hurry, Paige. Hurry. If I die because—"

"What was that?" She craned her neck to see up the face of the cliff. "I thought I heard a thump."

"Maybe they're coming back."

"I don't know why they would." The next wave sent water surging up to her chest, and her wrists slipped away from the protrusion when the tide dragged against her. "It might not be them. Start screaming while I work on the rope."

"If they come back—"

"Just scream, damn it!" Paige raised her voice and yelled, "Help! Help us! Help!"

A wave smacked her in the face, and she gagged on a mouthful of water. Choking and coughing, she shouted with all her might while she sawed the rope against the rock.

Blaze screamed and kept screaming until the next wave hit.

Holding her breath, Paige waited until the water receded. Her ears rang, and her hands had gone completely numb. Her hair clung to her face like seaweed, blocking her vision.

"Paige! Paige!"

Was she imagining the voice? She gasped for air and held her breath as another wave hit. She smacked her face against the rock and struggled to fight against encroaching blackness.

"She's tied to the rock." Hands cupped her face. "Hang on, Paige."

Quentin. In her dream, Quentin held her while she drifted, floating . . .

Another voice echoed from far away. "Take my pocket knife. I've freed the other woman."

"Hold your breath." Quentin spoke urgently against her ear.

Instinctively, she did as he asked. When the wave receded, her arms broke loose and floated at her sides.

"I have you. Hold on. Paige!" He gave her a hard shake. "Hold on to me."

She blinked and coughed and clung to Quentin as the world around her swirled back into focus. He clambered up the rocks to higher ground, never easing his grip on her. Finally, he stopped and leaned against the cliff.

"Are you okay? Talk to me."

"Yeah." She coughed again and gasped, dragging air into her lungs. "Yeah, I'm okay."

"Thank God. Oh, thank God." He brushed dripping

hair off her face and kissed her, holding her tight against his chest.

"Blaze seems okay. Do you need help?" Ryan called from above them.

Quentin smiled at her, his eyes filled with infinite relief and love. "Do we need Ryan's help?"

She let out a long, shuddering breath. "No. We've got this. Together, we've got this."

"Damn right we do."

Chapter Twenty-seven

After his meeting in the judge's chambers, Quentin left the courthouse and hurried down the sidewalk with a lightness to his step he hadn't felt in a long time. He truly was a free man since all charges against him had been officially dropped. As he approached the Poseidon Grill, he paused in the parking lot to look out over the cove at the three monolithic rocks guarding the entrance. The late afternoon sun sparkled off the breakers crashing on the shore. He wouldn't let the knowledge of what those powerful waves had almost done to Paige ruin his pleasure in the moment.

Pulling open the restaurant door, he entered the warm interior. The smell of the celebration prime rib he'd put in the oven earlier made his mouth water. Voices and laughter drifted from the dining room, and he couldn't stop smiling as he headed past the hostess stand to join his friends.

"Quentin!" Paige set down her glass and ran toward him. "How did it go?"

He slid an arm around her and bent to press a kiss to

her bruised cheek. Several abrasions marred her skin from smacking her face against the rock, and a nasty cut on one of her wrists was still bandaged. She was lucky she hadn't sliced an artery. Even the thought of how differently that day could have ended made him feel a little lightheaded.

"As my attorney promised, all charges were dropped. That nightmare is over and done with." He squeezed her waist. "Have you been keeping an eye on our dinner?"

Paige smiled up at him, her relief clearly visible as the tension eased from her body. "Nina's in the kitchen checking on everything. She said something about tossing the salad."

"Then our meal is in good hands."

They joined Leah, Ryan, and Teague near the windows, and Quentin accepted a congratulatory hug and handshakes. When Keely showed him the picture she was drawing, he admired it and gave her a high-five.

"Did you hear anything about the Stillwater brothers while you were at the courthouse? Have they been caught yet?" Ryan waited to speak until Keely went back to working on her picture.

"Nothing specific, but the district attorney had quite a conversation with Chief Stackhouse while we were waiting to see the judge. The chief seemed pretty excited, if the way he was waving his hands and had to keep lowering his voice was any indication. Of course, it could have been an entirely different matter, but they looked my way a time or two during the discussion."

"They damn well better find those bastards." Teague clenched his fists at his sides. "Before they hurt someone else."

"I never believed in an eye for an eye before this happened." Leah reached over to give Paige a fierce hug.

"But right now, I'd like to tie both those men to one of the Sirens out in the cove at low tide and leave them there to think about their fate for a few hours."

"I'd like to do worse than that." When Paige's cell dinged, she pulled it from her pocket and frowned. "Interesting. I wonder . . ." She typed a response then stuck the phone back in her pocket.

"Who was that?" Quentin asked quietly.

"Chris. He—"

"Quentin, you're back!" Nina hurried out of the kitchen and crossed the room to give him a quick hug. "Is it over?"

"Yep. All the charges were dropped."

"Thank goodness. Now we really can celebrate." She slid a hand over her stomach as she picked up a bottle of sparkling water sitting next to the champagne flutes on one of the tables. "Well, you can all celebrate with bubbly. Keely and I will drink milk with our dinner."

"Speaking of dinner, I should probably—"

"Relax and enjoy yourself. I have it under control, but I'll let you carve the roast beast." Nina's smile broadened. "That's what Keely calls it."

Leah nudged her friend. "I hope you're cooking a few vegetables back there for me."

"Don't worry. I've got your vegetarian needs handled."

When the two women moved away, Quentin glanced down at Paige. "What did Chris want?"

"I'm not sure. He asked where I was, so I told him."

"Is he going to crash our party? Maybe we should have had it at the house instead of here, but I wanted to give the new kitchen equipment a test run before I open the restaurant next week."

"I'm sure he won't—" She glanced over his shoulder. "Or maybe he will."

Quentin turned. "Perfect. Just the person I most wanted to see."

"You can't blame Chris for arresting you. He was only following orders. I'm prepared to forgive him since he didn't hesitate to jump in and search for me when you called him."

"True." Quentin raised a hand to wave the cop over when he paused in the doorway. "Hey, Chris. Come have a glass of champagne. We're celebrating the fact that Paige isn't fish food and I won't become some criminal named Big Bubba's girlfriend."

His lips curved slightly as he approached. "Charming. Actually, I came to give you an update on the Stillwater situation."

Paige drew in a sharp breath as the others broke off their conversations and gathered closer. "Did the police find them?"

He nodded then glanced over at Keely, who was staring in their direction with laser focus.

Nina held out a hand. "Let's go check on the food, hon. Quentin baked a cake this morning. You can help me decorate it."

"Can I put on lots of sprinkles?"

"You bet."

As soon as the two disappeared into the kitchen, Chris cleared his throat. "The brothers switched vehicles and left town the minute word broke that you and Blaze Campbell had been rescued. They stole a car from the garage where Justin works, which was how they got out of the area without being detected. Anyway, when they bought gas down in Northern California, an off-duty cop filling his tank recognized them from the photos we'd entered into the system."

"Did he arrest those bastards?" Quentin asked, his tone hard.

"Jonas had a weapon in his possession, and he drew it on the officer. The cop shot and killed him at the scene. Justin was arrested. This all happened yesterday."

"And you're only now telling me?" Paige's voice rose. "I've been worried sick those two were still a threat."

"I'm sorry, Paige, but I couldn't notify you any sooner. Justin is cutting a deal."

"You've got to be kidding." Quentin clenched his teeth so hard they ached. "The man left two women tied up to die. Surely—"

"Oh, he's going to do plenty of jail time. But the DA agreed to reduce the charges in exchange for information. Jonas killed half a dozen women over the years, including Clea Merrick. Justin knew the names of each one and where the remains were buried. We figured providing closure for those families was worth taking a few years off his sentence."

Paige reached down to twine her fingers through Quentin's and squeezed. "Definitely worth it. Honestly, I bet any decent attorney will use an insanity defense to get him off. My guess is Jonas had been mercilessly badgering his brother since they were young boys, telling him over and over that he had to stay loyal, no matter what. The psychological damage Justin was exposed to—"

Quentin turned to stare at her. "Do you feel *sorry* for him?"

"In a way, I do. I don't think he's inherently evil like his brother was, but I feel worse for poor Zeb. He shouldn't have to face knowing what his grandsons did."

"He won't have to," Chris said. "Zeb suffered a heart attack the day you were kidnapped. The officers who went out to the farm to search for the twins found him and called an ambulance. He's been in intensive care for a couple of days, but I'm afraid he didn't make it."

Paige released her grip on Quentin and pressed a hand to her mouth. Tears formed. "Oh, no. He was such a great guy."

Leah stepped closer and gave Paige a hug. "Maybe it's better he didn't have to learn the truth. I can't begin to imagine how horrible that would have been for him."

"Zeb would have been just one more emotional casualty." Paige swiped a hand across her damp cheeks. "So many lives lost. And everyone who loved the women Jonas killed will have to grieve all over again."

"It sucks, but better to know the truth than always wonder," Ryan said. "Right, babe?"

Leah nodded. "I agree. It's good that Justin talked."

The cop regarded them with sober eyes. "Sorry to deflate the party mood, but I thought you'd want to know."

Paige wiped her eyes again and gave him a weak smile. "I'm glad you stopped by to tell us. Thanks, Chris."

"You bet."

As he turned to go, Teague stepped up beside him. "I'll walk you out. You always seem to be the bearer of bad news in these situations."

"Let's hope it never happens again. This town has been through enough."

As the two men crossed the room, Quentin wrapped his arms around Paige and rested his chin on her head, needing to hold her. "I have you safe beside me. Honestly, right now that's the only thing I care about."

"Sounds good, Mom. Okay, we'll see you then." Paige laid her phone on the counter, walked over to lock the front door, then flipped the sign over to 'closed.'

"How are your parents doing?" Quentin stepped across Leo, who was stretched out on the floor, napping.

"Still a little frazzled. Thank God, they didn't find out I'd been kidnapped until after it was all over, but my mom still feels the need to check on me daily. I told her we'd have dinner with them tomorrow night."

She paused halfway down the aisle to touch the horse weathervane she'd purchased from Zeb, and a sigh slipped out. When Quentin took her in his arms, she leaned against his chest.

"What are you thinking?"

"How happy I am that you're in my life. How, despite everything, you make me believe in endless possibilities."

He tipped up her chin with one finger and kissed her. "That's beautiful. You're beautiful. Every inch of you, inside and out."

She threaded her fingers into his hair as she stood on her toes to kiss him back. "Since I'm still covered in bruises, I guess love really is blind."

He pressed his forehead against hers. "I was blind, all right. Blind not to see what has always been right in front of me. You're my best friend and the love of my life. Thank you for being patient."

"I'm willing to slow down to make this work. We're in this together, Quentin."

"No need. I'm finally up to pace." He cupped her face in his hands and kissed her so thoroughly she melted against him.

When he pulled back an inch, she was breathless. "Should we take this upstairs?"

"Not yet, because if we do, I'll forget the whole speech I planned."

"What the heck are you talking about?"

He grinned down at her. "One step at a time. First, I had a conversation with Nina about her house."

"Oh, yeah? What about it?"

"I want to buy it, so I made her an offer. No offense, but your apartment is on the small side. I want a place to call home in Siren Cove that will accommodate both of us . . . and then some."

Warmth filled her, and she couldn't stop smiling. "That sounds awfully permanent. Leo will be thrilled to have a fulltime yard."

"This is where I want to be. Not in Seattle. Not anywhere else." He stroked her cheek with his thumb. "Just here with you."

"What did Nina say about your offer?"

"She said she'd give me a break on the price with one stipulation."

"No loud parties? No letting Leo pee on their lawn? Free babysitting service for Keely and the new baby when it arrives?"

"Obviously, Nina didn't think through all her options. No, she wants your name on the title, too."

Paige pulled back and frowned. "I'm going to have a talk with my pal about overstepping her friendship privileges."

"No, you won't. I already agreed. Do you know what I want most?"

"What?" She could barely force out the word.

"I want our home to be the first thing we purchase together as husband and wife. You have your business, and I have mine, but a house should belong to us both, a place for our family."

Before she could say a word, he touched her lips with

his finger. "I love you, Paige. I want to marry you and spend my life with you. I want to have kids and grow old together. I want it all."

Tears ran down her cheeks. "Are you sure? Really, really sure?"

"Positive, and I could ask you the same question. Are you willing to take a chance on me?"

"I gave you my heart long, long ago." She smiled and blinked away the dampness. "Giving you my hand in marriage is a piece of cake. Of course I'll marry you, Quentin."

"About that." He gripped her fingers and brought them to his lips. "I didn't buy a ring yet. Knowing you, I thought you'd want something old and unique. I figured we could search for a ring together."

"Oh, thank God." She wiped away more tears. "Best call you've ever made . . . other than asking me to marry you."

"I'm not a complete moron."

"No, you're not. You're the only man I've ever truly loved."

"I plan to spend the rest of my life making you happy, Paige." He bent to kiss her. "I promise."

"And I'm going to spend the rest of my life making sure you never have any regrets." Her heart felt ready to burst with joy as she looked deep into his eyes. "Together, we've got this."

"Damn right."

If you enjoyed *Hidden Secrets*, be sure not to miss Jannine Gallant's thrilling Siren Cove series, including

LOST INNOCENCE

Artist Nina Hutton finds a lottery ticket on the beach, stuffs the crumpled paper in her pocket—then forgets all about it. Distracted and shaken by a series of break-ins at her home, Nina turns to her handsome new neighbor for help and protection again and again.

Since the death of his wife in a drive-by shooting, Teague O'Dell has moved from the city to the small town of Siren Cove, determined that his daughter will grow up in a safe environment. But when the intriguing woman next door is plagued by a mysterious vandal, he wonders if his new home harbors unexpected dangers.

The winning lottery numbers have been revealed, and the owner will do whatever it takes to claim the prize. And the closer Nina and Teague get to each other, the closer they may get to exposing a horror that could cost them everything . . .

Keep reading for a special look!

A Lyrical mass-market paperback and
e-book on sale now.

Chapter One

The day she'd dreaded had arrived. The roar of a diesel engine blasted through the tranquility of a May morning and sent the mother robin perched on her nest into flight. Nina Hutton dropped her paintbrush onto the ledge of her easel and scowled. Rarely did a vehicle venture down her dead-end street, let alone one emitting puffs of exhaust into the pristine coastal air and creating enough noise to frighten away the wildlife. Spinning on her stool, she rose to her feet and stared in the direction of the disturbance. Not that she could see squat from the seclusion of her backyard.

Finally, the rumble of the engine died, doors slammed, barking erupted, and a high-pitched squeal pierced the sudden silence. "Daddy, look! Our new house matches my dress."

A deep male voice responded, too low for Nina to make out the words over excited yelps and the clatter of metal against metal. She softly swore. The For Sale sign planted in the yard of the run-down Victorian across the street had disappeared the previous month. Apparently, the new owners had arrived. So much for peace and solitude . . .

Since the subject of her current painting was winging its way through the brilliant blue sky, there was little reason not to satisfy her curiosity as the voices faded in and out. Openly gaping at her new neighbors wasn't an option, not when she could spy on them from an upstairs window. After cleaning her brushes and stowing her paints, Nina left the easel where it stood near the big madrone tree with its nest of baby robins, crossed the yard to the back deck, then entered her house through the open sliding door.

Sunlight pierced the high windows in the main room, catching dust motes in the beams. She sniffed the aroma of beef stew slow cooking in the Crock-Pot as she skirted around the green suede couch and climbed the stairs to the second floor. Entering her bedroom, she dropped down onto the padded window seat, then adjusted the blinds to peek out.

A big yellow moving van stood in the middle of the cul-de-sac with a loading ramp leading from its rear to the ground. Beyond it, a dark blue pickup was parked in the driveway of the house across from hers. Two men in uniform shirts struggled to haul a tall armoire up the steps of the wraparound front porch, while a third man wearing a black T-shirt stretched tight across his broad back followed them, carrying a large box labeled *Books* in bold red marker. A series of expletives from one of the movers—unsuitable for the ears of the small girl running in circles on the weedy patch of lawn, chased by a white and tan ball of fur—drifted upward on the breeze.

She wondered where the child's mother was. *Probably inside, trying to figure out where to put the furniture.* The girl couldn't be more than six or seven, all arms and legs in a princess dress of pink tulle that was indeed the same color as the house. Blond hair had been pulled back in a ratty ponytail. Despite the girl's high-pitched shrieks, which complemented equally shrill canine yapping, Nina smiled.

The man in the black T-shirt emerged from the front entrance a few moments later—minus the box—and raised his voice to be heard. Thankfully, both the child and the dog piped down. When he reached the street, he fisted his hands on his hips and glanced in Nina's direction.

Nina quickly ducked out of sight. *Gorgeous* was the word that sprang to mind. The short sleeves of his T-shirt clung to well-defined biceps, while brown hair with a hint of a wave topped the most handsome face she'd seen outside a movie theater. Silvery eyes narrowed against the sun above a straight nose and strong chin. The man reminded her of Clint Eastwood back in his spaghetti Western days. All he needed was a battered cowboy hat, a poncho, and a cigar clamped between those white teeth.

"Wow. Just wow." She settled more comfortably against the cushions as her new neighbor disappeared into the moving van only to return a few seconds later carrying a white painted headboard in one hand and a box labeled *Kitchen* in block letters beneath the other arm. If she had to sacrifice the peace and quiet she'd enjoyed since the last tenant—a rock-n-roll wannabe who'd spent most evenings practicing on his drums—moved out, at least the new owner of the dilapidated Victorian was easy on the eyes. *Very easy.*

Best of all, she could enjoy his beauty with no internal pressure since he was obviously a family man and unavailable. She clenched her fist around the edge of the windowsill. Over the last six months, she'd honestly tried to put herself out there on the social front, only to wind up disappointed and aching . . . missing Keith. Accepting the fact that she was happier alone was easier on her and any potential suitors who invariably failed to live up to her unrealistic expectations.

When her cell phone chimed, she pulled it out of the pocket of her jeans, happy to escape her thoughts, and glanced at the display. A smile formed as she answered. "Hey, Leah."

"Hey, yourself. What do you have going on today?"

"I was working before my subject flew away. Why? Aren't you at school?"

"Recess. Can't you hear the kids screaming in the background?"

"Not over the commotion next door."

Nina glanced out the window as a string of oaths blistered her ears through the open window. One of the moving men stood at the end of the ramp next to a carved oak bookcase, rubbing his right shin. Thankfully, the girl and dog had disappeared, presumably ordered inside out of hearing range.

"What's going on next door?"

She returned her attention to the conversation with one of her oldest and dearest friends. "The people who bought the Victorian are moving in this morning. I can barely hear myself think over the ruckus, let alone focus on painting."

"Oh, yeah? What are they like?"

"The man is drool-worthy, probably a little older than us, and his daughter is cute but loud. Their dog is small and yappy. I haven't seen the wife or girlfriend or whoever yet. She must have gone inside before I set up watch from my bedroom."

"You're spying on them?"

"Of course. Wouldn't you?"

"I'd probably walk across the street and introduce myself. Did that thought ever occur to you? Maybe welcome them to the neighborhood."

"The guy's too busy flexing his muscles." Nina gave the hottie an appreciative stare as he hauled a rolled-up rug slung over one shoulder into the house. "Literally, since he's busy unpacking a moving van. I'm sure his partner is equally occupied. There'll be plenty of time to meet them later."

"I suppose so, but not this afternoon. The bridesmaid dresses finally arrived. Can you meet me and Paige at All Dressed Up for a fitting? Three o'clock sharp."

"Says the woman who's chronically late. Of course I can." She leaned an elbow on the windowsill. "I can't believe you and Ryan are getting married next month. The time has flown by since he proposed last fall."

"I know, right? I can't wait to say *I do.* Oh, crap, the bell is ringing. I need to herd the little monsters back into the classroom. See you this afternoon, Nina."

The phone went dead before she could respond. Sticking it back in her pocket, Nina glanced down as the movers finally maneuvered the bookcase inside. Spying was getting a little old. Maybe the mother robin had returned to her nest, and she could get back to work on the painting Miss Lola had commissioned. Sliding off the window seat, she headed downstairs but stopped when she reached the deck door.

The munchkin hadn't gone inside after all. She stood with her hands clasped behind her back in front of the easel while her furry companion sniffed the base of the tree before squatting to pee. Sliding open the screen, Nina stepped out onto the deck.

The child turned to regard her. "How come you didn't finish the picture? The bird's feathers look funny."

"Because the robin flew away when your moving

truck drove up." Nina crossed the yard to the young girl's side. "Does your mom know you're over here?"

Her uninvited guest rocked back and forth on pink tennis shoes. "Daddy says my mommy watches me all the time. She always knows where I am."

While Nina struggled to imagine any mother turning a child who couldn't be much more than six loose in an unfamiliar neighborhood, she didn't argue. "I'm Nina. What's your name?"

"Keely. It means beautiful. My daddy says I was a very pretty baby, but a mean boy in my kindergarten class told me I look like a giraffe because I have long legs."

"Calling people names is definitely not nice, but giraffes are graceful and majestic."

"Majestic. I like that word." She gave a little hop and a skip. "Where did Coco go?"

"Your dog?" When Keely nodded, Nina turned her to face an upended rump as the dog sniffed a clump of ferns, tail wagging. "There she is. She's very pretty, just like you."

The girl smiled. "Coco's a paplon. I love how the fur hangs off her ears. It's soft."

"You mean a papillon?"

"That's what I said, a paplon. Come on, Coco. Let's go."

"It was nice meeting you, Keely. Tell your parents I'll stop by to introduce myself sometime soon."

She opened her mouth, then shut it, and ran off without another word to disappear around the side of the house. After giving the ferns a final sniff, the dog followed.

When a chorus of cheeping erupted above her, Nina glanced up and smiled. The mother robin had returned, and the babies in the nest were making it clear they were on the verge of starvation. She settled at her easel and resumed work. Not that painting birds was her true passion, but sometimes artistic zeal took a back seat to paying the bills. Miss Lola was a steady customer and bird enthusiast with deep pockets, and Nina had learned the hard way you did what was necessary to survive.

Two hours later, she put the finishing touches on the painting. Shading the orange of the mother robin's breast and adding a protective gleam to her eye. Instilling a sense of urgency in the gaping mouths and stretched, scrawny necks of the hatchlings. Curling the edges of the thin bark peeling away from the madrone tree. Satisfied with the results, she cleaned her brushes, put away her paints, and then rose from her stool.

As she headed straight to the kitchen, her stomach rumbled. Probably because she'd had nothing but a yogurt for breakfast, and it was well past noon. After making herself a turkey sandwich on wheat, she peeked out the kitchen window. Silence reigned next door. Apparently the movers were on a lunch break since the truck was still parked in the street, blocking her view. No matter. She could squeeze her Mini Cooper around it. Maybe she'd drive down to the beach for a run before she met her friends for the dress fitting.

Biting into her sandwich, Nina climbed the stairs two at a time to her room, where she tossed her paint-stained shirt and jeans into the hamper before sorting through her dresser drawer for a pair of shorts and a tank top. She finished eating while tying on her running shoes, then paused downstairs at the kitchen sink to chug a glass of water.

Heading outside, she stopped at the end of her driveway and surveyed the limited stretch of pavement between her front lawn and the van through narrowed eyes. The Mini Cooper was small, but not that tiny. Backing out would seriously endanger either the car's shiny red paint or her grass. She rounded the end of the truck at a fast clip and smacked straight into a hard, T-shirt-clad chest. Her nose mashed against the pulse beating at the man's throat, and when she drew in a breath, a woodsy scent teased her nostrils. Strong arms closed around her as they both wobbled and swayed before her new neighbor steadied her and took a step back.

"Sorry about that." He assessed her from the top of her head to her running shoes, and a hint of appreciation entered those silvery eyes. "You make quite an impact."

"I guess I should look where I'm going." Her slightly breathless tone annoyed her no end. Getting flustered over a married man, no matter how hot he might be, was pointless. "I'm Nina Hutton." She extended her hand. "Welcome to our little corner of the neighborhood."

A warm palm gripped hers. "Nice to meet you. I'm Teague O'Dell." When he released her hand, he waved toward the thick woods surrounding them. "I love the seclusion here. It's the reason I bought this place. A far cry from the Southern California suburbs."

"You moved to Oregon from Los Angeles?"

"We lived in Encino, which is in the L.A. area. After . . . well, I wanted a complete change, small town instead of urban sprawl."

"Siren Cove certainly offers that."

"This house needs a lot of work, but I don't mind." He regarded her steadily. "I just want a safe place where I don't have to worry about my daughter if she wants to play in the yard."

"You found it." She gave him a quick smile, wondering if he was always so serious. "Uh, I'd love to meet the rest of your family, but I was on my way out for a run on the beach. Do you think someone could move the truck?"

"Of course. Sorry, I didn't realize we were blocking your driveway. I'll go get the keys, and hopefully we'll have the van unloaded and out of here in another hour or so."

"No worries. Nice to meet you, Teague, and good luck with the unpacking. I don't envy you that task."

"I'm sure we'll be hip-deep in boxes for weeks."

He hurried away, presumably to retrieve the keys, and Nina climbed into her car to wait. A minute later, the truck engine fired up with a roar, followed by a shout from Teague. Her gaze was glued to the rearview mirror as he raised the metal ramp, biceps bulging beneath the weight, to slide it into the truck before the driver pulled forward out of her way.

After backing to the end of the driveway, she returned her new neighbor's wave, then accelerated down the street. "Oh, my. Mr. Hottie O'Dell is eye candy with a capital *C*." She couldn't help wondering what Keely's mother looked like. *Probably Malibu Barbie.*

Turning at the corner, she pressed harder on the accelerator to send her little car flying down the coast road south of town. One thing was certain, she needed to stop salivating over attached men, no matter how hot. Since pulling off a relationship seemed beyond her capabilities, for now, she'd simply run off her frustrations.

Nina parked in the half-full lot above the beach and followed the winding trail down to the water's edge, then ran facing into the wind. Her shoes pounded the sand in a steady rhythm as the salt spray off the waves dampened her arms and legs. Out near the breakwater, the three monolithic rocks that gave Siren Cove its name stood sentinel over the town. Her breathing came in harsh pants as she passed a handful of young women watching toddlers build castles with buckets and shovels. She recognized a couple of the mothers and nodded in greeting but wasn't tempted to join them.

If Keith hadn't died, maybe I'd be part of that group. Or not.

She shook off the painful thought and ran faster past a woman bundled in a jacket bent over a tide pool to poke something with the tip of a stick while a blond girl sat alone on a nearby rock. Farther up the beach, a couple strolled hand in hand, their laughter drifting on the breeze. Sweat dripped down Nina's face and neck to pool between her breasts. Slowing to a stop, she braced her hands on her knees and forced air into her labored lungs.

What an idiot she was, letting her emotions get out of control and running like a woman possessed. Now she'd have to go home to shower before she could try on her dress for the wedding. Which meant she'd better head straight back to her car. Turning down the beach, she jogged to cool off and smiled at a fellow runner in a bright pink T-shirt going in the opposite direction. The young girl had left her rock to stand ankle-deep in water while the tide surged away from her bare feet. Up ahead, the group of preschoolers had abandoned their castles to chase seagulls, screaming like banshees as the birds flew away with equally harsh cries.

When a scrap of paper blew across her path, Nina bent to grab the piece of litter and thrust it into the pocket of her shorts, then picked up her pace again. The cool breeze off the ocean dried her sweat and soothed her soul. By the time she reached the trail up to the parking lot, she'd gotten over her attack of self-pity.

Until the next time.

* * *

Where had she put the lottery ticket? She turned the pockets of her jacket inside out but found only a few coins and a small clamshell, then searched through the open bag on the bench by the kitchen door. Bits of sand stuck to her fingertips as she pulled out the miscellaneous assortment that had accumulated since she'd last cleaned out her tote bag. Relief filled her when her fingers closed around a piece of paper, but it wasn't the magic ticket, only an old grocery receipt she wadded and chucked in the trash.

The lottery ticket must have blown away while she was on the beach, but she didn't have time to spare looking for it right now. Not if she didn't want to be late.

What were the chances her numbers would be the winning ones, anyway? She'd played those same numbers for years to no avail, but this time she'd felt lucky. Her lips tightened. Obviously not. The underlying feeling of nervous anticipation keeping her on edge must be due to summer drawing near. Memories of that humid day had become more insistent and dominated her dreams. She glanced toward the small head bent over the picture books open on the table.

The day of reckoning was almost here.

Romantic Suspense from

Lisa Jackson

Absolute Fear	0-8217-7936-2	$7.99US/$9.99CAN
Afraid to Die	1-4201-1850-1	$7.99US/$9.99CAN
Almost Dead	0-8217-7579-0	$7.99US/$10.99CAN
Born to Die	1-4201-0278-8	$7.99US/$9.99CAN
Chosen to Die	1-4201-0277-X	$7.99US/$10.99CAN
Cold Blooded	1-4201-2581-8	$7.99US/$8.99CAN
Deep Freeze	0-8217-7296-1	$7.99US/$10.99CAN
Devious	1-4201-0275-3	$7.99US/$9.99CAN
Fatal Burn	0-8217-7577-4	$7.99US/$10.99CAN
Final Scream	0-8217-7712-2	$7.99US/$10.99CAN
Hot Blooded	1-4201-0678-3	$7.99US/$9.49CAN
If She Only Knew	1-4201-3241-5	$7.99US/$9.99CAN
Left to Die	1-4201-0276-1	$7.99US/$10.99CAN
Lost Souls	0-8217-7938-9	$7.99US/$10.99CAN
Malice	0-8217-7940-0	$7.99US/$10.99CAN
The Morning After	1-4201-3370-5	$7.99US/$9.99CAN
The Night Before	1-4201-3371-3	$7.99US/$9.99CAN
Ready to Die	1-4201-1851-X	$7.99US/$9.99CAN
Running Scared	1-4201-0182-X	$7.99US/$10.99CAN
See How She Dies	1-4201-2584-2	$7.99US/$8.99CAN
Shiver	0-8217-7578-2	$7.99US/$10.99CAN
Tell Me	1-4201-1854-4	$7.99US/$9.99CAN
Twice Kissed	0-8217-7944-3	$7.99US/$9.99CAN
Unspoken	1-4201-0093-9	$7.99US/$9.99CAN
Whispers	1-4201-5158-4	$7.99US/$9.99CAN
Wicked Game	1-4201-0338-5	$7.99US/$9.99CAN
Wicked Lies	1-4201-0339-3	$7.99US/$9.99CAN
Without Mercy	1-4201-0274-5	$7.99US/$10.99CAN
You Don't Want to Know	1-4201-1853-6	$7.99US/$9.99CAN

Available Wherever Books Are Sold!

Visit our website at **www.kensingtonbooks.com**

Books by Bestselling Author
Fern Michaels

__The Jury	0-8217-7878-1	$6.99US/$9.99CAN
__Sweet Revenge	0-8217-7879-X	$6.99US/$9.99CAN
__Lethal Justice	0-8217-7880-3	$6.99US/$9.99CAN
__Free Fall	0-8217-7881-1	$6.99US/$9.99CAN
__Fool Me Once	0-8217-8071-9	$7.99US/$10.99CAN
__Vegas Rich	0-8217-8112-X	$7.99US/$10.99CAN
__Hide and Seek	1-4201-0184-6	$6.99US/$9.99CAN
__Hokus Pokus	1-4201-0185-4	$6.99US/$9.99CAN
__Fast Track	1-4201-0186-2	$6.99US/$9.99CAN
__Collateral Damage	1-4201-0187-0	$6.99US/$9.99CAN
__Final Justice	1-4201-0188-9	$6.99US/$9.99CAN
__Up Close and Personal	0-8217-7956-7	$7.99US/$9.99CAN
__Under the Radar	1-4201-0683-X	$6.99US/$9.99CAN
__Razor Sharp	1-4201-0684-8	$7.99US/$10.99CAN
__Yesterday	1-4201-1494-8	$5.99US/$6.99CAN
__Vanishing Act	1-4201-0685-6	$7.99US/$10.99CAN
__Sara's Song	1-4201-1493-X	$5.99US/$6.99CAN
__Deadly Deals	1-4201-0686-4	$7.99US/$10.99CAN
__Game Over	1-4201-0687-2	$7.99US/$10.99CAN
__Sins of Omission	1-4201-1153-1	$7.99US/$10.99CAN
__Sins of the Flesh	1-4201-1154-X	$7.99US/$10.99CAN
__Cross Roads	1-4201-1192-2	$7.99US/$10.99CAN

Available Wherever Books Are Sold!

Check out our website at **www.kensingtonbooks.com**